GINNY L. YTTRUP

FLAMES

A NOVEL

D1516120

SHELTERWOOD
PRESS

ISBN 978-0-9961447-0-4

This novel is a work of fiction. Names, characters, places,
and incidents are either products of the author's imagination
or are used fictitiously. All characters are fictional and any
similarity to people living or dead is purely coincidental.

Edited by Karen Ball and Julee Schwarzburg
Cover and interior design by Diana Lawrence and Flawed
People Press

Printed in the United States of America.

For Christina, Jeanette, Judy, Kim, and so many others…

By forces seemingly antagonistic and destructive, Nature accomplishes her beneficent designs—now a flood of fire, now a flood of ice, now a flood of water; and again in the fullness of time an outburst of...life.
John Muir

There is in every true woman's heart, a spark of heavenly fire, which lies dormant in the broad daylight of prosperity, but which kindles up and beams and blazes in the dark hour of adversity.
Washington Irving

The Valley

I lean into the embrace of the valley,
my sibling, my friend.
Shorn by the violence of time, the brutality of nature,
our fissures run deep.
Our peaks jut sharp.
The land bleeds our heritage
as the name wails our history,
Yosemite!
Together we stretch, grow, change, evolve.
Shaped by seasons.
Water. Ice. Wind.
Fire.
Embers glow, their dance hypnotic,
their song soft.
Complacency woos.
The older, wiser sibling does not succumb.
But I follow complacency's call,
wrapping myself against the assailing seasons.
I shift, uncertain.
Then settle. Again.
Until an angry wind stirs.
Embers ignite, flames erupt, and fire leads
the frenzied dance outside the circle.
Its staccato rhythm hisses and crackles.
I cast off my wrap and leap to my feet.
Instinct insists I fight.
But the howling gale,
the voice of the valley,
bids me otherwise.
Let fire have its way.
So I stand.
Tall.
Still.
Like the mighty sequoia.
Flames lap, singeing and searing.

Devastating.
Yet not destroying.
When fire yields and gives way to water,
rain falls.
And life begins anew.
In the valley.
In me.

*There is a love of wild nature in everybody, an ancient
mother-love ever showing itself whether recognized or no,
and however covered by cares and duties.*
John Muir

CHAPTER ONE

Jessica

 I PRESERVE LEGACIES.

Preserving remnants of the past because they inform
the present is more than just a job to me—it's who I am. It
plays into everything I do—each role I fill. Or, I sigh, is it
that I wouldn't know who I am apart from the roles I fill?
Wife, mother, archeologist. As I search for, study, protect,
and preserve items from the past, I'm beginning to
understand that it's the missing pieces of myself I seek.

But does it matter who I am?

Can I unearth *myself* in the search?

I've stared, unseeing, until the sounds of my family
stirring bring me back to the present, where dust motes
bounce in shafts of morning light. Attuned to the moment, I
shake my head as my face heats at my wandering thoughts.

Chet's steps echo on the stone floor in the hallway, then fall in the kitchen. As he passes the island where I stand, he swats my back end. "Looking beautiful as usual, babe. I love a woman in uniform."

I touch my hair, still damp and confined to its usual knot, and look down at my National-Park-Service, standard-issue green khaki pants and shirt, brown leather belt, and brown work boots. I smile. "I don't deserve you."

"Well, you're right there. Just lucky for you that I've always had a thing for rangers."

"I'm—"

Chet, standing with coffeepot in hand, winks. "I'm also partial to fire archeologists. So what natural or cultural resource in the magnificent Yosemite National Park will you save from the flames of destruction today, Ranger Jess?"

I shake my head. "I don't think you need caffeine this morning." I glance at the list. "There's lasagna, enchiladas, and a turkey-and-stuffing casserole in the freezer. I shopped yesterday afternoon, so there's plenty of milk, cereal, fruit, and lunch items for the kids. Laundry is done, and—"

Chet holds up one hand. "Whoa, Jess. I know the routine. Been there, done that. A few thousand times, remember?"

I nod. "The list is here, and oh"—I scrawl another note—"Tyler has a doctor's appointment tomorrow morning. It's his annual physical, so if I'm not here—"

"Sure, I can tag along with him. But he's almost nineteen, Jessica. He can handle it on his own."

"I like one of us to be there, just in case." How many of those annual physicals have I missed through the years? I'd rather not count.

"Right."

"Lightning is forecast for this afternoon."

Chet nods but I'm losing him—tossing too many details his way. His playful tone has turned impatient. "It most always is."

I leave the list on the counter, cross the kitchen, and sidle up to him. Slipping my arms around his neck, I'm careful not to bump the full mug of hot coffee he holds. "We haven't had much time together lately, but I do love you. We still have a tentative date to get away this weekend, right?" I kiss his neck, the scent of his aftershave as familiar to me as the feel of him.

"Gross, Mom!"

I back away from Chet and turn around. "Haley, you're fifteen. This won't always be gross."

"It's just gross when it's you and dad."

Haley, clad in *her* standard-issue uniform—cotton pajama bottoms and a T-shirt—opens the refrigerator and peers inside. She closes the fridge. "What's for breakfast?"

"I have to—"

"Go? What's new?"

"Drop the attitude, Haley." Chet sets his mug on the counter and grabs the griddle from the cabinet under the range. "Pancakes are for breakfast."

"Thanks, Daddy."

Chet and I mastered the art of tag-team parenting long ago. As a business owner—Mountain Play, a sporting goods store in Oakhurst—Chet sets his own hours, leaving the store in one of his managers' capable hands when he needs to be home with the kids. He's usually at the store during peak retail hours, evenings and weekends, but I'm home then. Well, depending on the season. If neither of us is available, then my dad and stepmom, Cretia, pitch in. *It takes a village*, as they say. We make it work.

"Hey, you two, if all goes well, I'll see you for dinner. But I'm on call, so if there's a fire…"

Chet's right, they know the routine. California's wildfire season began early, thanks to another year of drought. The forests are a tinderbox—if a lightning strike or anything else starts a fire this afternoon, it could be days, or even weeks, before I'm back home. "Haley, when your brother gets up, remind him to water Grandpa and Grandma's yard. They're gone until—"

"I know." Tyler mumbles as he staggers into the kitchen, his dark hair protruding in ten different directions, his eyes barely open. He feels his way toward the coffeepot.

"Here buddy, you look like you need this more than I do." Chet hands his mug of coffee to Tyler, who takes the cup, slurps a sip, and then sighs.

Chet and I look at one another and smile.

"What are you doing up so early, Ty?" He has to have a reason to be up before noon.

"He's going bouldering," Haley offers.

"Be careful." I reach for the pen to write one more thing on the list, but Chet crosses the kitchen and takes the pen from my hand. "Jess, we've got it."

"I know, I know. Oh, I'm making a presentation in the valley this morning, then I'm taking Johnny out to the site of that small fire last week. If you need anything, catch me before this afternoon. There's no cell service—"

"I know. What's with you this morning?"

"I just… Never mind."

I turn back and try to give Haley a hug, but she ducks. When her dark eyes meet mine, for just a moment, with her hair still mussed from sleep, I see the little girl she was rather than the hormonal young woman she's become. "Love you, Haley-bug."

She rolls her eyes but then cracks a smile. "Me too."

"Love you, Tyler."

He lifts his mug toward me as if in a toast, words too costly until the caffeine does its work.

I give Chet a hug and then make my way to the back door, but before I leave he stops me. "Hey, don't count on this weekend. I didn't get the store covered."

"What?"

He shrugs. "It was tentative, right? Just didn't work out."

"Okay." Disappointment, like a spring, bubbles to the surface, but I say nothing more. I bend to pick up a duffel bag packed with a change of clothes for this afternoon, then reach for my hat hanging on a peg. Once in the garage, I set my Smokey-the-Bear hat, as Chet calls it, on the passenger seat of the SUV and climb into the driver's seat.

I put the SUV into gear, do a three-point turn, and head out the gravel road to the highway, leaving my legacies to fend for themselves.

But not in the same way my mother left me.

My dad anchored my life. A wildland firefighter. Strong. Courageous. All parts of him that became a part of who I am. But my mother? What part of her genetic makeup is also mine? Native American, yes, but what else? How did her history inform who I am—physically, emotionally, spiritually? How am I supposed to navigate my future without a full road map of my past?

My mother robbed me of more than her nurture and care—she robbed me of half my heritage.

As I negotiate the highway's curves, Chet's question comes back to me: *"What's with you this morning?"*

I sigh as I consider the timeworn answer. It's the same thing that's always with me. Don't you know that by now? It's the phantom ache of loss.

I hike through the charred section of the valley, a day pack on my back, the acrid smells of burnt earth and ash an aroma forever etched in my memory, as familiar to me as the downy scent of my newborn babes. I veer around a boulder and then stop, look over my shoulder for Johnny who's coming up behind me, and then survey the landscape. Where others might view the blackened remains of a wildfire as death, I see new life, rich with possibility.

Maybe that's the perspective motherhood gives me. Yes, fire destroys, but it's also life giving—a force of nature as important to the ecosystem as sunlight and water. Something the Native Americans understood, but the white men worked against. The early settlers' ignorance is part of the legacy we live as our forests pay the price for a century of fire suppression. But now we understand fire and the life it engenders.

When Johnny reaches me, I point. "There." A granite slab flat as a tabletop lies ahead.

Johnny Shaw, senior spiritual leader of the Southern Sierra Miwuk Nation, nods. We walk the last hundred feet side by side, then stop just short of the site. I lift my pack from my back, set it down, and pull out my camera. I snap a couple of shots, then make my way to the granite outcropping. I kick aside a few pieces of scorched shrubbery—had the fire burned hotter, this bedrock may have exploded. Instead, the flames worked to reveal a piece of history by burning away the underbrush that kept it concealed. I sit on my heels and, with gentle strokes, brush ash from the rock revealing indentations in the granite. Then I stand back with Johnny and we gaze at what the fire left for us.

"Mortars."

I nod. "It's a kitchen." The flattened granite likely acted as a tabletop for food preparation—the mortars were used to grind acorns into flour. Further investigation will likely reveal an area of midden beneath the black crust of ground somewhere nearby—dark, rich soil where kitchen scraps were discarded generations ago.

Johnny stands tall, regarding the area. "My ancestors were here."

"Our ancestors."

"Yes."

I make a few notes, mark the site on my GPS, then lift my camera and frame a shot of Johnny, squatting on the granite, running fingers over one of the mortars, his expression reverent.

I lower the camera. How many photos have I shot through the years? I have stacks of albums at home and multiple files on my computer all of moments I long to capture. To hold. But moments, like smoke, can't be contained. I look beyond the burnt landscape to the azure summer sky and the granite monoliths standing guard around us, reminding me of the power of the Creator. I breathe deep of the cool, thin air. "It's a good day, my friend."

He stands. "Yes, a good day, indeed."

As I survey the rest of the site, making notes, Johnny perches on a rock. He is as familiar to me as my own father. Well, almost. They are friends—have always been friends as far as I know. I grew up with Johnny and his wife at our house more often than not, it seemed.

By late afternoon the sun has dipped behind El Capitan and long shadows stretch across the valley floor. I walk back to where Johnny waits. "Time to call it a day." I look toward Half Dome, where thunderheads so often build, but the sky is clear, proving this morning's forecast wrong. "I get to go home this evening."

He smiles, his two front teeth lapped one over the other. "It is always good to go home." He gets up and takes slow, stilted steps as I load my pack. I catch up to Johnny with easy strides.

"How's Dot?"

"Dorothy? She is well. Like me, a little stiff but still kicking strong." He chuckles.

"Good."

"Yes." He glances my way. "And Chet?"

"Fine. The usual." I shrug. "Busy." I slow my pace to keep in step with Johnny. "We were supposed to get away this weekend, just overnight, but…"

"You hesitate."

I stop walking and look at Johnny. "It was tentative. It's fire season, so…" I shrug again. "You know, all things are tentative this time of year. He didn't get the store covered—he'll work. It's fine."

"Your eyes tell a different story."

"No, really, it's fine. He has a lot on his plate with my schedule, the kids... He just forgot to arrange for a manager to cover the weekend." I start walking again.

"You make excuses for him, Jessica."

I turn and look back at him. "I do?"

"You always have."

After Johnny and I part ways, I climb back into my SUV to make the hour-long drive back to Fish Camp. Home. As I meander out of the valley, I take in the scenery—the Merced River, ribbonlike, dividing the valley floor, Bridalveil and Yosemite Falls cascading over granite cliffs—though this year their usual roar is but a trickle—and the lush meadows, so full of life, carpeting the valley floor.

During the summer months when tourists swarm to the valley, traffic is as slow as the lazy river in fall, which I don't usually mind as I am awed anew by the surrounding beauty each time I make this drive. But this afternoon, anxiety creeps in. My impatience is the clue that something's amiss and I turn my thoughts inward.

Johnny's comment bothers me, of course.

When Chet and I married, I determined I'd weave the colorful strands of our individual histories into one cohesive basket. In much the same way an Ahwahneechee woman would have twined materials stained with the blackened roots of a brake fern and the oxblood bark of the redbud to form an intricate and lasting pattern, I would create a pattern different than the one I inherited.

Our family basket would remain intact.

"You make excuses for him, Jessica. You always have."

Is it possible I'm so bent on preserving our basket that I excuse what I should consider? I tap the brakes as the line of cars in front of me slows again.

No, that's ridiculous.

As I work to dismiss what Johnny said, my dad's oft-spoken words intrude: *Johnny's a straight shooter—you can trust him to tell you the truth. If a man isn't truthful, he isn't your friend."*

I thrum my fingers on the steering wheel. Okay, so maybe Johnny's right. I occasionally excuse Chet's behavior. But isn't that a wife's duty? To believe the best about her husband, to defend him? That's different than making excuses for him.

I reach for my phone, plug it into the MP3 port, and tap a playlist. I turn off the air conditioner, roll down the windows, and breathe deep of summer's organic scents—dried leaves and pine needles mulching, dust, and the sharp bite of pines. I will myself to think about something else.

In two weeks, Tyler takes off for a road trip to the Grand Canyon with buddies on his way to his second year of college at ASU. Then they'll get themselves settled in the dorms, rather than having us help him as we did last year.

I shake my head. "I am not ready for him to go." They'll drive from here to the Grand Canyon, camping along the way. I protested, but Chet was right—it's time to let Tyler go, let him spread his wings.

And on August 18—just three weeks away—Haley begins her sophomore year at Yosemite High School. How can that be?

Haley...

If Johnny thinks *I* make excuses for Chet, he should hear Haley. She defends him, stands up for him, and fights for him at every turn. She is her daddy's girl—especially now as some of that normal mother-daughter angst sets in. At least, I think it's normal.

Did Haley learn to make excuses for Chet from me?

I've never felt the need to defend my father or make excuses for him. He's never given me cause. He is a man of his word.

What am I saying?

As I wend my way out of the valley and begin the twisting ascent toward home, questions nag.

What about Chet makes us run to his defense?

Why does he need anyone to defend or excuse him?

I swallow a rising sense of dread as I consider the real question: Is Chet, like my dad, a man of his word?

"If a man isn't truthful, he isn't your friend."

There's a difference between keeping your word and being truthful.

Chet's just...

He's just forgetful, that's all.

As I reach the highway, my foot seems to bear the weight I feel and the accelerator responds. But rather than check myself, I allow anxiety to speed me home.

There is at least a punky spark in my heart
and it may blaze...
John Muir

CHAPTER TWO

Haley

CHLOE AND I plop on my bed with my laptop. "What's it called?"

"I dunno. It's on my wall—just watch it from there."

I go to Chloe's Facebook wall. "That one?"

"Yeah. It's so funny."

I click on the video link, but instead of it playing I get a message that the video is blocked.

Chloe rolls her eyes.

I slap the cover of the laptop shut. "It's my mom—she put some parental-control thing on my computer. She's so annoying."

"Whatever. Here, watch it on my phone."

But just as Chloe hands me her phone, my phone vibrates. I grab it off the bed.

Chloe leans over and tries to see the screen. "Who is it?"

I shrug. "No one."

"Yeah right." Chloe grabs the phone. "Why's he messaging you?"

"Give it to me." I grab the phone back.

"What'd he say?"

I read the message out loud. "'You should be here.'"

"Where? Let me see."

I hold the phone out so Chloe can see the picture Zach posted with the message. "It's the mall, right?"

"Yeah, but—"

"What should I say?"

Chloe flips her long blonde hair over her shoulder. "Say, 'Why would I want to be there?'"

"No. That's mean." I look around my room—gray and white chevron-striped walls, small black chandelier, and turquoise accents. My mom helped me redecorate it as my Christmas present last year. She said since I was a freshman, it was time to make it look as grown-up as me.

I point my phone at my bulletin board—a huge frame we painted turquoise. I covered the corkboard with pictures of my friends, sayings I like, drawings I've done. Just stuff. Chloe's between me and the bulletin board, so that's the picture I take—her with my stuff in the background—then I reply to Zach.

She sits up and looks over my shoulder. "Wait! What're you saying?"

I show her the picture. "I told him *he* should be *here*."

Chloe smiles. "Whatever."

I look back at the screen as my phone vibrates again, but I don't say anything and Chloe doesn't notice. I toss the phone back on the bed. "I wish we could drive."

"Like your mom would let you drive all the way to Fresno?" She lies back down. "I hate this town. There's nothing to do and it's over an hour to the mall."

"It's not that bad."

Chloe's phone dings and she looks at the screen. "I have to go."

"Why?"

"My mom's here. I'm babysitting at two o'clock."

"Oh yeah, I forgot."

After Chloe leaves, I read Zach's last message again.

Why would I want 2 b there?

I message him back.

Haha.

But before I hit Send, I hesitate. Instead, I delete my message and don't respond at all. I mean, it's not like Chloe and Zach are going out or anything, but she is my friend and it wouldn't be nice to laugh at Zach's comment. I sigh. But...

I lean back against my headboard and pick up my laptop. I open it, look at Chloe's Facebook page again, and then click it closed. I don't care about the video—it's probably not something I'd like anyway. Even though Chloe's my best friend, that doesn't mean I always agree with her about everything. But sometimes...I don't know, I just feel like I have to act a certain way so she'll stay friends with me. Like saying my mom's annoying. I mean, she is, but she's not *that* bad.

Or...pretending I don't like Zach too.

I sigh as I close the laptop, then get up and set it on my desk and plug it in. It's time to do something else, something that will get me somewhere. Literally. I pick up the *Driver Handbook,* open it, and sit at my desk to study the contents. Again.

"Hi, Chipmunk."

I lower the handbook and turn around. "Dad, really?"

"Sorry."

"What are you doing home?"

"I spilled." He points at a stain on his shirt. "I have a meeting with a vendor"—he looks at his watch—"in about an hour, so I came home to change. What are you up to?"

I lift up the handbook. "You remember you're taking me to the DMV on Friday, right?"

"Yep. What time again?"

"One o'clock. You said an afternoon appointment worked best."

"Right."

"So if I pass, I'll have my permit and I can drive home from there, right?"

"I didn't say that."

"Dad..."

"Sure your mom can't take you?"

I sigh.

He winks. "She's the brave one. I don't know if I can handle having you behind the wheel."

"Very funny."

"I try. Driving home is a little ambitious for your first stint in the driver's seat. I'll take you to the store and give you a lesson in the parking lot. We'll see how it goes."

I smile. "Thank you, Daddy."

"Anytime, Chipmunk."

I shake my head.

"Hey, I might be late tonight. I've got some paperwork to catch up on after this meeting. If your mom comes home, let her know."

"Okay."

"Tyler's home if you need anything—"

"Yeah, okay."

"By the way, your friend Zach signed up for the climbing camp this morning."

I shrug.

"You're coming, right?"

I try not to smile, but I can't help it. "Duh."

When I was little, my mom worked a lot—not that it's changed or anything—so my dad was around more because his schedule was flexible. Maybe that's why I've always felt closer to him. Or maybe it's because my mom is harder—

she's the one with the big expectations and the one who sets the rules. Like not going out with a guy until I'm sixteen. Chloe and my other friends don't have a rule like that. Really, my dad even thinks it's kind of stupid. I mean, not that he's said that, but doesn't him telling me Zach signed up for the climbing camp kind of imply that?

It's not that my mom's rules are bad; she's just more strict and my dad's more fun. When Tyler and I were little, he started taking us to the store with him and we'd play around on the climbing wall—a huge wall that looks like granite with bouldering routes that change every month or so. It's what Mountain Play is known for—besides all the climbing and mountaineering gear they sell. As we got older, Dad let Tyler and me take climbing classes at the store, then he let us take classes in the park. He sometimes teaches classes for Yosemite's Mountaineering School.

Last summer, the space next to the store opened up, so my dad expanded the climbing area, adding a huge arch with some cool boulder problems, like stuff you'd encounter on a real climb.

That's when I met Zach.

It was the summer before my freshman year and Zach's sophomore year. He'd just moved here, and I was the only girl in the teen advanced climbing camp—well, besides Heather, the instructor my dad had just hired. I watched Zach all week. And Zach watched Heather. She is totally gorgeous. My dad watched Heather too, but only because it was the first class she taught at Mountain Play.

I didn't think Zach even noticed me until last fall when I started at Yosemite High School. I was standing at my locker with Chloe trying to get the stupid thing open when someone came up behind us, pounded a fist on it, and it popped open.

"Hey, Weaver, gone climbing lately?"

We both turned around and looked up at Zach. "Um..."

"We should go sometime." Before he started to walk away, he nodded toward my locker. "You're welcome." Then he left.

"Who is *that*?" Chloe grabbed my arm as she watched Zach walk down the hall.

"Just some guy I met at Mountain Play." I couldn't believe he'd remembered me. And all I could say was *Um...*? Heat crawled from my neck to my face.

"He is so hot. Did you see how blue his eyes are? He wants to climb with you?" She shook her head. "I gotta learn to climb. You have to teach me."

"You hate that kind of thing."

"So?"

Chloe's just like that about guys. You always know who she thinks is hot or who she likes. She went out with some other guy last year, but now she likes Zach.

I don't talk about that kind of thing as much. I mean, I don't know…it's personal, or special, you know? Something you want to keep to yourself. But now, it's this big problem because I knew Zach first, but Chloe's the one who said she liked him first. And it doesn't seem like he's all that in to Chloe. I mean, he might even kind of like me. But, like, how do I tell Chloe *that*?

I open my laptop and click Pinterest open and pin a few things to my boards. A couple quotes from *The Fault in Our Stars* and a photo of the cutest puppy *ever*. I pin a bunch of beauty stuff too—nail polish colors, eyeliner tips, and hairstyles.

Did Zach really want me at the mall with him?

I do a search for dresses and start pinning things I'd want to wear to Winter Formal if Zach asked me to go.

I stare at the dress I just pinned.

Chloe would freak if Zach asked me to Winter Formal.

I shut the laptop.

That's drama I don't need.

Winds are advertisements of all they touch, however much or little we may be able to read them; telling their wanderings even by their scents alone.
John Muir

CHAPTER THREE

Jessica

I WALK INTO the kitchen where Tyler stands peering into the open refrigerator. "Hi, buddy, where's your dad?"

Tyler pulls one earbud out of his ear. "Hey, you're home. What?"

"Your dad?"

"Working late, I think."

I glance at the clock on the microwave: 5:55 p.m. "Did he say how late?"

"I don't—"

Haley slumps in a bar stool at the island. "He has a meeting with a vendor, then he has paperwork to catch up on. You're not the only one who works, Mom."

"And hello to you too, Haley. I'm well aware that I'm not the only one who works."

She looks at the floor, then makes eye contact. "Sorry."

"I'm going to change, then I'll start dinner. You're both home for the night?"

I receive two nods in response.

Once in our bedroom, I go to my closet, undress, and slip into my favorite yoga pants and a fitted T-shirt, one I know Chet likes. Then I go to the bathroom, take my hair out of its knot, and run a brush through it. As I look in the mirror, I notice a bath towel hung over the shower enclosure behind me rather than on the towel bar. A habit of Chet's. I thought I hung his towel after he showered this morning. I set the brush back in the drawer and then go and grab the towel, which is damp. Weird.

"Mom?"

"In here."

"Can Chloe and Lexie spend the night?"

"I guess so. Will they be here for dinner?"

"No, Chloe's babysitting until seven. Lexie's mom will bring them over later."

"Okay." I fold the damp towel as Haley turns to go. "Haley, wait. Was your dad here today? Did he shower again?"

Haley shrugs. "Maybe. He came home to change. He spilled something on his shirt. He's a klutz."

"That he is." I drape the towel over the bar, turn to follow Haley, then stop and look back at the towel. Something about it nags at me...

I shake my head. He took another shower. So what?

On my way out of the bedroom, I pick up the phone and call Chet, but he doesn't answer so I leave a message. If he was doing paperwork, he'd have answered. It's kind of late for a meeting with a vendor, but it happens. They get to talking, and—

You make excuses for him, Jessica.

I set the phone back on the charging station and wander out to the kitchen, but I can't escape the sense of

26

unease…like a faint scent of smoke for which you can't identify the source…

"Where there's smoke, there's fire, Jessie." My father pointed at a twisting plume from the Henness Ridge Lookout where we stood. We'd just made the half-mile hike from the road up to the abandoned lookout. My little calves ached but my heart swelled with pride. Once we'd climbed the steps to the top, I did a slow spin taking in the view.

I stopped spinning and stood next to him. "Where?" Standing on tiptoes, I looked in the direction he pointed until I saw smoke billowing on the horizon.

"See the color of the smoke?"

I nodded.

"Brownish-red smoke tells you it's a brush fire. But if the smoke is dark gray or black, then you know something else is burning."

"Like what?"

"Probably a structure of some sort."

"Like someone's home?" I bit my lip and looked up at him.

"Could be a barn or something."

"Oh." I stood close to him, watching the smoke from the fire rise and then drift with the wind.

He draped his arm around my shoulder. "Smoke tells a story, Jessie. If you're going to fight fires someday, it's important you learn to read the signs."

When Chet eases himself into bed, it's after eleven o'clock and, lying on my side with my back to him, I let him think I'm asleep. He'd texted me around eight explaining he was buried under paperwork and would likely stay at the store until he'd finished. I didn't respond. Cretia, a retired counselor, would say my reaction was passive-aggressive. But I'm not sure.

I was confused.

Am confused.

Why was I angry? Why am I still angry? Was Haley right? Do I think I'm the only one who works hard? Chet has spent years building his business, and he's well respected in our area as both a climber and businessman. He's the go-to person in the western Yosemite area for all things mountaineering for both locals and tourists. When he's not working at the store, he's often teaching climbing classes for Yosemite's Mountaineering School. Of course he works hard, I know that.

When the rhythm of Chet's breathing is deep and steady, I roll onto my back, my movement methodic.

"You make excuses for him, Jessica. You always have."

I stare into the darkened room. I can't let it go because Johnny spoke a truth I've avoided for…how long? Too long. I make excuses for Chet because it's easier than facing…

What?

My disappointment in him?

Or is it more than that?

After work on Friday, I decide to drop in on Dad and Cretia, who should be back from their trip. I'm anxious to see them and hear about their time away. I'm also anxious for a few minutes alone with Cretia, to run a few things by her. As close as I am to my dad, I'm not ready to talk with him about whatever lunacy is taking over my thoughts about Chet. Early on, my dad adopted the Mama Bear role—a role in which he excels. There's no need to get him riled up.

I pull into their driveway, park the SUV, then sit for a moment. Chet and I were supposed to leave this evening, providing I was free to go. Dinner out, a room at a B & B, sleeping in on Saturday, lingering over a late breakfast…

Did Chet really forget to get the store covered, or was he avoiding the time together? Spending time with me hasn't seemed like a priority to him in recent months.

Or years.

When did he begin withdrawing? Is he withdrawing? His comment in the kitchen earlier this week whispers through me: *"Looking beautiful as usual, babe."* He's still attentive, right?

I shake my head. A fog of confusion rolled in this week—and I can't seem to find my way out. I sigh as I get out of the SUV and head for the front door, but before I get there, the door swings open.

"There's my girl!"

I square my shoulders and smile. "Hi, Daddy. How was the trip?"

"Good, but I missed you."

I stand on tiptoe as he wraps me in a hug. "I missed you too. I can't wait to hear all about it."

"We took lots of pictures to show you." He steps aside. "Come on in."

I step into the house and before I'm through the entry hall, Cretia rounds the corner from the kitchen. "Oh, there you are. We're so glad to see you. How are you? How are Chet and the kids? Tyler took such good care of my plants. Oh honey, come sit down, we need to catch up."

I follow Cretia and my dad into the living room.

My dad married Cretia during my senior year of high school—a time when I was desperate for a woman's nurture and input. At first, I was jealous of the time my dad spent with her, but soon I looked forward to seeing her almost as much as he did. Her presence also assuaged a worry I'd nursed since I began high school—leaving my dad alone when I went off to college. How could I leave him? What would he do all on his own? He was capable of taking care of himself, but...

He hadn't dated Cretia for long, maybe a few months, when he sat me down and told me he knew she was the one. They waited a full year before marrying, but he'd been right—Cretia was the one. For both of us.

After that, I assumed I too would experience that sense of knowing before I married. But it was missing when I married Chet. Or maybe I just didn't give it time to develop.

As we all go to sit in the living room, my dad stops. "Shoot. We've got three weeks' worth of mail piled up at the post office. That's where I was headed when you came up the walkway. I need to get there before five. How long can you stay?"

"As long as you want me. The kids have plans for the evening and Chet's at the store until closing—at least nine o'clock."

"Ted, you just go. We'll chat and you'll be back before we know it, and we'll all have a glass of wine together."

"Sorry to run off—"

"Go. I'll be here when you get back." I don't know whether to feel relief or dread that I'll get time alone with Cretia.

I sit on the sofa across from her chair. "Tell me about your trip."

"Oh, it was wonderful. But it will have to wait until your dad gets back—he'll want to tell you all about it. You just catch me up. What's going on with you?" She laughs. "Of course, he'll want to hear that too."

I scoot forward and take a deep breath. "Well, there was something I wanted to…" I hesitate. "While he's gone, I'd like to get your opinion about something."

"Well, sure. What is it?"

"It's…" I look at my hands in my lap. "I…"

"Jessica, what's wrong?"

I look back at Cretia, the words I'd wanted to say lost to me now.

"You know you can tell me anything."

"I know, it's just that… I don't know, I feel a little crazy."

"Crazy? You?" She shakes her head. "Not a chance. What's going on?"

I swallow. "It's probably nothing. It's just that Chet's seemed distant lately and… I don't know, I just wonder if…" My stomach knots. "You know what? Never mind. It's ridiculous." I shake my head. "Really."

"Why don't you let me decide if it's ridiculous or not?"

I exhale. "I don't know why it's even bothering me. Really, nothing's changed. It's just something Johnny said to me this week and it made me wonder if…Chet always tells me the truth."

"What's your intuition tell you?"

"Intuition?"

"Yes, you know, what's your heart say?"

"Cretia, you know me, I deal more in the realm of science—of facts, not intuition."

"Yes, you deal in science, but you also deal with history, and more important, you're also a woman, Jessica. We women listen to our emotions, our feelings, our instincts. Your intuition may be a little rusty, but you wouldn't be questioning Chet if it wasn't telling you something. So look at the facts and the history, but listen to your heart too. What's it telling you?"

I swallow the lump in my throat. "It's…it's telling me something's not right. But I can't back it up with facts or history. It's just a *feeling*."

Cretia leans forward. "Don't discount your feelings, Jessica. You can't live by them, but you can't ignore them either. Let your feelings lead you and then check things out."

"Okay."

"What is it Johnny said that got you all in a knot in the first place?"

My shoulders slump. "He said I make excuses for Chet."

"Ah…"

"I guess that's not new information?"

"No."

"Maybe I'm just facing it for the first time and wondering why I do that. You don't do it for Dad."

"No, I don't. Listen, honey. Johnny's observation was a good one. Maybe you were just ready to hear it. So ask yourself the tough questions. Ask Chet the tough questions. You'll work through it."

I nod. "You're probably right."

As I drive home Friday evening, after having stayed for dinner with my dad and Cretia, I consider her suggestion. Ask the tough questions. I try to rehearse those questions in my mind, and to imagine Chet's responses. But as I do, I realize I have no history to draw on. I've never really confronted Chet about anything.

I haven't ever asked him the hard questions.

I take a deep breath. I can, however, begin by facing a difficult question myself. Am I disappointed in Chet? As a husband? As I maneuver the shadowed twists and turns of the stretch of Highway 41, the answer, like a deer darting onto the road, catches me off guard.

I'm not disappointed.

I'm suspicious.

*I know little of men yet I venture to say that half our best
teachers are manufactured - so ground and pressed in the
mills of culture that God cannot play a single tune on them.*
John Muir

CHAPTER FOUR

Ted

CRETIA LOOKS OVER my shoulder as I import
our vacation photos from the camera SD card to my iMac.
"This is going to take a few minutes, you know."

"I know. I'm just watching. I want to see how they
turned out."

"Well, why don't you wait until I'm finished?"

"Oh, you!" She gives me a gentle swat. "Call me when
you're done."

Actually, there's more on the card than vacation
photos—these go back to our family barbecue in May. I
would've organized those photos sooner, but I got caught up
in planning for our trip—a road trip through Oregon,
Washington, and British Columbia. Beautiful country. So
now, I have a slew of photos to deal with.

Once they're done importing, I click through the images—they're so much easier to see on the twenty-seven-inch monitor. My eyes aren't what they used to be. When I come to a picture of Tyler towering over his mother, I stop and look at it a minute. He's a smart, strapping young man, that one—the definition of redemption, if you ask me.

When Jessie told me she was pregnant all those years ago, well, I was none too happy about it. First thing I asked was why the baby's father wasn't standing by her side as she told me. In his defense, she hadn't told him yet.

But that's when I stopped defending Chet.

It's a man's job to protect a woman. And Chet didn't have enough self-control to protect Jessie. Sure, it takes two to tango, but the man's supposed to lead that dance. And Chet should have told Jessica there'd be no dancing until they were married, if you know what I mean. If *he* wasn't going to say no, then I certainly taught that daughter of mine how to say it.

Ah well, I let go of all that a long time ago. I'm also a man who believes in forgiveness. And look at that boy now. Tyler is a good kid. His father on the other hand, well…he still has some work to do. Jessie too.

Chet wasn't good enough for my Jessie. Cretia might say I wouldn't have thought anyone was good enough, but that's not true. I've met some fine young men in my day— men who walk their talk. Men who believe in something or someone bigger than themselves. Men who put others first.

As far as I can tell, Chet's always put himself first.

And Jessie's let him.

I run my hand over the stubble on my chin. I taught her better than that. Or I tried to. But I guess I fell short somewhere. I look back at the picture of Tyler and Jessie again. Her smile is genuine. She loves that boy. Haley too. She's a good mom. A good woman. But for some reason, I'm not sure she's ever believed that about herself.

"How're you coming in there? Can I see them yet?"

I shake my head. That woman doesn't give up. "Come on in. They're all here, but I haven't organized them yet."

"Well, what are you doing?" Cretia comes in and stands next to the desk.

"I'm thinking. Why is it you suppose that Jessie doesn't...?"

"Doesn't what?"

"Why doesn't she respect herself more or... I don't know, I can't put my finger on it."

"Look at all she's accomplished. She wouldn't be where she is without respecting herself."

"I'm not talking about as a professional or even as a mom—she's confident in those roles. I mean as a woman. She doesn't respect herself as a woman or as a wife."

Cretia pulls over a chair from the corner of my den and sits herself down. "Maybe it's because she didn't have a woman in her life all those years, a role model to follow."

"I did all I could."

"Of course you did, Ted. But you couldn't make up for the mother she didn't have—the mother who walked out on her. A girl needs a mother, plain and simple. How's she supposed to form her identity as a woman without another woman leading the way?"

I shake my head, as I do every time I've thought of Jessica's mother since she left.

"What got you thinking about all this anyway?"

"I was just looking at this picture." I point to the photo on the screen.

Cretia gets up and comes around behind me and looks at the photo. "It's a good shot."

"It's a fine shot. But it got me remembering when Jessie told me she was pregnant with Tyler." I look over my shoulder at Cretia. "Remember how angry I was?"

"Yes, I remember. But you didn't let her see your anger. I was proud of you."

"Well, that did take some self-control." I chuckle. "What I never understood was why Jessie went and let that happen in the first place. But that's water under the bridge. What's bothering me now is that even though I forgave them both, I've never trusted Chet since."

"Ah, so we're back to that." Cretia puts her hands on my shoulders and gives them a squeeze. "You sure this is about Chet?"

I lean back in my chair. "'Course it is. What else would it be about?"

Cretia holds up her hands. "I'm just asking. And I'm not saying you're wrong about Chet, just check yourself." She gives my shoulders another squeeze. "Now's a good time to do that."

"Why now?"

"Just a sense I have. I'm going to make us a fresh pot of coffee. You call me when those pictures are organized."

I begin deleting duplicate photos and those not worthy of viewing. As I do, I take Cretia's suggestion. If that woman has a sense about something, I know enough to pay attention. Though I don't have to give it much thought to know she's right—my mistrust of Chet is as much, maybe more, about something else than it is about him. Though, I'm still not thoroughly convinced he's trustworthy.

It was the truth what I told Cretia, that the picture of Jessie and Tyler got me to thinking. But it wasn't the whole truth. I open a drawer in my desk, bottom left, and reach into a file toward the back of the drawer. An empty file except for one thing. I feel around until my hand lands on the envelope. I pull it out of the file and look again at my name scrawled across the front in handwriting that at one time was as familiar as my own. Well, almost that familiar. I turn the envelope over and run my finger across the still-sealed flap.

Why now? What on earth is the purpose of this? I sigh, then drop the letter back into the file and close the drawer.

I may tell myself I'm a man who believes in forgiveness, and I do, but… When I pulled that letter out of the pile of mail that stacked up at the post office while we were gone, well, it wasn't forgiveness I felt.

No, sir.

That letter's what got me to thinking about Jessie. And especially about Chet. Of course I need to open it and read it, but that's best done when I'm alone. When I have some extended time to think on what's inside.

Whatever hogwash that may be.

I am only a baby slowly learning my mountain alphabet.
John Muir

CHAPTER FIVE

Haley

 "BELAY?" I CALL to Zach.
"Belay on."

"Climbing."

I make my way up the face of the arch, leaving Zach beneath me holding the rope attached to the harness I'm wearing. Jake, our instructor, paired me with Zach for the camp since we climb at about the same level. Really, I'm the better climber, but Zach's pretty good.

"Haley, you're a better climber than that," Jake yells up to me. "Stretch yourself."

I glance down, then swallow. Jake is standing next to Zach, and they're both staring up at me.

"Trust Zach. He won't let go of the rope. He's got you." Jake slaps Zach on the back. Then loud enough for me to hear, he says to Zach, "She's trusting you, man. Prove you're worth her trust."

I look back up and plan a more challenging route than the simple one I'd begun. As I reach for the next hold, I know Zach is watching me because that's his job. But it's sort of distracting because, you know, he's watching me. I pull my T-shirt down, a pale pink North Face shirt that's bunched up under the harness. The T-shirt looks good with my black Spandex shorts. And for once, I'm glad I have my mom's skin, 'cause my long legs are tan. It's hard not to think about stuff like that when Zach's down there.

I figure out a new route and make my way toward the top of the arch. Zach tightens the rope or gives me slack as I need it.

"You got it, Haley," Jake yells. He took Heather's place after she left last year. I smile. It's easier to trust Zach as my belayer knowing Heather's gone and he's not watching her.

When we're done, Zach hangs around talking to a couple of guys while I get my backpack and stuff together. I pull the key ring with our car keys on it out of my backpack—my dad gave me the key ring and car keys after I got my permit on Friday. Then I leave to go find my dad who said he'd let me drive home with him.

"Haley."

I stop and turn around and look back at Zach who jogs over to meet me. "Hey, so you want to grab coffee or something?"

My heart starts beating crazy fast. "Um…"

"No big deal if you don't want—"

"No, I want to." I swallow. Great. That probably sounded desperate. "Let me check with my dad—I, um, I've started working here a couple afternoons a week and I don't know if he needs me or"—I lift the keys so Zach can see them—"if I'm heading home."

"Cool."

"Yeah, um, I'll be right back." I turn to go. "Oh, wait, where were you thinking? Like, Brew's Up?" I point toward the parking lot.

"Sure, that works."

Much better to say we're just going across the parking lot instead of having to ask if I can go with Zach somewhere in his car. Maybe Dad will say yes if it's not like some big deal. I look for him near the registers, but only see one of his employees, so I go back and find him in his office. "Hey…"

He holds up a finger and writes something down, then looks at me. "How'd it go?"

"Good." I shrug. "So like, if you don't need me for anything, I'm going to go get a coffee with Zach and then I can, you know, just hang around until you're ready to take me home." I already know he doesn't need me to work this afternoon because he told me so this morning. I mean, it's not like I really work here—I can't until I'm sixteen—I just kind of help my dad with stuff sometimes.

"With Zach? Who else is going?"

"We're just going to Brew's Up."

"Since when do you drink coffee?"

I roll my eyes. "Dad…"

His phone rings and he reaches for it. "Sure, go ahead."

I leave before he has time to change his mind, but as I walk back to where I left Zach, my stomach starts doing flips, like it's on a trampoline. I walk slower and take a deep breath. I want to go with Zach, but, I mean, like…what are we going to talk about all that time? Climbing, of course, but what else? I stop, turn around, and head to the restroom where I stare at myself in the mirror.

I set my backpack on the counter, wipe my palms on my shorts, and then dig through the backpack looking for lip gloss. Wait, does putting on lip gloss look like…like I'm trying too hard? Oh man, I'm gonna throw up. I take a few deep breaths. Chloe's so much better at this kind of stuff.

Oh. Chloe…

Bummer.

I leave the restroom and as I cross the store, my stomach calms. I come up beside Zach and smile. "Hey, sorry it took me so long. I…um, I can't go. My dad needs me here for a while."

"Maybe tomorrow?"

"Oh…sure."

"Nice."

I bite my lip as I watch Zach walk out of the store. *Tomorrow?* It's only Monday and the climbing camp goes through Friday.

My stomach starts doing flips again.

"Chipmunk had a date today." My dad winks at me and then takes a bite of his spaghetti.

My mom's eyes seem like they're going to pop out of their sockets.

"No, it wasn't a… We were just going to get coffee. Anyway, I didn't go. Dad was going to bring me home, but then Tyler picked me up, right?" I look at Tyler who, mouth full, nods.

"Chet?" My mom takes the napkin from her lap and sets it on the table.

Great. My heart pounds.

"What?"

"We agreed she's not going to date until she's sixteen." My mom turns from my dad to me. "Haley, you know that."

"Mom, it's not even called dating anymore. Anyway, I didn't go."

She sets her fork down and stares at my dad but doesn't say anything else.

After dinner I clear the table and put the dishes in the dishwasher. But as I do, my phone is exploding in the living room. I want to go see who's texting me, because they are seriously intent about whatever they're saying, but my mom made a no-phone-at-the-dinner-table-or-until-the-dishes-are-done rule. I rinse the last plate, load it, then dry my hands.

As I go into the living room, I can hear my mom and dad talking in the den. Talking loud, which is weird because they don't fight. Ever. I stand still and try to hear them, but even though they're loud, I can't really make out what they're saying, but I assume it's about the whole date thing, which is stupid, because I didn't go. And I'm not going tomorrow either. I sigh. At least, I guess I'm not.

I grab my phone. Chloe's texted me six messages.

> OMG! U will nvr guess who asked me out!

> Hello? Where r u? I need my bff!

> Ok, I'll tell u. Grant VenDeven! OMG!

> Haley?!

> Seriously, where r u?

> We're going rafting 2morrow! Hello?

Grant asked her out? I text Chloe back.

> What about Zach?

I get an almost immediate response.

> Zach who? LOL! Call me!

The battle we have fought, and are still fighting...is part of the eternal conflict between right and wrong, and we cannot expect to see the end of it.
John Muir

CHAPTER SIX

Jessica

THE NIGHT I met Chet, I was sitting in a bar with the guys. We weren't there to party; it was just the one place in town where we could go after work still smelling of smoke. And we didn't have to get cleaned up after training behind the station, where we'd worked the hoses that day. After a long week, we came to hang out, shoot the breeze, and play a little pool. With the exception of a long ponytail down my back and a couple of barely detectable anatomical differences, I was just another one of the guys.

But Chet noticed me anyway.

He walked up behind me at the bar, two pool cues in his hand. He tapped me on the shoulder and I turned around and looked into eyes the color of a summer forest—variegated greens, with flecks of brown and yellow. He smiled and heat rose to my face. I was grateful for the dim lighting.

He held up the cues. "Wanna play?"

The guys down the bar hooted and whistled. Randy, the guy on the stool to my left, called out, "Jess has herself a live one!" Amidst the roar, I nodded and followed Chet to the table where I watched as he leaned the cues against the wall and then racked the balls. When he was done, he grabbed the cues and came over and handed one to me. "So, what's a girl like you doing with all those bums?"

I laughed because I had no idea what to say.

I'd grown up in a world of men and was comfortable there. Most of my friends were guys and men dominated the profession I'd chosen. And yes, there were a few along the way I was attracted to, but if they noticed me as anything other than one of the guys, they didn't let on.

Chet was another story.

When he walked me out to my car later that night, he leaned in close and whispered in my ear, "You smell like a smoldering campfire under a starlit sky." Then he kissed the tip of my ear—a kiss so light, so tantalizing, it set me ablaze. When he turned and walked away, I wanted to follow him into the night every night for the rest of my life.

After dinner I find Chet in his den. I walk in, take a deep breath, and close the door. "I was surprised you told Haley she could go out for coffee with a guy. Haven't we always said she can't date until she's sixteen?"

Chet looks at me. "You're challenging me on this?"

"I'm…" My voice shakes. Why can't I have a simple, adult conversation with my husband? *It's time to grow up, Jessica.* "I want to discuss it—to understand your reasoning."

"Fine. Understand this—he's a good kid and they wanted to walk across the parking lot and get coffee. It was harmless. I said she could go."

"Maybe you could have called me so we could have talked about it."

"Talked about it? Half the time you're somewhere in the backwoods where I can't reach you. I've had to make a lot of parenting decisions without you, Jess. That's because of your choices, not mine."

Mouth dry, I struggle to swallow. "I know I'm hard to reach sometimes, but—"

"Sometimes?"

"Chet…"

"Either you trust me or you don't. Period."

Tears prick my eyes and I turn away so he won't see them. *How did this go so wrong?* I wipe the back of my hand across my eyes and turn to face him. "I work…" My voice shakes again but I have to get this out. "I work to help support our family. It isn't a choice *I* made—it's a choice *we* made."

"Is that what you tell yourself?"

I stare at him, my mouth open. *What?* "Chet…" Tears threaten again. "What's…happening to us?" The question comes out in a whisper.

"What's happening to *you*? I can't believe you'd question a decision I made concerning Haley."

"I'm…sorry. I am. I didn't mean to question your judgment. I just…" I wipe away the tears I'm no longer able to hide. "I…thought we could talk about it."

His shrug dismisses the issue. And me.

I turn to go, but as I do, anger roots me. I straighten my back and stand still. Chet's turned away and sat down at his desk. When he looks up and sees I haven't left, his brows lift. I just catch the look, but it's enough to spur me on.

"Chet, this is about Haley—her well-being. This isn't about us." We need to get back on track. "We want to protect her. We've talked about that. We want to keep her from situations she's not mature enough to handle."

He nods.

He's listening. "I don't want her to get involved yet—I don't want her in a position where she feels pressured and ends up"—I lift my hands, palms up—"like we did."

"So you think I pressured you? Is that it? You're blaming that on me too?"

"What? That's not what I said."

"It's exactly what you said. We were adults, Jess. And the way I remember it, you were a very willing participant. You know what? I'm done here. If you don't like the way I parent, then you take over." He gets up, grabs his keys off the desk, and walks out. The door to the garage slams and…

He's gone.

I wrap my arms around my waist and try to catch my breath and stop the flow of tears. What just happened?

"Was that about me? Was it?" Haley stands in the doorway of the den, hands on her hips. "Really, Mom? You made him leave over me having a stupid cup of coffee with a guy? Which, news flash, I didn't even do!" She grabs the door and slams it shut.

"Haley!" When I hear her bedroom door slam, I double over and my tears sprinkle the floor.

"Mom?"

I lift my head and see Tyler, hands on the door frame, leaning into the den. "Are you okay? What happened?"

He comes in and tries to put a hand on my shoulder, but I turn away. His concern for me is too much. "I'm sorry, I'm…fine. I am. We just had a little… It was just a thing, that's all it was."

But I know, even as I try to reassure Tyler, it was more than a *thing*. I just experienced the repercussions of confronting my husband. No wonder I've never done it before. I must have known, in some part of my being, that it wasn't allowed.

I take another series of deep breaths, hoping they'll settle my stomach.

🌲

After I get myself together, I tap on Haley's bedroom door, then open it. She's lying on her bed, facedown, her arms crossed and her head resting on them. When she looks up at me, her eyes are puffy and red. "Hey…" She doesn't say anything so I venture in and go sit next to her on the side of her bed. I put my hand on her back and rub gently like I did when she was little and couldn't sleep. "I'm sorry about whatever it is you overheard. None of it was your fault. Sometimes a husband and wife just disagree. Fortunately, it's a pretty rare event around here."

She turns her head toward me. "Did he come back?"

"Not yet. He needed some space and went for a drive— he'll probably end up at work." I sound more confident than I feel. Not that I doubt Chet will be back. It's just that I have no real idea where he's gone, but I want to reassure Haley.

"I don't get what the big deal was anyway."

"I've been downstairs thinking about that and I'd like to tell you what the big deal is."

She rolls her eyes. "Oh, great." Then she turns and rests her forehead back on her arms.

"It might surprise you."

Her words are muffled. "I doubt it."

I push ahead, knowing I need to be truthful with her. "I'm scared. That's it. I'm scared to let you grow up. I'm afraid that what happened to me will happen to you."

She turns her head and, though she doesn't look at me, I know I have her attention.

"What do you mean?"

I take a deep breath. "Want to sit up and I'll tell you?"

She looks at me for a minute as she decides, then she pushes herself into a sitting position and leans back against her headboard.

"Here"—I hand her a tissue—"I needed a few of these myself earlier."

She takes the tissue and wipes her nose.

"Your dad and I have never talked about telling you this. I think we just assumed you'd figure it out, like Tyler did, and ask. Maybe we should have—"

"Ask what?"

I shift to get comfortable. "How old is Tyler?"

"Almost nineteen, why?"

"And how long have your dad and I been married?"

She shrugs, thinks for a moment, then raises her eyebrows. "No way."

I nod.

She shakes her head, then puts her fingers in her ears. "Too much information, Mom." She takes her fingers out of her ears. "Wait. So like, did Grandpa want to kill you?"

"Probably, but fortunately for you, he didn't." I smile.

"So that's why I can't go out with a guy until I'm sixteen?"

"Sort of."

"That's really lame. Anyway, you were older than sixteen when you…you know."

I nod. "I was twenty-three."

"Anyway, I'm not going to do *that,* and if I did, I mean, there's birth control. Duh. How did you not know that?"

"I did know about birth control, but in the moment, I…"

"You what?"

Have I ever really answered that question for myself? What did happen? I sigh. Who am I kidding? I know what happened. I just don't like thinking about it. But a sense of knowing envelops me, and with it the willingness to not only think about what happened, but also to share it with Haley. It is one of the most important things I can share with my daughter. I inhale. "I knew your dad wanted to—"

Haley holds up one hand. "Don't!"

I shake my head. "No details, I promise. I knew your dad wanted *something,* and I was afraid that if I said no, I'd lose him." I tuck a strand of hair behind one ear. "How's that for lame?"

"Why would you lose him? I mean, if he really loved you."

I stare at Haley as I marvel at her insight—so beyond my own at her age, or at twenty-three for that matter—and I grasp for an answer. "I...don't know. Maybe I didn't trust that he really loved me."

"But he did."

"Of course." My response is automatic. But something gives me pause and I bookmark the moment so I can think about it again later.

Haley pulls one of her pillows onto her lap and picks at a thread on the pillowcase. She focuses on the thread as she asks her next question. "So did you get pregnant the...you know, the first time?"

"Yes."

We're both quiet for a moment, then I ask her a question I've been wondering about since dinner. "So who's the guy you were going to have coffee with?"

She looks at me, then looks back down at the pillow. "No one."

I'd hoped she'd tell me, trust me with the information. But rather than let her see my disappointment, I prod a little more. "Is that why you decided not to go with him, because he's no one—not important?"

"No."

"Then why?"

Haley looks at me as though she's weighing whether or not to tell me. She puts the pillow aside. "His name is Zach. I met him at climbing camp last year. He goes to my school too—he'll be a junior."

I don't say anything. I don't want to interrupt her and risk stopping the flow of words, which is so rare these days.

"I kind of knew he might, you know, like me, but Chloe likes him. Or she did." She picks up her phone and looks at the screen, and then groans.

"What?"

She shakes her head. "She texted me. She's going out with some other guy. So now it's going to be this big problem."

"What problem? Zach?"

"Mom." She rolls her eyes. "He's going to ask me to go to Brew's Up again tomorrow after camp. So what am I supposed to say?"

"The truth?"

"Like, really?" She throws her phone back down onto the bed and rolls over.

I stare at her rigid back and try to remember what it felt like for a fifteen-year-old girl to tell the older guy who asked her out that her parents won't let her date yet.

Definitely not good. Still… "Haley, turning your back on me isn't going to get you anywhere."

She doesn't respond. But then she turns back over and stares at the ceiling. When she finally looks at me, tears glisten in her eyes.

I put my hand on her leg. "Let's see if we can figure something out."

When we try to pick out anything by itself, we find it hitched to everything else in the Universe.
John Muir

CHAPTER SEVEN

Haley

BEFORE I WENT to bed, my mom said she called my dad and he'd gone to work, so I wasn't worried exactly, but I also couldn't really sleep knowing he was still gone. When I hear the garage door go up, I roll over in bed and feel around my desk until my hand lands on my phone. I pick it up and look at the time—1:38 a.m. How mad was he that he stayed at the store until 1:30? I mean, was whatever my mom said to him really that big a deal? I put my phone back on the nightstand and roll onto my back. Maybe he just had work to do.

They never fight and the one time they do, it's about me? Great. I put my hand on my tummy and rub back and forth, trying to make the knot inside go away.

But it isn't just him being gone that was keeping me up. It's a bunch of stuff.

Like what my mom said about getting pregnant, that she'd been afraid if she said no, she'd lose my dad. I can so see Chloe doing something like that. But my mom? Like my dad says, she's the brave one. She doesn't fight many wildfires anymore; she mostly stays at the staging area or command center or whatever it's called. She tells the fire crews where important cultural resources are and how they need to avoid them with their bulldozers, or where to cut fire lines to protect something. In a way, her whole job is about telling guys what to do or what not to do. When she first started working as a fire archeologist, she told me that a lot of the time she was one of the few women on-site.

Kind of like me and climbing.

Oh.

I've always thought I was more like my dad because he's a climber, but maybe I'm sort of like my mom too. I'm not afraid of climbing to the top of the arch, or of taking the hardest routes on either the arch or the walls or when we do a real climb in the park.

But...I'm scared to go out with Zach.

I sigh, roll over, and pull the blanket up around my chin. I mean, I wouldn't have gone out with him when Chloe liked him. But now that she's into some other guy, I don't have a reason to tell Zach no, especially since my mom told me tonight that I could go to Brew's Up with him: *"We'll take it one day at a time, okay?"*

So now...

If I tell Zach no again, will he stop liking me?

*Most people are on the world, not in it—have no conscious
sympathy or relationship to anything about them—
undiffused, separate, and rigidly alone like marbles of
polished stone, touching but separate.*
John Muir

CHAPTER EIGHT

Jessica

I ROLL OVER, kicking the sheet and blanket off
as I do. *Where is he?* I look at the digital clock again, as I
have at least every five minutes since climbing into bed.
After I finished talking with Haley, I went downstairs and sat
at the desk in Chet's den and called him several times, but he
didn't answer. I didn't know what to do with myself, so I
turned on the computer on his desk and rested my fingers on
the keyboard. After a few minutes, I typed a name into the
search field: *Sandra Marie Martin.*

A variety of listings displayed, but none of them what I
was looking for.

I tried another name: *Sandra Marie Shreeve.* My
actions were rote. I waited, but again, what I was looking for
didn't appear.

She didn't appear.

I closed the window on the screen and went to bed.

In areas where there's an increased frequency of fire, like during years of drought, native plant species can be eliminated from an area altogether and are often replaced by a non-native, invasive species.

What once was, is no longer.

My mother was eliminated from my life. And anxiety was the invasive species that took over.

I put my hand on my chest as an almost physical ache settles there. A familiar ache. My breath catches. Eyes wide, I stare into the dark void of our room.

How many times have I typed her name? How many times have I searched for her?

What if, like my mother, Chet…

Tendrils of fear tighten their grip around my throat.

Stay calm.

I swallow once, twice, and then gasp for air.

Just breathe.

My heart thumps in my chest as its rhythm pounds in my ears. I try to inhale, try to suck air into my lungs, but my throat constricts and is, I'm sure, cutting off my airway. I drop my arms from around my knees and swing my legs over the side of the bed. I steady myself, palms flat on the mattress, arms shaking, fingertips tingling. I close my eyes and try to visualize another place—another time—but my mind is locked on one moment. No, two moments.

The first time.

And now.

Though there were times in between, I can pinpoint the exact moment—can recall just where I was and what I was thinking the first time this happened.

Terror cackles—its hot breath reeking of sulfur.

No. Please, no. I reach for the bedside lamp. My fingers, now damp, slide off the chain as I tug at it. I pull again and just catch the lamp as it tilts and falls. I right it and light floods the room. I gulp for air and then raise my hands to my chest and push against my sternum with my palms.

The first time, I was eleven years old and I'd realized she was never coming back.

What if…?

I push again on my sternum—the pressure reassuring somehow. I stand. *Water, just get a drink of…* The room begins to spin with dizzying speed. I close my eyes as I grab for the nightstand.

Breathe.

"Jess?"

Chet. I open my eyes and pivot to face him. I'm aware of him crossing the room, but I turned too fast.

"What the…?" Chet reaches for me and breaks my fall. He holds me tight.

I flail, trying to pull away from him, but his grip is too firm.

"Jessica, stop. Stop it!" He lifts me toward the bed. "Sit. Jess, sit on the bed." He sets me down, his hands on my shoulders now, making it impossible to move.

"Go…go away." Still gasping, I swat at him. "I can't…I can't…breathe."

He reaches past me and grabs the phone.

"No!" I bend at the waist and drop my head low, and this time as I try to suck air into my lungs, my chest rises. I exhale and my chest falls. I inhale again as the vise around my throat begins to relax its hold.

"I'm calling 911."

I hold up one hand and grab his arm with the other. "Wait…"

I take another breath.

"I'm calling."

"I'm…" I lift my head and make eye contact with him. "I'm…okay." I drop my hand from his arm. "Really, I am." I take a deep breath and though I'm still trembling, each successive breath comes more easily. "See. I'm okay. It's just…it's nothing."

"Nothing? It doesn't look like nothing." He steps back. "What's wrong with you?"

I shake my head. "Nothing. I just…" I shake my head again. "Nothing." I stand, my movements slow. I plant my feet. "Nothing is wrong with me." I read the confusion on his face, then I turn, deliberate this time, and take slow steps toward the bathroom. "I'm fine."

I close and lock the bathroom door, then slump to the floor. With my back against the door, certain Chet can't get in if he tries, I…breathe. And then when Chet doesn't try to come in—doesn't even ask again if I'm okay—

I cry.

The first time, I'd just come home from school, walked in the front door, and gone straight to the kitchen expecting to find the college-aged girl my dad had hired to keep me company when he was working. At eleven, I refused to let my dad call her a babysitter. Instead, there was someone else standing at the kitchen sink.

A woman.

Long, dark hair cascading down her back.

"Mom?" I whispered. With the water running she didn't hear me, so I said it again, louder. "Mom." Tears flowed as I threw my books on the counter and ran to her, but when she turned around…

It wasn't her.

I tried to swallow, but hope lodged in my throat and my heart beat so fast I was sure it would explode. I took a step back, opened my mouth, and tried to suck in air, but not only couldn't I swallow, I couldn't breathe.

Instead of my mom, Dot—Johnny's wife—stood at the sink.

The thing I remember most was watching Dot watch me. Her lips falling from the curve of a smile to a straight line, then a frown. Her eyes went from dark brown to black, and her brow furrowed. Yes, her features were similar to my mother's, but not my mother's at all.

"Jessica, breathe. Breathe, baby."

She reached for a dishcloth, ran it under warm water, then guided me to a chair at the kitchen table. She helped me into the chair, then went to stand behind me. She reached down, put her arms around me, and pressed the warm, damp cloth against my chest.

"Breathe with me, baby. C'mon, just breathe. It's easy. In, out, in…" She whispered the words in my ear as she inhaled and exhaled, inhaled and exhaled, holding me tight, her breath damp against my cheek, the warmth of the cloth pressed against my sternum. "In and out…"

It felt like hours, but was likely just seconds, before I caught her rhythm and was able to breathe again. When I finally quieted, I slumped in the chair and cried and cried. She finally led me to the sofa, had me lie down, and then covered me with an afghan. She sat with me the rest of the afternoon, her hand on my back, rubbing small circles between my shoulder blades.

Later, after our family doctor poked and prodded, he told my father what Dot had instinctively known—I'd likely had a panic attack. It could happen again or not. Time would tell.

The last time I had one was during college, long before I married Chet. I never told him about the attacks. They were something from my past—something that no longer mattered.

Until tonight.

I remember my mother as an outline, a caricature void of shade or dimension. My father added very little to the picture, so I was left to fill in the color. Sable hair, ebony eyes, and skin the burnished reddish-browns of fall. A physical composite wasn't difficult to create—my father had a few black-and-white photos taken when they were married and one or two of my mother holding me soon after I was born. I could look at those photos and assign my own coloring to the faded prints.

But an emotional composite required creativity.

I've spent a lifetime imagining scenarios that would make my mother think I was better off without her rather than succumbing to the evidence that selfishness was her driving force.

My memories of the day she left are some of my earliest and are sensory in nature: the sound of my dad and Dot talking in the living room, the sweet scent of cornbread baking, followed by the acrid smell of it burning, and later, the feel of my stomach clenching as I vomited. My daddy holding my shoulders as I bent over the toilet.

My body must have known what my mind was too young to comprehend.

My body, it seems, has always comprehended what I want to deny.

That awareness came as I sat slumped on the bathroom floor last night. The panic attacks, so long dormant, point to something I'd rather ignore. Or maybe…I grasp for another explanation—our raised voices, Chet leaving last night…it all simply triggered the memory of the day my mother left. And my body reacted.

My phone vibrates on my desk, interrupting my reverie. I glance at the phone. It's Chet. He was still asleep when I left early this morning. I pick up the phone, get up from my desk, and head outside where others won't hear the conversation. I answer as I go. "Hey." My tone is guarded—I can't help it.

"How are you feeling? You scared me last night."

"Fine. I'm fine. It was nothing. Not nothing, just…you know, stress maybe."

"Okay, if you're sure."

"I'm sure."

"Jess, listen, I don't like how last night went down. It shouldn't have happened. The kid Haley wanted to have coffee with is a good guy. I'd rather give her permission to spend time with a guy like that than have her go behind our backs and hang out with a jerk, you know?"

"I know."

"Good. So we agree."

Chet doesn't ask if we agree, he states it as a fact and I don't argue the point, but there is something I can't let go. I stand in a patch of sunlight in the parking lot outside the Resources Management and Science building, close my eyes, and take a deep breath. "So...where did you go last night?"

He hesitates. "What do you mean?"

What do I mean? Isn't that obvious? "When you left. Where did you go?"

"I drove around. Then went to the store and worked. Why?"

It's my turn to hesitate. "I...just wondered. I called but you didn't answer."

"Jess"—there's an edge to his tone—"are you accusing me of something?"

"What? No. I just...no. Why would you think that?"

"Because that's how it sounds. I don't even know you this week. Where's my wife?"

"I'm...sorry. I..."

"Yeah. I'll talk to you later." Chet hangs up.

For the second time in less than twenty-four hours, the same thought hits me: How did the conversation go so wrong? After all, he did call to apologize, and...

I replay the conversation in my mind. Did he apologize? No. He stated that he didn't like how things went last night. But didn't he mean he was sorry for how he reacted? Or is that just what I wanted to hear?

I stand in the parking lot, which is surrounded by thickets of trees and dotted with granite outcroppings. How I long to put on my hiking boots, grab a pack, and lose myself in those trees—feel the embrace of the forest, where the sounds of nature deafen me to the constant din of my mind.

I turn to head back into the office, our conversation still troubling me. When I asked Chet where he'd gone last night, he was...what? Defensive? *Was* I accusing him of something? Maybe he's right, it's me—I'm just not myself. If I'm honest, I sense that too. I'm on edge, no longer willing to let things go, to retreat to please him. I'm no longer willing to bury my head in the sand, as they say.

Why?

And if I'm not myself, then who am I?

"You're losing yourself, Jessica." Cretia's words come back to me now.

Several years after Chet and I married, Cretia confronted me.

"What are you doing?"

I'd shrugged, confused by her question. "What do you mean?"

"With Chet—in your marriage—you're losing yourself. It's like you're a chameleon. You become whatever color matches Chet's fancy."

"I don't know what you mean."

She leaned forward. "Jessica, you're a strong woman—stronger than most—"

I shook my head, looked around Brew's Up where we were talking over lattes, and whispered, "You know that's not true. You know about the anxiety—the panic attacks I used to have."

"Oh for goodness sakes, Jessica, you struggled with some anxiety induced by a traumatic event. And, may I remind you, you overcame your mother's leaving. Does it still hurt? I'm sure it does, but look at yourself—look how far you've come, and I'm not just talking about your career. But, with Chet, the lines are blurring. You're no longer yourself. You're becoming a weak copy of him."

"Isn't that how it's supposed to be? Don't a husband and wife become more like each other as time goes on?"

"Sure they do, honey, but one doesn't give up herself— her thoughts, her opinions, her desires, just to please the other. In a healthy relationship the couple grows together. Instead, you're ceasing to exist."

Cretia was right.

But I didn't hear her. Or maybe I couldn't hear her.

Until now.

Man must be made conscious of his origin as a child of Nature. Brought into right relationship with the wilderness he would see that he was not a separate entity endowed with a divine right to subdue his fellow creatures and destroy the common heritage, but rather an integral part of a harmonious whole.
John Muir

CHAPTER NINE

Ted

"WHERE ARE YOU off to?" I set my coffee cup in the sink.

"Oh Ted, it's Tuesday, you know perfectly well where I'm going."

"Bridge."

Cretia puts her purse over her shoulder and then comes and gives me a peck on the cheek. "And don't you pout about it. I'll be home in time to make your lunch."

"What are we having?"

"Meatloaf sandwiches."

"Good. Then you're forgiven for deserting me."

Cretia laughs, gives me another kiss, and then sashays out of the house like she's off to a party. Which, in a way, I guess those bridge games are. I stand at the window in the breakfast nook until I see her drive out the driveway and down the street, then I make my way to my office. I have some unfinished business waiting for me in my file drawer.

I sit at my desk and flip on the scanner so I can listen for local fire activity. Once a firefighter, always a firefighter. I pick up on local Cal Fire activity and National Park dispatches on this broadcast, so I know when Jessie's likely to get a call.

Jessie.

I lean back in my chair and eye the drawer as a dispatcher relays a call.

Honestly, I'd prefer to just forget that letter ever came, and it better not have anything to do with Jessie. I guess the only way to find out is to deal with it—whatever it is. I lean forward, open the drawer, and pull it out. As I slit the envelope with my letter opener, I hope I'll find it's just a piece of business—something about the divorce. This many years later? I shake my head. No.

The only time I've heard from her since she left was the one time the bank made a mistake and didn't automatically deposit her spousal-support payment. Isn't that just the way—she leaves us and then to add insult to injury, every month for the next several years, I had to make a payment to her? California—a no-fault state. Well, I'd like to tell the state of California who was at fault, because believe you me, I know exactly whose fault it was.

I grunt. One thing's for sure, whatever this is about, it won't be simple. Nothing about that woman is ever simple. I pull out what looks like two sheets of paper, unfold them, and begin reading.

🌲

Cretia stands in the doorway between the house and the garage. I turn the table saw off. "What'd you say?"

"I said, what are you doing?"

I brush my hands together to rid them of sawdust. "What does it look like I'm doing?" My tone is gruffer than I intend.

"Don't get smart with me. Obviously you're cutting something. But what and why?"

"Well, you said you'd like a few shelves for the closet in the guest bedroom. Said you thought that'd be a good idea, didn't you?"

"Yes, I did. So…what's wrong?"

"Nothing's wrong."

"Ted?"

"That fire over off of Highway140 has taken off."

"Is Jessie involved?"

"She's on call, so if she hasn't already been dispatched, she will be soon. They're calling for strong winds again later this afternoon."

Cretia comes down the steps and walks over to me. She puts a hand on my arm. "What else is going on?"

"Isn't that enough?"

"Sure it is, but that's old hat to you."

"Can't a man come out to his own garage to cut a few shelves without getting the third degree? How was bridge?"

Cretia stares at me a moment. "Bridge was fine. Dot sent home some of that chicken salad she makes that you like so much. And Johnny said to tell you it's time for the two of you to meet up for coffee."

I ignore her comment about Johnny—or try to. "That chicken salad will make a nice snack."

She pats my tummy. "Or we could have it for lunch."

"With the meatloaf?"

"No silly, we'll save the chicken salad for lunch tomorrow."

"I guess we could do that too. So, you going to let me finish this project?"

She stares at me a few seconds, then nods. "Yes, I am. But I'll be right inside if you decide you'd like to talk about anything."

I turn the saw back on and line up the next cut. The best thing Sandra ever did, besides giving birth to Jessie, was leave me so that when Cretia came along I was free to pursue her. Come to think of it, it was the best thing she ever did for Jessie too. Though I don't think Jessie can see it that way. It's just too bad Cretia didn't come along earlier in Jessie's life.

It's too bad she didn't come along earlier in my life.

Sandra just made a mess of things. And if the damage she caused by leaving wasn't enough, now she's—

I push the board against the blade of the saw, forcing it rather than guiding it, and it buckles back on me.

She's destroyed everything.

I throw the switch and turn the saw off, then pull off my leather gloves and throw them to the floor.

Everything!

Why couldn't she just leave well enough alone?

I put my hand on my chest, over my heart, like it will lessen the ache that's settled there, and tears blur my vision.

She left me and Jessie. She should have just kept it that way—stayed away for good. Why'd she have to go and send that letter? I stand for another few minutes, staring at that board on the table saw, then I bend, feeling every one of my years in my bones, and pick up my gloves. I jam my hands back into the gloves, right first, then left. I turn the saw back on and cut another length, letting the saw do the work this time.

I find slight satisfaction in the clean cut of the board, but it isn't enough to dull the pain that letter—that woman—inflicted.

By the time I've finished with the saw, I've got three more shelves than we need.

But I still haven't worked out what to do about what I now know.

It's California law that a home has a defensible space of one hundred feet to help protect it from wildfire. Cal Fire breaks it down like this: The immediate thirty feet surrounding a home is the critical area and requires clearing of flammable foliage. Fuel clearing for the remaining seventy feet involves creating a horizontal and vertical space between plants. In other words, you can leave your trees as long as you remove all the plants beneath the trees to eliminate a fire ladder. Basically, they expect people to use their noggins, though that's expecting a lot of some folks.

After I finished the shelves, I decided it was time to clear an area of dry weeds around the back of our property. I cleared them once this season already, then we got one afternoon of rain. We need the rain, but it wasn't enough precipitation to do any good—just enough to cause the weeds to sprout again.

I put on a pair of goggles and power up the Weed Eater and begin the work of clearing the area. I also noticed a dead branch on one of the oaks near the house—it needs to go. The branch, not the tree. Though the chance of Cretia letting me get on a ladder with a chain saw is about as good as the chance of a deluge of rain in California during the month of August. One can only hope.

The problem with that letter from Sandra—well, one of the problems—is that it has me thinking about that time in my life, something I've done a good job of avoiding. Too good a job, Cretia would say. But what's the point? Why dwell on failure when you can look ahead to success? That's my motto and it's served me well. Though, as Cretia has also pointed out, I don't know that it's served Jessie well.

Maybe I should have talked more about her mother. Told her what she wanted to know. Maybe I should have told her what happened, but it wasn't about her and I didn't want her ever thinking it was. And who am I kidding? I didn't want to talk about it. It hurt too much. But it was more than that—it didn't just hurt, it also brought up questions—doubts—I couldn't quell. When it finally stopped hurting and I'd silenced the doubts for good...well, why bring it up and risk having to deal with it all over again?

I kick a rock out of the path of the Weed Eater. Maybe if I'd given it more thought I'd have realized how selfish that decision was. Jessie deserved the truth. She still does.

Problem is, I'm a coward.

Or maybe the problem is that I barely remember the truth after all these years. I grunt. It's a combination of both—I'm an old coward who can't remember what's important. Oh, Cretia would have my hide if she knew I was thinking like this. *Stinking thinking* is what she'd call it. So…what was the truth? What is the truth?

I shut off the Weed Eater, wipe the sweat from my forehead with the back of my hand, and stand and look out at the forest surrounding our property—oaks and pines and a dozen other varieties of trees. Underneath it all is manzanita, weeds, dry brush—a fire waiting to happen with this heat and lack of humidity. If something sparked, would a hundred feet of defensible space save the house? It might. No guarantee. But it just might.

And that's the truth of what happened.

I didn't clear a defensible space in my first marriage. When something ignited, there was no stopping it. And the destruction was inevitable. And complete.

For the first time since Sandra left, I realize that maybe she wasn't the only one to blame for what happened. I sigh. Maybe I had some responsibility too. I suppose if I'm going to tell Jessie the truth, I have to tell her the whole truth, whether I like it or not.

But there's someone else who holds a good deal of the responsibility, though Sandra didn't mention him by name.

It's a fact I can't yet fathom.

It just doesn't add up.

Never did.

The warm, brooding days are full of life and thoughts of life to come, ripening seeds with next summer in them or a hundred summers.
John Muir

CHAPTER TEN

Haley

"YOU LOOKED A little beat on the wall today. I mean, you looked great, but…" Zach gazes at me over his iced mocha. "I probably could have said that better, right?"

I smile. "It's okay, really. I stayed up too late last night. I just didn't have it in me today."

"Yeah. That happens."

I take a sip of my iced vanilla latte, the coffee still overpowering the vanilla and the three sugar packets I added. Why do people drink this stuff? I don't know what to say next and I swear my palms are sweating even against the icy cup. This is just so awkward. Even more awkward was my dad's reaction when I told him Mom had told me I could go with Zach today.

"Oh, so now she agrees with me?"

What was that about? Don't put me in the middle of your stuff. Not that I really said that, but…

After my dad got home last night, or more like this morning, I decided I might as well have coffee with Zach and get it over with instead of worrying about it forever. It was either that or not show up for camp today, and that would have just delayed the whole thing.

"So we're climbing in the park tomorrow. What've you climbed? Probably everything, knowing your dad."

Zach leans back in his seat, seeming totally at ease. I wish I felt the same. "I haven't done that much, really. He keeps pretty busy between the store and teaching for the mountaineering school. I go bouldering with my brother and his friends sometimes, but my mom gets kind of freaked about it. I mean I've done climbs with my dad, but"—I smile—"it's not like I've gone up the face of El Capitan." I pause. "Yet."

He laughs. "Good to know. Someday, though. How awesome would that be?"

"I know, right?"

Zach runs his hand through his curly blond hair. "I haven't done anything yet. Like the cables up Half Dome, I gotta give that a try. The view would be killer. I wonder if you get cell reception up there. Good place to take a selfie and post it." He laughs again.

I like how he doesn't take himself too seriously. I set my cup down. "You get reception up there. Look…" I pull out my phone and scroll through my Facebook photos. I find what I'm looking for, then hold out my phone for him to see.

"Check you out. When was that?"

"Last summer. We did it as a family—we've done it a few times. My mom's not a climber, but she loves that hike and the cables are no problem for her. We hiked up from the valley, camped at Little Yosemite Valley, summited, and then took the Panorama Trail over to Glacier Point the next day. My grandpa picked us up there. We were total tourists, but it was cool."

"Could you do the whole thing in a day?"

"Sure. That's what we usually do—go up the Mist Trail from the valley, then back down. It's a long day, but it's amazing."

"Want to do it with me sometime? Before school starts?"

"Sure. I mean, you know, maybe."

"So what does maybe mean?" He smiles at me and I notice again how white his teeth look against his tanned face. "Like maybe yes, or maybe no?"

I take another sip of my drink as I decide how to answer him. "You have to have a permit for the cables and it's too late to apply unless you apply for the daily lottery."

"How does that work?"

"They give out something like fifty daily permits. You have to apply two days in advance of the date you want to hike, then they let you know if you get it by that night."

"Cool. So it's still possible. You want to do it?"

"Yeah, but…"

"What?"

I hesitate, then make my decision. "Okay, so"—I roll my eyes—"I don't know if my parents would let me."

Zach nods. "I get why they might not."

I stare at him. "Really?"

"Yeah, I mean, people have fallen from there and died. It's a big deal." He lifts his drink, puts the straw up to his mouth, then stops. "Oh wait, is that what you meant? Or did you mean you don't know if they'd let you go with me?"

I look down at the table and then back to him. "Maybe both."

"Hey, doesn't hurt to ask, right? And if they say no, then maybe they'll let us do something else."

I smile. "Thanks."

"For what?"

"You know, for coffee, and not, like, thinking I'm a baby."

He lifts one hand, palm up. "Hey, I have parents too. I get it."

I set my coffee cup on the table. "So what else do you like to do besides climbing?"

He stretches out his long legs. "Surf, mostly."

I laugh. "Surf? Um, you're kinda in the wrong place for that."

"Yeah, no kidding. My mom likes the small-town stuff, and when she got an offer to teach up here, she asked how I'd feel about living here." He shrugs. "It's cool with me. It's a new adventure. My dad lives in Laguna Beach, so I surf when I'm with him."

"Oh. So…your parents are…?"

"Divorced."

I try to think how that would feel. I could barely take hearing my parents fight last night. "Wow… Sorry."

"Nah, it's fine. They split when I was little. I hardly even remember them being together, so this is my normal. I hang at my dad's a few weeks every summer and then again at either Thanksgiving or Christmas. Sometimes he'll fly me down for a weekend. Whatever. It's cool. And the surf's good there."

"So that's why you haven't done much in the park? I mean, your mom, she's not…" I stop. Am I dissing his mom?

He laughs. "No, she's not really into the outdoorsy stuff. We've driven through the valley a few times and had lunch at the Ahwahnee once. Swanky place."

"Yeah, we go there for special occasions sometimes." I lean back in my seat and sort of settle in.

This isn't so hard after all.

After we have coffee, Zach offers to drive me home, but I tell him I have to go back to the store to help out for a few hours. The last thing I need is my parents flipping out at me—or worse, at each other—because I got in a car with a guy. Anyway, my dad said he'd let me drive home this afternoon rather than just drive around the parking lot which, since I got my permit on Friday, is all he's let me do.

When I walk back into Mountain Play, my dad is near the registers talking to someone. I walk past them on my way back to the office to wait for him, and I recognize the woman he's talking to. I mean, sort of. I've seen her here a lot recently.

When I get to the office, I sit at my dad's desk and sign in to my Facebook on his computer so I can message Chloe and tell her about Zach. Not that there's much to tell, but I might as well let her know I hung out with him while she's focused on another guy.

I stare at the computer screen. *There's not much to tell?* Yeah, right! I just hung out with Zach Landrum! Seriously! And it was only a little awkward. But my fingers pause over the keyboard. Will Chloe be happy for me?

"Why the frown?"

I jump. I didn't hear my dad come into the office.

"How was coffee, Chipmunk? Looks like it didn't go very well."

"Are you ever going to stop calling me that?"

"Probably not. Coffee?"

"Coffee is gross. Even with sugar."

"It's an acquired addiction, but that's not what I meant."

I shrug.

"C'mon. Spill it. How was your time with Zach?"

"Good."

"Good?"

"Yeah, good. So…who was that?" I point toward the registers.

"Changing the subject, huh?"

I raise my eyebrows.

He looks out the office door. "Her? She's a North Face rep, why?"

"I've seen her around here a lot lately."

"Yeah, well, North Face is one of our main lines."

"So I get to drive home, right?"

"That depends. Are you going to tell me about your date?"

I roll my eyes. "It wasn't a date. Who even says *date* anymore besides you and Mom?"

"Other old people like us. You want to drive, you have to share information."

"That's bribery or blackmail or something."

"Yes it is." He grabs his car keys off the desk and dangles them in front of me. "Speak."

"Really?"

"Yep, really."

"It was fine. He's fine. Okay?"

"Details." He jangles the keys again.

I try not to smile, but he can tell and laughs. "I hold all the power."

"Whatever." I get up from the desk, then walk past my dad and grab the keys out of his hand.

"Hey!"

"I'll tell you on the way home."

"Deal."

Once we're in the car and he's made a huge show of buckling his seat belt like he's sure he's going to die, I pull out of the parking space, and then out of the parking lot onto the highway.

"Nicely done."

"Thank you. Hey, so like, do you have to be eighteen to get a wilderness permit—a day permit to climb Half Dome?"

"No changing the subject. We had a deal."

"I'm not changing the subject. I'm asking for Zach."

"Nope, no age restrictions on permits. He planning to go?"

I shrug. "Maybe."

"Oh, aren't you the coy one."

"Coy? You are so old." I glance at him. "He was just talking about doing some stuff in the park because, you know, he hasn't lived here all that long, and I told him he'd need a permit."

"So you like this guy?"

I shrug. "He's okay. I mean, you know, he's nice."

"Nice is good."

I glance at him again. "Yep."

"Hey, keep your eyes on the road. Stop talking and focus."

I laugh. "No problem."

"So are you planning on hiking with him?"

I stare straight ahead. "Sorry, I can't talk. I'm focusing."

Earth has no sorrow that earth cannot heal.
John Muir

CHAPTER ELEVEN

Ted

I WAS THIRTY-SIX years old when I married for the first time. I was fit, able-bodied, and still doing a young man's job, jumping out of airplanes to fight fires. But I was an old workhorse to Sandra's filly. She was twenty-five, long-legged, spirited, and with eyes so black they concealed her every thought and emotion. A woman some men would say needed breaking. But I've never been that kind of man.

When she got pregnant right away, I was thrilled. She was less so. But I figured she'd come around to the idea of a baby. I figured wrong. The pregnancy was hard on her, and the way she screamed when she delivered Jessie, I thought she might just up and die on us.

I know I don't have a clue about how it feels to birth a baby, but plenty of women make it through just fine. Sandra didn't. She was never the same and she seemed to blame that fact on Jessie. And me.

When I finally told Cretia about Sandra and the whole mess, she got me to thinking about something I hadn't considered.

"You know, Ted, hormones can wreak havoc with a woman's system during pregnancy. She may have suffered with postpartum depression too."

But I reason now, as I have a hundred times since that conversation with Cretia years ago, if Sandra had suffered from postpartum depression, wouldn't she have eventually gotten better? Wouldn't she have come to her senses at some point and realized what she'd done by leaving? Not to me, but to her daughter?

"Ted?"

"What?" I look over at Cretia who's sitting in her chair—the one right next to mine in front of the television. She's got the remote pointed at the TV and she's paused the game.

"What's the score?"

"The score?"

"Yes, what's the score of the game we're watching?"

I look at the screen, but the score isn't posted. "Why are you asking me? You're watching the game too."

"It seems I'm the only one watching the game. You're somewhere else."

"How can I be somewhere else when I'm sitting right here?"

"You know perfectly well what I mean. It's time you stop stewing and talk to me. Something's bothering you. I've given you several days to mull it over, whatever it is. Now, it's time to talk."

I take my baseball cap off and smooth my hairs back, all fourteen of them, then put the cap back on. I get up out of my chair and head for the office.

"Honey? Where are you going?"

"I have something to show you. Just sit tight, I'll be right back."

Cretia folds the letter, slips it back into the envelope, and sets it on the coffee table. "Oh, honey, no wonder you've been moping around here."

"That all you have to say?"

"No. But I'm going to withhold what I want to say. I need a few minutes to process it all. But I will say this. Even if it's true, Ted, it doesn't change a thing." She gets up out of her chair.

"Where you going?"

"How about a cup of coffee?"

"Do we have any of those cookies you made?"

"Yes, and"—she points to the letter—"having read that, you deserve as many as you want." She goes to the kitchen, and I get up and take the letter and tuck it back into the filing cabinet in the office. As least that letter's good for unlimited cookies.

And that's about all it's good for.

I meet Cretia back in the living room, where she's set a plate of cookies on the coffee table. I down two before she comes back with my coffee. Once she's handed it to me, she settles back in her chair. "I'd like to just burn that letter, pretend it never came."

I slurp a sip of the coffee. "Me too. But it did."

"Well, like I said, it doesn't change anything. Are you going to tell Jessie?"

I lean back in my chair. "I suppose I have to. I owe her that, don't I?"

"Oh, honey…"

I grab another cookie and pop it into my mouth. "She deserves—"

"Don't talk with your mouth full. And yes, you're right, she deserves the truth, but how do you know the truth?" Cretia sets her mug of coffee down. "This just makes me angry. So angry. Here Jessica's longed for word of her mother all these years, and this is what she'll get?"

"Yep. And you're right, I don't know what's true, but I intend to find out." Cretia may say this news doesn't make an ounce of difference, but it sure feels like it makes a difference. A big difference.

I reach for another cookie.

Nearly all the park is...full of charming company, full of God's thoughts, a place of peace and safety amid the most exalted grandeur and eager enthusiastic action, a new song, a place of beginnings abounding in first lessons of life.
John Muir

CHAPTER TWELVE

Haley

TODAY, ZACH ASKED if I could go to lunch with him after our last climb in the park tomorrow. The group from camp all meets there, but he'd drive himself. He said we could grab burgers at one of the concessions by Yosemite Lodge, hang out, and then he'd drive me home before dark. Before dark means I'd spend the whole day with him.

Yeah right. Like that's going to happen.

But after having coffee with him on Tuesday and being with him during the rest of camp this week, I really want to go. I look at the clock on my phone: 9:23 p.m. If I don't ask now, my parents will go to bed and it will be too late.

It's now or never.

When I get downstairs, my dad is on his computer in the den and my mom is in the kitchen. I know there's no sense in talking to my dad without my mom, so I go to the kitchen.

"Haley, can you grab the mustard out of the fridge?" She's standing at the island making a sandwich.

"Who's that for?"

"You. For after camp tomorrow."

"Oh." I hand her the mustard. "Um, yeah, about that."

"Camp?"

"Yeah, well, after…"

She puts a few slices of turkey on a piece of bread, and when I don't say anything else, she stops what she's doing and looks up at me. "What's up?"

I shrug. "It's just…I need to ask you something."

She smiles. "So ask."

"No, like both you and dad. Together."

She looks at me for a second, her eyebrows raised like she's going to ask me something, but then changes her mind. "I'll get your dad." She wipes her hands on a towel on the counter and then leaves the sandwich and goes to the hallway. "Chet, can you come here? Haley wants to talk to us."

His chair scrapes against the stone floor in the den. He comes into the kitchen, leans against the island, then looks from me to my mom. "What's up?"

They both stare at me and wait for me to answer. I take a deep breath. "Okay, don't freak out or anything. Promise?"

"Nope." My dad winks at me.

"I'm serious."

"So am I." He reaches over and takes a piece of turkey off the sandwich my mom was making and pops it into his mouth.

"Haley, we can't promise anything until we know what you're going to ask. So rather than keep us in suspense, why not just get it over with?" She puts another piece of turkey on the bread.

"Okay, so Zach asked if I could hang out with him tomorrow—you know, after camp."

My dad shrugs.

"Where?" Of course, my mom wants details.

"In the valley—for, you know, lunch at the concessions and...whatever."

"Just the two of you?"

My stomach clenches. "Maybe. I don't really know." I mean, Zach didn't mention anyone else, but that doesn't mean other people won't be there too.

My dad reaches over and takes another piece of turkey off the sandwich. "Looks like she won't need this."

"Chet..."

He smiles at her, then shrugs. "I'm just saying..." She raises one eyebrow and he holds up his hands. "Okay, okay." Then he turns to me. "So, how would you get home and when would you get home?"

"He'd bring me home." I don't look at my mom. I can't look at her. "And I'd be home before dark."

"Before dark? It doesn't get dark until nine o'clock."

I glance at her then and look back at my dad. "So what time would you want me to be home?" I give myself a mental pat on the back for my brilliant strategy of allowing them to name a time.

"Well, I think dinnertime is reasonable."

"What difference does a couple hours make, Jess?"

She sighs. "I'd like to know who else is going. And I'd also like to know more about Zach—about his family. I know you've met him, Chet, but do we really know anything about him?"

"He's a polite kid. Seems responsible. Good climber."

That's not the information my mom's looking for, I know. "His mom's a teacher—um, she teaches fourth grade, I think, at Oakhurst Elementary. His parents are divorced—he lives with his mom and his dad lives in Laguna Beach. He says he has a good relationship with both his parents. Dad's right, he is responsible, because he's like, you know, the man of the house."

I'm on the right track, I can tell by my mom's expression. "He's also really respectful. I mean, he said he'd get it if you wouldn't let him drive me home, but he said to tell you he's a good driver and that he'll take the curves slow."

She nods. "Okay."

"Okay, I can go?"

She looks at my dad and then sighs. "Okay, you can go, but I'd like Zach's home phone number and his cell phone number, and you need to keep your phone on and check in with us. Let one of us know when you're leaving the valley and heading home. And don't go anywhere else. Straight home, okay?"

I nod. "Okay." Then I go around the island, take the rest of the turkey off the bread, and smile at my mom as I put it in my mouth. With mouth full, I mumble, "Thank you."

"Zach..." My dad puts out his hand and Zach shakes it. "Good climbing today."

"Thanks."

"I hear you and Haley are going to stay in the valley for lunch."

"Yes, sir."

He nods. "Good. Have fun." He turns to me. "See you later, Chipmunk."

My face gets hot and I hang my head. He laughs, ruffles my hair, and then turns to leave. "Take care of her, Zach, or you'll have her mother to deal with."

"Yes sir." Once he's gone, Zach turns to me. "Chipmunk?"

I shake my head and continue to look at the ground. "He's called me that since I was little. It's so embarrassing."

Zach laughs. "It's so cute."

I glance up at him and then roll my eyes. "What...ever."

He comes over to me and throws one arm over my shoulders like it's no big deal. "C'mon. I'm starved."

We walk through the village with his arm around me. He talks—says some stuff—but I don't really hear him. All I can think about is how tall he is, and how his blue eyes sparkle in the sunlight, and how I don't feel all that awkward with him, and…how he has his arm around me like I'm his…girlfriend.

But I'm not. Am I?

I stop walking and his arm drops from my shoulders. "Um, just a minute, I have to make sure my phone is on." I pull my phone out of my backpack and look at it. "Okay." Then when I start walking again, I keep a little distance between us. It's not that I don't want to be his girlfriend; it's just that I want to be the one to make that decision.

We have burgers at the Village Grill, then after lunch Zach asks what I want to do.

"What have you done?"

"Besides lunch at the Ahwahnee with my mom and the climbs I've done during camps, nothing."

"Wow, okay. Well, we could take a tour of the valley on one of the buses, there's a cool movie about Yosemite at the Visitor Center, there's the museum and the Indian Cultural Exhibit—"

"I'm not much of a museum guy."

"Okay, good, 'cause I've been there like a million times. My mom loves that exhibit."

"Why?"

I shrug. "It has a bunch of cultural resources, plus people doing demonstrations on things like basket-weaving." I lift my hands, palms up. "She loves that stuff. We're part Native American—my mom is—and preserving that heritage is super important to her."

"Really? That's cool."

"It is?"

"Sure."

"She says our roots go back to the original Ahwahneechee people."

"So, you're a total local."

I laugh. "I guess so. C'mon, I want to show you something."

We leave the village and I lead Zach to the Sentinel/Cook's Meadow trail, and we take the short walk to Sentinel Bridge—the old stone bridge that arches over the river. Once we reach the middle of the bridge, I stop and point. "See?"

"Whoa… That's incredible."

"Yeah, especially this time of year when the river is slow and smooth—see the reflection?" From the bridge you see straight to Half Dome and the dome's reflection shimmers on the river. "This is one of my favorite places." I look around. "It's so…peaceful, you know?" The river burbles over rocks beneath us as a warm breeze rustles the nearby trees.

He nods and looks from the reflection up to the sheer granite face of Half Dome. "What are those dark streaks on the face of the dome from, do you know?"

"They're Tis-sa-ack's tears."

"Who?"

I laugh. "It's a legend. My mom used to tell us the Native American legends as bedtime stories."

"Tell me." He turns away from Half Dome, leans against the bridge, looks at me, and waits.

"Really?"

"Yeah, I want to hear it."

I look down and kick a pebble across the road. "Okay, so Tis-sa-ack and her husband, Nangas, heard about the beauty of the valley and they decided to come and live here, but it was a long way from"—I pause…it's been a long time since I've heard this one—"well, from wherever they lived. So Tis-sa-ack packed a burden basket filled—"

"Wait, what's a burden basket?"

"Oh, um it's a basket a woman carried on her back to keep her hands free—she'd collect stuff and put it in the basket during the day, like berries, and…I don't know, just stuff. Then when she got home, she'd hang it near the front door and when people came to visit, they were supposed to leave their burdens in the basket…or something like that."

"Huh. Okay, keep going."

I shake my head. "Why do you want to hear all this?"

"Because it's cool."

I laugh. "You'll love my mother." I pull my long hair off my neck and put it in a ponytail with the ponytail holder I keep around my wrist.

"C'mon, tell me the rest."

I smile. "Okay. Tis-sa-ack carried a burden basket filled with acorns and a papoose on her back. I don't remember what Nangas carried, except for a stick—like a walking stick or something. When they finally got to the valley, they were exhausted and Tis-sa-ack did something or said something that made Nangas mad, so he hit her with the stick."

"Nice guy."

"Yeah, really. Anyway, it wasn't the Indians' way to hurt their wives, so Tis-sa-ack got scared and ran off. She ran through the valley and the path she followed became a stream, I think, and the acorns that fell out of her basket as she ran grew into oak trees. Then when she reached Mirror Lake, she was so thirsty that she drank all the water in the lake. So when Nangas caught up with her and saw there was no water in the lake for him to drink, he got even madder and he hit her again."

"So that's it?"

"No, there's more. After Nangas hit her the second time, she ran again. But he followed her and continued beating her, which made the gods really mad because Nangas and Tis-sa-ack had broken the peace. So they decided to turn them into granite. Tis-sa-ack became Half Dome and Nangas became Washington Column. The place where she threw off her burden basket so she could run faster became Basket

Dome, and where she dropped the papoose became Royal Arches." I turn, look up at Half Dome again, and point. "The streaks are the tears Tis-sa-ack cried as she ran from Nangas."

"Wow. What other legends do you know?"

I laugh. "A bunch, but that's the only one I'm telling you today."

He gazes back to Half Dome. "We have to do that hike. What does it feel like up there?"

"It's pretty amazing. The top is bigger than you think it's going to be. And you can see forever. It's an intense hike though. Going up Sub-Dome, with all the switchbacks, is enough to thrash your calves, then after that, you go four hundred feet straight up."

"The cables?"

I nod. "We use our climbing gear and clip to the cables, but a lot of people just take their chances. But if you fell…"

"Not good."

I shake my head. "I think it's eighteen miles round trip from the valley. And you have to do it early—like start at sunrise, or even earlier, in case of thunderstorms in the afternoon. You don't want to be up there when there's lightning."

He turns to me. "Haley, you've got to ask your parents if you can go with me. We've got to plan it before school starts. Please?"

"I don't know. Don't you have some guy friends you could do it with?"

"Yeah, but…" He reaches over and gently tugs on a piece of my ponytail. "I want to hike it with you."

Before I can think about it, the obvious question is out of my mouth. "Why?" Then I feel like an idiot. "I mean—"

"Because, I like you. You're not like other girls, you know?"

Heat creeps from my neck to my face. "I wasn't…I didn't… I mean, I wasn't asking how you…feel about me. I just…" I shake my head and stare at my feet. "Whatever."

"That's what I mean. You're not all stuck on yourself. You're not afraid to get dirty and sweat and have fun. I like that. And you don't get how cute you are…" He pauses, then laughs. "Chipmunk."

I look up at him. *"What?"* I swat at his arm. "Do *not* call me that!"

"Aw, c'mon, Chipmunk."

I lift my arm to swat him again and, laughing, he grabs both my arms and pulls me close to him. "Okay, okay, I'll stop on one condition." He leans down and whispers, "Promise to climb Half Dome with me and go to Winter Formal with me too. Deal?"

"Winter Formal's like a million months from now." My skin tingles where he's holding my arms, and I'm so close to him I swear I can feel his heart beating. When I look up at him, his expression has turned serious.

"Deal?" he says again.

For some reason, I'm out of breath now and all I can do is nod.

And wonder.

Is this, maybe, what love feels like?

Few in these hot, dim, frictiony times are quite sane or free;
choked with care like clocks full of dust, laboriously doing so
much good and making so much money, or so little, they are
no longer good for themselves.
John Muir

CHAPTER THIRTEEN

Jessica

I SPENT HALEY'S first birthday at an Incident Command Post, bent over a desk relaying the GPS coordinates of a tree where a spotted owl had nested. There were other natural and cultural resources in the fire area, of course, but it's the owl I remember. I fought for the owl, rooted for her, and in the end, I envied her. While I worked, she nurtured her hatchlings.

At home, Cretia baked a birthday cake and my family gathered to celebrate Haley's milestone without me as Chet insisted they celebrate on Haley's actual birthday, not that she'd have known the difference. I lived the experience later through videos my dad took: Haley in her high chair, face smeared with frosting, a toothy grin on her face. Haley toddling across the kitchen, her chubby little hand clasped in

Chet's. And the moment when Chet let go of her hand and Haley took her first steps on her own before falling back on her well-padded bottom. When they sang *Happy Birthday* to her, I sang along with the video, tears choking me. Later, I baked her another cake and celebrated with her myself.

What was I sacrificing for a job I loved? I consoled myself with the assurance that it would get easier as the kids grew older—they'd understand why I missed an occasion every now and then. What I didn't count on was the way the sense of loss would weigh on me more each passing year. But the truth was, it was more than a job I loved. It was a job we needed.

But oh, how I still grieve those missed moments.

This afternoon, the grief is palpable as I pull into the ICP—Incident Command Post—which is like driving into a small town. Vehicles, trailers housing offices, portable cell towers, satellite dishes, tents, and portable restroom and shower facilities, are all in place. Caterers will prepare and serve meals throughout the day to exhausted firefighters and personnel who will camp here until the fire is contained.

Based on what I know so far, I'll be here three or four days at the least. At the most, I'll be here fourteen days. After two weeks, the law imposes a day off, which means if I care to make the drive, a night in my own bed and, if I'm lucky, a meal or two with my family. And if the fire still rages? I return to the ICP the following day.

While there's a serious nature and even an urgency to the situation at hand, there is also a sense of camaraderie that prevails at an ICP—we leave one family to join another made up of individuals from multiple agencies partnering together, focused on a single purpose. But the adrenaline that keeps us going has yet to kick in for me. Instead of the usual anticipation that accompanies being dispatched, today my companion is an albatross of grief. As I made the drive from the office in El Portal, rather than concentrating on the upcoming task, I could only think of what I'm missing at home: news of Haley's lunch date with Zach, or whatever she'd call it. At her age, this new relationship could end before I return home to hear the details.

While I missed Haley's first birthday, she didn't really miss me.

Will she miss me this evening? Will she want to share details of hanging out with Zach? Probably not. But I'd like to be there anyway to attempt to coerce the details out of her. The sense of grief is familiar, but I'm carrying something else as well. Something less familiar.

Dread?

I slip the notch of the word into place, like a puzzle piece, and it fits.

But why?

A change is taking place within me, and with it comes uncertainty and anxiety, which are more familiar than not. However, anxiety isn't visiting alone this time—it's brought its cousin dread along too.

But why now? Again, the question waves like a red flag.

I cross the parking area—a field of dry grass trampled by cars, trucks, and equipment. What's on the horizon that I can't see? Anything? Or is my mind running amuck?

"Weaver." The planning section chief spots me and waves me over. I take a deep breath and tuck my thoughts away for later.

Later, when I wrestle in the confines of a sleeping bag.

Later, when sleep eludes me.

Later, when fear ferrets its way through the dark to gnaw at my soul.

I point to the computer monitor on the desk in the temporary office set up at the ICP. "That won't work." I glance up at Frank O'Leary, the planning section chief. "There's a historic railroad grade in that area—railroad ties. We have to protect that area if we can." I read the frustration on O'Leary's face, but the law mandates my decision.

He leans over me and points to another area. "Can we cut a line here?"

"That's good."

"Yeah?"

I nod and he slaps me on the back and makes the call. Yesterday the winds died down and for the first time since the fire broke out we gained ground. It's burned 5,600 acres thus far but is now 62 percent contained. We have a long fight ahead, but at least the wind and humidity levels are working in our favor. At least for today.

I lean back, close my eyes, and then rub them. When I open them, the computer monitor is a blur. I need a good night's sleep. I get up from the desk, lift my arms over my head, and stretch my back. Then I go to the coffeepot and pour myself another mug.

This fire impacts more people than I can count—in our camp alone there are hundreds of people who have loved ones at home, families filling the gaps left in their absence. But that's just the beginning—there are the families whose homes are in the path of the fire, now evacuees living with friends, family, or in shelters until it's safe to return home. A local school has become a shelter and is staffed with volunteers who've disrupted their usual routine to serve others. Air-quality specialists, water-resource managers, media personnel—the list is endless. And once the fire is contained and life seems to go back to normal for all of us, then we begin planning for erosion, flooding, landslides…

I set the mug of coffee on the desk and lean my head to one shoulder and then the other, stretching the tight tendons in my neck. As many people as are impacted by this fire, this time my focus is on myself. Not my preference. But I can't seem to remain focused on anything but what may be going on at home in my absence.

Or more specifically…

What is Chet doing while I'm gone?

As age comes on, one source of enjoyment after another is closed, but Nature's sources never fail.
John Muir

CHAPTER FOURTEEN

Haley

CHLOE'S SPRAWLED ACROSS my bed with my laptop open in front of her, her skinny jeans low on her hips and her top cropped high. I pull my long T-shirt down. "So, how's Grant?"

She shuts the laptop and rolls onto her back and looks at the ceiling. "He's boring."

"What? I thought he was the hottest thing since…" I hesitate. "Who'd you compare him to?"

"I don't remember. But he's not. I mean, he's hot, but he's still boring. All he wants to do is play his stupid video game—*World of War Zones*, or some lame thing."

"World of Warcraft."

"What?"

"Never mind."

She sits up and looks at me. "The only way I can get his attention is to make out with him. And you can only do that for so long, you know?"

Um, no, I don't. "Why are you making out with him if you don't really like him?"

Chloe stares at me like I'm some kind of freak. "So what have you been doing? I haven't seen you in *forever*."

"It's only been a little over a week, Chloe."

"A lot can happen in a week. Look at Lexie."

"What do you mean?"

"OMG, where have you been? Her brother came out!"

"He's gay? He's only, like, nine or something, right?"

Chloe doubles over laughing. "No, you dweeb! He's not gay. He came out of his room. Remember he was holding a hunger strike because he said Lexie's stepdad, who is his real dad, liked Lexie better than he liked him? Then when he finally came out of his room, his dad told Lexie's mom that Lexie should go live with her dad for a while to give her brother a break."

"What? Where's her dad live?"

"Alaska!" Chloe, the Queen of Drama, stands up and puts her hands on her hips. "Can you imagine Lexie in Alaska? Where would she shop? Or tan?"

"Is she okay? Does she really have to move?"

Chloe shrugs. "Beats me. So, back to you."

"Oh." I guess I can't avoid the topic forever. "I've just been hanging out, you know, with"—I turn away from Chloe and act like I'm looking at my phone, which is plugged in next to my desk—"Zach." I say his name kind of quiet. Okay, I mumble his name hoping she won't care enough to ask me to repeat it.

"Who?"

Zach's name gets caught somewhere in my throat. I turn back and look at her.

"Did you say Zach?"

I shrug. "Yeah, but you know, it's not like a big deal…exactly."

Chloe stares at me and then she gets that look—the *how could you?* look. "You knew I liked him."

"I know, but you're with Grant. Anyway, I told you I hung out with him, remember? We went for coffee."

"Are you going out with him?"

I plop down on my bed. "I don't know. I mean…" I look at Chloe and see the anger in her eyes, which makes me angry. "Yes, I'm going out with him." Am I? I'm not sure but… "I thought you didn't like him anymore. When you did like him, and I knew it, I stayed away from him, but now you've moved on."

I might as well get it all out. I take a deep breath. "I've had coffee with him, then spent Friday in the valley with him after climbing camp. And I'm going to Winter Formal with him. I mean, if we're still going out by then. But he asked me, so…"

Chloe stares at me, her mouth hanging open. "Whatever. I have to go."

"Go? You just got here."

She grabs her purse and heads for my bedroom door.

"Chloe?" I follow her to the top of the stairs, my anger increasing with every step. "Wait!" I startle myself with the strength of my voice, and I can see I startled Chloe too. She stops on the top stair and turns back to look at me. "You went rafting with Grant." I lower my voice. "And you're making out with him, and, by the way, after only one week. Chloe, that means you're with him. You can't be with him and still want Zach too. It doesn't work that way."

I swallow the lump that's formed in my throat. "Can't you…be happy for me? You're my"—tears puddle in my eyes—"best friend."

Chloe's shoulders slump and she exhales. Then she comes back and puts her arms around me and hugs me. "I'm sorry. I just… I think I just went out with Grant hoping to make Zach jealous or maybe I just knew…you know, that he had a thing for you. It was kind of obvious. I just didn't want to admit it."

I pull back from Chloe and wipe the tears off my cheeks. "So?"

Chloe smiles. "So I'm happy for you." She grabs my hand and pulls me back toward my bedroom. "You have to tell me everything. Every detail!"

We go back into my room and I close the door. I stand with my back against the door. "I'll tell you everything, but first you have to answer the question I asked you."

She rolls her eyes. "What question?"

"You know. Why are you making out with Grant if you don't really like him?"

She hesitates. "I…don't know. I mean, he's okay, and I don't want him to dump me."

"Chloe, you have to respect yourself more than that. If he doesn't like you unless you do stuff like that with him, then he isn't worth it. You don't need him. You're better than that." I go sit next to her. "I care about you and I don't want to see you do anything stupid."

"Nobody's ever said that to me before." Chloe's eyes fill with tears but she doesn't say anything else.

Am I getting through to her? She's not talking and I can't tell. So I do the only thing I can…

Hope.

After Chloe leaves, I go out to the woods behind our property. Something's bugging me and I need to figure it out. I head for the old tire swing my dad hung from a huge oak tree when Tyler and I were little—clouds of dust puff as my feet scuff the ground. When I reach the swing, I put one leg through the tire, then the other. I wrap my arms around the tire and lean my cheek against the warm rubber, the oily scent a reminder of all the summers Tyler and I spent out here, my dad pushing us on the swing.

When I told Chloe she needed to respect herself more, it made me think of my mom—in the same way I thought of Chloe when my mom told me about getting pregnant with Tyler.

My mom and Chloe are nothing alike. I mean *nothing*. But… I lean back in the swing so my long hair almost drags in the dry leaves and pine needles on the ground. I push off with one foot and the tire sways back and forth. When I close my eyes the movement is dizzying.

Or, like, disorienting.

It's almost as disorienting as comparing my mom and Chloe. I laugh. With my eyes still closed, I push off again, holding tight to the tire. Or as disorienting as hearing my parents argue the other night. I put my foot down, stop the swing, open my eyes, and sit up.

That's it.

My mom acts with my dad the way Chloe acts with guys. It's like they become someone else. I've never thought about it before, but my mom isn't the same with my dad as she is with everyone else. I mean, she's like this in-charge person with Tyler and me and in her job. She's totally respected at work—I've heard the way my grandpa and some of her work friends talk about her. But with my dad, she's not like that. I don't ever remember hearing her even disagree with him about anything. Until a couple weeks ago. Or is it that I've just never paid attention?

And that's how Chloe is when she's with a guy. It's like she's not really there and she wouldn't even think of saying no or disagreeing.

I think back to the argument my mom and dad had— how it began while we were having dinner and how the whole, like, atmosphere got tense. I mean, really, what was the big deal?

I get, after my mom explained it to me, why she has some issues or fears or whatever about my going out with a guy. So why didn't my dad get why Mom was concerned? And even if he didn't get it, why not just let her talk about it instead of getting all mad and storming out?

Why are my mom and Chloe like that? Grandma Cretia isn't that way. At all. She says whatever she wants to my grandpa. I mean, she's not rude, but she's just…herself.

Chloe's response when I told her I cared about her comes back to me now: *"Nobody's ever said that to me before."*

Maybe—I hug the tire—maybe, you have to know you're loved in order to respect yourself?

But... My mom knows my dad loves her.

Right?

I pull my legs out of the swing and stand next to it for a minute before heading back toward the house. As I walk, I take deep breaths, trying to calm myself and ignore the thought that's landed in my brain. But it doesn't work. Instead, the thought takes flight and buzzes around my mind like an annoying fly. I want to swat it away. Smash it. But all I can do is focus on it:

Does my dad *really* love my mom?

*As we go on and on, studying this old, old life in the light of
the life beating warmly about us, we enrich
and lengthen our own.*
John Muir

CHAPTER FIFTEEN

Ted

 "HI, KIDDO."

Haley drops herself into the chair on the other side of my desk.

"Where's your grandma?"

"She's out front talking to one of your neighbors."

I chuckle. "Social butterfly."

Haley pulls her legs up and curls into the chair.

"How was school?"

She rolls her eyes and wears that sullen teenager look.

"That good?"

She sighs. "It was okay. I just miss summer, and having Tyler home, and my mom's been gone so much, I'm even kind of missing her. But don't, you know, tell her that."

"Your secret's safe with me, kiddo."

"I wish I could drive. It would make life so much more interesting. More options, you know?"

"Right. Well, from what I hear, you're driving all over these mountains now and soon you'll be driving on your own. In the meantime, there's never a dull moment at Grandma and Grandpa's."

Unimpressed, she glances down at her phone—the one glued to her hand.

"Who're you communicating with now?" When she looks back at me, she smiles—a smile that makes her look so much like her mother did at that age that it's almost unnerving.

"Just a friend."

"A friend, huh? What friend?"

She hesitates. "Um…Zach."

I lean forward. "Zach? Don't tell me you went out and got yourself a boyfriend."

"No. I mean…" She sinks a little lower in her seat.

"C'mon, fess up. No holding back with Grandpa."

"He's a boy, but he's just a friend…sort of."

"Sort of?" I lean back in my chair, "Uh-ho. Well, you better tell me about him. I'm going to need to meet him too. I have some pretty rigorous standards he'll need to live up to if he's going to date *my* granddaughter. Think he's man enough to stand up to the scrutiny?" Her cheeks have turned fire-engine red and she giggles. "I'm waiting. What qualifies this young man to go out with you?"

She swings her feet back to the floor and sits up straight. "Well, he's…nice, and"—she raises her eyebrows—"he's cute." She laughs.

"That's not enough."

"Okay, he's a good climber and a good student, I think, and he's…" She pauses and her expression grows serious. "He's respectful—of me and my mom and dad. Their rules, you know?"

"Good. That's what I like to hear. So, do you think you're in love?"

She blushes again. "Grandpa!"

"What?" Her face is almost purple now. This is great fun.

She shakes her head. "I don't know."

"Well, you like the boy. He's *cute*"—I try to mimic the way she'd said it, which gets another laugh out of her—"and you share common interests. Most important, he's respectful. If he doesn't treat you with respect, then what you feel doesn't matter—you kick him to the curb."

"Kick him to the curb?"

"You dump him."

"Oh."

"If all the important qualities are there and you can't stop thinking about him and you get fluttery feelings in your gut—then it might be love."

"Fluttery feelings in my gut? What's my gut got to do with anything?"

"Now, don't go and get all literal on me. I suspect you know exactly what I'm talking about."

She seems to think for a moment. "Grandpa, what does respect look like? I mean, how do you know if someone really respects someone else?"

"That's a fine question, and an important one too. Respect means you take one another's feelings into consideration. You listen to one another's opinions. You work together. You compromise. And as far as a man goes, he treats a lady like a lady. I know that probably sounds old-fashioned with all the talk of equality, but a man can still consider a woman his equal and treat her with tenderness and care. In my book, that's respect."

Haley's brow furrows. "But sometimes couples just, you know, disagree. If they don't compromise does that mean they don't respect each other?"

"Well"—I rub the stubble on my chin—"I think both parties need to be free to speak their minds, to share their thoughts and opinions. It's when one demands his own way that trouble brews. Listen up, Haley. The way I define love is when a couple is willing to sacrifice for each other, when they're willing to put the other's needs above their own. There's a lot more to love than the fluttery feelings in your gut. And respect is an important part of that." I lean forward and put my elbows on the desk. "Here's the most important thing for you to remember…"

Haley leans forward.

I point at her. "You are too young for love. Much too young. You need to wait at least, at the very least, a couple more decades before you fall in love."

Her eyes go wide. "A couple *decades*? I'll be thirty-five by then."

"That sounds about right."

She giggles.

Wasn't she just toddling around and getting into mischief? Now look at her. She's a young woman. And a wise one at that, it seems.

After Cretia and Haley leave for a trip to the grocery store, I'm left on my own. I have some research to do—some things I need to figure out about the news Sandra revealed in her letter, so I settle back at my desk.

But before I do a Google search for the information I need, I click open my photo app and scroll through some old photos I scanned a while back. It takes me a few minutes before I find the one I'm looking for. When I do, I lean in close to the monitor. It's a photo of Jessie when she was about Haley's age. The resemblance is remarkable—high, broad cheekbones, eyes so dark you can't tell the pupils from the irises, and that ebony straight hair they both, to this day, wear long. But when I look at Haley, as much as she looks like her mother, there's also evidence of Chet—he's there in the shape of her nose and the crease of her brow.

Then I search for another photo, one of the few I have of Sandra, taken shortly after we married—a photo I kept for Jessie, should she ever want it. Sandra was just twenty-six when the picture was taken, older than Jessie and Haley in their photos. Yet when I maneuver the pictures on the monitor and line the three of them up side by side, with the exception of the obvious differences in the eras the photos were shot, they could all three be the same person. Well, almost.

But as I stare at Jessie and compare her features to those of her mother, what I'm really looking for is missing.

I study the photo.

But…it's just not there.

One must labor for beauty as for bread here as elsewhere.
John Muir

CHAPTER SIXTEEN

Haley

WHEN MY GRANDMA drops me off at school on Friday morning, Zach's waiting for me in the parking lot.

He smiles and gives me a hug. "I thought you'd never get here."

"What's up?"

"I applied for Half Dome permits this morning through that lottery system you told me about. If we get them, we could do the hike on Sunday. Have you asked your parents yet?"

"You're really serious? I mean, I knew you were, but…"

"So you haven't talked to them?"

"Zach, I've been at my grandparents' house, remember? My mom's still working that fire—she's not even home." I'm not irritated with Zach, exactly. Just with the situation.

"So ask your dad."

I hesitate. Maybe this is the perfect time to ask, while my mom is away, because there's no way she'd let me do that hike without an adult. "I don't know. I'll have to see."

"Haley, you've done the hike before and the cables are nothing compared to climbs we've done during camps. What if I call and talk to your dad—you know, do the whole respect-the-parents'-authority thing? Seriously."

"No! No...don't call my dad. Just...just let me think about it, okay? We probably won't even get the permits. I mean, it's a weekend, what are the chances? When you find out, call me and I'll figure it out then."

"Yeah, sure. But if we get them, and you want me to talk to your dad, let me know. I'm totally willing."

I smile. "Thanks."

On Saturday afternoon, my grandpa drives me home and drops me off. My dad, who's been working long hours all week, said he'd be home tonight. So I decide to go home and do my homework, and anything else that will keep me from thinking about the text Zach sent late last night telling me we got the permits.

After I finish my homework, I sign on to the National Park Service's website for Yosemite and check the weather and trail conditions for tomorrow. They're good. Of course. Then I click over and read the fire updates, especially the fire my mom's working. It looks like she should be home soon, maybe even tonight or tomorrow.

Half Dome? There's just no way that's going to happen.

Or could it?

I've had, like, this battle going on in my head all day. The weird thing is, I'm pretty sure my dad would let me go if I asked him. But then what if my mom shows up tonight? Anyway, if I know my mom wouldn't approve of my doing the hike with Zach, then doesn't my dad know that too? And if he does, then why doesn't that matter to him? I mean, I know I'm assuming all this because I haven't even asked him, but that's almost not even the point.

It's just… I don't get my parents' relationship.

I guess I've never thought about it until now, but now that I am thinking about it, it's totally bugging me.

I get up from my desk and head downstairs to get something to eat, which, I know, is just another excuse to ignore Zach's texts asking me if we're going tomorrow or not. I haven't responded to him since I got home today. I don't want to disappoint him, but I know I'm going to.

It's just too big a deal to go without my mom knowing and approving—I'd get in way too much trouble when she found out.

I rummage through the pantry and then go to the fridge and pull out some leftovers. I'm standing at the microwave waiting for the food to warm when my dad comes in.

"Hey, Chipmunk, you're back. It's been pretty lonely here all by myself."

"I thought you were spending all your time at the store?"

"More time than I'd like. Fall's one of my busy seasons—you know, getting things ordered for the Christmas rush."

"Whatever." I pull the plate out of the microwave.

"What's with you?"

I shrug. "Nothing."

"What's for dinner?"

"Leftovers." I settle on a bar stool at the island.

He goes to the fridge, opens it, then closes it and opens the freezer. "I guess I need to shop. Think your mother's ever coming home?"

"Eventually."

"Want to go out?"

I lift my fork and raise my eyebrows.

"Right. You're already eating. You're a barrel of fun, you know that?"

I take another bite and just look at him. I don't know why I'm mad at him.

I just am.

Few places in this world are more dangerous than home.
John Muir

CHAPTER SEVENTEEN

Jessica

BECAUSE FIRE SEASON began so early this year, at early September, the season feels endless. And after fourteen to sixteen-hour workdays for fourteen straight days, it feels like forever since I've walked into my own house. Since I've fulfilled my primary roles as wife and mother. The few brief phone conversations with Chet and Haley rather than sate my desire to hear their voices—to enter their lives—only stirred the longing more.

Especially my longing to connect with Chet. To get our relationship back on track and once again enjoy the companionship, intimacy, and security that've marked our marriage. They *have* marked our marriage, haven't they?

I drop my duffel bag in the hallway and run my hand along the top of the pine-paneled wainscoting leading to Chet's den. Whatever that sense of dread was, it's gone. I determined I'd leave it at the ICP. I shake my head and laugh. It was nothing—just fatigue. Tired of leaving Chet and

Haley, missing Tyler. Burnout. Whatever name I want to give it, it was temporary.

I'm home now.

I plop onto the desk chair in the den, pull the pins out of my hair, and my hair unwinds from its knot and falls over my shoulders. I lean back in the chair and close my eyes— my body is weary, physically drained, yet my mind is still on overdrive. When I'm overly tired, as I am now, I've learned I must distract my mind, lull it into a state of rest, so I can sleep—otherwise, regardless of how tired I am, I'll toss and turn all night. And as much as I'm looking forward to my own bed, I'm looking forward most to *sleeping* in that bed.

Late this evening, with the fire nearing containment, a resource advisor relieved me. By the time I grabbed my gear and got on the road, it was already late and I had a long drive ahead of me. I called Chet and told him I was coming home but to go on to bed without me.

I open my eyes and scoot toward the computer keyboard. I swipe my fingers across the trackpad and the monitor comes to life. A few games of solitaire should do the trick to transition my mind. But before clicking on that app, I open my e-mail in-box and stare at two weeks' worth of unopened posts. Most of them are junk since anything important goes to my work address, but I still need to sift through these in case something personal awaits my attention. Although, really, I don't have the mental energy to go through the posts now. They'll wait another day.

I move the cursor to close the in-box, but as I do a name jumps off the screen: heathercopolo@gmail.com.

Heather Copolo? Why would she e-mail me? My shoulders tense. I met her at the store once, maybe twice. Chet introduced her to me one afternoon when I dropped by. She was a climbing instructor. I only remember her because… I lean my head toward my shoulder, a stretch I hope will relieve the tension that's climbed from my shoulders to my neck. I remember her because I reacted to her with unusual force.

I didn't like her.

But that was crazy. I didn't even know her, beyond hearing Haley talk about her after one of the camps she attended. Later, Chet told me I'd been rude to Heather. I'd wanted to argue the point with him, but I didn't.

I never do.

The feeling of dread is back with a new force. But that's ridiculous. Isn't it? Yes, it is. I click the in-box closed and get up and pad my way to the kitchen, grateful I left my boots in the garage so I can wander the house without waking Chet and Haley. I grab a glass, fill it with water, and run a little water into the empty pan sitting in the sink—looks like it's from one of the casseroles I left in the freezer. Seems like Chet or Haley would have thought to let it soak. I shrug. Oh well.

I go to the island and flip through a stack of mail. Whatever Heather has to say can wait until tomorrow. It's probably just business—something meant for Chet but accidentally sent to my e-mail address. Our personal e-mail addresses are similar. But why would she send something to Chet's personal e-mail address? His business stuff doesn't come to the home computer—he says he doesn't want to bother with work stuff when he's at home. I take a sip of water, leave the glass on the island, and walk back down the hall to the den.

I stand in front of the computer. *Go to bed, Jess. Let it go until tomorrow.* But the unopened post is magnetic. I reach for the trackpad again and reopen the in-box. I sit back down in the desk chair and stare at the monitor.

This is silly. It's nothing. Open it or you'll never get to sleep tonight.

I'm right, I know. If I don't open it, I'll go to bed and perseverate on what the e-mail may or may not contain.

I lean forward, click open the e-mail, and see the note is addressed to me. How did she get my e-mail address? Does it matter? I read on:

Jessica,

We only met once, briefly, a couple of years ago, but based on the circumstance, I assume you'll remember me, and likely wish you could forget me.

Why would I wish I could forget her? I sigh. I don't have this kind of energy right now. I look away from the screen and consider, again, the feelings my brief encounter with this woman triggered. Why was Chet angry that I'd been rude to her? I try to recall the details of that day. Had I really been rude? Not exactly. I was polite, but brusque. I was there to see Chet, drop in at the store, and *take an interest for once*—not chitchat with one of his employees. Though, in Chet's defense, I knew what he wanted was for me to step into his world with genuine interest. When I, in fact, was just there to check something off one of my lists. Drop in at the store to make Chet happy. Check.

Am I defending him again? Taking responsibility that isn't mine to own? I lean my head back and close my eyes. The truth is, I've always taken an interest in Chet's business and have dropped in when my schedule allowed. The other truth is that I hadn't liked Heather and yes, my behavior may have been rude.

Guilt jabs at me.

I open my eyes and return to the e-mail.

I'm writing to apologize for my involvement with your husband.

My stomach twists. Like a premonition of a horrible accident, I know what I'm about to read will wreck me.

I wanted to contact you at the time but feared causing more damage. When you discovered the affair and gave Chet that ultimatum...

Affair. The word blazes on the screen and I can read no more.

I push back from the computer and double over in the chair, arms wrapped around my abdomen. I gasp for breath. *An affair? Chet?*

No. No. No. I must have misunderstood. He wouldn't... I sit up and look back at the screen and continue reading.

> I realized then the reality of what I'd participated in. When he confessed that I hadn't been his first involvement outside his marriage, in an odd way, I felt cheated too and got a glimpse of how you might feel.
>
> Anyway, I am very sorry and felt it was time to own my actions. I'm working through my own recovery from issues that...

My stomach cramps and my mouth fills with saliva. Fearing I'm going to vomit, I stand and run toward the bathroom down the hall, gulping for air as I go. I stand in front of the toilet, fighting the urge to relieve my stomach of its contents. I inhale again, and again. I wrap my arms around my shuddering body and then wipe the unbidden tears from my face.

I reach for a tissue, hands shaking. Still breathing deep, my stomach calms a bit.

Okay. I'm going to be okay. Keep breathing.

Wait. What else had she said? Chet said she hadn't been his first... My stomach cramps again. I drop the tissue and lean over the toilet for what I can no longer control. As I heave, and heave again, I know my retching is futile.

I cannot purge myself of the information I've just digested.

I back away from the house, slam the transmission into Drive, and then turn and race down the long, shadowed driveway, gravel spraying the forested areas on either side of the road. When I reach the highway, I crank the steering wheel to the right and pull into the lane in front of two glaring orbs of light. A truck bears down on my SUV, horn howling. My foot heavy on the accelerator, I pull away and leave the truck behind me.

"Just drive, Jessica. Don't think. Just drive." I wind my way over the twisting road, drifting into the opposite lane as I take the curves.

I drive blind to all but my raging emotions.

"No. No!" My hands shake on the steering wheel and then pound against the hard acrylic. How could he do this to me? How could he do this to—a sob catches in my throat—to Tyler and Haley?

Tears blur my vision of the highway in front of me. I lift my foot off the accelerator and, frantic, look for a turnout in the road, but I can see nothing in the pitch of night. Then as I round another curve, my headlights bounce off what looks like a turnout. But I swerve onto the shoulder too soon, my perception skewed by my tears. I grab hold of the steering wheel with both hands and crank it hard trying to correct, but the SUV propels forward on the loose dirt while the back end shifts in the opposite direction.

I hit the brakes, turn the wheel again, and then lose control of the car. It spins in the dirt and slides toward what I fear may be a cliff.

I open my mouth to scream but instead hear a nightmarish silence against the backdrop of wheels crunching dirt and rocks as they slide.

I close my eyes tight.

Help!

The SUV slams into something and I lurch to the side as the sound of metal screeches and glass cracks. Then everything is silent—a dead halt to movement and sound—except for the pounding of my heart in my ears.

When I open my eyes, it appears one headlight is pointing askew into a forested area. The other light seems to have gone out. I lean my forehead on the steering wheel and then realize the air bag didn't deploy. I'm surprised but also relieved. Maybe the damage is minimal.

I lift my head and reach for the glove compartment, but my hands are still shaking so much that I struggle with the latch. Finally, I get a firm grip, pull the latch, and the compartment pops open. I reach inside and feel for the flashlight I keep there. Once I find it, I switch it on and shine the light toward the passenger door. A tree branch is where the side mirror should be—the window has cracked but remains intact, though the door is pushed in against the passenger seat.

My heart, like a hammer, pounds against my chest. I gulp for air, realizing I've been holding my breath in anticipation of tumbling over a cliff to my—I try to swallow—death. But my throat constricts, blocking my airway.

No.

No. Please…

I put my hands on my sternum, sure my heart will beat through my chest. Breathe. I have to breathe. My nose is plugged with mucus from crying and my throat is tight. I open my mouth, gulping for air again as the interior of the car seems to spin like a carnival ride. I gasp again and again, certain I'm not getting air into my lungs.

A latent memory, lost somewhere in the dense fog of my mind, tries to push through to a place of cognition but then slinks back. I reach for it, straining, then chase after the memory, sure it's something that will save me. Some piece of information I need to…live. I trip through the dark, grasping for the recollection, following it, I realize too late, into a dark abyss.

I somersault over a cliff, and fall, and fall, and fall…

The wrongs done…wrongs of every sort, are done in the darkness of ignorance and unbelief.
John Muir

CHAPTER EIGHTEEN

Haley

A LITTLE AFTER midnight, I get out of bed, grab a sweatshirt, pull it on over my pajamas, drop my phone into one of the pockets, and go downstairs. A couple of hours ago, I finally texted Zach and told him I couldn't go tomorrow. Then he sent like a hundred texts trying to talk me into at least asking my dad.

Okay, maybe he sent two texts trying to talk me into it and ninety-eight about other things. Just stuff. I smile. He was totally disappointed, like I knew he would be, but he didn't pressure me. He said he'd think about finding a friend to go, but seeing as we were done texting, like just now, I don't think he'll find anyone.

I tiptoe down the stairs, careful not to wake my dad. The house is quiet but when I get downstairs, I see the light in the den is on and my mom's duffel bag is in the hallway by

the laundry room. I stop at the den and peek in. "Mom?"
She's not there.

I head to the kitchen and for the first time, I'm relieved
I made the right decision about the hike. How would I have
explained to my mom that I was leaving at 4:30 a.m.? At the
least, it would have caused another blowup between my
parents, and I don't want to be the cause of one of those
again.

I walk into the kitchen. "Mom?" She must have gone
straight to bed. I get a glass out of the cabinet, open the
fridge, and pour myself some milk. Then I grab a granola bar
from the pantry. I go back to the den, walk in, and drop into
the chair in front of the computer. I set my glass on the desk,
unwrap the granola bar, take a bite, and then tap the trackpad.
I sip my milk while the computer does its thing. Chloe posted
another video on my Facebook page but told me to watch it
on our big monitor. I roll my eyes—Chloe and her videos.

I set my glass back down, this time reaching for a
coaster. My mom would kill me if I didn't use a coaster.
When I look back at the monitor, it's come on and there's an
open e-mail on the screen. I reach to click it closed but as I
do, a line snags my attention.

I'm writing to apologize...

I keep reading.

*Will human destructions like those of Nature—fire and flood
and avalanche—work out a higher good, a finer beauty?*
John Muir

CHAPTER NINETEEN

Jessica

I SHIVER AND reach out to pull the blanket over me, but my hand hits something hard, cold. I move to sit up but...I'm already sitting. I open my eyes, the action slow. Where am I? My body shudders again and I wrap my arms around myself. When I move my head, my neck aches. Out the front windshield, I'm surrounded by nothing but the dark of night. Unwelcome fear intrudes, knocking at my soul.

What happened?

Then memories, less welcome than fear, fly at me.

Losing control of the car.

The panic attack.

Trying to remember what to do or not to do.

I lift my hands to my head and press against my temples. It comes to me then... Hyperventilating during a panic attack can cause fainting—too little CO_2 and too much oxygen. That's what I was trying to remember when I passed out. I learned, as a teenager, to try and slow my breathing, taking shallow breaths to reduce the amount of oxygen intake.

And then the memory of why I was in the car to begin with slaps me.

Chet…

My head throbs—my sinuses swollen from crying. I turn the key in the ignition of the SUV and the dash lights blink, then steady. I check the clock—12:37 a.m. I turn the ignition off again and slump in my seat, still shivering. Am I cold or is my body reacting to the events of the night?

I recall getting the flashlight out of the glove compartment and feel for it on the console. When my fingers find it, I switch it on and survey the damage to the car again, at least what I can see from the driver's seat. Then I give the key in the ignition a full turn, but nothing happens. I try again but still nothing. I'll have to call a tow truck.

But…then what?

I'm not ready to go home, not ready to face Chet.

Not yet.

I click the lock button, making sure I'm locked in, then I lift myself off my seat, and turn and reach for a sweatshirt I keep in the back along with a few other emergency provisions. When I find it, I turn back and do the hard work of wiggling into it while still sitting in the driver's seat. As I do, I realize the night isn't all that cold, but the T-shirt I'm wearing isn't enough to stave off the slight chill.

I recline my seat, then turn the ignition off. I want to at least save the battery. I try to get comfortable for the long hours ahead. When day breaks, I'll deal with my predicament.

Or predicaments.

Sleep. All I need is a little sleep, then I can figure out my…life.

I close my eyes and attempt to shut off my mind, but the contents of the e-mail taunt me and questions pester. What did Heather mean about me giving Chet an ultimatum?

It's clear she thought I knew of their affair. What had Chet told her?

Where do his lies begin and end?

Who is Chet?

Do I know him at all?

I spend several restless hours grappling, wrestling with an elusive truth—a truth I can't unravel until I confront Chet. With the thought of confronting him, fear returns. But what choice do I have? The only way to discover the truth is to unravel the lies.

Finally, in the gray of predawn, I give up on sleep. Cold and stiff, I need to move. I unlock the car doors, reach for my phone, and move to get out. I take slow, stilted steps to the front of the car, where now I can see the damage—the car is wedged against a tree, the side mirror dangling and both the front and back doors crushed.

My shoulders slump with the weight of emotional and physical weariness. I stare at the car, then I turn, trying to determine where I am. I can just make out the highway to my left, which is deserted at this hour, and to my right, beyond the tree, is a clearing of some sort. I take a few steps in that direction. What I feared last night was a cliff is actually a meadow.

Something about the area is familiar.

I stumble through tall grass, making my way to the middle of the meadow. Once there, I stop and for a moment I view my surroundings rather than my own interior devastation. I'm standing in the meadow where, in conjunction with members of the Southern Miwuk Nation, we facilitated a prescribed burn several years ago. It's a meadow where tribe members have gathered native plants for generations, until the Himalayan blackberry bush took over—strangling and endangering the native flora.

The blackberries moved in where they were never meant to be.

They took over territory that was not their own.

They suffocated the very life out of plants meant to thrive here.

Smoke curls and coils within as betrayal's embers smolder, threatening to destroy all I've worked and fought for. The meadow, through fresh tears, wavers like an inferior mirage above hot asphalt. I swipe at the wetness falling down my cheeks and then reach down, wrap my fists around stalks of dry grass, and yank until the clumps break at the roots. I lift the fistfuls of grass over my head and throw them with all my might, but the loose grass catches a breeze and flutters back to the ground just in front of me.

I kick at it, and then kick again so hard that my feet go out from under me and I land on my backside. A sharp stab sends surges of pain through my upper thigh and down my leg. I groan and then roll off of whatever I've landed on and see a rock—or rather a pointed shard of granite. My leg throbs where I discover the piece of granite cut through my jeans and pierced the back of my thigh. I pull my hand away from the back of my leg, fingers sticky with blood.

Rage, a smoldering wick, gives way to an inferno and bursts from me as a guttural, primal scream that sounds, to my own ears, as though it will split the atmosphere.

I take a breath and then scream again. The first yell bounces off the sheers of granite surrounding the meadow on one side and echoes back to me. On my hands and knees, tall grass swaying around me, I pound my fists on the ground, dirt and bits of rock imbedding the flesh of my fists. I pound and scream and pound and scream until, exhausted, I roll onto my side, curl into myself, and pray my tears will extinguish the rage.

I lie there, unaware of time passing, surrounded by the now-thriving native grass, the very grass we saved by burning the blackberry bushes, until a sound, a buzzing or vibrating noise, pulls me from my stupor. As I sit up, I wince at the pain in my leg. I listen and the vibration sounds again.

My phone.

It must have come out of my back pocket when I fell. On my hands and knees, I scour the grass, feeling for the phone until I find it just a few feet from where I'd landed. When I see Chet's name on the screen, I lift my arm with the intent of hurling the phone as far away from me as I can throw it, but before I release it, I realize I may need it. Instead, I drop it back into the grass letting Chet's call go to voice mail.

I have nothing to say to him.

Yet.

My movements slow, I stand up and assess the damage to my leg—the wound isn't deep, just painful. I take small steps in a circular pattern to make sure I can walk, then I bend and pick up the phone from where I dropped it. I shove it into my back pocket and plod my way back toward the car. My throat burns, raw from screaming, and my abdominal muscles announce their own anger.

Spent, it takes me several minutes before my steps become steady. My phone vibrates again. And again I ignore the call and let it go to voice mail. Then it begins its vibrations for a third time and my anger wells. I stop, yank the phone from my pocket, and answer it. *"What?"*

"Where *are* you?" His tone indicates anger near the level of my own. "Jessica!"

"Don't—"

"Jessica, listen! I need you to listen! Haley is missing."

To live without human love is impossible.
John Muir

CHAPTER TWENTY

Ted

 "TED, HONEY. TED."
Cretia nudges me and I stir. "What?"

"There's someone at the door. The doorbell rang. There it is again, hear it?"

"What…time is it?"

"Almost six thirty. We overslept. But who would be here this early?"

Groggy, I pull myself up, throw the blanket back, and reach for my robe as whoever's at the front door begins banging on it. "Something's wrong. Stay put." I insert my hearing aids as I make my way down the hallway toward the entry hall.

"Dad!"

Jessie? Now wide-awake, I bound for the door and open it. Jessie, wild-eyed, stands with fists raised ready to bang on the door again.

"What's wrong? What's happened?"

"Haley. It's Haley. Chet…can't find her. She's gone! She's…I don't…know. She's just gone. She…"

Jessie's breathless, rambling, and is in quite a state—eyes red and swollen, hair wild, and her jeans and hands are covered in dirt. I step out the door and put my hand on her arm. "Jessie, honey, slow down. Everything will be okay—"

She yanks her arm away from me. "No!" She sobs. "No, you don't…understand!" She raises her fists again, this time aiming them at my chest and pounds me. "Nothing…*nothing* will ever…be okay again!"

"Jessie!" She flails, hitting at air as I sidestep her attack. Then I step around her and wrap her in a bear hug from behind, confining her arms. I pull her close as she fights against me. I may be old, but I'm still bigger and stronger, it seems, than my girl.

Cretia stands in the doorway, her tone alarmed. "Ted, what's happened?"

"I don't know."

Jessie surges forward, kicking and trying to pull away from me.

I tighten my hold on her. "Jessica! Stop!"

She responds and seems to calm a bit, then she tries to turn toward me. I give her just enough space to turn within the circumference of my arms, and she collapses against me, hiccupping, sobbing, and wetting my robe with her tears.

Cretia puts her hand on Jessie's back. "Let it out, honey. Just let it all out."

We stand there as Jessie cries, then Cretia nudges me and points to Jessie's SUV parked askew in front of the house, the passenger side smashed, window cracked, and the side mirror dangling.

I look at Cretia and shake my head. *What in the world is going on?* "Come on, we're going inside." Keeping one arm firmly around her shoulders, I guide her into the house.

"Jessica, your leg…"

Cretia, following behind us, must see something I can't. Once we're in the entry hall, Cretia skirts around us and heads toward the bathroom. She comes back with a damp washcloth and a box of tissues. "Here, let me…" She hands me the tissue box to hold and I step back from Jessie, who stands, head down, looking at the floor, shoulders shaking with her sobs.

Cretia comes close, lifts Jessie's chin, and tucks her hair behind her ears. Then she uses the washcloth to wipe Jessie's face. "Shh, honey. Shh…" Cretia gently wipes away Jessie's tears. "Take a deep breath. That's it. You're going to tell us what's happened, and then we're going to get you cleaned up. We need to look at that wound on your leg. We're going to take care of everything, honey."

"Jessie, where's Chet?" I need to know what's going on.

She shakes her head—a violent motion.

"Honey, stop. Be still. Shh… Just be still." Cretia shoots a pointed look in my direction. "Here, blow your nose." She grabs a few tissues from the box I'm holding and then hands them to Jessie.

Jessie wipes her nose and, despite Cretia's look, I prod. "Tell us about Haley."

She sniffs and wipes her nose again. "She…she was gone when Chet got up this morning. She's just…gone. I don't know where she is."

"Okay. What else?"

Jessie looks at me, really looks at me, for the first time since I opened the door. The agony I read in her eyes tells me there's more going on here than a teenager who left the house without telling anyone where she was going.

"He got up early, around five fifteen he said, and she wasn't there. Chet said she went to bed last night around ten o'clock."

I nod. "What happened to your car? And your leg?"

She glances toward the front door and then down at her leg. When she looks back at me, her eyes fill again.

"Jessie?" My voice cracks. I clear my throat, trying to rid myself of the emotion lodged there. Though, truth be told, it's more than emotion—it's fear. As a firefighter, Jessie was trained to handle emergencies, trained to respond rather than react. She's a strong woman, levelheaded, one who bears almost no resemblance to the crazed woman standing in front of me. Has she had a breakdown of some sort? Lost her mind?

"I was…careless. I took a curve too fast. I was…tired."

"Honey, that's not like you. Were you upset about something else?"

Thank God for Cretia. Maybe she can get somewhere with her. But Jessie doesn't respond—she just looks back at the floor. It's time to get practical. "Have you called Haley's friends? Checked with that boy she's been spending time with?"

"Boy?"

Cretia and I exchange a concerned glance, but then I remember that Jessie's been camped at an ICP for near two weeks now. "Zach's his name. Have you checked with him?"

"I…I don't know. Maybe Chet…"

Again I wonder where Chet is, but before I can ask again Cretia takes Jessie's arm. "Let's go sit in the kitchen and figure this all out. I'll fix you a cup of hot tea and we'll work through it."

"Tea?" I traipse behind them, grumbling, "I need something a lot stronger than tea."

Cretia glances over her shoulder. "Black coffee for you."

That will have to do.

After Cretia got a cup of hot tea down Jessie, she also got her to agree to let her look at that wound on her leg. She mentioned a hot shower too. But we still know little more than what Jessie told us in the beginning. She got home around eleven thirty last night, was there briefly but didn't see Haley. Then, for reasons she won't disclose, she left the house. Chet called her just after six this morning and told her Haley was missing.

What's really missing is the truth.

I run my hand over my head and, when I hear the bathroom door click shut and know Cretia and Jessie are occupied for a few minutes, I pick up the phone and punch in Chet's cell phone number.

He answers on the first ring. "Ted, is Haley with you and Cretia?"

"No. But Jessie's here."

Chet's silent.

"Are you there? Or did I lose you?"

"No, I'm here. What's Jessie told you?"

"Not enough. Just that you don't know where Haley is. But Chet, your wife is a wreck. What in blazes is going on? And don't mince words—you tell me everything you know."

"Haley's upset. She…left me a note. She's taken off and we have reason to be concerned. I know you want details, Ted, but I can't take time to fill in the blanks now. I need to go. I have more calls to make. Tell Jessica we need to work together on this. Have her call me."

With that, the line goes dead.

Work together? Why *wouldn't* they work together to find their daughter? What craziness has taken over? And what's my granddaughter upset about? If that boy, Zach, hurt her, he'll have me to deal with. I amble down the hallway and rap on the bathroom door. "Jessie?"

"Just a minute, Ted. I'm helping her into the shower."

A few minutes later, Cretia emerges from the bathroom, Jessie's clothes in her arms. "Well?"

"Well, nothing. All I know is that she fell on a sharp rock. She's sore, but the cut isn't deep. I left some ointment for her to put on it along with a bandage."

I follow Cretia to the laundry room, where she throws the pile of clothes into the washing machine. "I called Chet. He said Haley was upset about something, though he wouldn't tell me what. He said they have good reason to be concerned about her. He wants Jessie to call him."

Cretia turns on the washer, then faces me. She puts a hand on my arm. "They must have had an argument for Jessie to leave like she did last night—something has her pretty upset."

"An argument? Good. Maybe that means Jessie stood up to him for once. Though from the looks of her, I'd say she lost the fight." I shake my head. "I know this isn't the time to be thinking about that letter from Sandra, but—"

"Well, you certainly can't tell her about it now."

"Don't I know it."

"Oh, honey, this is a lot for you to handle. I'm so sorry. Jessie's your girl, you hear me? And she needs you now more than ever. Let's just focus on what we can do to help."

I nod. And then I take my wife into my arms and hold her there—letting the warmth of her comfort me.

The freedom I felt was exhilarating, and the burning heat,
and thirst, and faintness could not make it less.
John Muir

CHAPTER TWENTY-ONE

Jessica

I STAND UNDER the showerhead, water pelting me, punishing me with its heat. I don't turn the temperature down because I can't afford to linger here. The shock of the searing water is what I need—a cleansing in more ways than one. I use the few minutes I'm in the shower to gather myself, to push the jeering facts aside for now. But just for now. The temptation is to bury them forever—to pretend I never read that e-mail.

But it's too late.

I can't pretend. Nor should I. Isn't pretense what's landed me here? Chet's. And my own, in some ways.

Fate has forced our hands.

Chet told me that when he woke this morning and realized I hadn't come to bed, he got up to look for me. He didn't tell me much, just enough that I can imagine the scenario. He walked through the house, noticed the light on in the den, walked in, and saw a note taped to the computer monitor. The part I can't imagine is what Haley wrote in her note to Chet. I replay what Chet said to me when he called.

"Evidently you received an e-mail and left it open on the computer. Haley saw it and left it for me to find along with a note from her. What were you thinking, Jess? Didn't it occur to you she might find it?"

He accused *me*?

I'd run from the meadow back to the SUV pressed up against that tree, and the morning sun filtering through the branches made the cracked glass of the passenger window shimmer with the beauty of a filigreed snowflake.

Only, there was no beauty in the situation.

I climbed into the car and willed it to start. Turning the key in the ignition once, twice, only then realizing the car wasn't in gear. It must have stalled on impact. I shifted the car into Park, then turned the ignition again and the engine rumbled. I leaned my forehead against the steering wheel. The first sense of relief I'd felt since I returned home last night acted as a stimulant.

I raised my head, shifted the SUV into gear, and then tried to ease it away from the tree. The tires only spun in the dirt. As I put more pressure on the accelerator, the car groaned and metal screeched as it scraped against the tree, but it moved.

Once I'd pulled away and determined I could drive the car, the full impact of what Haley had discovered hit me. How could I have been so stupid? Why hadn't I closed the e-mail? Shut down the computer? I drove, blinded by anger and deaf to all but the condemning voice in my head. I drove on autopilot until I found myself in front of my dad's and Cretia's.

Of course. Where else would I go?

I turn my back to the showerhead, the water stinging the cut on my leg, the physical pain an appropriate companion for the emotional pain of the knowledge I now hold regarding Chet and our marriage. And, of course, my concern for Haley.

What must she be thinking?

Feeling?

Where would she go?

I turn the water off, reach for the towel hanging outside the shower, then dry off and step out to dress the wound on my leg and put on the sweats Cretia loaned me until my own clothes are out of the wash. As much as I dread doing it, I have to call Chet again. See who he's talked to, what he's done to find Haley. It's time to focus—to put the issues between us aside until we find our daughter.

She is the priority.

My single focus.

And, yes, I may have left that e-mail open on the computer. But...this is *not* my fault.

The fault belongs to Chet.

I emerge from the bathroom a different woman than the one Cretia dragged in there. Now, I have a purpose. I go down the hallway, out the front door, and to the SUV where I retrieve my cell phone, and out of my stash of emergency gear, a phone charger. Never knowing when I'll be called to a fire means always being prepared. I'd have clothes with me too if I hadn't carried my duffel bag into the house with me last night so I could do laundry this morning.

Laundry? Whoever thought I'd long for a mundane task like laundry? I straighten. Now isn't the time to wish circumstances were different. As I head back toward the house, I call Chet.

I don't bother saying hello. "Any news?"

"No."

I hear the stress in his tone but can't let it get to me. "Who've you called?"

"Everyone. Chloe, Lexie, her other friends—everyone I could think of."

"What about Zach?"

"Of course, I called him too. Called his home, but there was no answer, and I called his cell phone. No answer there either. I'll keep trying both numbers."

"And the sheriff's department?"

He hesitates. "Jessica, she wasn't kidnapped."

My shoulders tense, and I stop short of the front door, not wanting my dad or Cretia to hear this conversation. "No, she wasn't. She was upset—quite upset. The police will consider her a runaway. I'll call them. The sooner we engage them, the better."

The sneer in Chet's tone is clear. "Oh, I see, so you've gone into emergency-responder mode. Always the professional. Too bad you weren't in that mode last night. If you'd thought to delete that e-mail, maybe this wouldn't have happened."

"Are you blaming...?" I stop, take a deep breath, and refrain from spewing the sentence that came to mind. Now isn't the time. "The police will want to see the note she left—don't destroy it. I'll be home in fifteen minutes."

"Jessica—"

I hang up on him, but as I push End, my hands tremble. Taking a stance with Chet, taking control by telling him I'll do what he should have already done, shutting him down by hanging up on him—these are new and unfamiliar actions that leave me shaking.

But, in the midst of this chaos, another new and unfamiliar sensation surges through me.

Is it power? Not exactly.

I breathe deep, air expanding my lungs. Then I exhale.

Not power, but...

Freedom.

However, as soon as I identify the feeling, it flees like a scared jackrabbit.

Undeterred, I make a call to report my daughter missing.

I assure my dad and Cretia that I'll keep them posted. Then I get back into the SUV and head for home.

Home.

The word makes my stomach churn, but I can't let myself think about all home means—or has meant. Instead, I must remain focused. Chet was right about one thing: Now's the time to address reality with professionalism, with the training that's become second nature.

Not with the emotion of—I swallow—a mother.

Or maybe now is the time to fan the smoldering embers of betrayal, allowing them to rage so the force propels me forward.

I push my foot on the accelerator and pick up speed. The velocity of the wind hitting the dangling side mirror causes it to hit against the passenger door.

It bangs like the rhythmic beating of a drum.

Like an Ahwahneechee would beat a drum during a ceremonial dance.

A war dance.

When I pull into the driveway, I'm infused with strength, purpose, and resolve. Chet can play all the games he wants, but I won't join him. I don't know who I am or who I'm becoming and I can't take the time to analyze it now. All I can do is act—do what needs to be done.

I put the SUV into Park, turn off the ignition, and get out and head into the house. I bypass Chet, who must have heard the garage door opening as he is holding the door for me as I come in. I say nothing and head straight for our room—my closet—where I change into jeans, a T-shirt, and tennis shoes. Once I have the shoes on, I look at my feet, kick the shoes off, and exchange them for a pair of work boots. The T-shirt is different, but this feels like my standard field wear.

I have work to do.

I go to the bathroom and run a comb through my still-damp hair. Just as I'm pulling it into a ponytail, the doorbell rings. I drop the comb into the drawer and make my way to the front door as Chet opens it for the two officers standing on our front porch.

"Mr. and Mrs. Weaver?"

"Yes." Chet responds and opens the door wide. "Come in."

The four of us stand in our foyer for a strained moment before one of the officers begins asking questions.

"You reported that your fifteen-year-old daughter is missing? A runaway? What are the circumstances? And do you have a photo of her?"

"Let's sit down."

Chet and the officers follow me into the living room and take seats. I remain standing. "I'll get a photo of Haley. Chet, where's the note she left?"

"I can tell them what it said."

One of the officers looks at him. "We'll need to see it."

Chet sets his jaw. "I'll get it."

We go in separate directions—Chet to his den, while I head to the family room and pull a recent photo of Haley out of an album. With the photo in hand, one of thousands I've taken through the years as a means of preserving our family and its heritage, I realize how worthless the attempt at control was. No matter how hard I worked, how many photos of perfect moments I captured, it all crumbled, shaken out of my control. I turn on my heel and return to the living room where Chet has Haley's note and starts to hand it to one of the officers.

"Wait, I'd like to see that. I haven't…" I falter, then take a deep breath. "I haven't had a chance to read it yet."

Chet, ignoring me, gives it to the officer who in turn hands it to me. I take the note written on a torn piece of notepaper with the Mountain Play logo on it and read Haley's familiar scrawl.

I hate you! I hate you! I hate you! How could you do this to us?! I thought you loved us, but I guess I was wrong. Now you've lost us—or at least me. How does that feel?

H.

Tears blur my vision and I keep my focus on the note until I gain control. Then I look up and hand the note back to the officer who also reads it. When he's done, he glances at me, then at Chet. "I assume this was meant for one of you?"

I point to Chet. "It was for him." It's my first acknowledgment, in front of Chet, of his actions.

The officer holds up the note. "Where did you find this?"

Chet drops into an armchair across from the two officers. He runs his hand through his dark hair. "It was taped to the computer monitor in the den."

"What precipitated the note? Did you argue with her about something?"

Chet's gaze shifts to the ground. "No."

The officer looks back to me. "Ma'am?"

"She read an e-mail meant for me. I'd read it and then forgot to close it. It…upset her."

The officer glances from Chet to me again. "Ma'am, the more you can tell us, the better. What was in the e-mail that upset your daughter?"

I wait to see if Chet will respond, but he says nothing. I steel myself by refusing to think or feel. I simply report facts. "It indicated her father was involved in an extramarital affair. Or affairs."

He nods and jots a few notes on a pad.

When I dare to glance back at Chet, he's staring at me and his expression isn't one of contrition, but anger. My heart flip-flops in my chest and then beats double-time. I wipe my damp palms on my jeans, then cross my arms across my chest in a posture of resolve. I may not feel the bravado I'm demonstrating, but I refuse to let Chet see anything else.

The officer asks a few more questions about friends and who we've called—that type of thing—then tells us they'll be in touch.

"That's it? I mean…"

"Ma'am, I know you're concerned. If you think of anything else that may help, give me a call." He hands me a card with his number on it. As I walk the officers to the door, Chet gets up and heads toward his den.

Once the officers are out the door, I turn toward the den. "Chet…"

But he's closed the door.

*Most people who are born into the world remain babies all
their lives, their development being arrested
like sun-dried seeds.*
John Muir

CHAPTER TWENTY-TWO

Ted

THE NIGHT JESSIE was born, Sandra's screams woke me from a deep, groggy state of denial.

I remember the moment of cognition.

But her screams demanded my attention.

I'd woken to the sound of fear—Sandra crying out from somewhere. She wasn't beside me in the bed. I sat up, the rapid beat of my heart pounding in my ears. I flung the covers back and started for the bathroom, where her screams originated. I pushed open the door to find her curled on the bathroom floor, arms wrapped around her protruding abdomen.

"Is it time? Are you in labor?" I knelt beside her. She only whimpered, like a baby herself. She wasn't due for almost a month, so I wasn't sure if she was in labor or something else had happened. "Talk to me, Sandra." When I stroked her hair, she jerked away from me.

I sat down next to her and took stock. Her forehead was damp, but not hot. She didn't appear to have fallen or to be injured in any way. If it was labor, another contraction would come in time. And sure enough, a few minutes later, Sandra screamed again.

I timed the contractions by her screams and realized soon enough that we didn't have much time. "C'mon. Let's get you to the hospital." I got up and tried to lift her shoulders, tried to help her get up. But when I touched her, she jerked away from me again.

"Johnny! I want John!"

I let go of her, stepped back, and looked down at her. *John? What the—?*

Her next scream deafened me to all but the moment. Then she looked up at me and her gaze seemed to focus. "Ted... Help me."

She was confused, that was all. Right?

There wasn't time to ponder Sandra's words—those cried out in her delirium.

The pain drove her to incoherence.

That's all.

"I'm calling an ambulance. The contractions are too close—I don't want to drive you to the hospital." The hospital was in Fresno, almost an hour away. "I'd rather deliver the baby here than chance having to do it on the side of the road somewhere. But hopefully the ambulance will show up first." I left her on the floor and went back to the bedroom where I dialed 911.

Thirty-five minutes later, Sandra, with my hand crushed in hers, gave birth to Jessie. A paramedic caught the baby, cut the umbilical cord, and then lifted her to Sandra's chest.

Sandra didn't seem to know what to do with her, so I reached for her, wrapped her in a towel, and held her close.

Her dark eyes stared up at me as her head bobbed. Her mouth was open, seeking, and finally found her own fist.

I was smitten by this little life. My little girl.

With the help of the paramedics, we'd gotten Sandra off the bathroom floor and moved her to our bed, where she'd pushed all six pounds, one ounce, of Jessica into the world. Later, mother and baby were loaded into an ambulance and taken to the hospital in Fresno. I followed behind them in my own car, but I didn't want to let that little girl out of my sight for even that long.

After twenty-four hours, we were sent home. The baby was strong, and the doctor told me Sandra was fine. *"Just tired,"* he'd said when I asked about her seeming aversion to the baby. *"She'll be herself in a few days and then she'll bond with the baby. Nothing to worry about."*

Only, she wasn't herself ever again. Or maybe I'd never really known who she was. As for bonding with the baby, it didn't happen. She didn't even want to name her—told me to name her whatever I wanted. I chose the name Jessica, after my mother. And when Jessie cried in the night, I was the one to get up and feed her a bottle. When she needed changing, I did the job. And that first time I had to leave for a fire, well, I almost worried myself sick. I asked a neighbor to come by several times a day and check on Sandra and Jessie—told the woman Sandra wasn't feeling well. Maybe she wasn't. I was groping for explanations.

But after she'd recovered from giving birth, or at least had ample time to do so, she seemed to slip into denial. Denying she even had a baby at all.

When she finally left us, it seemed an easy choice for her.

Denial was a comfortable place to live. Who could blame her? Not me. I'd moved there myself after consulting Sandra's obstetrician about the baby's due date and her early arrival. He'd shrugged. She was small but close to full term. Projecting due dates is still an imperfect science. And forty-plus years ago, that was true. I chose to accept his explanation because to do otherwise was unfathomable. I'd worked a raging wildfire for several weeks around the time Jessie would have been conceived if she were truly full term.

All these years later, I've learned something about denial, though I didn't fully understand it until I read Sandra's letter. It isn't something that happens to you or something you slip into. It's something you choose.

Denial is a shield you pick up to protect yourself from the flaming arrows of truth.

Sitting in my office, with Cretia banging around in the kitchen and the voices on the scanner the backdrop for my thoughts, my mind wanders, again, to that darned letter. Haley's antics, and I'm hoping that's just what this mess is all about—teenaged antics—gives me an out for today. I don't have to deal with the contents of the letter yet. But when Haley's found and assuming all ends well, I have a call to make before I sit down and talk to Jessie.

The first person I need to confront is my friend.

I rub my hand over my head and sigh.

I need to have a conversation with Johnny.

While Jessie was still here this morning, I checked my phone hoping maybe Haley would have called or sent me a text. She hadn't, so I texted her. Twice. And I've checked my phone every five minutes since then, at least. In between checking my phone, I pace the length of my office, which is all of ten steps. "Doggone it!"

"Ted?" Cretia calls from the kitchen. She rounds the corner into my den, a dishtowel in her hands. "Honey…"

"I should be doing something to help find that little gal."

"Ted, all we can do right now is wait."

"Wait? What good does waiting do? What in the world would have her so upset that she'd just take off? Haley's not like that. She knows we'd worry."

"Yes, she does know that."

"And that's what has me so worried. This just isn't like her. My guess is when they find that boy, they'll find Haley. Maybe he's brainwashed her or something."

"Oh, honey, I know you're upset, but jumping to conclusions doesn't help anything."

After Cretia goes back to the kitchen where, I know, she's baking something in an attempt to appease me, but also to keep herself occupied, I plop down in my chair and try to focus on the scanner. If there's anything going on in the area, I'll hear about it. I glance at my watch—by now Jessie's called the sheriff's department and reported Haley's absence. If they find her, it's even possible I'll hear that on the scanner. And Jessie promised to call as soon as she knew anything. Or if she came up with something I could do to help.

But the only activity I'm hearing on the scanner this morning is fire related, including a natural burn in the park that the blasted wind has stirred up.

The whole darn state is burning up.

*Briskly venturing and roaming, some are washing off sins
and cobweb cares of the devil's spinning in all-day
storms on mountains.*
John Muir

CHAPTER TWENTY-THREE

Haley

AT THE TOP of Nevada Falls, we stop for another water break and I pull my cell phone out of my backpack and turn it on and check the time: 7:50 a.m. I stand in a clearing where I kind of remember getting cell reception when I did this hike before—reception is mostly nonexistent on the trail.

I shouldn't check my messages. I mean, that wasn't my plan, but I do it anyway. Part of me wants to know my dad's worried about me so I can ignore his messages and make him worry more. Knowing him, he's probably been up a couple hours by now and has found my note. I guess making him worry is the only way I know to punish him for what he did. Or what he's done. Because things are, like, never going to be the same.

I don't listen to the messages. Instead I just look at who the messages are from. Three from my dad, two from my mom, and two from Chloe. I'm sure they called Chloe when they figured out I'd left. Then I check my texts. Again, I have texts from my dad, my mom, Chloe, Lexie, and—uh-ho—two from my grandpa. I'd better read those.

> **Haley, we're all concerned about you. Where are you?**

I guess I was so upset that I didn't think about how my grandparents would feel when they heard I was gone. I only thought about my mom and dad. I read the next text from him.

> **Honey, just let me know you're okay.**

"We better keep going." Zach swings his pack onto his back.

"Yeah, just a minute." I can't let my grandpa worry about me, but if I text him back… Whatever. I begin punching keys.

> **I'm ok don't worry abt me. ILY.**

I press Send. I don't want my grandparents to worry—none of this is their fault. I switch my phone off. I'll try to send the text again if I can get reception somewhere. I may have to wait till we reach the top of Half Dome. I know I can't ignore everyone forever, but…

I do a slow turn, taking in the view—Nevada Falls and the rocky climb we just made below us, and a zillion trees and granite outcroppings ahead of us.

There's nothing here but space, that's for sure. I inhale and my lungs fill with the cool morning air. The sky is clear and blue and the tree branches bounce.

Zach's looking at the trees too. "It's windy."

"Yeah, kind of. Hey, I'm sorry I've been…you know. I'm glad I came. Thanks for talking me into it."

"Really?"

"Yeah, really." I smile, and for the first time today, it's real. I mean, there's a lot of stuff on my mind, but being here, on the trail, surrounded by the rocks and forest, it's distracting in a good way and I feel a little better than when we started out.

We didn't get off to a great start this morning. We hit the trail from the valley around five thirty, made the hike up the Mist Trail, including the seven hundred or so steps up the side of Vernal Falls. When we were about halfway up the steps, I pulled up my hood, making sure it didn't cover the lamp on my head lighting the steps, and then jammed my hands into the pockets of my sweatshirt. Even with the physical exertion of following the trail up out of the valley, then climbing at least three hundred steps, I was cold.

The falls weren't full because of the drought and this late in the year, early September, the stairs were mostly dry. But it was still dark and I was cold. If we'd hiked in June or July, the spray from the falls would have soaked us and made the granite stairs slippery.

Zach reached over, touched my arm, and stopped me. "Are you okay?"

Sunrise wasn't until around six thirty, so it was still dark, and when I turned to him, my headlamp shone in his eyes and he squinted and turned away. "Sorry." I shoved the lamp to the side and peered into Zach's eyes. "I'm fine, why?"

"You're just, you know, really quiet."

I shrugged. What did he want me to do, chat all the way to the top of the falls? Give me a break. I sighed. Okay, my bad mood had nothing to do with him, so I tried to smile. "Not enough sleep."

"Tell me about it." Zach laughed. "But I was so glad to get that last text from you, even if it was late."

"Yeah, sorry about that. My mom came home and, well, you know the rest." I bit my lip. I didn't like lying to him, but there was no way I was telling him the truth. My stomach clenched for like the thousandth time since... I didn't want to even think about it. "Hey, did you turn your phone off?"

"No, why?"

"If you want service when we reach the top—you know, to post a picture or whatever—you better save your battery now."

"Good call." We stood as close to the granite wall as we could get, so other early morning hikers could pass us on the stairs carved into the wall, and Zach pulled off his backpack, grabbed his phone out of an outside pocket, and turned it off.

Good.

I smiled at him. I didn't need my parents calling him— I turned my phone off before I left the house. I couldn't deal with my parents yet. This was their problem, so they could just figure it out without me. "We should stop and eat something at the top of the falls. There's this great pool—we can take a short break up there before we go to the top of Nevada Falls."

"Sounds good. You're in charge."

We climbed the rest of the stairs at a steady pace without saying much else because our breathing was labored and it got hard to talk. Which was a good thing for me, because I didn't want to talk.

When we reached the top, I led Zach to Emerald Pool, where I dropped my backpack on one of the flat granite rocks surrounding the pool. I plopped down, switched my headlamp off, took it off my head, and attached it to one of the clips on the outside of the pack. Though the sun hadn't risen over the mountains yet, there was finally enough light to see. I was a little warmer, but I left my sweatshirt on. I didn't need my muscles getting cold and tight.

"Want some trail mix? Or…" I stopped and unzipped my pack, looked inside, and dug through the contents, which included a mechanical water filter and my dad's GPS unit. Just in case. Really, it's almost impossible to get lost with so many people making the hike, though there were fewer people on the trails this time of year.

"Or how about a protein bar? I have blueberry—that's sort of like a breakfast flavor." I pulled a bar out of my pack and handed it to him.

Zach set his pack down and then sat next to me. "Aren't you eating something?"

I shrugged. "I'm not really hungry."

"You're the one who said we should eat something. Here..." Zach broke off a chunk of the protein bar and handed it to me. "You have to chow down some calories to account for what you're burning, you know? Want an apple? I brought two."

"No, thanks." I broke the piece of the protein bar into small pieces. I put a bite into my mouth and chewed, but it was hard to swallow. Still, I knew Zach was right—I needed to eat and make sure I drank enough water.

"Haley...I don't want to bug you, but are you sure something's not wrong? I mean, are you mad at me?"

I got the bite to go down and then shook my head. "No, why would I be mad at you?"

"I don't know. It's just the vibe you're sending out."

"Vibe? You sound like some kind of surfer dude."

He laughed and then took in our surroundings. "We're a little short on waves, but this is cool too." He got back up. "I'm glad it's getting light so we can see all of this. It's amazing." Zach was quiet for a few minutes as he finished his protein bar, then he looked down at me. "Haley..." He hesitated. "Is it your time of the month? I've heard that whole hormonal thing can be pretty bad."

Really? Did he really just say that to me? My face got hot. Too bad there wasn't a hole somewhere I could crawl into. "Um..." I pulled my knees up and buried my face in my hands. "I cannot believe you just asked me that."

"Why?"

He was so clueless! I dropped my hands from my face and looked up at him. "Really?"

"Hey, it's a fact of life, right? The way women are made? I just figured it might account for your mood."

Tears, which I so didn't want him to see, pricked my eyes and I looked away. Then I grabbed my backpack and dug through it again, like there was something important I needed to find. I took a deep breath and willed the tears to stop, but one slipped down my cheek anyway. I brushed it away the way I might swat at a fly that's landed on my face.

"Oh, man, did I make you cry? I'm so sorry. I didn't mean to—"

"No." I continued digging through my backpack. "I just…I have…something in my eye. I'm looking for…eyedrops."

Zach sat back down, scooted next to me, put his arm around my shoulders, and then pulled me close. I tried to pull away but his grip was firm. I jerked away and his arm dropped, and then I got up, fast, and walked away from him. I could tell by the sound of his footsteps that he'd gotten up too and followed me.

"Haley, I'm sorry." His tone was so, like, serious. "I didn't mean to upset you more than you already are."

I spun around. "How do you know I'm…?" I hiccupped and wiped at the tears flowing down my face.

His expression turned all tender and caring, which made me cry even more. "Just…can you, like, just…leave me alone? Please."

He held one hand up and took a step back. "Yep."

I turned away from him again and took a few more steps, then stopped. My nose was running and I didn't have any tissue. I considered wiping my nose on my sweatshirt, but I didn't want to live with snot on my sleeve all day. I sniffed, then sniffed again. But the tears wouldn't stop.

I took a deep breath through my open mouth, just as Zach's hand reached over my shoulder—in it was a wad of tissue. I turned around and grabbed the tissue and wiped my eyes and nose.

He put one hand on my shoulder and with the other he tilted my chin up so I'd have to look at him. He smiled and that little dimple on the right side of his mouth puckered. "You look like what's her name."

I sniffed again. "Like…who?"

"The Half Dome Indian girl."

"What?" I wiped my eyes again, then I saw the black streaks on the tissue and realized the mascara I'd put on this morning was probably running down my face like the streaks on the face of the dome. I'm such an idiot! Who puts on mascara at four in the morning for a hike anyway? But I couldn't sleep and thought it might make my eyes look less puffy. Nice try. "Shoot." I took another tissue and rubbed under my eyes and my cheeks.

Zach turned back, went to his backpack, and wet a tissue with his water reserve. Then he came back. "Here, let me help."

He began wiping my face, and I reached to stop him, but then…I just let him. The water cooled my hot cheeks and I couldn't see my face to get the mascara off anyway, so I just stood there. When he was done, he looked at me, then leaned down and kissed my forehead. He put his arms around me and pulled me into a hug. He didn't say anything—he just held me.

And I cried some more.

Zach didn't ask me any more stupid questions. He just handed me more tissue when he could tell I needed it. When the tears finally stopped, I pulled away. "Sorry. I so hate drama. I am not a drama queen."

"I know you're not. But sometimes drama just happens and you can't help it."

Without looking at him, I nodded. Then I turned away from him and blew my nose. When I finally felt like I kind of had it together, I turned back. "So okay, like obviously I'm not in a great mood. But can we just not talk about it? I mean, I don't want to ruin the day, you know?"

"You won't ruin it, but if you don't want to talk, that's cool."

I shrugged. What good would talking about it do? "Okay. Thanks. And, just for the record, it's *not* my time of the month. It's just...stuff."

"Got it."

We walked back to where we left our packs. I picked mine up and slung it over my shoulder. "We better get going." My eyes were heavy from crying and my nose was stuffed up. I felt more like crawling into bed and pulling a blanket over my head than hiking another fourteen or more miles. But my bed was at home, and I wasn't going back there.

At least, not today.

Zach looked up at Nevada Falls. "It looks like a steep climb."

"The whole hike is steep. We'll gain over forty-seven hundred feet."

"How do you know all this?"

"My parents, of course." My response was automatic. I've always thought of my parents as one—a unit—but when I said the word, I wondered how much things were going to change.

"Hey, that climb up here didn't do you in, did it?" Zach points down at the trail alongside the falls.

"No, I was just..." I shake my head and smile. "No, I'm fine."

"Okay, let's do this. We have a mountain to climb."

I follow him. But I know I'm not really fine at all.

Nature is always lovely, invincible, glad, whatever is done and suffered by her creatures. All scars she heals, whether in rocks or water or sky or hearts.
John Muir

CHAPTER TWENTY-FOUR

Haley

FROM THE TOP of Nevada Falls we hike until we reach the trail junction, where the Mist Trail and the John Muir Trail merge. I stop and pull my dad's old copy of *One Best Hike: Yosemite's Half Dome* from my backpack. I find what I'm looking for, then point at the page. "Look."

Zach leans over my shoulder and reads. "What? We've only come 2.7 miles? Whoa… It feels like a lot more. I thought we'd never get to the top of Nevada Falls."

"I know. The trail flattens out now for a little while. When we get to Little Yosemite Valley we're at the halfway point. We can use the compost toilets there"—I point to the left—"this way."

Zach and I walk side by side. He kicks a pebble on the trail, then slows and looks around. He sniffs. "It's smoky up here. Smell it?"

I stop. "Yeah, a little." I shrug. "There's always a fire somewhere." I start walking again and Zach falls in step next to me.

"Did you check for trail closures before we left?" He looks around again.

"I checked last night. What? Are you nervous?" I laugh. "It's fine. It's just a little smoke. You're a SoCal boy. You should totally be used to smoke in September."

"Yeah, I guess."

"It's from a small fire they're letting burn over that way somewhere." I point, though I don't really know where the fire is exactly. I read about it yesterday when I was checking on the conditions of the fire my mom was working.

"Why not put it out?"

"Ask my mom."

"No, really, why don't they put it out?"

"They call it a natural burn. It was started by lightning. If it isn't a threat, they let it burn—it's good for the forest."

"How do they know whether it's a threat or not?"

"They base it on what's around the area. You know, buildings or campgrounds, popular trails, and on weather conditions. Stuff like that."

"It must be pretty cool having a mom who does what your mom does."

"I guess."

"So when do I get to meet her?"

"I don't know."

"Maybe when I drop you off tonight?"

"No." I answer too fast, and I can tell by the look on Zach's face that my tone is too…something. "I mean, I don't think she'll be home."

"Oh, okay, well, I'll meet her another time. So hey, what are we going to do for your birthday?"

"My birthday?" Thank goodness he's moved on from asking questions about my mom.

"It's next month, right?"

I smile. "Yeah."

"Okay, so you'll officially be sixteen so your parents should let you go out with me, right? I mean, if they let you do this."

I shrug. "Probably." Guilt nags at me like a mosquito.

"I want to plan something special."

"You do?"

He slows his pace and looks at me. "Of course."

I stop walking again. "So are we…? I mean, you want to do something for my birthday and take me to Winter Formal and… Are we, like, together?"

He smiles at me and takes a step toward me. "I hope so."

"Oh." This is what I've wanted, right? So why do I feel so weird?

"Or maybe not? I don't want to pressure you or anything, but Haley, you know how I feel about you."

"I know, but…" It's not that I don't feel that way about Zach, it's just… "What if, you know, when we're together you decide you want to be with someone else? I mean, what if—?"

"We'd talk about it." He shrugs like it's no big deal. "Is there someone else you want to go out with? Is that why you're not sure?"

"No. Really." I shake my head. "There's only you."

He smiles again and moves even closer. Then he leans down, kind of slow, like he's going to…

I take a step back. "Wait."

"What?"

"Um, I don't know." I put my hand on my stomach.

"Are you sick?"

My stomach flip-flops. Oh. My grandpa's words come back to me about love and a fluttery feeling in the gut. I smile at Zach. "No, I'm definitely not sick." I take a step toward him, put my hands on his shoulders, then stand on my tiptoes. As I do, he leans down, and I close my eyes just as his lips, which are warmer and softer than I expected, meet mine.

Now I'll have something to tell Chloe. Only—I smile—I probably won't.

"Where's a faucet?" Zach looks at me, then looks around as we stand in line to use the compost toilets in Little Yosemite Valley.

"Faucet?"

"Yeah, you said we needed to refill our water bottles. So where do we do that?"

I laugh. "There aren't any faucets up here. We get water from the river—this is a good place because it's flat and the water moves slow. I have a filter."

"Oh, I knew that." He raises his eyebrows. "I was just testing you."

I give him a light shove. "Yeah, right."

After we're done using the toilets, we get back on the trail. The Merced River meanders through the valley to the right of us and—

"Look, there it is." I point to a clearing where Half Dome towers above.

"Whoa, it's mammoth."

We find a place along the river where it's easy for me to filter water into our bottles, then I sprinkle a packet of powdered Gatorade into each one.

"What's that?"

"Gatorade. We need the electrolytes."

"Cool. You thought of everything."

We find a dry, sandy spot along the riverbank where we sit for a short break. Zach opens his backpack and pulls out two squished sandwiches. "Lunchtime." He hands me one.

"Lunch? It's only like eight o'clock or something."

"Yeah, but we've been up since four."

True. I met Zach at the end of the road that leads to our house at four thirty this morning. And I never really did sleep much. "So did you make this?" I unwrap the sandwich and the scent of peanut butter makes my stomach rumble. I guess I am hungry.

"Yep. My mom is out of town this weekend for a teachers' conference."

I take a bite of the sandwich. "Mmm, grape jelly is the best."

"It's the only jelly for a PB & J sandwich."

"Agreed." I cover my mouth and yawn.

"Hey, stop it. We have a mountain to climb." Zach smiles, then we quiet as we eat our sandwiches. Until Zach jumps. "Hey! Knock it off!" He gets up, holding his sandwich close to his chest.

I laugh as I watch him swat the air.

"Get out of here!"

I laugh again. "Oh yeah, I forgot to tell you about the blue jays. They attack."

Zach's still swatting at the air and yelling when the jay dive-bombs for his sandwich again. "What do I do?"

"Eat your sandwich. Fast." I giggle again when he stuffs the whole rest of his sandwich into his mouth and then tries to chew and swallow the sticky bread while still watching for the pesky intruder.

When he finally gets the sandwich down, he comes and sits by me again. "Why'd he go for mine and not yours?"

"He knows you're a rookie."

"Very funny."

When I'm done with my sandwich, I take both our sandwich bags and ball them up and stick them in an outside pocket of my pack. "Leave no trace."

"Right."

I pull my phone out of the pocket of my backpack, turn it on, and wait for it to power up. When it does, I try again to send the text to my grandpa, but a little red exclamation mark next to the text lets me know it still won't go through. I'll just have to keep trying. I turn the phone off and put it away, then I lean back, the palms of my hands flat against the cool sand. I turn my face toward the sun, which is up over the granite mountaintops now, and I close my eyes. The sun warms my face. "I could go to sleep right here."

With my eyes closed, I sense Zach close to me, and then his lips touch mine. His kiss is brief and then he whispers, "Wake up, Chipmunk."

My shoulders tense and I open my eyes and lean away from him. "Don't call me that. Really."

He can tell I'm serious and holds up his hands. "Sorry."

"It's just…" I sigh. "Can I, like, ask you something personal?"

"Sure."

"What happened with your parents? Why'd they get divorced?"

Zach shrugs. "They fought a lot. I was really little, but I remember times they argued. My mom says she's a better person when she's not with my dad." He studies me. "Why?"

"I just wondered. Is it…hard? I mean, not having your family together?"

"I don't know. It's been so long. I guess I'm used to it, you know? It's hard living so far from my dad, but"—he shrugs again—"he doesn't have much time for me anyway. He has two little kids with his new wife. That's his family now. He still loves me, I guess, but it's just different. He's pretty good when we're together. We surf together and do some stuff." He laughs. "I'm kind of like his escape now when he needs to get away from the trophy wife and toddlers."

"Trophy wife?"

"Yeah, you know, the younger, hotter wife. She's like a trophy for an old guy."

"Oh. That's weird."

"What about your parents? Do they get along?"

I stare at the river before responding. "They had their first fight a few weeks ago—or at least the first one I've heard. But I don't know if that means they get along or if it's just because my mom…" I turn and look at Zach. "I don't know." I don't really want to talk about this anymore.

"Your dad seems like a cool guy."

I pick up a rock and toss it into the river. "He's not that cool. I mean, I used to think he was, but…"

"But what?"

"Never mind. We better get going." I get up, brush off my hands and the back of my pants, then grab my backpack. "We want to get up there before any weather comes in—lightning, you know?"

He doesn't seem to notice that I changed the subject. Or if he does, he doesn't push me. Instead, he just gets up and follows me.

Before we hit the forested section of the trail out of Little Yosemite Valley, I take a last look around at the sheer granite mountains surrounding this small valley—the same mountains that overlook Yosemite Valley below. The same mountains that have stood, like, forever. I mean, at least since the glaciers carved them into what they are now. They're like superheroes—strong, invincible, watching and waiting, ready to protect us from harm.

And somehow, the thought of all that power standing ready to fight for me makes my parents' problems seem less heavy.

Like maybe they aren't mine to carry.

Or at least like maybe I don't have to carry them alone.

We cannot forget anything. Memories may escape the action of will, may sleep a long time, but when stirred by the right influence…they flash into full stature and life with everything in place.
John Muir

CHAPTER TWENTY-FIVE

Jessica

AFTER CHET HIDES away in the den, I'm not sure what to do, but standing still isn't it. I need to *do* something. I go to the kitchen, grab a pad of paper and, standing at the island, make a list of Haley's friends to make sure we haven't missed calling anyone. When I've added everyone I can think of, I make my way upstairs to Haley's room to see if I can find anything that might lead me to where she's gone, or maybe lead me to friends of hers I haven't met. Maybe someone from school.

When I open her bedroom door and walk into her room, the sweet scent of the perfume she began wearing last year wends its way to my senses. Like a swirling waft of noxious gas, it knocks out my fledgling resolve. Tears prick my eyes and my breath catches. I take a slow, intentional breath, then another. I can't afford another panic attack—not now. As I inhale the scent of Haley, my heart returns to its usual steady rhythm and my breathing follows suit, as though there's no need for panic.

Maybe my body knows something my mind can't grasp? I long for that thought to become truth.

I stand in the middle of the room and take note: Her bed is made, which is Haley's way, though it looks as though she made it in haste. The comforter is pulled up over lumpy sheets and blankets. And the pillows, which she is careful about placing just so look as though she tossed them in the general direction of the head of the bed. A pair of print cotton PJ bottoms lay across the foot of the bed.

I go to her closet and riffle through the clothes hanging there to see if I'll notice anything missing, though now that she does her own laundry, I'm not as familiar with what she keeps in her closet. I run one hand over her favorite Roxy T-shirt, then look for her gray-and-neon-pink North Face hoodie, also a favorite—which I don't see. But maybe that's not unusual. It's a little warm for a sweatshirt, although if she left in the middle of the night as Chet suspects, then maybe she'd have worn it.

I shuffle through the closet again, making sure it isn't pushed to the back, but I don't find it. Of course, that doesn't mean it isn't in the laundry or folded in one of her drawers. But for now, I take a mental photo of the sweatshirt and drop it into a file in my mind marked *Missing*.

The same file—fear clenches my heart and squeezes— where I guess I'd have to place Haley herself. I mentally scratch out the word *Missing* on the file label and replace it with a less daunting word: *Misplaced*.

After a quick search of her dresser drawers, I sit at her desk—the desk was mine as a teenager. When we redecorated her room, she wanted a desk and my dad still had this one in the storage shed. He helped Haley refinish it. I run my hand over the smooth painted surface—white, with edges sanded to reveal the natural wood under the paint, giving the desk an antiqued patina. Haley's laptop sits on the desk, along with a collage frame of photos of Haley with Chloe, another with Chloe and Lexie, and a shot of Haley with Tyler at his graduation ceremony.

Tyler.

Would Haley call him and tell him what she'd discovered?

I pull my phone out of my back pocket.

Tyler was a tornado as a toddler—spinning in and out of my line of view as I attempted to nurse his newborn sister. The nursing didn't last long. One afternoon, while Chet was working and Tyler was napping, I spent a few precious moments with Haley at my breast taking in the sustenance my body provided. Just as I'd switched her from one breast to the other and she was suckling with eyes wide and focused on mine, the doorbell rang and she startled in my arms.

"Shh…" Her eyes blinked several times, but her gaze never left mine. "Shh…" I rubbed my hand over her downy head and determined whoever was interrupting this quiet moment could come back another time.

Then the bell rang again and soon I heard voices. "She in dere wid my sister."

Tyler? How'd he get out of his crib? Before I had time to process that my two-and-a-half-year-old could now climb out of his crib by himself *and* answer the front door, a woman stood before me.

I pulled the blanket I had wrapped around Haley up and over her and my exposed breast.

"I'm sorry if this isn't a good time…" The woman's smile seemed unnatural, nervous, and she held a gift in one hand. A box wrapped in pink paper.

"It's…fine."

"I'm Olivia. I work with Chet."

"Right, yes, I know. Excuse me for not getting up." I ran my free hand through my hair, which needed washing, and licked my cracked, pale lips. I wished I'd at least brushed my hair or bothered with mascara or even a little lip gloss. The stiff collar of Chet's oxford shirt, which was roomy enough for my postpartum figure, chafed my neck, and the spot where Haley had spit up on my shoulder when I burped her was beginning to sour. As I sat there, I slid my feet, clad in wool socks, into worn slippers.

"I have a gift for the baby. Congratulations." Her gaze met mine for just a moment, then she seemed to take in my appearance as she looked me up and down, finally resting her gaze on the lump of Haley hidden under the blanket. Her black nylon sweatpants hugged her toned legs and back end, and her tight fleece pullover was zipped just high enough to cover the necessities but low enough to reveal her ample cleavage. Her long, shiny blonde hair was pulled back, revealing almond-shaped, chocolate-colored, perfectly lined eyes and her creamy, flawless complexion.

I, the mother of a newborn and toddler, made the mistake of comparing myself to the young, fit, and beautiful—what was she? Climbing instructor? Sales rep? Goddess?—who worked with my husband.

"Well, here." She sat the gift next to me on the sofa while Tyler sat at my feet rolling a Brio train engine back and forth across the carpeted floor. When Olivia, or *Liv* as I recalled hearing others refer to her, placed the gift next to me, her hand shook, just barely, but enough to let me know that perhaps she wasn't feeling as superior as I'd imagined.

"Thank you. This is so kind—"

"It's nothing, really. I'll let you get back to…" She didn't seem to know what to say. "I can show myself out."

"Great. Thanks, again. I'll let Chet know you came by."

At the mention of Chet's name, the young woman's gaze darted around the room, then she turned and left.

As soon as Haley had finished nursing, I'd gotten off the sofa and set the dead bolt on the front door—the bolt Tyler couldn't yet reach. Then instead of waiting for Chet to get home to watch Tyler and Haley, I put Haley in her carrier and picked up a bucket of blocks and carried both the baby and the bucket into our master bathroom, encouraging Tyler to follow me as I went.

Once there, I locked the three of us in the bathroom, where I showered and washed my hair, keeping an eye on Tyler as he piled up blocks and Haley cried herself to sleep. I even put on a little makeup and found a sweater of my own that I could squeeze into. By the time I finished, Tyler, who was bored and hungry, was crying and his cries woke Haley.

I desperately needed a nap, which I didn't get.

But what struck me then, and what strikes me again now, all these years later, is how I felt when I got out of the shower that afternoon. My hair once again smelled like the floral shampoo I used and my shaved legs were smooth for the first time in over a week. But while the hot water and lemon-verbena soap cleansed me physically, they didn't wash away the unease Olivia's visit left in my soul.

Or Chet's reaction later.

"One of your employees came by today with a baby gift."

"Oh yeah, who?"

"Olivia."

Chet looked away and busied himself with something, but before he turned, there was a look in his eyes, something I couldn't quite define. What I did recognize was the way his gaze didn't meet mine—the way he wouldn't look me in the eye. The same way Olivia hadn't looked me in the eye. But with a toddler and a newborn to care for, a boss waiting for my return to work, a mortgage to pay, debt to catch up with…I couldn't afford to dwell on the reason I felt unsettled. So I did what I was already becoming adept at doing.

I dug a hole in my soul and buried the feeling there.

It felt like survival, but Cretia, I know now, would call it denial.

I'd bet now that Olivia was another of the affairs Heather referred to in her e-mail. I may not have felt I could afford to deal with the reality at the time, but now, with a teenage daughter watching and learning from me, I can't afford *not* to deal with the knowledge of Chet's affair. No…

Make that affairs.

My cell phone vibrates, startling me out of my reverie. Haley? I look at the screen, my heart beating overtime. But the call isn't from Haley.

"Chloe? Have you heard from her?"

"You still haven't found her? She has to be with Zach. But I've texted them both like a hundred times, but neither of them is responding."

"Where would they go? Do you have any ideas?"

"I dunno, the mall maybe?"

I sigh. "Chloe, the mall wouldn't even be open yet on a Sunday."

"Oh yeah, well, maybe they, you know, went out for breakfast or something first."

"Maybe. Thanks for checking in with me. If you hear from her, or from Zach, let me know."

"Okay. And Mrs. Weaver, I don't think you need to worry about Haley—she's the solid one, you know what I mean? She's smart, the one who gives the rest of us advice and keeps us from doing anything too stupid. She probably just isn't thinking that you'd be worried."

I smile, though the action requires energy and reminds me how little sleep I've had. "Thanks, Chloe."

I press End and start to tuck my phone back into my pocket when I remember Tyler. I key in his number and listen as it rings. When his voice mail answers, I leave him a message. Then I send him a text—sometimes he responds to a text before he'll return a call. And on a Sunday morning, he's probably still sleeping.

> Ty, have you heard from Haley this morning? We're not sure where she is and we're concerned.

I set the phone on Haley's desk and then open her laptop. I turn it on—no password necessary. This morning, I'm grateful for the rules I've set regarding electronics. If a program requires a password, like Facebook, then the kids need to use the family password we've established. Although, once Tyler turned eighteen and left for college, I abolished that rule for him. As hard as that was for me, I trust his discernment. I trust him.

And with that thought comes the comfort of knowing I can trust Haley too. Though her emotions in this situation are unpredictable.

I check Haley's e-mail and Facebook messages to see if there's anything that may give me a clue as to where she's gone, but I learn nothing, except that Chloe is right—Haley has a good head on her shoulders. But then, I knew that. Even so, the reminder is comforting.

My phone vibrates again, this time it's a response from Tyler:

Haven't heard from her, but I wouldn't worry. ILY

But would he worry if he knew why Haley left? The thought of having to tell Tyler about his dad makes my heart ache, but now isn't the time to think that far ahead.

"Stay in the moment, Jessica," Stay in the moment? How often have I avoided the moment? Like those moments with Olivia and Chet?

Denial has been my coping mechanism of choice.

But no longer.

I lay my head on my arms on top of Haley's desk and consider what letting go of denial really means. As I do, my stomach cramps and I begin to perspire. It will mean confronting Chet. And then staying in the moment for his response.

Or reaction.

I close my eyes.

The thought is overwhelming.

Now, in the deep, brooding silence all seems motionless, as if the work of creation were done. But in the midst of this outer steadfastness we know there is incessant motion. Ever and anon, avalanches are falling from yonder peaks.
John Muir

CHAPTER TWENTY-SIX

Haley

THE STRAPS OF my backpack are starting to dig into my shoulders, so I hitch it higher. I'm glad it's just a day pack. I'm too tired to carry the weight of a loaded pack. My legs feel like bricks. I yawn again, then glance at Zach. "Sorry."

He nudges me with his elbow. "You better be careful. It's when you're tired that you have an accident or get injured."

"Says who?"

"Beats me."

I shake my head at him. "There's a long section of switchbacks up ahead that'll wake me up. Anyway, that injury thing when you're tired only applies to old people."

Zach laughs. "Yeah, you're probably right."

We walk in silence, then Zach turns to me. "So, is it something with your parents that has you bummed today? Are they having problems? I mean, I get it if you don't want to talk about it, but sometimes it, you know, helps. Based on what you said back there"—he gestures behind us—"I just figured it's about your parents."

I sigh. "I don't see how talking about it can really help anything." I shift my backpack again. "I just…" I stop walking and Zach, a few steps ahead of me, stops and turns around and waits. I shrug. "I don't mean to, you know, keep it from you or anything. I just don't want to talk about it." I look at the ground.

Talking only makes it seem more real.

He nods. "Okay, no problem. But I'm here if, you know, you change your mind."

That is so not going to happen.

As we start up the switchbacks, the late-morning sun has warmed the trail and dust stirs, then settles again with each step we take. The sunshine filtering through the treetops makes shadowed patterns on the trail and forest floor. We're making good time and keeping a great pace—faster than when I've done this hike before. "I don't smell smoke as much anymore, do you?"

"Nope. Mostly just dust and forest stuff."

"Forest stuff?" I laugh.

"Yeah."

"Like, um, trees?"

He grins. "Yeah, and…"—he sniffs, then shrugs—"other stuff too."

I sniff. "It smells…organic."

He laughs. "Organic, it is."

"So how come you never asked Chloe out?"

"Whoa, way to change the subject." He holds a water bottle in one hand and takes a swig, then wipes his mouth. "Chloe? Why would I ask her out?" He slows as he tucks the bottle into an outside pocket of his pack.

I raise my eyebrows. "Really? Because she's gorgeous, she's popular, she's fun."

"She's high maintenance."

I swat his arm. "No, she's not. She's my best friend."

"Well, she seems high maintenance. Anyway, she's not my type. You're my type. But I thought you'd never go out with me."

"Why?"

"Because you were totally ignoring me."

"I didn't ignore you. I just couldn't...you know..."

"Because of Chloe?"

"You knew?"

"That she liked me? She's not exactly subtle."

I laugh. "I guess not. Well, yeah, since she liked you, I kind of had to ignore you a little bit." I laugh again. "I mean, Chloe and I have been friends since kindergarten. That means something."

"See, that's what I like about you. You're not one of those girls who'd stab her BFF in the back over a guy."

"Yeah, because friendship or relationships"—my voice catches—"are about trust."

Zach looks over at me. "You okay?"

I nod but don't say anything else until I'm sure I can say it without crying. "It's like climbing."

"What do you mean?"

"It's the 'brotherhood of the rope'—that unspoken bond between climbers—we've got each other's back. If I've got the brake rope, I won't let go, no matter what. When we're climbing, we trust our partners with our lives."

"Yeah, right. So?"

"So remember the story my dad told us during climbing camp that first year you were there?" I stop. *My dad?* I swallow the lump that's formed in my throat. "The story about the three guys climbing Apron Jam on Glacier Point?"

"Sort of."

"I've heard him tell it *so* many times."

"You sound mad."

I take a deep breath, "It's just…" I sigh, then begin again. "Pete Terbush, Joe Kewin, and Kerry Pyle were climbing. Pyle led, Terbush belayed, and Kewin was at the base, remember?"

Zach nods.

"Just as Pyle neared the anchor, something like five hundred tons of rock broke off above and to the right of him and came crashing down. Some of the rock, as it fell, broke apart and went in all directions. Kewin ran for cover near the wall, right? But Terbush knew Pyle was still on belay and if he let go, Pyle could fall. So even with rock spraying down on him, he held his position. He didn't let go of the brake."

The pitch of my voice rises, and I wipe tears from my cheeks. I don't even try to stop myself from crying this time. "He stood firm, Zach. Terbush didn't cave, you know? He didn't just take off and do what he wanted to—he didn't just think of himself. He thought of the person he was supposed to take care of!" I sob. "He took care of the person he was supposed to…to protect!"

The sobs are making it hard to talk now. "Pyle was hit in the head, his scalp was cut and bleeding. If he'd fallen, and Terbush had let go—" I hiccup and swipe at my nose and then wipe my cheeks with my palms. "But he didn't let go. He…he *died* down there. He took a direct hit in the head and it killed him. Later, Kewin had to pry Terbush's fingers off the rope to get Pyle down. Terbush hadn't let go! Even as he died! Isn't that what marriage is supposed to be about? The whole 'until death do us part' thing?"

We've stopped on the trail and Zach's watching me, a look of confusion on his face. He takes a step toward me but then stops. "So…we're not talking about you and Chloe or climbing anymore, right?"

Everything I've held in since reading that e-mail breaks loose and explodes to the surface with energy I totally cannot control. I ball my fists and stamp one foot, the force of it sending slivers of pain through my heel into my calf. Then a scream roars from my chest, up my throat, and through my clenched teeth. I turn away from Zach and with head down and tears blurring my view of the trail, I trudge my way up the next switchback.

But just as I reach the turn, the toe of my boot catches on something.

And before I can catch myself…

"Haley!"

A yowling noise, like a dog would make when someone's stepped on its paw, sounds in my ears, as my face hits the ground. Hard. The cry, I realize, is coming from me. I gasp for air, but when I do, my chest aches. Puffs of dust swirl around my face so when I catch my breath, my nose and mouth fill with fine, dry dirt.

"Oh, man…Haley." Zach, who's caught up with me, kneels next to me and puts his hand on my back. "Don't move, okay. Just hang on for a second."

My bottom lip throbs. "Oww…" I groan and then try to roll over.

"No, seriously, don't move. Just give me a minute." Zach has gotten up and his voice sounds like it's coming from down by my feet now, where I'm sure someone is jabbing knives into my ankle.

"Whoa…" He comes back and kneels beside me again. "Okay, so your ankle is…um, it's tweaked. It's turned at a weird angle." He puts his hand on my back again.

"Oh no…" My tears wet the dirt. I lift my head a little and try to look at Zach.

"Oh man, your face is bleeding. Here, hold on, let me—"

"Looks like you two could use a hand."

Zach gets up. "Yeah, she just fell. I think her ankle's broken."

"Looks that way."

I listen to the conversation between Zach and some guy—another hiker who must have come up behind us. Zach tells him we've both had some first-aid training through climbing classes, and the guy says something that I can't hear.

After a few minutes of talking about me like I'm not even there, the guy leans down. "Hi, I'm Dave. I'm going to help your friend here. Give us a couple minutes. We're going to make a splint for your ankle—to keep it from moving." He puts his hand on my shoulder. "Anything else hurt?"

"Mostly just my ankle. And my face."

"Okay. Sweetie, what's your name?"

"Haley."

"Nice to meet you, Haley. But next time, let's meet under better circumstances. Deal?"

"Yeah."

He gets up and I listen to them rustling around. The zippers on a backpack zip and unzip a few times as they talk about what they're going to do. Then one of them walks by me, and pretty soon I hear a couple of snaps, like the crack of wood breaking. Then Dave kneels next to me again.

"Haley, first let's get your pack off." He lifts each of my arms just enough to slide the straps of my backpack off, then lifts it off my back. "Okay, I'm not going to lie to you. This is going to hurt. We'll be as gentle as possible. Your friend's going to lift your leg, and I'm going to splint it using a couple of tree branches and an ace bandage. You kids were smart to pack a few first-aid supplies."

Dave gets up and I'm guessing he goes to where Zach already has his hands on my injured leg.

Zach's voice drifts to me. "Haley, I'm going to lift your leg. I'll try not to move your ankle, but it's still probably going to hurt."

In a second I realize what an understatement that is. Pain rips through my ankle as he lifts my leg and I scream, then groan, nauseated. I try to take deep breaths as I cry and try not to groan again. I don't want them to think I'm a baby or can't handle this, but it hurts so much.

"You doing okay, Haley?" Dave asks.

I can't say anything.

Once they have the ankle wrapped, Zach tells me they're going to help me roll over. "I'll hold your leg and Dave will help you roll. Okay?"

"Okay."

"Take it slow." Dave counts to three. "Ready?"

My heart is pounding, making my chest thump against the ground. I close my eyes tight. "Okay, ready." I twist my shoulders and torso as I try to roll myself over, and Dave lifts my hips as Zach turns my leg. It hurts, but not as much as it did before they wrapped it. Once on my back, tears slip into my ears and the sun shining in my eyes blinds me. I lift one arm to shield my eyes as Zach eases my leg back down.

"Good girl. Now take a few more deep breaths." Dave is kneeling beside me and now Zach comes and stands over me, blocking the sun.

I take a deep, ragged breath, then another.

"Looks like you bit your lip—that's the blood I saw. But it's not too bad. Your face is fine—just a little scratched up." Zach leans down and brushes dirt from one of my cheeks. Then straightens and looks around. "So there's a tree right behind you, just off the trail. If you sit up, you can probably scoot yourself back and lean against the tree. Want to try?"

Not really, but I don't want to just lie in the middle of the trail either, so I nod. "Okay."

"We'll help you." Dave comes around behind my head and slowly lifts my shoulders as I push off the ground with my elbows.

"Ow! Wait! Just…wait a minute." I take a few more deep breaths.

"Here, let me hold your leg so it doesn't drag." Again, Zach lifts my leg.

"Okay…" With Dave lifting my shoulders, I use my hands to push myself into a sitting position, with my legs out in front of me. I bend the knee of the leg that's not injured and pull it to my chest, then use it to push myself back through the dirt, inch by slow inch.

The pain in my ankle, throbbing now, leaves me out of breath and a wave of nausea rolls over me again, but, after several minutes, I make it to the tree and lean my back against the hard ripple of bark.

"Here." Zach folds the sweatshirt he tied around his waist earlier. "Lean forward a little." Then he puts it between me and the tree. "Better?"

I nod.

"Good job, Haley." Dave smiles at me, then pulls a cell phone out of a side pocket of his cargo shorts. "No reception. Do either of you have cell reception?"

Zach checks his phone. "Nah. Which means she won't either—we have the same carrier."

"Tell you what. I'm going on. There'll be a ranger posted at Sub-Dome checking permits. I still want to make the summit and we're just as close, if not closer, to Sub-Dome as we are to the ranger station at Little Yosemite Valley. I'll notify the ranger. You two stay put." He winks at me, knowing I don't have a choice.

"Thanks, man." Zach puts out his hand and Dave shakes it.

"She's lucky you're with her. Sit tight." He takes off around the bend.

I lean my head back against the tree and close my eyes, my whole body shaking because of the pain. Zach wraps my sweatshirt around the front of me—he must have dug it out of my backpack. Then he pulls a shirt out of his backpack. "Good thing I packed an extra." He wraps it around the splint they put on my leg. "The padding will help it stay in place and protect it a little more." Then he lifts my leg again and slips my backpack under my wrapped calf and ankle.

"That'll help support your ankle and keep it elevated a little bit."

Tears slip down my cheeks, but I just ignore them. Crying is the least of my problems now.

"Here, take these."

I open my eyes and stare at the two little pills in the hand Zach is holding out. "What is it?"

"Ibuprofen. They'll help with the pain, and maybe the swelling."

"My boot or the splint is too tight. It hurts."

He bends over and puts his fingers between the splint and my leg. "It's not too tight, but your ankle's probably swelling. Sorry."

I take the ibuprofen and the water bottle he hands to me. I swallow the pills and hand the bottle back. Then he takes a couple of pieces of tissue, wets them with water from the bottle, and, for the second time today, he cleans my face.

"I don't want to hurt you, but I want to get the dirt out of those scrapes on your cheek and your lip. Your lip is pretty swollen."

"Here…" I take the tissue and gently wipe at the areas around my lip and cheek. "How bad do I look? I mean, am I getting the dirt off my face?"

Zach smiles. "Sort of." He grabs a couple more tissues and starts to wet them.

"Don't use all your water."

"It's okay, we probably won't need it. Anyway, we're close enough to that spring you mentioned, right? I can get more if we need it." His touch gentle, he cleans the rest of my face. Then he takes a small first-aid kit out of his pack, digs through it, and comes up with a packet of antibiotic ointment. He tears the corner of the packet and, with a clean tissue, dabs some on the scrapes on my cheek.

"There's not much I can do for your lip. It'll just have to heal."

I nod. "What happened?"

Zach turns around and sits next to me, then he points to the trail, back the way we came. "See that thing sticking up? Looks like a stick?"

I nod.

"It's a tree root. It had grown under the trail, but the middle of it must have broken through the dirt. You caught it with your foot, I guess, and then went flying. Only, your foot was stuck under it. When you fell forward with your foot stuck"—he shrugs—"even with your boots on, I think it snapped your ankle. I mean, that's my guess. It happened pretty fast."

I shake my head and then lean it back against the tree again. "I'm so…tired."

A steady parade of hikers pass us, some stopping to make sure I'm okay, others ignoring us.

"Try to rest. It's going to take that guy a while to get to Sub-Dome and then time for someone to get here, right? What'll they do? I mean, how will they get you down? Back to the Valley?"

"They'll get someone up here, stick me on a litter, and take me down."

"A litter?"

"Yeah, that's what they call it. It's like a stretcher thing on fat wheels. They'll just roll me down."

Zach's eyes get wide. "Down all those steps we came up?"

Even with all the pain, Zach's question makes me laugh. "No, silly. They'll take me down the John Muir Trail."

"Oh, right, but still, it'll be a bumpy ride. But hey, lucky you, you get a ride out of here. I have to hike."

"Yeah, poor you." I smile. "Hey, I'm sorry I, like, totally ruined your day."

"You didn't ruin it."

"But you're not going to make it to the top if you stay here with me."

"I'm not leaving you. We'll do it another time."

"Maybe."

"Maybe?"

It's time to tell Zach the truth. He'll find out soon enough anyway. "My mom is going to ground me for the rest of my life."

"What? Why?"

I try to shift my leg, which is beginning to cramp. But even the slightest movement causes the throbbing in my ankle to turn to stabbing pain again. My puffy lip makes me talk funny and my eyes and sinuses are swollen from crying. I sigh. "She didn't know—I didn't ask her if I could come. I didn't get permission."

"Wait, what? You said you did. What about your dad? You at least got permission from him, right?"

I shake my head, then turn and look at Zach. "I…lied. I'm, like, I'm so sorry."

Zach runs his hand through his curly blond hair. "Oh man, that's not good. I mean, they're going to hate me—"

"No. No, it's not your fault and, believe me, they already know that. If it's, like, anyone's fault, it's my dad's." I lean back and close my eyes again.

"Why is it his fault? Is this what's been bothering you all day? Did he do something?"

"Yeah." I open my eyes and stare straight ahead. "He had an affair. Or…affairs, I guess."

Zach doesn't say anything, so I turn to look at him. He's staring at me, like he doesn't believe me.

"Really, he did."

He shakes his head. "Whoa, Haley…I'm so…I mean, whoa."

"Exactly. And, oh wait, it gets better. Remember Heather, our climbing instructor from last year?"

Zach's eyes get wide, then he turns his head and stares out at the trail for a second, then nods. "He had an affair with her." It's a statement, not a question.

"You knew?"

"Nah. I'm just not surprised." He looks at me again. "She's really, you know, she's…hot."

"What?"

"Well, yeah…" He lifts his shoulders. "But it was more than that. I remember watching your dad talking to her, and I just had a weird feeling, like maybe things weren't on the up-and-up. But then I figured that was crazy. Anyway, most of the guys there were looking at her and trying to get her attention, so I just figured your dad was, you know, flirting." He shrugs again.

"So just because a girl's hot, guys think they have a right to—?"

"No, I didn't say that. But some guys are like that."

"That's so wrong." I shake my head again. "She e-mailed my mom and told her about having an affair with my dad. And last night, I found the e-mail."

"So that's why you asked about my parents?"

I nod. "Yeah, I guess my dad's on the hunt for a trophy wife of his own."

Zach just stares at me.

"You don't have to say anything. There's nothing to really say."

"I was just thinking about those climbers on Apron Jam, and here's the thing—sometimes climbers just fall. They do, Haley, we both know that. And it's not because of a rockslide or some major thing—it's because of a stupid mistake. Something they did wrong. Maybe your dad just, you know, made a stupid mistake. Like, he didn't think through the consequences."

"Yeah, but when you make a stupid mistake, you can take others down with you."

"Right, but it's not like you mean to. You know?"

I look down. That would be so great if Zach was right about my dad, because maybe there'd be some hope…

But no. He's wrong.

And there's no hope.

My mouth is dry and my throat aches from the lump lodged there. I take a sip of water, then look back at Zach. "I get what you're trying to say. But this wasn't a stupid mistake my dad made once. It wasn't just one time! She, *Heather*, said there were others. Like, he's done it before with other women, so…that's different. It's like when you're belaying for someone and you take your hand off the brake to do something and nothing happens so you figure you can do it again, and again, until that one time when the climber's on belay and you take your hand off the brake to scratch your ear or reach for a soda, and oh, oops, the climber falls and dies! Like, that's what happened. My family just fell off the wall and died while my dad, who was so selfish and stupid, was scratching an itch!" Hot tears fall down my cheeks.

Zach's tone is serious. "Wow. Sorry. So…what about your mom?"

"What do you mean?"

"She knows?"

"Um, yeah, I guess." I sniff. "I mean, it looked like she'd come home. Her duffel bag was there. When I went into the den to look for her, the computer was on and her e-mail was open and *that one* was on the screen. So, like, I guess she'd read it."

"Did you talk to her?"

"No, she wasn't there." I shift again and the sweatshirt behind me slips down—a lump pressed against my lower back. "I…I haven't really…thought that much about her. I mean, I know that sounds really bad—it is really bad—I just was, like, I was so upset."

I shake my head again. "That's so warped, I know. I just…" I lift my hands, palms up. "I don't know. I just wanted to get out of there. That's when I texted you and told you I could go today. I just needed to…leave. I didn't want to, you know, deal with it."

Zach scoots close to me and puts his arm around my shoulders. "It's okay," he whispers. "It's okay."

But I know it's not.

And it won't ever be okay again.

*Thousands of tired, nerve-shaken, over-civilized people are
beginning to find out that going to the mountains
is going home...*
John Muir

CHAPTER TWENTY-SEVEN

Jessica

MY SHOULDERS TWITCH, then lurch upward.
My neck aches as I raise my head. I open my eyes and try to
focus—try to figure out where I am. I look around. Haley's
room? My phone vibrates and skitters across her desk. As it
does, reality returns—and with it comes dread, rearing its
head like a fire-breathing dragon, singeing the sense of peace
I'd found in sleep.

But I don't have time to sleep. What time is it? I rub
my eyes, then reach for my phone, hope, like an anchor,
steadying me for a moment. Haley? But when I look at the
screen, *Dad* is displayed there.

I clear the sound of sleep from my voice. "Hi, Dad."
"Have you heard anything?"

I sigh. "No, nothing. But I think she's okay. Just intuitively, I think she'll be okay. She wouldn't do anything…stupid."

"No, she wouldn't. Though it isn't like her to take off without telling anyone where she was going."

"I know, but she was pretty upset."

"Jessie, I don't know what's going on over there or what had our little gal so upset, but you know—"

"I know, Dad. I know." I know he'd do anything for me—for us—but to hear it right now will only stir my emotions again, and I need to focus. "What time is it?"

By the way the sun is shining into Haley's room and by the ache that's formed in my neck, I fear I slept awhile.

"Just before noon."

"Noon?" Already?

"By the way, in case you haven't heard, there's a fire that's taken off inside the park this morning. It was a natural burn that NPS was letting run its course, and now it's headed for some of the most popular trails in the park, which means shutdowns. Well, you know how all that works. You're not on call, are you?"

"No, thank God. I have enough to deal with at the moment."

"That you do. Keep us posted, Jessie."

"I will, Dad. Thanks."

I close Haley's laptop and get up from her desk, but as I'm walking out of her room, it occurs to me that I didn't check the search history on her computer. I turn back, open the lid of the laptop again, and sign on to her browser. Then I click *History*.

And there, I discover my first clue.

In the garage, I check the shelf where our hiking boots are lined up. There were four pairs of boots until Tyler left for school. Then there were three. This morning, there are only two pairs of hiking boots on the shelf. I open a large plastic container next to the boots where we keep hiking gear—water bottles, water filters, first-aid kits… Several items are missing.

I stare into the container and peace flutters, like a dove, and then lands once again in my soul. Of course she'd escape to a trail—to the mountains. She's my daughter. Our daughter. As much as I'm loathe to admit it right now, Chet's influence on Haley is as marked as my own, and we've passed our love for the grandeur of the mountains to our kids.

I close the container, grab my own backpack off an upper shelf, and head back inside.

What trail beckoned you, Haley?

I set my pack on the kitchen island and toss in provisions—likely the same things Haley packed: trail mix, a couple of granola bars, an apple, and a few cheese sticks. Whatever we have on hand that will keep me going for…

How long? Where am I going? And what makes me think I can find her?

Wait…

What did my dad say?

A fire is threatening popular trails in the park? "Chet!" I run down the hallway and burst into the den, the French doors banging against the walls as I push through them. "She's hiking. Her gear is gone. Where would she go? Is her climbing gear gone too?" I turn back, intending to go back to the garage to check if her gear is still here.

"Jess, wait! How do you know she's hiking?" Chet's up and out of his chair.

I ignore his call to wait and jog down the hallway to the garage, Chet close behind. "I checked the history on her computer. She checked for trail closures in the park this morning at 3:47 a.m."

"Slow down! Jess!"

I stop at the door to the garage and turn back and look at Chet.

"If she's hiking she's fine. Calm down."

My heart, like a jackhammer, pounds. *Do not* tell me to calm down." I speak through clenched teeth. "There's a fire. It's threatening some of the popular, and therefore most populated, trails in the park. Think, Chet, where would she go? Would she hike or climb?" I swing open the door between the house and garage and head back to the shelf where we keep gear. I open another container that holds the kids' and Chet's climbing gear. "Is it all here?"

He skirts around me, grabs the container, and riffles though the contents. "Yeah." He nods. "Yeah, I think it's all here."

"Okay. She's hiking. Where would she go?"

"Where's the fire?"

"I don't know. I haven't checked yet. My dad told me. Just think, where would Haley hike?"

Chet runs his hand through his mussed hair and sighs. "I don't know, she could go anywhere. Likely somewhere we've been, but we've hiked all over Yosemite through the years." He shrugs. "I don't know."

"Chloe thinks she's with Zach. Have you gotten through to him or his mother yet?"

"No, still no response on his cell or at his home number."

"So maybe he and Haley are together."

"Yeah." Chet turns to head back into the house, then stops mid step and turns back to me. "I know! Half Dome. Zach wanted to do the hike to Half Dome. Haley asked me about applying for permits. That's it!"

"Did she ask you if she could go with him? Mention him doing the hike this weekend?"

"No."

"Then that doesn't make sense. She wouldn't just call Zach and take off early this morning without a permit."

"Maybe they'd already applied for a permit. Who knows?"

"I'll find out where that fire is—can you check to see if a permit was issued to either Haley or Zach for today? You must have a contact in that office, right?"

"Sure, but it's Sunday. No one will be there today. I'll make a few calls—see what I can do."

I follow Chet as far as the living room, then he closes himself in the den again, using the doors as a barrier between us. Maybe he understands that he needs the protection—but then that would mean he understands he's responsible for his actions and, at the core, that place of knowledge deep within each of our souls, I know he'll never own what he's done.

Somehow, he'll blame me.

As I stare at the closed doors, grief, a harbinger of reality, accosts me. For just a moment as we discussed Haley, it was easy to believe we were working together to solve a common, benign issue, like a stopped-up kitchen sink—there was a brief moment of camaraderie, which makes the intrusive reminder of reality all the more bitter.

Chet and I may never share a sense of camaraderie again.

Though, we'll always be our kids' parents, so...

I make my way to the living room and drop onto the sofa and close my eyes. *Stay in the moment, remember?* Jumping ahead to what may or may not happen to my marriage isn't going to help anything right now.

What may or may not happen?

It's already happened. Remember that, Jessica.

There will be time enough to ponder the repercussions later.

I pull my phone from my pocket and call my dad back, killing two birds with one stone—he knows where the fire is and I can update him at the same time. I'm praying it isn't the natural burn I think it is, because with the direction the wind is blowing this morning...

He picks up after the first ring. "Honey?"

"Hi again. Hey, we think Haley's hiking today—probably with her friend Zach."

"Ah, well that would make sense wouldn't it? Do you know where they headed?"

"Possibly Half Dome. Haley mentioned to Chet that Zach wanted to do that hike." I wait for his response, but there's only silence on the other end of the line. "Dad?" When he clears his throat, my nerves rattle again.

"Jess, you need to make a few calls. The Meadow Fire is headed toward Half Dome—they're talking about sweeping trails, shutdowns, you know the routine. NPS does their job well, you know that, so there's probably no need to worry, but it doesn't hurt to alert Search and Rescue—let 'em know your daughter may be out there."

"I…I can't believe this. Dad…" I don't know what else to say.

"Honey, I'm pretty sure there's a lot going on that you're not telling me and that's okay, but I want you to listen up. You keep your head on straight. Let SAR do their job. Haley's going to be fine. I feel it in my bones, just like you did earlier. Okay?"

"Okay. But Dad, what if…?" My voice cracks.

"*What-if* questions aren't going to get you anywhere right now, Jessie. Let's just focus on finding her and getting her home. We're here for you—for all of you."

"I know. Thanks, Dad."

I look at my watch. If Haley and Zach did make the Half Dome hike, they'd have likely ascended via the cables by now. In the past, we've summited by noon and Haley would follow suit, I think. If they're on top, she'd have cell phone reception.

I text her again.

> H, if you get this, I need to know you're ok. Fire near Half Dome. Worried. Pls text me.

I wait a few moments, praying she'll respond. But when I hear nothing, I make a few calls. Following the chain of command, I get briefed on the fire situation in the park— weather conditions, expected fire behavior, trail closures, and rescue operations—and, at the same time, report that Haley may be in the vicinity of Half Dome. I'm assured, as my dad already mentioned, that they're sweeping trails in the area for hikers, and those who've already summited will be airlifted off Half Dome sometime this afternoon. All procedures I'm familiar with.

Too familiar.

That information signals how serious this fire is. The expense of such a rescue is—I shake my head—staggering. I pull out the business card one of the deputies handed me before they left and call and report what we know: Haley is hiking with a friend in the area of the Meadow Fire.

When the deputy questions me, I have to admit to him, and to myself, that no, we don't know that for sure. It's just our best guess.

And for now, a guess is all we have to go on.

Lie down among the pines for a while…
John Muir

CHAPTER TWENTY-EIGHT

Haley

MY HEAD ACHES, so I keep my eyes closed as I lean against the tree. When I open my eyes, Zach is standing on his toes on a boulder trying to see something. "What are you looking at?"

"Smoke." He turns toward me, jumps off the boulder, and comes back and sits down next to me. "Hear those planes?"

I close my eyes again and listen, then open my eyes and nod. "Sounds like a helicopter too."

"Yeah, I saw one—red and white—like a Cal Fire chopper. So I got up there to look around. There's a humungous cloud of smoke"—he points—"that way. That must be what we smelled in Little Yosemite Valley. Some of the smoke probably settled there. Haley, it's bad."

I lift my head and focus on the tree branches above and watch them sway in the wind. "How far away do you think it is?"

"I don't know. I mean, close, but I don't know how close. And with the wind—"

"It's probably a long way off. Smoke can seem closer than it really is." Too bad I'm not as confident as I sound. "Did you try your phone over there, on top of that boulder? Can you get reception up there?" A sliver of fear imbeds itself somewhere in my chest.

"Let me try." He unzips his backpack, grabs his phone, then gets up, crosses the trail, and climbs back to the top of the boulder. He shakes his head. "Still nothing."

My mom would know about the fire. Mom…how is she doing? What is she thinking and feeling? The thoughts feel kind of weird. I'm used to her worrying about me rather than the other way around. Where did she go last night after reading that e-mail? Where is she now? Does she even know I'm gone? Would my dad have told her about the note I left for him?

"Zach, maybe you should go on ahead—go until you get phone reception. You can call my mom, let her know where we are so, you know, she doesn't worry. I should've called her or something last night or this morning. I was just so…"

"She'll understand."

"I don't know. Anyway, she'll know about the fire."

Zach comes and stands next to me. "I don't think it's a good idea for us to get separated. Who knows if I'll get reception anywhere?"

"I told you, I got reception at the top."

"I'm not going all the way to the top and leaving you here, Haley. That would be stupid. What if something happened to you? What if a rescue team never shows up? No way."

"It's not like I'm alone out here. Have you seen how many people have passed us?"

"So we'll ask the next group of hikers if they have cell reception. I'm not leaving you."

No one's going to have reception here, but I stop arguing—it's obvious there's no point. "Do you have a pencil or pen in your backpack?"

"I can look. Why?"

"I'm going to write down my mom's number and give it to the next group of hikers that pass by. They could call her or give the number to a ranger to call or something."

"Okay."

He digs through his backpack and finds a pen and a napkin. I write down my name, my mom's name, her title with NPS, and her cell phone number—she always has her phone with her. Then we wait.

And wait.

But no one comes. After what seems like a hundred people have passed us since I fell, now there's no one.

We are out here all alone.

All that is necessary to make any landscape visible and therefore impressive is to regard it from a new point of view, or from the old one with our heads upside down.
John Muir

CHAPTER TWENTY-NINE

Jessica

HAVING MADE ALL the necessary calls, there's nothing to do now but wait. I don't even tell Chet what I've learned. I don't want to face him again. With energy waning, I drag myself back up the stairs where I curl into myself under the covers of Haley's bed.

I struggle to catch my breath.

And my heart pounds like a sledgehammer.

With the covers pulled over my head, I try to ignore the questions hissing in my mind. What if something happens to Haley? Why isn't Chet showing signs of remorse? I gasp for air. Does he understand that Haley's in danger because of what he's done? My throat constricts. Why does he think it's okay to treat me this way? I gasp again. Why do I let him treat me this way? A veil of sweat forms on my upper lip. No, not now. Please.

I pull the covers tight, but whatever new thing is birthing itself in my soul won't leave me alone to lick my wounds in the dark, quiet confines of the warm pocket I've crawled into.

Nor will it let panic threaten to suffocate me any longer.

I throw back the sheet and blanket and sit up. I inhale.

"No!"

And exhale.

"No more!"

I inhale again, my lungs filling with life-giving air.

As my heart finds its natural rhythm, I swing my legs over the side of the bed.

Why *have* I let Chet treat me this way?

The dying embers of determination crackle and spark to life.

I will not allow myself to fall into dismay. I can't let panic rule. Instead, it's time to act.

For Haley's sake.

And my own.

For the second time in an hour, I don't knock or even tap on the door of the den before opening it, and I've always offered Chet the respect of a knock.

But the winds have changed course.

Chet sits hunched over his desk, looking at his phone. He sets it down and leans back in his chair as I come in and stand in front of him.

"The fire is expected to head up the back of Half Dome. They're shutting down trails in the area, sweeping for hikers, and prepping for a rescue operation off the summit." Employing every ounce of self-control I posses, I relay the information without emotion. "Have you heard anything about permits issued?"

"No. Why a rescue off the top?"

"Because…the fire's cut off, or is close to cutting off, return access to the valley via the trail system."

"Great."

"Great? There's nothing *great* about this, Chet." My tone sharpens.

"Obviously, Jessica." He raises his brows. "Ever heard of sarcasm?"

I shake my head. "You know she could be—"

"She's fine. Okay? She's fine. You're the one always blowing YOSAR's horn—if she's in that area, Search and Rescue will find her."

"You're..." Rage like a fire whirl spins within—its heat rising in my chest, neck, face. The swirling vortex of fury threatens to cut a swath of destruction, leaving nothing but ash in its wake. "This is all your..." But no, now's not the time. I take a deep breath and instead, I turn to go.

"Watch yourself, Jess."

For as long as I've known Chet, I've let comments like that go. And though now isn't the best time, I can't just walk away any longer. I turn back. "Watch myself?"

Chet stares at me, daring me to say more.

But I don't need a dare. "It seems to me you should have watched yourself. *You*, Chet. Not me. But instead, you did exactly what you wanted, and now, you'll have to pay the consequences. I just pray one of those consequences isn't our daughter's life!"

"How dare—"

"No! How dare *you."* I hiss the word. "I gave you everything—everything I had. All of me. Was I the perfect wife? No. But my biggest mistake was letting you think the world revolved around you. Well, no more. I did not, I do not, deserve what you did with Heather or with anyone else. Our children don't deserve that either. Your actions were thoughtless and selfish. You thought only of yourself."

He gets up out of his chair and as we stand eye to eye, I see anger sizzling in his eyes. But the heat of his anger can't match the firestorm of mine. I turn away and walk back toward the door of the den.

"Where do you think you're going?"

When I reach the door, I turn back to him. My tone conveys a strength my body doesn't yet feel. "I'm going to the valley. I'll see if Haley and Zach show up among those rescued."

"I'm going with you."

"No." I take a deep breath. "No, you are not. I'm not sure you'll ever go anywhere with me again."

"You can't—"

"Chet, I said no."

His expression registers confusion, then his anger fumes again—his expressions reveal all. Have I ever said no to him before? It doesn't matter. I'm saying it now.

"Someone needs to stay here by the phone. Reception is too spotty down there. And I won't sit here and wait a minute longer. Besides that, I don't want you with me."

With that, I close the door, hard—its slam the exclamation point to my no. My hands tremble, but my resolve is set. *How dare I?* Oh, Chet, this is just the beginning. Your actions woke a sleeping bear, and now you'll have to deal with it.

We both will.

I take Chet's keys hanging on a peg next to the keys for my SUV. If he has to go somewhere, my SUV is still drivable, but I don't need the banging side mirror as a constant reminder of last night's events.

As I'm pulling out of the garage, my phone rings. "Dad?"

"I heard from our girl."

"What?" My shoulders drop as the tension I've held there eases. "Where is she? What did she say? Did she call—?"

"Hold on, honey. Hold on. I'd texted her a couple of times this morning—told her we were worried. I just got a text back. She didn't say much, only that's she's okay and not to worry."

"That's it? She didn't say where she is? I texted her too, but she didn't contact me."

"Her text just came through and that's all she said."

"Okay. Well, that's something. That's good news. But that means she's somewhere with cell reception. Maybe she's not anywhere near that fire. Maybe our assumption was completely off." Or maybe, as I thought earlier, they reached the top and she sent the text from there. "I'm just leaving to head down to the valley—Ahwahnee Meadow—to wait. They're executing a rescue of the hikers in the Half Dome area, and those waiting on the top, they'll drop them at the meadow. I was hoping she and Zach would show up there."

"Well, you don't have anything else to go on. There's no harm in going down there. Is Chet going with you?"

"No."

"Want me to ride along?"

As I pull onto the highway, I consider my dad's offer, knowing he wants to go. But what if Haley is there? We'll need to talk and with my dad there… "I don't know, Dad. I…"

But if she *is* there, then Zach will be with her and conversation will be limited anyway. "Actually, sure, I'd love your company. Pick you up in ten minutes?"

"I'll be waiting."

I pull to the side of the highway, check both lanes, then pull back out, make a U-turn, and head in the opposite direction of Yosemite Valley.

When I reach Dad and Cretia's, they're sitting on the front porch. Cretia follows my dad out to the truck, gives him a good-bye peck on his cheek, then comes around to the driver's side.

I roll down my window. "Thanks for your help earlier—and your clothes. I'll get them back to you soon."

"Oh honey, there's no rush. You just go find Haley and take care of yourself too." She pats my arm, then looks past me to my dad. "Call me if you can. Keep me posted."

"Will do." My dad blows her a kiss. As she makes her way back up the walk, he buckles his seat belt. "She's a good woman, that one."

"You got lucky."

He chuckles. "You know it."

I update my dad on what I've learned about the Meadow Fire, and he relays information he picked up from the scanner just before I arrived. Then we settle into a comfortable silence until he shifts in his seat so he can look at me.

"Jessie, you weren't yourself this morning. I know you were upset about Haley, but I also know there's more going on. You ready to tell me about it?"

I glance in his direction, then fix my eyes on the road. I knew he'd ask and I'm prepared to talk. In fact, I need to talk. I take a deep breath, "Chet...had an affair. Or maybe affairs. I found out late last night, just after I got home." I state this as fact rather than feeling.

When he doesn't respond, I glance his way again. He's turned his face toward the passenger window and seems to be staring out that way.

"Did you hear me?"

He looks back at me, his features etched with an emotion I've seen only a few times in my life, but one I remember well: anger. "I heard you. Haley knows? That's what she was upset about?"

I roll my shoulders back, trying to relieve the tension pinching them again. "She knows." I swallow the lump in my throat. "It's my fault—"

"Jessie, nothing about this is your fault!" He all but growls the words.

The road in front of me wavers as tears, unbidden, well. But I can't cry again, not now. My dad reaches over and puts his big hand on my shoulder. "I'm sorry."

"I just meant that Haley finding out is my fault, although really, I guess that's also Chet's responsibility. She only found out because Chet..." I shake my head. "The woman e-mailed me to apologize. How do you apologize for something like that? Anyway, it seems Chet told her I knew, that I'd found out about them. Maybe that was his way of ending it with her. I don't know." I look over at my dad. "How many lies has he told? I can't…I can't believe I was so naive."

The words I've held back since last night pour out of me now. "It was a young woman he worked with, one of his climbing instructors. She said she knew she wasn't the first woman Chet had been with outside his marriage. Why would she tell me that? Why would Chet tell her that?" I pause to catch my breath.

"Do you wish she hadn't e-mailed you?"

I weigh my dad's question. "No, I wish the affairs never happened. That I wasn't married to the kind of man who would do something like that to me, to his kids, even to himself. Dad, I don't know who Chet is. And although the responsibility for the affair or affairs is Chet's, I've been so focused on preserving the legacy of my family that I've feared standing up to him. Feared doing anything that might rock the boat or drive him away. We don't have a marriage." I shake my head again. "I haven't been Chet's partner—his equal. I haven't spoken up or even dared to disagree with him *because* I've so feared losing him—losing our family and everything that means to me. And now, I stand to lose it all anyway.

"And somehow, I've lost myself in the process. That e-mail? It woke me up. It's hard to explain, but"—I glance at him again—"I checked out of reality the day I married Chet. Today, I checked back in."

"But will you stay checked-in?"

I tighten my grip on the steering wheel. "It's going to be hard. Like navigating a foreign land without knowing the language. There will be days when I feel lost. And days when I want nothing more than to give up and go back to what's familiar. And"—I reach over and grab my dad's hand—"I'll need someone to hold me accountable. Someone who will encourage me to keep going. You. And Cretia."

"You've got it, of course. Chet may have started this fire, but you control it, Jessie. Remember that."

"Okay." I glance at my dad again. "The other thing I've realized is that between my job and the kids and the way I've focused on Chet, I haven't allowed myself time for friends. It hit me early this morning that I wanted to pick up the phone and call a girl friend—yell, scream, cry on her shoulder—but there was no one to call. I'm grateful for you and Cretia, you know that, but—"

"You need more. You're not telling me anything I don't know or haven't observed. And it isn't any secret that I've had my doubts about Chet from the beginning."

"You haven't been very vocal about your doubts."

"Well, not to you. But Cretia's had to listen to me gripe about Chet for years. Maybe I should have said more to you. I was just never sure if…" He turns and looks out the window again.

"If what?"

He's quiet a moment, then turns back. "If what I thought I was seeing was skewed by my own experience."

"What do you mean?"

"My experience with your mother."

The cause of my mother's abandonment still hangs, all these years later, as a question mark, life-sized, in my mind. It is the question my father never answered. But now, maybe for the first time, I realize I wasn't the only one she left. My mouth has gone dry and my heart pounds, but I work to steady my voice and make my next question sound natural. "What does that have to do with Chet?"

He takes off the baseball cap he's wearing, runs his hand over his head, then puts the cap back on. "Jessie, there's a lot I should have told you through the years—I've realized that the last few weeks. You aren't the only one who buried her head in the sand. I fear that's a practice you learned from me, and I'm sorry about that. There's a lot I need to tell you, and I will tell you, but now isn't the time. Once Haley's back home and settled, you and I will sit down and have a talk. I promise."

I nod.

"What are you going to do about Chet? About your marriage?"

I shake my head. "I don't know. I haven't had time to even process it all, let alone make decisions. But I know this, things have to change. I have to change. For now, that's the only decision I've made."

"Well, you can't change Chet. Cretia would say something smart about you only being able to control your own choices, so it sounds to me like you're heading in the right direction." He gives my shoulder a squeeze.

In the silence that follows our conversation, my mind struggles to grasp all that's occurred in the last twelve hours. I've learned I don't know the man I've spent the last almost twenty years with, and that I may be facing the end of a marriage I swore I'd preserve at all costs. Even if it meant losing myself, it seems. The changes in Haley brought on by Chet's choices—changes I can't even imagine yet—haunt me. And now, my dad's promise to talk with me about my mother—to, perhaps, hand me the answers I've sought most of my life.

I no longer recognize the landscape of my life. It's like the charred remains following a forest fire, and I don't know where, or who, I am.

I don't know what comes next.

The familiar landmarks that have guided me are gone. And in their place all that remains are…

Ashes.

*I became nerve-shaken for the first time since setting foot on
the mountains, and my mind seemed to fill
with a stifling smoke.*
John Muir

CHAPTER THIRTY

Haley

 "WHAT TIME IS it?"

"It's a little after one. I checked a few minutes ago." Zach circles the section of trail we came up before my fall. He's like one of those cars at an amusement park going around a track. He makes another lap, then stops. "Doesn't it seem weird that we saw hikers all morning, now there's no one?"

"Yeah, kind of." A haze has settled along the tops of the trees, like fog—but the smell tells me it's smoke. I don't say anything about it to Zach, though I'm sure he's noticed it too. "Maybe you should help me get up and we can see if, like, I can hop or something? I mean, we can't just sit here."

"Yeah, okay. Maybe if you lean on me..." Zach comes and stands over me. "Here, I'm going to put my arms under yours and then lift you up. Don't put weight on your ankle."

He bends down and, like a forklift, he slips his arms under mine and then lifts. I push off with my good ankle. As he lifts me to my feet, I hold my other foot off the ground. But as the blood rushes to it, pain explodes. "Oww!" I take a few deep breaths, hoping they'll keep me from throwing up, because that's what it feels like is going to happen.

Zach holds me close, his arms now wrapped around my waist. "The pain's really bad?"

I nod hard.

"Just stand here for a minute—give yourself time to adjust. Maybe it'll get better."

All I can think of as I stand with Zach, my ankle throbbing and smoke settling in around us, is how much my mom is going to kill me if I end up dying in a forest fire.

And how guilty my dad will feel.

Zach looks from the path to me. "Would they close the trail?"

"What?"

"Is that why we haven't seen anyone? They closed the trail because of the fire?"

Maybe. He could be right. "Or for other reasons."

"What other reasons?"

"Like a rockslide. Or—"

"Haley, it's the fire. They closed the trail because the fire's coming this way. That's why we haven't seen anyone. They're probably sending people back when they reach Little Yosemite Valley. Or maybe they're stopping them at Happy Isles. We can't pretend there isn't a fire. But wouldn't that Dave guy have told the ranger about us? He wouldn't just leave us hanging out here, right? He seemed like a stand-up kind of guy."

"Even if he didn't tell the ranger, they would send someone to check the trails. That's what they do when there's a fire or other hazard." My tone is more confident than I feel, even though I know what I told Zach is true. "But yeah, it seems like we'd have seen someone by now, so…you're probably right."

Zach, still holding on to me, comes around to my side. "Here, put your arm around my waist and try to hop. If you can hop, we could maybe make it back to the ranger station at Little Yosemite Valley, right?"

"Maybe." It would be slow going, but it's better than sitting here. I lift my bad foot up and then push off with my good foot and take a tiny hop, Zach takes a step with me as I do. But even with the improvised splint, the movement causes my ankle to bounce and I double over with the pain. Tears prick my eyes again.

"Oh, man. That's not going to work."

Zach rubs my back as I gulp for air. When the pain lessens a little bit and the nausea passes again, I stand up straight and look at him. "I'm sorry."

"What if I carry you? Like a piggy back ride? I could maybe hold your leg steady enough that it wouldn't bounce."

"What about our backpacks?"

"We'll leave them here. Or you can put yours on. We'll just keep it light. Leave anything heavy here."

The rumble of a plane sounds in the distance, along with the whir of helicopter blades. I look up but can't see anything through the cover of trees. We're hearing the planes and helicopters more often now. Forgetting about the split in my lip, I bite my lower lip, causing it to throb. I try to think of another way out of here, besides having Zach carry me but can't come up with anything.

"Haley, it's the only way. Here, sit back down for a minute." He helps lower me to the ground and then goes to work rearranging things in our backpacks, leaving one pack and a pile of stuff by a tree. Before he helps me back up, he slips the straps of the backpack over my shoulders, then does the forklift move again. Once I'm up and steady, he turns his back to me. "Here, put your hands on my shoulders."

With my hands on his shoulders, Zach bends over, links one arm around my bad leg, then tells me to pull myself up as he lifts me onto his back. I wince again as the movement jostles my ankle, but this time I can handle the pain. I wrap my good leg around Zach's waist and then lean into him, clasping my hands loosely around his neck. He hikes me up a bit, then supports my bad ankle with his arm.

"Are you okay?" he asks over his shoulder.

"Um, yeah. Are you?"

"Yep. Let's go."

With his head down, he starts walking back the way we came. I rest my chin on his shoulder and close my eyes. Thank goodness we're, like, doing something about getting out of here. But then Zach slows down and then he stops. I look back over my shoulder and I can still see the pile of our stuff by the tree.

"Haley...I don't think...I..."

"I'm too heavy?"

"No...well. I mean, it's...just—"

"Look!" I unhook my hands from around Zach's neck and point. Coming up the trail from the direction of Little Yosemite Valley is a man wearing one of the NPS T-shirts my mom wears when she's doing fieldwork. "It's a ranger!"

Zach sets me down, turns around, and plants a kiss on my forehead. "Cool..." He inhales. "We're saved."

When the ranger sees us, he calls out, "Haley and Zach?"

Zach yells, "Yeah." Then he says to me, "You better sit down again." He helps lower me to the ground, and by the time I'm situated, the ranger has reached us.

"Looks like you took a tumble. A hiker notified the ranger at Sub-Dome—we got word at the station in Little Yosemite Valley."

"I fell—I'm sorry." Heat rushes to my cheeks and I look down at the ground.

"She tripped on a tree root. Part of it was sticking up across the trail, just enough for her to catch the toe of her boot under it."

"No need to apologize. Unfortunately, accidents happen. I'm Greg."

When I look back up, the ranger has stuck his hand out for Zach to shake, then he bends down by my feet and studies my ankle. "Nice splint." He glances up at Zach. "Think it's broken?"

"Totally broken."

Greg looks at me. "How's your pain level?"

"Um, it's pretty bad."

"Okay. Well, let's get you a ride out of here, and the sooner the better."

"Are you going to dispatch a litter?"

Greg smiles at me. "You know the lingo."

"My mom works for NPS."

"Ah, who's your mom?"

I tell him and though he hasn't met her, he's heard her name. I almost want to cry. "Can you call her?"

"Dispatch can get word to the IC, and they'll relay a message to your mom."

"IC?" Zach looks at me.

"Incident Commander."

Zach frowns. "Incident?"

"There's a fire heading this way. Which is why the litter I'd guess you're thinking about isn't going to be your chariot ride out this time. Today, you're being airlifted—hoisted."

"Hoisted?" Zach looks down at me. "That's so cool!"

He has to be kidding! "Seriously? It sounds, like, terrifying."

But the ranger is already pulling a radio from his belt. He holds up one hand and then relays information to someone about my injury, my mom's name, and the need to get a message to her. When he's done he looks down. "Okay, here's the plan. Your ride is on the way, my friend." Then he glances over at Zach. "And you sir, are going to the top of Half Dome with me."

"What? Why can't I go with her?"

"That would be the preference, but there's no place to land to pick you up—either of you. They'll drop a litter." He looks at me. "There's more than one kind of litter. I'll get you set in the litter, then they'll pull you into the ship."

"Ship?" My voice cracks.

"Helicopter." He looks at Zach. "Then you and I will hike to the top, but it's your lucky day, because you'll also get a ride out. Because of the fire, we've closed the trails in the area and are airlifting out those hikers who are above the closure points."

"Score!" Then Zach gazes back down at me. "I mean, I wish I could go with you, but at least…you know."

"It's an adventure, right?" I try to smile at him, but my mind, and stomach are still focused on the idea of being hoisted out of here. It's not like I'm afraid of heights, but something about dangling from a helicopter doesn't sound like the kind of adventure I want.

Zach seems to read my mind. "Hey, it won't be that much different than rock climbing. Just pretend you're hanging off the side of a mountain."

"Um, yeah." But somehow that isn't comforting.

Before long, the whirring sound of helicopter blades can be heard, but instead of hearing them off in the distance, the sound gets louder and louder. "So"—I swallow—"how's this going to work?"

"They'll drop the litter, I'll help you get into it, and then they'll pull you up and in. Piece of cake, Haley. You'll do great."

"Where will they take me?"

Greg raises his voice to be heard over the helicopter, which is now hovering above us. "Ahwahnee Meadow. They'll transport you to the medical clinic from there. And Zach, you'll land there too."

"Come see if I'm still at the clinic when you get there, okay?" I yell to Zach.

He nods, then watches the litter being lowered from the helicopter. He looks back at me. "You'll do great." He bends down and grabs my hand. "Really. It'll be fine. It'll be a great story too. I'll take some pictures as they're lifting you up, okay?" He reaches behind me and takes his cell phone out of one of the outside pockets of the pack on my back.

"Okay." But I'd rather not, like, have a great story to tell or pictures to remind me of this day.

Once the litter is on the ground, Greg yells instructions into my ear and then helps me into the litter, which, with my ankle the way it is, takes some maneuvering. Once I'm in and know that any minute they're going to lift me, my heart pounds so hard I'm sure it will, like, come right out of my chest. When I try to swallow, my tongue sticks to the roof of my mouth.

Greg leans over. "Ready, Haley?"

I look up at the helicopter hovering and then over at Zach. I can't respond—can't get anything to come out of my mouth. I look back to Greg and close my eyes. Tight.

He must take that as a sign that I am ready because he yells, "Enjoy the ride."

Then I feel myself being lifted off the ground and my stomach feels like it jumps into my chest. I hold my breath, eyes still closed, as the litter swings in the air. I scream, but no sound comes out of my mouth, or if it does, I can't hear it over the roar of the helicopter.

Man as he came from the hand of his Maker was poetic in both mind and body, but the gross heathenism of civilization has generally destroyed Nature, and poetry, and all that is spiritual.
John Muir

CHAPTER THIRTY-ONE

Ted

AFTER JESSIE'S TALKED herself out, we ride in silence, both lost in our own thoughts. And there's plenty to think about. I know at almost eighty-two I'm of another generation, but I'd sure like to know why things have changed so darned much. Men of my generation were raised with manners and morals, and now it seems both are absent from the lives of younger men. Oh, I know I can't lump every man younger than me into the same category, but there are a lot of ill-mannered men who lack morals and, after what Jessie's told me, I'm putting Chet at the top of that list.

I've always appreciated the attributes of the opposite sex, the emotional and spiritual attributes, that is. But I only appreciate the *other* attributes when they belong to my wife.

And only my wife. Chet seems to have missed that piece of common sense.

I ball my fists. I want to pummel him. But what good will that do? It won't change anything. It's just that I know how Jessie's feeling, and I know some of what she'll feel in the months and even years to come. That kind of betrayal— the way it hurts—never really goes away. Oh sure, time is a healer, but there's always a scar.

I take my cap off and smooth back my hair. Once things settle, I need to let Jessie know I understand. There's a lot I should've told her a long time ago, but maybe, besides not wanting to reopen old wounds myself, I wanted to protect Jessie from the truth—the truth of who and what her mother really was.

And is.

From the tone of that letter she sent, she hasn't changed one iota. Her focus is still on herself and her own needs and desires. She certainly isn't thinking about anyone else, that's for sure, and least of all Jessie. Sandra didn't want her daughter until now, when she's old enough that she doesn't have anything else to focus on. Probably has alienated everyone else in her life and wants someone to take care of her. But it isn't just that she wants Jessie now.

It's that she wants to take her away from me.

Cretia would tell me my assumptions are just making an ass out of me, but my assumptions about Jessie's mom are based on my experience. Cretia never knew her. I did. And the only good thing that woman ever produced is the woman who sits next to me now. Facts are facts. I had to forgive Sandra—had to let go of the pain she caused me—for my sake and for Jessie's. Otherwise bitterness would have just hurt both of us more than Sandra's abandonment. But forgiveness doesn't blind me to the facts.

And now, I'm going to have to forgive her all over again. I sigh, then clear my throat. "You know, you're going to have to forgive Chet."

"What?"

"You'll have to forgive him."

"I know, I heard you. But Dad…I can't even—"

"I'm just saying, down the road, you'll need to do that, but you need to know now that forgiving him doesn't mean forgetting what he's done. Don't let yourself be blinded to who he really is. It's one thing if he's truly sorry, but somehow I don't think you'll see that kind of humility from him."

"Sounds like you may have to forgive him too."

"Huh, you got that right," I grumble. "You'll also have to remember that forgiveness isn't a feeling; it's a choice."

Jessie looks at me, then she chuckles.

"What?"

"Only you could make me laugh at a time like this."

"What's so funny?"

"You, parroting Cretia."

"Well, she says some good things."

"Yes, she does. And I will think about what you said, later. Right now, I'm too angry and"—she glances my way— "for now, I think anger is good."

"It is good. Stay that way for as long as you need to, Jessie. Anger will push you forward. Let it." As we come through Wawona Tunnel, I point. "There." Smoke, like a mushroom cloud, rises behind Half Dome in the distance.

Jessie slows the car as she takes in the view. "I hope we find her."

Her whispered words almost break my heart. "We will, honey. We will."

It was a letter that let me know Sandra had left me— left us. Is it any wonder I dreaded opening the one that came in the mail a few weeks back? I've only had two from the woman, and they are bookends of bad news.

It was a Tuesday in January. At least she'd had the decency to wait out fire season. I'd put in a day at the station and was back home in time to help get Jessie up from her afternoon nap. But when I pulled into the driveway, instead of the '69 used Buick I'd bought for Sandra, Johnny's Ford truck sat in the driveway. What was he doing at my house in the middle of the day? The memory of Sandra calling out his name the night of Jessie's birth slapped me in the face as I pulled in next to the truck. I entered the house through the back door, then eased it shut, my footsteps light on the wood floors, my shoulders tense, my mind wracked with suspicion.

But it wasn't Johnny I found.

It was Dot—the woman Johnny had started dating a few months back. She was sitting on the sofa thumbing through one of those ladies magazines.

"Dot?"

She startled when she heard her name, looked up, put the magazine down, then stood. "Hi, Ted. I didn't hear you come in."

"What are you doing here? You waiting on Sandra for something?"

She shook her head, her eyes telling a story I didn't think I wanted to hear.

"No." She bent and picked up an envelope off the coffee table and then walked over and handed it to me. "She left you this. She…she called and asked if I could babysit until you got home. Asked me to give you this."

"Where'd she go?" My grip on the letter was too tight, crumpling the edge of the thing.

"She wouldn't say, but…" Dot took a deep breath. "I…I don't think… I'm sorry, Ted." She shook her head and then took her leave. When she reached the front door, she turned back. "Jessie's still sleeping and there's a pan of cornbread I made in the oven—don't forget to take it out." Then she was gone.

I dropped onto the sofa, knowing full well there was nothing in the letter I'd want to read, but read it I did.

What choice did I have?

None, it seemed.

Not about the letter, or her leaving.

As Jessie drives past Ahwahnee Meadow looking for a place to park, I take a gander at the wide grassy area. "Not much activity. Looks like a couple of rangers out there is all."

Jessie's phone beeps a couple times. "We have service again and it sounds like I have a couple of messages. Cross your fingers." She pulls into a parking spot, puts the truck in Park, then pulls out her phone and listens to her messages. As she listens, I watch her face, trying to read her expression. Then she reaches over and puts her hand on my arm. "It's the IC!" Tears fill her eyes as she finishes listening to the message. When she turns to me, the tears spill onto her cheeks. "She's hurt, but she's okay. She's okay, Dad."

"Hurt?"

"They have her at the clinic. She was airlifted off the trail. He said she's injured. That's all I know." She sets her phone on the middle console, throws the truck in gear, and starts to pull out of the parking space, then hits the brakes. "Wait. I want to check my texts."

She picks up her phone again and then smiles though her tears as she reads a text to me, "'I'm okay so don't freak out, but I'm at the Yosemite Medical Clinic. I hurt my ankle. I'm really sorry, Mom. I...'" She stops and reads the last two words in a whisper, "'...love you.'"

"Well, what are you waiting for? Let's go!"

*No miles of any measurement can separate
your soul from mine.*
John Muir

CHAPTER THIRTY-TWO

Jessica

IT TAKES ONLY a few moments to drive from the meadow to the clinic, but the trip feels endless as I search for a parking space again in busy Yosemite Village.

"There's one." My dad points to a car backing out of a space in front of the clinic.

The adrenaline that's alternately coursed through my veins and left me exhausted since reading that e-mail last night is pumping again. I park the truck, unbuckle my seat belt, and get out and head for the clinic. When I reach the front, I turn to look for my dad, who's just getting out of the truck.

He waves me on. "Go!"

I dash in only to have to wait behind someone else before I can let the receptionist know who I am. As I wait, I pull my phone out of my pocket to text Chet, but then I hesitate. Of course, he has a right to know Haley is okay, but the desire to punish him by withholding what I know almost overwhelms me. I want to hurt him as much as he's hurt me. Is that possible? As I slip the phone back into my pocket, my dad comes up behind me.

"Text him, Jessie. Let him know she's okay."

I shrug as though I don't know what he's talking about. "I will. I want a few details first." I look down at my feet. I can't hold eye contact with my dad and tell him something that isn't true. He knows me too well. I sigh as I concede. "Okay."

I text Chet and tell him that I've found Haley and she's okay, as far as I know, and I'll send details later. As I put the phone back into my pocket, I make a silent vow to myself: I won't make Haley or Tyler pawns in this game with Chet.

After waiting as long as my patience, or lack thereof, will allow, I edge my way around the young man talking to the receptionist and interrupt. "I'm sorry, but my daughter was brought in—can I just go back?"

"Your daughter's name?"

"Haley. Haley Weaver."

The receptionist keys Haley's name into the computer. "She's in radiology. Take a seat and as soon as she's done, you can go back."

"Take a seat? Can't I just—"

"It won't be long."

My dad puts his hand on my shoulder. "C'mon. I'll get you a cup of coffee. Just sit for a few minutes."

"Okay, but no coffee." I hold out one hand and show him how it's trembling. "I don't think caffeine is my friend right now."

"No, probably not, but it is mine. I'm going to grab a cup for myself and call Cretia."

Instead of finding a seat in the waiting room, I pace in front of the receptionist's station, where she can't help but notice me and remember I'm waiting. Soon, a woman about my age dressed in scrubs stands at the double doors leading to the back of the clinic—the examining rooms, I assume. "Mrs. Weaver?"

"Yes." I dash to where she stands. "Is she okay? May I see her now?"

"She'll be fine. I'm Dr. Sanchez. Your daughter took a fall and her right ankle is broken. I just looked at the X-rays, and it's a clean break that should heal well, but she'll be off her feet for a while."

"That's all? Just her ankle? She's okay otherwise?"

"She has a scrape or two, and a laceration on her lip, but overall she's in good shape."

I exhale. "Oh…" I lift my hand and place it across my chest. "I'm so relieved."

"I need to set the ankle and put a cast on, but you can sit with her. She's been asking for you."

"Thank you." She's been asking for me? When was the last time Haley sought me out or desired my presence? Not since her teen years. Unless, of course, she needed a ride somewhere or money for something. The thought makes me smile, until I remember why she's here. She fled after reading the e-mail from Heather. It seems mother and daughter reacted in the same manner. I wonder if Haley realizes I had the same reaction. I ran. But running isn't an option anymore. No, as I follow the doctor into Haley's room, I determine it's time to stand.

Stand firm.

Until I see her.

Then I cry.

Haley is lying on a gurney—her bottom lip swollen, an angry, red scuffmark on one of her cheeks. Does Chet have any idea what could have happened to her?

I wipe my tears and try, oh I try, to keep my tone light. "Hey…you okay?" I walk over to her and put a hand on her shoulder.

Her swollen bottom lip protrudes even more and tears fill her eyes as she shakes her head. "No."

I smooth her long ebony hair back rather than respond for fear my tears will turn to sobs.

"Am I...in trouble?" Tears cling to her thick lashes as her dark-brown eyes search mine.

I shake my head and then take a deep breath. "I understand why you..." That's all I can get out, but it's enough.

She reaches for my hand and holds it tight, as though she were two years old again and trying hard to act brave when what she really feels is terrified.

"We'll...we'll get through this, okay? You and me. We'll...make it." Then I remember we're not alone. I look over my shoulder to where Dr. Sanchez is hovering over supplies on a counter behind me. It's clear she knows we needed a moment.

I squeeze Haley's hand and raise my voice. 'So...Dr. Sanchez says it's a clean break—that's good news. Well, sort of good news." I smile through my tears, then release Haley's hand and dig in my purse for a couple of tissues for each of us.

On cue, Dr. Sanchez joins us and explains to Haley what comes next in terms of her ankle.

I wish she could explain what comes next for the two of us. For our family. But there are, I suspect, no simple explanations or cures for what we face.

*In God's wildness lies the hope of the world—the great fresh
unblighted, unredeemed wilderness. The galling harness of
civilization drops off, and wounds heal ere we are aware.*
John Muir

CHAPTER THIRTY-THREE

Ted

I SWALLOW THE last gulp of sludge—or coffee,
as it's sometimes called—then drop my second empty paper
cup into the bear-proof trash can outside the clinic. Good
thing Cretia isn't here to see how much caffeine I've
consumed this late in the day. After seeing Haley for myself,
I poured myself a second cup from the pot in the waiting
room, came outside, and now I've circled the clinic twice.
Waiting isn't my favorite activity. Just as I'm about to head
back inside, an old truck, the tailgate covered in bumper
stickers, backs into the tight spot next to where Jessie parked.

A young man, all lanky limbs, gets out, slams the door,
and hurries toward the clinic. He looks familiar—like the boy
Haley showed me a picture of on her phone, maybe? Then I
take a gander at the bumper stickers. A surfer? Yep, that's

him. I've been half expecting him. Fact is, if he hadn't shown up, well…

I follow him into the clinic and before he can make his way to the receptionist, I intercede. "Young man?"

He turns. "Yes, sir."

Sir? Smart kid. "Zachary? Haley's friend?"

He steps toward me. "Is she still here? Is she okay?"

I note the lines of concern creasing his forehead. "Yes and yes. I'm her granddad—Ted Martin." I keep my hand at my side, gauging his response.

He puts out his right hand. Another smart move. I lift my hand and shake his, impressed by his firm grip and the eye contact he holds. "Yeah, I'm Zach. Nice to meet you. So, is she okay?"

"Her ankle's broken, but it's a clean break. Should heal fine. But you two gave us quite a scare. We didn't know where Haley was. Then to discover she was traipsing up the side of a mountain during a nearby wildfire, well now, that about gave her mother a heart attack."

Zach sighs and then runs one hand through his dirty blond hair. "I'm sorry. Really. I thought"—he looks down at his feet for a moment, then raises his gaze to mine again—"I mean, I'm sure you were worried. I'm really sorry."

I nod. He could have blamed Haley but didn't. She already confessed that she'd lied to Zach about getting permission to hike.

"I wish… If I could have done something to keep her from getting hurt… She tripped and—"

"Well, from what I heard, you did what you could."

"Yeah, but they wouldn't let me come with her. I would have stayed with her. But they made me hike to the top."

If Cretia were here, she'd have my hide for the tone I'm using with this kid, but I need to see what he's made of. If Haley has her eye on him, then he's got a test or two to pass. "Got yourself a ride off the top though, didn't you?"

"Well, yeah, but…"

It's a little soon to tell, but so far, I like this young man, so I give him a break and chuckle. "Not a bad way to come off the summit, is it?"

He stares at me a moment, then cracks a smile that seems beyond his control. "It was pretty cool. But really, I would have stayed—"

"I believe you, son." I stick my hand out again. "Thanks for taking care of her. She told us." I shake his hand once more, then pat him on the back. I glance over at the receptionist who has her nose to her computer screen. "C'mon, I'll sneak you in. You can see her for yourself, then be on your way."

As Zach walks alongside me down the hallway, Jessie comes out of the room where they were working on Haley— casting her ankle, I assume. Her head is dropped, she looks at the ground as she walks, and her shoulders sag. Then I see her swiping at tears on her cheeks. Probably not a great time to introduce Zach. She passes us without even seeing us.

I stop in the hallway and point. "Haley's in there—you go on in." Then I turn and follow my girl down the hallway, through the waiting room, and out the front door of the clinic. I don't say anything, just walk up behind her and put my arms around her as she collapses against the hood of Chet's truck in a fit of sobs.

My guess is that it's all hit her. She had to stay strong for Haley—to find Haley. Now that she knows she's okay, the emotions and questions are boiling over, and none of them good, except, of course, that Haley's safe. Add a whopping dose of fatigue to the reality she faces at home, and it's a miracle Jessie's still standing.

Although, from the way she trembles in my arms, I'm not sure if I let her go that she wouldn't crumble to the ground.

So I tighten my hold.

There's criteria that mandates whether home owners shelter in place or evacuate during a wildfire. If the property surrounding the home is cleared of flammable debris and the home is constructed of fireproof materials like stucco and tile, well then, during a slow-moving ground fire, residents may stay on their property and work to protect their homes from stray embers. Makes sense. But if the home is surrounded by ladder fuels and dense canopies?

It's time to get out.

Period.

Of course, there's always the one guy who ignores the evacuation order, putting firefighters and emergency personnel at risk.

I run my hand over the late-afternoon stubble on my chin and then shake my head. I pull my phone out of my pocket and punch Chet's number into the thing. As his line rings, my grip tightens. "Chet is just the kind of moron who'd—"

"Ted, everything okay? Jess texted me. You found Haley?"

"Yes, we connected with her. She'll be fine, though she's pretty uncomfortable at the moment." For more reasons than a busted ankle.

"Jess didn't have time to tell me much—is Haley hurt?"

Didn't have time? My foot. She didn't want to text you at all. You're lucky she gave you the time of day. "Her ankle's broken. Other than that, she's okay…physically." I take a breath. "Listen, Chet, Jessie and Haley are exhausted, among other things, and they're going to need some space. We're leaving the clinic in a few minutes. I suggest you pack a bag and check yourself into a motel for a few days. Thought I'd give you a heads-up in case you hadn't already thought of that yourself."

Chet's laugh, or snort, or whatever it is in response to my suggestion, doesn't strike me as humorous.

"I don't think so, Ted. I have an injured daughter I plan to see and spend some time with. Maybe you've forgotten, but this is my home. Anyway, it seems Jess took my truck and—"

Okay. Enough. "I am not going to mince words. You get out. Now! Neither of them wants you there. You've got a raging fire on your hands, man, one you started. If you have any ideas about saving your marriage—your family—then you *will* evacuate the premises, you hear me? Even if you do so, total destruction is a good possibility. But if you hope to have anything to return to, you better get out now. You got that?"

"Fine, but just for tonight."

"I have nothing more to say to you." I push End on the cell phone, my index finger shaking with contained rage. Responded just like I thought he would. I shove the phone back into my pocket.

"Dad? You ready?"

I turn back toward the front of the clinic. Jessie's holding a pair of crutches, and Zach's pushing Haley in a wheelchair, her casted leg extended in front of her. Good, Zach and Jessie seem to have met.

Jessie clicks her key fob, unlocking the doors of Chet's truck, and Zach rolls Haley to the passenger's side.

"Here, let me help you." I go around and open the door for Zach, who then helps Haley inside. I look back at Jessie. "I'll drive."

She nods, her eyes puffy, her expression blank.

Zach whispers something to Haley, then backs away from the truck. "I better go. I'll move my truck so you can get in, Mr. Martin."

"Thanks, Zach. Hope to see you around soon."

I lean into the truck, help Haley scoot to the center of the bench seat, then motion for Jessie to get in beside her. "Here, get in, then lift Haley's leg onto your lap—let it rest there as we drive home. Keep it elevated."

Again, Jessie just nods. The only indication that she heard me.

I climb into the driver's seat and Haley, at an awkward angle with her leg across Jessie's lap, leans against my shoulder. I help buckle her in, then I start the engine and pull out of the parking space. By the time we're outside Yosemite Village, both Jessie's and Haley's heads are bobbing. As they both give in to fatigue, I glance over at Jessie.

In sleep, she looks more like Sandra than ever.

It could be her mother sitting here in the cab of the truck with me.

As I drive and they sleep, I'm left in silence. And my own mess of thoughts and emotions threaten to boil over.

The clearest way into the Universe is through
a forest wilderness.
John Muir

CHAPTER THIRTY-FOUR

Jessica

THE CRUNCH OF tires on gravel pulls me from the respite of slumber. I lift my head from where it rested against the passenger-side window and then rub my stiff and aching neck. My legs tingle, asleep beneath the weight of Haley's casted leg. The gravel road to our house lies ahead, but the sense of anticipation I usually feel as I approach home has fled. Instead, dread, my new companion, accompanies me.

What will I say to Chet?

What will he say to Haley?

What comes next?

Haley stirs at my side, then lifts her head off my dad's shoulder. Her eyes focus and she takes in her surroundings. When she's recognized the gravel road into our property, she closes her eyes again. I rest my hand on her knee and try to think of something encouraging to say, but nothing comes to mind.

My dad slows as we approach the house and then leans into Haley, giving her a nudge with his shoulder. "Guess it's the master bedroom for you—the only downstairs bedroom in the house, huh? Not bad. And if I were you, I'd demand a bell to ring when you want something. You can't be expected to get to the kitchen yourself, now can you?"

Haley looks up at him and smiles.

"Watch it, Dad, or I'll send her over to your place with that bell. All your bedrooms are downstairs."

"Good point." He nudges Haley again. "Well, you know we'd be happy to have you. Grandma Cretia would dote on you to no end."

"Dad, you can drive my SUV home, if you don't mind the damaged mirror. Chet may need his—"

"Chet's not here."

"Dad's gone?" Haley looks at me and I read the fear in her eyes. Or is it relief? I can't tell.

"I suggested he give you two some space."

Haley doesn't respond to Dad's quiet comment, just looks down at her lap. I look at my dad, hoping he can read the gratitude in my expression.

"Cretia's coming to get me. I called her before we left the clinic and told her to meet me here in an hour. She'll be here anytime now. We'll get you two settled, then be on our way. I didn't want to leave you without a vehicle."

"Thanks, Dad. I'm glad you went with me today."

He looks over Haley's head at me. "Glad to be of help. You know who to call if you"—he clears his throat—"if you need anything." Then he looks away.

The emotion in his voice stirs my own and tears well again. I know he'd do anything for me. So would Cretia. But my husband? The days ahead, the decisions to make, pull on me like an anchor tied to my ankle. I take a deep breath, will the tears away, and square my shoulders as my dad parks Chet's truck in the driveway. "I'll pull it in the garage later."

"You sure? No problem to do it now."

"It's easier to get Haley out in the driveway—more space." I unbuckle my seat belt. One task at a time—that's my focus now. It has to be. Get Haley out of the car. Get her settled in the house. Make something for her to eat.

The mundane demands of life, the normalcy they represent, will save me.

Soon I'll have to deal with Chet—with what he's done. And I'll have to help my daughter deal with it. And then there's Tyler.

I open the passenger-side door, slide out, and then reach behind the seat for the crutches they fitted for Haley before we left the clinic. My dad comes around and helps Haley out of the truck, and as she leans on him, I hand her the crutches.

"I don't know how to use those. I don't know if I can do it."

I meet her eyes. "You can. You'll learn."

We both will.

One step at a time.

I help Haley into the deep tub in our master bathroom, a black plastic garbage bag taped around her cast. After hiking most of the day, a bath is a necessity rather than a nicety. "Okay, hold on to the edges of the tub and slowly sit down. Keep your leg up, then rest it on the edge of the tub."

"This is impossible." She clings to the towel covering her body.

"Here, give me the towel and then let me help hold your leg."

"I'm not giving you the towel."

"Haley, I've seen it all before. Give me the towel. I won't look."

Exasperated, she tosses the towel to the floor.

Bent over the tub, I reach for her leg and support it as she works to sit while keeping her cast out of the water. I pray she doesn't slip as she eases herself down into the hot bubble bath.

"You're not helping. Just let go of it." She jerks her leg away from my grasp, or tries to.

I ignore her. It's not the time for an attitude check. She's in pain. "Use the strength in your arms to lower yourself into the water."

"I know. I'm not stupid."

Again, I swallow the words I'd like to spout at her. She's tired.

She finally maneuvers so she's seated in the tub, with her leg hanging over the edge. I reach for the towel she threw on the floor, fold it, then set it on the ledge surrounding the tub. "Here, rest the heel of your cast on this. What else do you need?"

She looks at me, eyebrows raised. "Soap? A washcloth? Duh."

I sigh and hang my head. She's upset, I know. But... I shake my head. I will not continue making excuses. For anyone. I look back to her. "I won't put up with your attitude, young lady. So stop it. I am not the enemy here. I'm trying to help you."

"Oh, right, so *who* is the enemy?"

Her expression singes me, but then tears fill her eyes. She opens her mouth to say something more, then seems to think better of it.

"There is no enemy, Haley."

"Really? Because I thought it was…Dad. At least, that's what I thought you'd…" Tears spill down her cheeks, and she chokes out the last word, "think." Then she slaps the water and it splashes across the bathroom. "And"—she swipes at the tears—"and what…what am I…supposed to do if…if he's the…the…?" She puts her hands over her face and sobs.

I'd stood to get a washcloth for her, but now I kneel next to the tub and reach out to put my hand on her shoulder, which is covered in bubbles. I consider the question I've avoided since we got home. I guess it's time to ask. "Haley, do you want to talk about it? About the e-mail?"

She drops her hands from her face and sniffs a few times. I get up from the side of the tub and reach for a box of tissues, then hand her a few. She blows her nose, then hands the damp wad back to me.

"Nice."

She looks at me, and for the first time since we got home, she cracks a smile. Her nose is red and her face blotchy. Then her eyes fill with tears again. "I can't talk about it. Not now. I'm too"—she shakes her head—"like, way too tired."

My shoulders drop. Thank goodness. "We're both too tired. Tomorrow?"

She nods.

I drop the used tissue in the trash can under my sink, wash my hands, then I hand Haley a bar of soap and a washcloth. "Why don't you call me when you're done and I'll help you get out, okay?"

"Okay."

I turn to leave, to give her some time alone.

"Mom?"

I turn back.

"I'm…I'm sorry. For everything. I mean, for my attitude and for what happened with…Dad. You know?"

I nod, hoping I can respond without losing it. I swallow. "I know." I nod again. "Me too, Haley-bug. We'll get through this." But as I turn and walk out of the bathroom to the bedroom, I'm not sure what I've said is true. I'm not sure we'll get through this. I can't imagine how we'll survive. But then, I'm so tired, I'm not even sure how I'll get through the next five minutes.

Haley doesn't linger in the tub, and after I help her out, I give her one of the pain pills the doctor at the clinic prescribed and get her settled in my bed. Then I shower and get myself ready for bed. When I tiptoe back into the bedroom and take my pillow off the bed with the intent of dragging myself up the stairs to sleep in Haley's bed, she stirs.

"Mama?"

I stop at the bedroom door and turn toward her. *Mama?* She hasn't called me that in years. "What?"

"Where are you going?"

"Upstairs. I'll sleep in your room."

"Can't you…?" She pushes herself up on her elbows, her eyes heavy with sleep. "Can't you just sleep here? I mean, you know, what if I need something?"

"Oh, sure. I didn't think you wanted me to sleep with you." I walk back toward the bed, grateful to fall into it for the first time in over two weeks. As I pull the sheet over me, Haley rolls toward me, lifting her cast and propping it back on the pillow I put under it. As I settle in, Haley reaches out and runs one hand through my hair, then she twists several strands of it around her index finger, just as she used to do when she'd crawl into bed with us as a little girl after waking from a nightmare.

Something about her simple act unhinges me.

As the rhythm of her breathing steadies and she falls back to sleep, with my hair wrapped around her finger, silent tears slip down my cheeks.

Will I ever wake from the nightmare that's accosted me?

I reach out, eyes still closed, swatting in the direction of the buzzing sound. I miss whatever it is, because it buzzes again. One more time, I reach and swat, this time my hand hitting the corner of something. Ouch. I open my eyes, close them, then rub them. When I open them again, the gray light of early morning peeks through the upper windows in our bedroom.

"Get it."

I jump at the voice coming from the other side of the bed. I tilt my head to the side and see Haley next to me.

"Get your phone," she grumbles.

My phone. That's it. I turn the other way and grab the vibrating phone off my nightstand. But as soon as I pick it up, the vibrating stops. The screen shows a missed call. From Chet. At 6:29 a.m. Great. I guess twelve hours is all the space I get.

I set the phone back on the nightstand and, still groggy, lie back down. But just as my head hits the pillow, the phone vibrates again—this time a short series of vibrations. A text. Also from Chet, I'm sure. Patience isn't one of his virtues.

I close my eyes, willing the text to disappear, but when I open my eyes and reach for the phone, the text is waiting for me. I lift myself up on one elbow and read what he's sent.

Jess, you know I love you. We need to talk.

I glance over at Haley who's pulled her pillow over her head and seems to have fallen asleep again. Ignoring the text, I set the phone on the nightstand, lie back down, and close my eyes. I gently roll onto my side, facing away from Haley, pull the covers up around me, and determine that I *will* fall back to sleep too.

All I want to do is sleep. Forever.

I shift my pillow under my head.

Is he sorry? Won't he apologize? I want to believe he's hurting over how much he's hurt me. But if that were true, if he were sorry, why didn't he say so yesterday, even in the midst of the crisis with Haley? Wouldn't I have seen signs of remorse? I move my feet out from under the covers.

"We need to talk."

Talk? Talking isn't going to fix this. No, this will take… What? I don't know what it will take, but whatever it is, it will take time. I put my hand on my chest.

Hurt this deep doesn't just disappear, Chet. It has to heal.

I push the blanket and sheet back.

"You know I love you."

My phone jitters across the nightstand again. I reach out, grab it, and sit up. I don't need to look at it to know it's Chet again. He isn't used to having me ignore him unless I'm at an ICP or out of cell range while working. He'll deal with the inconvenience of not reaching me as long as I'm making money.

It's the first time I've let that thought fully form in my mind. Is it true?

I swing my legs over the edge of the bed. Sleep won't come again this morning. Taking my phone, I pad to my closet, grab my robe, and slide my feet into my slippers. Then I close the bedroom door making sure it doesn't bang and wake Haley, before making my way to the kitchen where I put on my robe and slip my phone into one of its pockets.

I won't respond.

I go to the coffeepot, fill it with water, and open the airtight canister on the countertop, the scent of ground coffee a comfort this morning. I scoop coffee into the filter and set the pot to brew. Then I realize I've made enough for two, and Haley won't drink any.

And Chet isn't here.

"You know I love you."

Why do I perceive those words as an accusation rather than a declaration? I sigh. The phone in my pocket pulls on me like an impatient toddler. *Ignore it, Jessica.* The muscles in my neck and shoulders tighten at the thought. I know the consequences of ignoring Chet.

All too well.

I reach into the pocket of my robe and wrap my fingers around the phone. I hold it there for a moment, then pull it out of my pocket and read the last text—just one word:

Hello?

I prescribe Chet's sarcastic tone to the message. He's angry. My stomach knots. I type a quick text in response to his:

> **Sorry, I was with Haley when you called** and didn't want to wake her. Can we talk this afternoon?

With finger poised above the Send icon, I hesitate. What did I say to my dad yesterday? That it was time I checked back into reality and made changes? Two days ago, I'd have sent the text I just typed to Chet.

Today?

I need to change the way I respond. But what will that cost me?

I set the phone on the counter, reach into the upper cabinet, and pull out a coffee mug. I wait as the coffeemaker gurgles and the final drops of coffee sputter into the pot, then I fill my mug. I stand for a moment, steaming mug in hand, and stare at my phone.

I set the mug down, pick up the phone, and delete my response to Chet. I drop the phone back into my pocket, pick up my coffee, and head outside to enjoy, or at least experience, the morning.

Fear not…the mountain passes. They will kill care, save you from deadly apathy, set you free, and call forth every faculty into vigorous, enthusiastic action.
John Muir

CHAPTER THIRTY-FIVE

Haley

BY THE TIME I've crutched my way to the kitchen, I'm already exhausted. I hate my life. "Mom?"

The coffeepot is on and the door to the back patio is cracked. Great. I have to go all the way outside to find her. I lift the crutches, set them on the floor a few inches in front of me, push myself up with my forearms, and swing myself forward. Or something like that. The whole process is way too much work. When I make it to the back door, I lift one of the crutches and push the door open with it—just wide enough for me to get through.

"You're up? Here, let me help you." My mom jumps up from the chair where she was sitting.

"I've got it." I take the last few steps, then plop into the chair next to where she was sitting. She takes the crutches from me and leans them up against the wall behind the chair.

"Wow. You did it." She pats me on the head like I'm a Labrador. Then she adjusts the ottoman in front of the chair so I can rest my cast on it. "I thought you'd sleep in. What happened?"

"Dad happened."

"Oh. Were you thinking about…everything?" She sits down next to me.

"No. I couldn't sleep because he keeps texting me. Is that who called you earlier?"

She nods.

"Did you talk to him?"

"Not yet."

"Like, what does he think? That he can just call or text and everything will be okay? How clueless is he?"

"Haley—"

"No, really. I mean it. He can't just call and expect everything to be okay." I slump down in the chair, my hair falling over my face. I push it back, then look at my mom. From the expression on her face, it's obvious she isn't loving this conversation, or my attitude, or something. "Don't tell me to be respectful."

"I wasn't going to. I'm angry too. But—"

"But what? It's not like you can just pretend it didn't happen. It happened. With Heather, and who knows who else? He probably did it with that North-Face rep who's been hanging around the store too."

"*Did it*? Haley…"

"I'm not going to let you ignore this."

"I won't ignore it. I wish I could, but I can't. I won't. And what North-Face rep?"

I shake my head. "Forget it."

"What about her?"

I throw my hands up. "Well, *she* said there were others. And this rep is always hanging around and talking to Dad and giggling. And he acts the same way with her that he acted with Heather. And I wasn't the only one who noticed it, you know? Zach noticed. He wasn't even surprised when I told him about Dad and Heather. Anyway, his dad has a trophy wife so, like, he gets it." I shake my head.

"A trophy wife?"

"Yeah, it's some young—"

"I *know* what it is. I just… You told Zach?"

I shrug. "I wasn't going to, but he knew something was wrong and—"

She holds up her hand. "No, Haley, it's okay. If you needed to talk about it, I'm glad he was there. And if his dad…" It's her turn to shake her head. "Did Zach's dad have an affair?"

"No, I think he met the trophy after he and Zach's mom divorced."

"Haley, you can't… We're women. I don't want you to ever see yourself or anyone else as a trophy." She sighs. "How did we get here? I can't believe we're having this conversation."

"Mom, I'm not a baby anymore."

"I know. That's not what I mean. I can't believe we're having this conversation about your…dad." Her last word comes out in a whisper.

I don't say anything else, because what is there to say? We're quiet for a few minutes as we stare out at the forest beyond our yard. The tire swing my dad pushed Tyler and me in so many times when we were little hangs from the tree. For some reason, those memories don't feel special anymore—like my dad hasn't just ruined the present and the future, but he's also made the past seem like it wasn't real.

"Are you hungry?"

I shrug. "Kind of." Then it hits me. "Um, it's Monday. You know that, right?"

She nods.

"School?"

"I thought you needed to rest, and the doctor said to take it easy for a couple of days and keep your ankle elevated, remember?"

"Oh, right." I shrug again. "Well, at least the ankle isn't a total waste—I mean, if it gets me out of chemistry." But chemistry isn't the only thing I want to avoid.

"How's it feeling?" She gestures toward my leg. "Do you need another pain pill?"

"Not really. It's okay right now."

"Okay, I'll make you something to eat."

But instead of getting up and going to the kitchen, she goes back to staring at the trees.

"Mom?"

"Hmm?"

"So, like, what are you going to do? I mean, about dad?" I watch her face. Her eyes are puffy and have dark circles under them and her lips sag at the corners. When she turns and looks at me again, there's no spark or, like, life in her eyes. She looks way older than she did when she left for that incident a couple of weeks ago.

She sighs, then lifts her hands, palms up. "I don't know, Haley. I don't know."

"You have to stay mad."

She stares at me. "I do?"

"Yeah."

"Why?"

"Because people have energy when they're mad, you know? Anger will keep you going. You have to use that energy."

She studies me a moment before saying anything, then she smiles, but the smile doesn't reach her eyes. "How'd you get to be so smart? And grown up?"

I shrug and look back at the tire swing, which blurs when tears fill my eyes. Again. I lay my head back against the chair cushion. "Anyway, feeling mad is better than"—I sniff—"the alternative." My stomach clenches. I turn my head toward my mom without lifting it off the cushion and then swipe at the tears that have fallen on my cheeks. "I'm not really hungry."

My dad's texts aren't the only ones I've ignored today. Zach texted and called too. I grab the TV remote next to me on my mom's bed and hit Mute. I set the remote back down and pick up my phone. It isn't Zach's fault that I don't want to talk to him. It's just... I don't know. Everything is so overwhelming right now.

After getting back into bed this morning, I slept for several more hours. I check the time—1:35 p.m.—then punch Zach's number into the phone, but he doesn't answer, so I leave a message. "Hey, it's me. Thanks for your calls and texts. I'm doing okay—just hanging out and catching up on some sleep. Hope you're not too sore from the hike. So, maybe I'll talk to you tomorrow, okay? Oh, and thanks for everything yesterday. Really. Okay, talk to you later."

I exhale, relieved I could just leave a message. But then, that's why I called when I did—when I knew he would be in class. I toss the phone back onto the bed. I don't plan on responding to my dad at all. I don't have anything to say to him. I mean, not yet anyway. I don't know what he expects.

I don't even know what *I* expect.

"Are you ready to eat something? Macaroni and cheese?" My mom comes in with a plate on a tray. "And chocolate milk."

My favorites. "My ankle's throbbing."

"That's why you need to eat something. You can't have any more of the ibuprofen the doctor sent home without something in your stomach. So eat this, then I'll give you another pill."

"Okay."

"Mind if I join you while you eat?" My mom comes around and sits on her side of the bed, then leans back against her pillow and closes her eyes. "I was thinking about something." She opens her eyes and looks at me.

"What?" I take a bite of the macaroni and cheese.

"You and I did the same thing after reading that e-mail."

"Yeah, we both left." I talk with my mouth full. "But"—I swallow the mac and cheese—"I don't get something."

"What's that?"

"That -email said that you knew about the…" Somehow I can't make myself say the word. "About what was going on and that you gave dad an ultimatum. So if you knew, why did it freak you out last night? Why did you leave?" Before I even finish my sentence she's shaking her head.

"I didn't know, Haley. I never even suspected. I don't know what that was about. The only thing I can think of is that your dad told her that to get out of the…affair. It's one of the questions I have for your dad when I'm ready to…discuss all this with him."

"Oh."

She pulls at a thread on the bedspread, then looks at me. "Anyway, back to what I was thinking about… Have you heard of the fight-or-flight response?"

"No."

"Well, I don't know the actual psychological definition, but I think it's something about a reaction to stress or trauma. And it appears you and I react the same way. We flee."

"Okay, so?" What is she getting at? I take another bite of mac and cheese.

She sits up and turns toward me. "Haley, I don't want to flee anymore. I realized this morning that I've done that my whole married life. Whenever I perceived any change in your dad—whether he was angry or disappointed—I fled. Not literally, but *who I am* ran away. Me." She points to herself. "Do you understand?"

"Yeah, I mean, I've seen you do that. But why? Why don't you just, you know, be yourself? Speak your mind, or whatever?"

"I don't know. I've just been so afraid of losing him—of losing our family. Maybe it has something to do with losing my mother." She shrugs. "I don't know. It's something

I want to figure out. But in the meantime, I want to make a pact right now. Okay?"

I can do that. I nod.

"We're not going to run away from problems anymore. We're going to fight. We're going to stand up for ourselves. We're going to stare hardships in the face, whatever or whoever they are, and we're going to realize that we're worth fighting for."

"Um, yeah, okay." I set the fork back on the tray. Yeah, I ran. Once. I don't have a problem with what she's saying—it sounds good. But can she really do it?

She leans forward. "The most important thing to me now, even over preserving the legacy of our family, is that I teach you and Tyler the importance of being who you were created to be. To love yourselves enough to fully love others. This is one of those Do-as-I-say-not-as-I've-done times. Deal?"

I look at her. "Are you going to change? Are you going to stop running and stand up and face things? Even Dad?"

She takes a deep breath, then nods. "Yes. I'm going to try."

"Pinky swear." I hold out my little finger.

She hooks her pinky around mine. "Pinky swear. Haley, you are a beautiful, unique, valuable young woman. And if anyone ever treats you in a way that makes you feel like anything less, then there's something wrong. That's when you have to promise me that you'll fight for yourself. Fight for you."

"Okay. I promise. By the way, just for the record, you ran before I did. So I sort of already get all this. There's a difference between running away and needing space." I lift my eyebrows and smile at her. "So, you know, you're not a total failure as a mother."

She laughs. "Thanks." Then she pulls me forward with her pinky still hooked around mine and plants a kiss on my forehead.

When I pull away, I have to ask. "But…" I look away.

"What?"

I look back at her and my shoulders droop. "Is there any way, I mean, do you think… Are you and Dad going to get a…divorce?"

She stares at me for a second and her eyes fill with tears. "I…I don't know. I just… I don't know."

I push the plate with the macaroni and cheese on it away.

That wasn't the answer I was looking for.

*The rocks where the exposure to storms is the greatest, and
where only ruin seems to be the object, are all the more
lavishly clothed upon with beauty.... In like manner do men
find themselves enriched by storms
that seem only big with ruin.*
John Muir

CHAPTER THIRTY-SIX

Jessica

AFTER GETTING HALEY to eat a few more bites
of her lunch, I give her an ibuprofen, then carry her tray back
to the kitchen where I rinse her glass and plate and load them
into the dishwasher. The mundane tasks I longed for
yesterday aren't enough to keep my mind from the question
Haley posed today.

The question I've avoided.

The question I've run from.

But I made a deal with Haley—no more fleeing. So
what *does* lie ahead for our marriage? Isn't divorce the
standard response to an affair? I wander out of the kitchen,
back to the porch, where I drop into the same chair in which I

spent much of the morning. I put my feet up on the ottoman, lean my head back, and close my eyes.

Some couples work through infidelity—some marriages even come back stronger after an affair. I've heard of that happening. There was that guy, a firefighter, who had an affair. His wife was suspicious and tracked him to a motel—one of those little ones along the Merced River, outside the park. It was all the gossip at an ICP a few weeks after it happened.

I lift my head and open my eyes. A couple years later, I overheard that same firefighter talking about his wife—telling one of the guys that after some counseling and time, they'd worked through it. What had he said? *"It took a lot of work, but now we're not only married, we're best friends."*

His comment struck me. Because, and I had to admit this, I've never shared that kind of relationship with Chet. But…could we? And why haven't we shared the closeness of best friends? I sigh. Because, as I told Haley, I ran. I hid. Rather than dare be myself with Chet, I assumed a role from the beginning. First I was his girlfriend, then his lover, then his wife. I became whoever I believed he wanted me to be.

Myself?

Who is that?

Do I know? Have I ever known?

I know Cretia would tell me I can't own Chet's behavior, and I'm not. But it is time to own my actions. And it is long past time to discover who I am—to decide who I am—and to develop that. The first thing I discovered about myself came as a surprise. Though I've worked, strived even, to preserve our family unit—to preserve the legacy of an intact family—the legacy I didn't receive—it is more important that Haley and Tyler embrace who they were created to become. That came to me this morning as I sat staring at the forest beyond our yard. It was the first time in years I've allowed myself the time to sit and let my mind and soul wander.

If my children are to embrace themselves for who they are, then I must do the same.

With that thought comes the old, familiar heartache. Loss. If a mother leads the way for her children, is it any wonder I struggled to find my way? To find myself?

It's time to have that conversation with my dad—the one he promised me about my mother.

Somehow, I know that's my next step. But before I call him, I pull out my phone and text Chet, who, it seems, finally gave up on me after I ignored his attempts to reach me. I've half expected him to show up all morning. But maybe he's trying to give us what we need—the space my dad declared for us. With my finger poised over the keys of my phone, I consider what I want to say to him. And how I want to say it.

> Chet, we have a lot to work through. I need some time to think, rest, and take care of Haley. I expect you to respect my need and stay elsewhere until you hear from me again.

I stare at the message for a moment, then push Send before I can change my mind. I am not asking for anything but respect. He can at least afford me that. If not in the past, now.

Then I call my dad and ask if I can come over and have that talk about my mother.

After I hang up, I realize that in the same way I've run away, so has my dad. He's run from telling me the truth about my mom all these years. But things are about to change. For both of us.

I smile. Maybe I do know who I am after all.

I am my father's daughter.

After making Haley promise not to get out of bed, and making certain she has all she needs to stay settled for an hour or two on her own, I make the drive to my dad's and

Cretia's. I roll down the windows in the truck rather than turn on the air conditioner and I breathe deep. The dry, late-summer air is scented, as it often is, with smoke. The news coverage of the Meadow Fire we saw this morning was sobering.

"Mom! Come here!" Haley had called from my bedroom where she was watching TV. "Hurry!"

I ran from the kitchen, hoping she hadn't fallen. "Are you okay?"

"Yeah. You have to see this."

I dashed into the bedroom and saw her pointing at the flat-screen TV that hangs over the small fireplace in our room. "Oh. Wow." The newscaster was reciting statistics about the number of acres burned so far and the number of hikers evacuated from the trails and the top of Half Dome yesterday. I already knew all that. But what caught my attention, and what Haley wanted me to see, were the photos they were showing of the area surrounding the trail where Haley was rescued. It looked like a charred moonscape.

"What if we hadn't—?"

"Don't, Haley. I can't think about that." I put my hand over my heart. "Oh, it could have been so much worse. For so many."

We continued watching in silence. The last photo they showed was taken last evening, from a vantage point near Glacier Point.

Taken at twilight, an ink-blue sky was the canvas, while Half Dome stood as the subject, regal and imposing, silhouetted against the orange glow of acres and acres of burning forest. Gray smoke billowed over the mountaintop. The contrasting colors were striking, capturing the art of nature.

The photo captured all the elements fire embodies: beauty, terror, awe, destruction, and necessity. As I stared at the image, my skin prickled. I wrapped my arms around myself and wondered, again, what my body knew in that moment that my mind hadn't yet grasped.

I ponder the image again as I drive but don't come up with any new insights. Then I chide myself for my silliness—looking for things that aren't there. The power of fire inspires, it always has, nothing new there.

By the time I reach my dad's and Cretia's, I've forgotten the photo and have instead fixated on what my father will tell me. I assume my mother also had an affair, which would explain, maybe, why she left. I've wondered about that for years. But now I'll hear the details, I hope, and can begin putting the shards of information into some sort of form, like taking broken pieces of pottery and creating a mosaic. The picture may not be perfect, but perhaps it will offer some perspective.

When Cretia greets me at the door, she hugs me tight and holds me there a moment. "Your dad told me everything. I am so sorry, honey. But you know we're here for you."

"I know." I pull back from her. "Thank you. I'm going to need your wisdom."

"Well, you've got it. You know that. I'm always ready to listen and offer whatever I can."

And she's right, I do know that. But for now, I'm here to talk about my mother, somehow hoping that information will inform, in some way, my situation with Chet.

My dad comes out of his office, takes off his baseball cap, smoothes back his hair, and then gives me a quick hug. He turns toward the living room without making eye contact with me and motions for me to follow him. He sits in his recliner and I take a seat on the end of the sofa closest to his chair.

"Can I get you some coffee, Jessica?" Cretia looks from Dad to me.

"No, thank you."

"Ted?"

"No, thanks. You just sit there next to Jessie." He waves her toward the sofa. "Jessie, I asked Cretia to join us because, well, just because. That okay with you?"

I smile at Cretia, who reaches over and gives my hand a squeeze. "Of course it's okay."

"Good. I might need her"—he clears his throat—"for moral support. She already knows everything I'm going to tell you."

I nod. I expected she would. "So Dad"—my heartbeat quickens—"yesterday, when I told you about Chet, you said you had some things to tell me about my mother. Is what's going on with Chet somehow related? I had the sense that maybe you understood what I'm"—I sigh—"going through."

He takes his cap off again and sets it in his lap, where he then runs his fingers around the brim, over and over.

I lean forward, my throat thick. "I know this probably isn't easy after all these years, but I really need to know what happened. Why she left. And, just for the record, I finally understand that I'm not the only one she left. I'm sorry, Dad."

Still looking down at his hat, he nods, then looks up at me. His expression is so full of…pain. "Well, to tell you the truth, I didn't know why she left. Not really. I had my suspicions, of course. But I didn't know for sure until…" He stops and looks over at Cretia.

"Go on, honey."

He licks his lips. "Well, I didn't know for sure until I got a letter from her. It came several weeks back, while we were on vacation, I guess. I found it in the pile of mail when we got home."

For a moment, I'm too stunned to respond. "She wrote? She's still alive?"

"Oh, well, yes, yes, she is." He puts his cap back on and then reaches into his shirt pocket and pulls out an envelope that looks folded in half. He holds it tight in one fist.

I hold out my hand. "May I?"

My dad glances from me to Cretia. Then he stuffs the envelope back into his pocket. "Just let me…let me get through this first."

I sit back, though I don't relax. I wish he'd just get on with it, but I can see how difficult this is for him. Why does my mother's leaving still cause him so much pain all these years later? "Dad?"

"Right. Well, here's the thing. I'm just not sure this is the right time to tell you all this. You have enough to deal with right now."

"But yesterday you said—"

"I know what I said."

"Dad—"

Cretia puts her hand on my arm. "He's worried about hurting you more when you're already dealing with painful circumstances." Then she looks at Ted. "Honey, you're not in control of the timing, or of what Sandra or Chet did. Providence has arranged this."

"Oh, all right. Let's get it over with." He leans forward in his chair. "Jessie, yes, your mother had an affair. Like I said, I didn't know it for sure at the time, but I suspected. When she left, well, I just assumed she'd followed some man. But it isn't as simple as that. It wasn't as simple that."

I lift my hands, palms up. "What happened? What does the letter say?"

"I'll get to that." He clears his throat again and then relays the details of the day she left—him coming home and finding Dot, the note Dot handed him from my mother. "I knew Sandra, your mother, was having a hard time. Seemed like as soon as she got pregnant, she changed. Or things changed. She wasn't herself. I wrote it off to hormones and the fact that she was young and not sure she was ready for motherhood. But I was a just a fool."

"Ted"—Cretia wags a finger at him—"you weren't a fool. You were, and you are, a good man."

"Well, not good enough for her, I guess." He looks down at his lap and seems to consider something, then looks back at Cretia. "Though if she hadn't left, I wouldn't have ended up with you, and that would've been a tragedy." He looks to me. "You remember that, Jessie. When things are at their worst, when everything seems impossible, you just never know what's ahead."

I nod and swallow the lump in my throat. Suddenly, I'm no longer sure I want to hear the story I've pined for all of my days—or at least for as long as I can remember.

"So, as I was saying, when your mother got pregnant, things began to change. Then when you were born, she went into what today I'd call a depression, but I didn't know it then. Again, I wrote it off to hormones and thought things would get better. Don't get me wrong, I didn't just ignore the situation. I did all I could. I helped out, took care of you, and when I couldn't be home, I had a neighbor come and watch you.

"Or"—he hesitates—"Dot. She had just started dating Johnny about the time Sandra went into her funk." He stares off somewhere beyond where Cretia and I are sitting, seeming to think about that. Then he shakes his head. "Anyway, I came home that day, and Sandra had packed a bag and was gone. I didn't hear from her again till I got served with divorce papers."

As I follow my dad's story, I also work to figure out what he isn't saying. "So…" I glance at Cretia, then to my dad. "When did she have this affair? Just after I was born?" I shake my head. "I can't imagine having the energy or even the desire to bother just after having a baby."

"Well, that's the thing." He shifts in his chair and then reaches for the envelope he'd tucked back into his pocket. He looks at Cretia.

She nods. "Give it to her, honey. She has a right to know." Then she looks at me. "We never would have planned this for you, Jessica. The timing, the circumstances, but we trust something greater than ourselves is at work here. And remember what your dad said: You just never know what's ahead or why some things happen."

My mouth has gone dry. "You're scaring me. You're both scaring me."

Cretia reaches over and gives my hand another squeeze. "Take the letter, honey. Read it."

"Fine. I just want this over with." My stomach feels as though it's tied in knots and my hand shakes as I reach for the envelope my dad holds out. I take it, unfold it, and then pull the sheets of notebook paper from the envelope. I run my hand over the words scrawled on the page. Words written by the woman I've longed for my entire life. Now, I have a piece of her here, in my hands.

Tears pool in my eyes as I try to read, but the words blur on the page. I blink, take a deep breath, and then begin reading.

Dear Ted,

These words should have been spoken many years ago, though at the time silence lured me. Why speak what would only wound? So I carried the truth like a stone as punishment for my actions and protection for you and our child. But now my shoulders bend like the willow and my strength wafts on the breeze. I must release the stone so I can rest.

It is a selfish act. But I see no other path. And I have wandered many paths, including the path that led me away from you.

I strayed. A seed was planted. And it grew in my womb.

But who'd planted the seed? I was uncertain. Or was I certain?

As the seed took root, I wanted to flee, but the
sapling grew within me. There was no escape. So I
stayed for a time, attempting to set my own roots,
but the soil was unyielding, fertilized with my lies.

I stop reading, my whole body shaking. "What…what
does this *mean*?" I throw the letter down and swipe at my
tears.

Cretia puts her arm around my shoulders,
"Shh…honey. It's going to be okay."

"No. No! It's not going to be okay." I pull away from
her. "This isn't okay!" I sob. Then, through my tears, I look
over at my dad. Tears are streaming down his cheeks too, and
then he buries his face in his hands. "Daddy?"

He shakes his head.

Then I choke out the question I have to ask.
"You're…you're not my…father?"

Nature's tables are spread and fires burning. You must go warm yourselves and eat.
John Muir

CHAPTER THIRTY-SEVEN

Jessica

FOR REASONS I can't yet explain, I need to see the Meadow Fire for myself. Though I promised Haley I'd no longer flee, I am running. But rather than running away, my sense is that I'm running *toward* something, though I'm not sure what.

The National Park Service reports that 2 to 3 percent of all wildfires account for 95 percent of the acreage burned annually. These large wildfires feed the myth that fire destroys the environment, when instead, fire is a necessary element for environmental and ecological health.

I rehearse the fire facts I know so well, hoping the familiar will center me in the unfamiliar realm I find myself—a realm where everything I've known has crashed in on me.

Without fire, our forests become overgrown, keeping sunlight from the forest floor. That, in turn, changes the natural order of the land by stunting the understory growth, which is the primary sustenance for many species of wildlife.

My head aches from the tears shed with my dad and Cretia.

As of this morning, the Meadow Fire had burned over four thousand acres of land and was only 10 percent contained.

Before leaving my dad and Cretia's, I called and checked on Haley, who told me Chloe was on her way over with a pizza. So instead of returning home, I followed the highway toward the park, then took the turnoff to Glacier Point.

Chloe could take care of Haley, and Cretia assured me she'd take care of my dad.

"You take some time for yourself this evening, Jessica. Your dad's had time to process all this—now you take some time. I'll take care of him. You take care of yourself."

Though I long to block out the conversation with my dad, snippets replay in my mind.

"I will always be your father, Jessie, regardless of what genetics say."

"But who am I? If I'm not your daughter?"

Cretia had leaned toward me. *"Jessica, we don't know that for sure. Her letter just says there's a chance he isn't."*

"From what she wrote, it sounds like it's more than a chance," I shot back.

"We can find out, Jessie, if you want to know, then if...if I'm not, your mother's address is on the envelope, maybe you can contact her and find out who..."

My dad's voice trailed off, leaving the unfinished sentence hanging between us.

I roll my shoulders back hoping to ease the tension.

As I near my destination, I pull onto the shoulder of the road where I get my first view of the Meadow Fire from this elevation. I flick on my hazard lights, put the truck in Park, then get out, go to the side of the road, and look out over the horizon.

From this vantage point, Tis-sa-ack stands in profile, her tear-streaked face hidden to me. The sun, just setting, reflects against the billowing cloud of smoke, coloring the sky with the hot hues of flames, making it easy to believe that not only is the earth on fire, but that all the universe is ablaze.

I stand and watch for several minutes, then go back to the truck, get in, and follow the road out to the point.

I park the truck in the Glacier Point parking area. When I get out, I'm no longer alone, but surrounded by a group of onlookers—tourists, photographers, and media personnel all here to see what I've come to see. I find a place of solitude, alone amidst the throng, and stand witness to the spectacle.

As the sun makes its descent, the fire in the sky is doused by the deep indigo of twilight. Tis-sa-ack stands strong, skirted by the orange glow of the burning forest, threatened but not consumed. Her eternal tears are just visible in the graying light of dusk.

The Native American people understood the necessity of fire for maintaining a healthy environment. But when fire threatens all you've known, is it possible to stand tall, threatened but not consumed, and let fire have its way? To trust something good will bloom after the blaze?

I wrap my arms around myself and stare, unseeing now.

I have no tears left to shed.

Nothing with which to quench the fires surrounding me.

Letting them rage is my only choice.

Only a few generations separate us from our grandfathers
that were savage as wolves.
John Muir

CHAPTER THIRTY-EIGHT

Haley

"OMG! THAT IS so romantic!"
I look at her. "Chloe, how is it romantic? I was hot, sweaty, and covered in dirt. Look at my lip, it's still split, and look how fat it is. It was bleeding and my ankle was turned in the opposite direction of what it was supposed to be. And it was smoky—the fire was coming our way. We were starting to freak out." I shake my head, then take a piece of pizza from the box Chloe had set on top of a magazine on my parents' bed.

"Yeah, but the two of you ran off without telling anyone where you were going, and then, after you fell, he took care of you. I mean, really, like he probably saved your life." She closes her eyes and sighs. "It's like a movie. Plus he's so cute."

I roll my eyes. "Whatever." I didn't tell her why I took off without telling my parents.

Chloe's sitting on my mom's side of the bed and leans into me. "Anyway, you told me you two kissed."

I *so* shouldn't have told her that. But I caved—she wouldn't quit asking if we'd made out yet. "It was one *little* kiss, Chloe." Anyway it didn't mean anything—at least, not to me.

She takes a bite of her pizza and chews for a minute. "Next time, at least tell me when you're going to do something like that so when your dad calls me, like a bazillion times, I can tell him you weren't kidnapped, or murdered, or something."

"You're such a drama queen."

"Hey, I just report the drama, I don't create it." She puts her hand over her mouth and laughs. "That was good, right?"

I nod. "Yeah, that was pretty good."

"So did he come over after school today?"

"Who?"

"Really? Haley, hello? Zach. Did he come over?"

"Oh, no."

"Why not? He wanted to—he told me."

"You talked to him?"

"Duh. I saw him at his locker after second period. Then I hung out with him at lunch."

I flip the lid closed on the pizza box.

"Don't you want another piece?"

"No."

"What's wrong? Haley, you're so, like, chill. I mean, it's like you're not even excited that the hottest guy at school is so into you." She looks at me like I'm an idiot. "Oh, are you in pain? Is that it? Here, what can I do? Do you need another pillow under your ankle?" She reaches behind her and grabs the pillow she's leaning against.

I hold up my hand. "No, I'm fine—"

"Haley, Chloe…"

I jump. I don't believe it. "Dad…what are you doing here?"

"Last time I checked, I lived here." He nods toward my leg. "How's the ankle?"

"Um, it's okay."

He smiles like it's just another day at home. "Hi, Chloe."

"Hey, Mr. Weaver. Want some pizza? Haley's not hungry."

"No, thanks." He looks at me. "Where's your mother?"

I shrug. *Like you care.* "At Grandma and Grandpa's, I think."

"Okay." He turns to leave.

I cannot *believe* him. "Wait. Are you... I mean, are you staying?"

"Like I said, I live here. By the way, you know that phone of yours that I pay for?"

I look at my phone lying next to me on the bed, then look back to him.

"Yeah, that one. Consider responding when I call or text. If that's too much trouble, we'll get rid of it. Deal?"

He walks out of the room and I reach for my phone. When I pick it up, my palms are damp.

"Whoa..." Chloe gazes from him to me. "What was that about? Is he still mad that you took off with Zach?"

Heat rises from my neck to my face. I swallow. "Um, yeah, I guess." I look at Chloe. "You better go. I need to talk to him."

"Yeah, okay, I'm pretty sure I don't want to be here for that."

"Thanks for the pizza. Why don't you take it with you."

"You sure?"

I work to keep my tone normal. "Of course. Sorry I didn't eat much, I'm just... I don't know."

"It's totally fine."

She scoops up the box, flips the lid shut, and sails out of the room. Watching her I can't help thinking...

I'll never be that happy again.

I wait until I hear the front door close, then I get out of the bed and reach for my crutches. I wasn't ready for him to come home yet—didn't expect him. But since he's here, I have some things to say to him.

No more running, right?

Holding my crutches in one hand, I grab my phone off the bed and slip it into the pocket of my gym shorts. Then I hobble my way out of the bedroom to go search for him.

If he can't understand why I didn't answer his calls or texts, then he can have my stupid phone. My heart beats fast as I go. Suddenly I have energy when I haven't had it all day.

And then I realize why.

I make it to the doorway of the den. He's sitting at his desk, as usual. I take a few steps into the den, then lean on my crutches. "Thanks for embarrassing me in front of Chloe. I can't believe—"

"Do not talk to me in that tone, young lady."

Who is he kidding? "No, Dad, *you* don't talk to me. In any tone!" My whole body shakes. "You gave up your right to respect from me! You don't deserve my respect! You just listen!" My blood pumps, throbbing in my temples.

He stands up and takes a step toward me.

I take a step back, but I keep talking. "You've ruined everything. *Everything!* Don't you *get* that? How could you do what you did to Mom? To me and Tyler? How could you *do* that to our family?"

My voice cracks and emotion clogs my throat, but I'm not done. "You know what? I'm only fifteen, but I'm more mature than you. When I first started liking Zach"—I take a breath—"Chloe liked him too. She'd liked him for a while. So you know what I did?"

He just stares at me.

"*Do* you?"

He shakes his head. "Don't—"

"I did nothing. *Nothing,* Dad! I didn't go behind her back. I didn't go out with him when he asked. I did nothing!

Because Chloe is *my friend.* And that means something to me. We're your *family* and that should mean something, but obviously, it's like, nothing…to you."

I'm crying now, choking out words between my sobs. "I waited, Dad. I waited until Chloe liked…some other guy. I barely even…talked…to…Zach…until"—I hiccup—"until it was…okay." I lean against the sofa in his den and then double over, crying.

But I'm still not done. I force myself to straighten back up and through my tears, I yell, "How…how is mom ever supposed to…trust you? Huh? Tell me that! And how…how am I ever supposed to trust you…again? Did you…did you ever…think of that?" I turn my head and wipe my face on the sleeve of my T-shirt. "You ruined everything! There's no…way to *fix this*!" I'm screaming at him.

He looks down his nose at me. "Are you finished? Huh? Finished with your little lecture?"

I look up, see the expression on his face, and then take another step back. I don't know what I expected, but…

His anger fills the room. "You're right, Haley. You're fifteen. *Only* fifteen. You have no idea what real life is like— the stress, the pressure, and"—he chuckles, but there's no humor in the laugh—*"marriage."* He hisses the word. "You can't possibly understand. So get out of my face. And as far as respect goes—"

"Stop!"

I jump, startled for the second time tonight. I spin to see my mom standing behind me. She glares at my dad. "Just stop, Chet!" She moves forward and puts her hand on my shoulder. "Whether you take responsibility for your actions or not is your choice, but I will not let you take this out on Haley. Or me, for that matter." Then, through clenched teeth, she says it again. "So just stop."

Her hand on my shoulder trembles, and I'm pretty sure it's not from fear, but from anger. "C'mon, let's get you back into bed." Her tone is calm, but stern. Then she looks at my dad. "You wait here. We're not finished yet."

I cry all the way back to the bedroom, my mom walking with me. She doesn't say anything—she's just, like, there for me.

When we get into her room, she pulls back the covers on her bed. "Why don't you use the bathroom and then wash your face. I'll wait for you."

I nod and hobble toward the bathroom. After blowing my nose and washing my face, the tears finally stop. When I go back into the bedroom, she takes my crutches and helps me get settled back in bed. Then she sits on the edge of the bed next to me.

She rests her hand on my leg. "I'm sorry you have to go through this."

She's sorry? She didn't even do anything. And my dad? He's not sorry at all. He's just mad. "It's not your fault."

She just stares at me. She still looks kind of wiped out, but there's something else in her expression now. I don't know what it is, but she seems different than when she left this afternoon.

"Are you"—it's a weird question to ask my mom, one I've never asked her before—"you know, are you...okay?"

Again, she just looks at me for a few seconds. "I think I've reached the end of myself. Grandpa told me something this afternoon that"—she shakes her head—"it was sort of the last straw. But I will be okay. And so will you, regardless of what happens."

"What did Grandpa tell you?"

She pats my leg. "I'll tell you later. Right now, I need to get back and...discuss things with your dad."

"Is he...? Where's he going to sleep?"

"I'm going to grab a few more things for him out of his closet and suggest he spend some time...away."

I remember the look on his face. "Um, good luck with that."

"Yeah, thanks."

Then she leans down and puts her forehead on mine, like she used to when I was little and she'd tuck me in at night. Then she turns her head. "I love you, Haley-bug." The whisper is warm against my ear.

And I whisper back, "Love you too."

*Whence comes the annihilation of bonds that seemed
everlasting?*
John Muir

CHAPTER THIRTY-NINE

Jessica

AS I LEAVE the bedroom, I shut the door behind me. There's no reason Haley needs to hear anything Chet and I may say to one another. I don't plan to make any life-altering decisions tonight. When I do, I want her to hear those decisions from me directly, rather than overhearing them.

I stand outside the closed bedroom door, holding a bag with more clothing and toiletry items for Chet. Am I really going to tell him to leave? Queasy, I put my hand on my stomach. Haley's right—he won't go without a fight. But why? I take a deep breath. Does he really think he has a right to be here after…?

And he had the audacity to tell Haley *she* was disrespectful?

I take a deep breath. No, he has to go.

I walk back to the den, my strides sure, but Chet isn't there. I find him in the kitchen, leaning against the island, a glass in one hand. I set the overnight bag I packed for him on the counter.

He takes a sip of whatever he's drinking as he eyes the bag, then he gestures to it. "What's that?"

"More clothes and things for you."

"I don't need those."

"Yes, you do." I try to keep my tone even. "I asked you to afford me the respect of some time—time to rest and think. So, I don't know what you're doing here." Inside, I'm quivering, but I work to keep my voice steady. "It seems odd you'd ask Haley for respect when you refuse to offer it to her or to me."

He chuckles. "Did you hear her attitude?"

I ignore his question. "Please leave."

His eyes narrow, then his expression softens. "No, babe, I need to be here. You said it in your text this afternoon. We have things to work through. The longer we put it off, the harder it will be. We just need to make a fresh start. Put the past behind us and move forward." He sets the glass down and walks to where I stand. He moves in close. "I blew it, okay? Is that what you need to hear? Things have just been rough—we're both too busy. But you know I love you." He buries his face in my hair.

I pull away and move to the other side of the island, needing a barrier between us. *I know he loves me?* The shaking inside stops and my tone—as well as my resolve—becomes steely. "How exactly am I supposed to know you love me? Because discovering you're sleeping with another woman, or *women,* does nothing to assure me of your love, Chet."

He holds up one hand. "Whoa…whoa… Who said I slept with Heather? Or anyone else, for that matter? I may have gotten a little too emotionally involved with her, but"—he shakes his head—"sleep with her? No. No way."

"What?" What is he talking about? "But...her e-mail... She referred to an affair. She said she wasn't the only woman you'd been with." Did I just assume...?

He looks down at the floor, clears his throat, then looks back to me, but just for a moment. He picks up the glass again and walks toward the sink, talking over his shoulder. "Yeah, I liked her. I spent some time with her. Maybe let my heart get involved. But nothing more."

He sets the glass in the sink, then turns back toward me. "C'mon, Jess, you know me better than that. Did you tell Haley I slept with Heather?" He runs his hand through his thick hair. "No wonder she's so mad. Great, thanks, Jess."

I raise my eyebrows. "*Thanks?* I've said nothing to Haley. She read the same e-mail I read. It seemed clear—"

"Well, it may have *seemed* clear to you, but I'm telling you you're wrong. Either you choose to believe me or you don't. Anyway, I did the right thing."

"*What?* In what respect?" I reach out for the countertop, my hand shaking. *The right thing? Are you* kidding *me?*

"You read her e-mail. I broke it off with her. Told her you knew how I felt about her and that I had to end it. I let her go. Gave her a couple months of pay—severance—and let her go."

"So you lied to her and paid her off?" I hiss. "You really believe you did the *right* thing?"

"You just don't get it." There's an edge to his tone now.

Questions dart at me like arrows—Heather, Olivia, the North-Face rep Haley mentioned. How will I ever trust him again? The questions threaten my sanity, but anger is my shield. "No!"

His expression registers surprise.

"No, you're the one who doesn't get it, Chet! *You!*" I'm trembling now as currents of anger course through me.

"Are you really going to believe one e-mail written by a disgruntled former employee, or are you going to believe me, your husband?" He sneers.

A disgruntled... Is what he's implying possible? Would someone do what Heather did as an act of revenge? The questions continue their attempted assault. The bag I packed for Chet sits on the counter between us, standing as a reminder that I wasn't going to have this conversation tonight. What happened?

I walk around to the other side of the island, pick up the bag, and hand it to him. "I told you to go."

He takes the bag and then sets the bag back onto the counter.

My tone is more forceful as I repeat myself. "Go." But as I say it again, I realize I have no way of making him leave. What will I do if he refuses?

He leans against the counter again, appearing calm. His tone is cool. "You're willing to take that risk?"

"What risk?"

He lowers his voice. "If you push me out now, Jess, there's no guarantee I'll come back."

I clench my fists. *"Go!"* I lean over the counter and shove the bag at him. "Just go! Get out!" Heat rises to my face and my voice trembles. "I mean it!" I pound the countertop.

He grabs the bag off the counter, holds it, and stares at me. Then he laughs.

He laughs at me.

"Fine, have it your way, Jess. But know this, you're making a big mistake." Then he turns and walks out of the kitchen.

My body trembles and I grab on to the edge of the countertop to steady myself.

Chet's footsteps echo in the hallway, and then the door between the house and the garage opens. I hear him laugh again. Then the door slams so hard every window in the house rattles. The diesel engine of his truck rumbles in the garage as he pulls out. He's left the dented SUV for me.

I sink onto one of the bar stools, put my head in my hands...

And weep.

After turning off the lights and locking the doors, I curl up on the sofa in the living room. My eyes and sinuses are swollen from the tears I shed with my dad and Cretia this afternoon, and the tears I shed again after Chet left. My head pounds. Shutting up the house for the night took my last reserve of energy. The thought of getting ready for bed and making the climb upstairs to Haley's bed is too much.

I pull the afghan off the back of the sofa and drape it over myself and close my eyes against the images of the day that insist on flashing before me. I wish I'd thought to grab my own pillow off my bed earlier, but I make do with a throw pillow. As my mind and body melt into sleep, a vision of Half Dome, surrounded by fire, fills my mind.

Soon, I'm weeping.

Running. And weeping.

I look over my shoulder to see if he's gaining on me, but no one's there. I quicken my pace anyway, my heart hammering and my breath coming in short bursts. My lungs burn. And on my tongue, I taste the salt of tears.

I stop, for just a moment, trying to catch my breath. My shoulders ache from the burden I carry on my back. A basket. It weighs on me, slowing my escape. Do I dare take the time to rid myself of it? I look over my shoulder again but see nothing except the river flowing behind me. All else is veiled in thick fog.

Or is it smoke?

I pull the straps of the burden basket off my arms and drop it to the ground, and as I do, the contents slosh over the sides. It is filled with tears.

My mother's tears.

My tears.

My daughter's tears.

No! No more! Then the assault begins again. I put my arms up to cover my face as arrows sail toward me. I turn and run again, but as I do, I realize arrows aren't shooting at me.

No. It's only words. I slow my pace, too tired to do more than trot now, and I try to discern the phrases wafting on the fog.

I can't make out the words. But I recognize the voice. My heart stills. It's only Chet. Of course. Why am I running from him?

But when I hear him call my name, when he slings his words my way again, a warning swells in my soul, and I turn and take off. I must not let him catch me, for if he does, he will beat me.

With his words.

He will destroy me.

With his lies—

I bolt upright, my heart pummeling my rib cage. My lip damp with sweat. *Where am I?* I throw off the blanket covering me, my finger catching in strands of yarn. The afghan. I'm on the sofa. I swing my legs over the side of the couch and then work to catch my breath. I inhale, but my throat begins to close.

No.

I inhale again and my throat relaxes.

No more.

Never again.

My breathing returns to normal. My heart rate steadies. And as I stare into the ink of night, understanding comes.

In the dream, I am Tis-sa-ack.

No.

I shake my head.

I will not cry eternal tears.

And neither will my daughter.

"Does it matter?" Cretia takes a bite of the fresh berries she ordered.

I look at her across the coffee cup I hold. *"Does it matter?"* I set my cup down. "Of course it matters." But then I really consider her question. "Doesn't it?"

"I don't know. Honey, it's a question you have to answer for yourself. You're the only one who can do so."

The murmurs of others in the small café are a white noise drowning out the intimate nature of the conversation we share. When I called Cretia and asked if she could meet me for coffee, she suggested our usual haunt: Brew's Up. But running into Chet, who often walks across the parking lot for a cup of coffee, wasn't on my agenda for today. I haven't heard from him since he came to the house on Monday night. And the distance is giving me room to breathe. So I suggested to Cretia that we meet at a new place I'd heard about.

I lean back in my chair, the usual tension pinching my shoulders. "If he slept with her, it means he broke our marriage vows. It makes a difference."

"Is he telling you the truth?"

I sigh. "I don't know. I feel crazy. I was sure after I read that e-mail that they'd had a full-on affair. But…"

Cretia shrugs one thin shoulder. "Listen, honey, first of all, you're not crazy. Second, you could e-mail her back and ask her if she slept with Chet. But will her answer satisfy you? Is that what you really need to know? You told me yourself that Chet admitted to having an emotional affair with her. How does that make you feel? Is the act of sex with someone other than your spouse the only act that breaks the covenant of marriage?"

I turn and gaze out the window to the parking lot. "Either way, trust has been broken." I look back at Cretia. "Not only don't I trust it won't happen again, emotionally *or* physically, I can't even trust that he's telling me the truth." I laugh—a short, staccato burst of air. "He even lied to *her* by saying I knew about the affair." I lift up my hands.

Cretia nods.

"But the details…" I lean my arms on the table, the solid foundation assuring. "They're keeping me up at night. I try to remember what Heather looked like and whether she was prettier than I am or built better than I am. How much younger is she? And if he did sleep with her, was she better in be—?"

"You stop right there. Those questions will destroy you, Jessica. Do you hear me? Comparing yourself to someone else is rarely a healthy act. And when an affair is involved, it's completely destructive. Anyway, you'll never get the answers to those questions, even if you really did want to know the answers. Listen honey, those are the wrong questions to ask." Cretia leans forward and puts her hand on my arm. "Ask constructive questions."

"Like what?"

"Like are you satisfied with who you are as a wife? As a woman? Are you content with the example you're setting for your daughter? And if you want to ask Chet questions, ask him what he'd like to see change in the marriage." She waves her hand. "Heck, ask him if he's glad you found out about the affair or affairs. Maybe he's relieved he doesn't have to hide anymore. Decide what's important, determine if it's helpful, then ask those questions." She pats my arm, then leans back in her seat.

"Okay."

"One other thing, those questions keeping you up at night?"

I nod.

"They won't just go away. It's up to you to tune them out. Do whatever it takes, but discipline your mind to ignore them. Otherwise, you'll just spiral downward. You hear me?" She puts her hand over mine. "If Chet accepts responsibility for his actions, your marriage has a chance. If not…" She shrugs.

"I hear you." I pick up my coffee and take a sip, then set the cup back on its saucer. "Cretia, he just wants to move on. Start fresh. He doesn't want to deal with any of this or even admit any fault. I don't see any remorse in him. There's no genuine grief for hurting me. Or Haley. Our family. He said he blew it, but…" I stare down at the dark liquid in my cup. "I don't believe he's sorry. Am I being unrealistic?"

"Oh, honey, what do you think? Unrealistic? Hardly. Listen to your intuition, Jessica. What's your heart telling you?"

"That's easy. It's telling me to run. Fast."

"Well then…"

"Cretia, I can't just pick up and run. I have to face things, deal with them. I have children to consider."

"Of course you do. But honey, running isn't always a bad thing. Sometimes it's exactly the right response. Listen, I'm not suggesting you abandon your marriage or your family. What I am saying is that it might be time to ask yourself if walking away from your marriage is the healthiest choice for you. And for your kids. Maybe for Chet too, for that matter."

"But—"

"I'm not saying walking away is the easy choice. But you've done easy and where did it get you? Set some boundaries, Jessica. Whether you tell Chet you've set them or not is your decision. But determine for yourself what you need to see from him to move forward—to work on making the marriage work. It sounds like, from what you've said, one of the criteria is seeing some genuine remorse in the man."

"Okay, that makes sense. Thank you. You've given me some things to consider. But I can't make a snap decision."

"No, you can't. You need to take your time."

I nod, but fear, like a mosquito, jabs me. "He told me on Monday night that I was taking a risk when I told him to leave." I rock back and forth in my seat as I wait to see how Cretia will respond.

"A risk?"

"He said he might not come back. It's Thursday and I…haven't heard from him. I expected a barrage of texts, but…" I wrap my arms around myself.

"Well, that would be *his* choice, wouldn't it?"

"But…I was so angry. Maybe I—"

"Jessica." She puts her palms down, flat, on the tabletop. "Sometimes anger is the only appropriate response.

And it's more than time you responded with anger. If he doesn't come back, well then, that sort of solves your problem, doesn't it?" She leans back. "I'm sorry. That was insensitive. You're seeing a bit of my own anger toward Chet. Use the time to your benefit, honey. Figure out what you want."

"Okay. The peace is nice. I didn't realize how much I walk on eggshells when Chet's around."

"Well, that tells you something, doesn't it?"

"It tells me I have a lot to figure out." I take another sip of coffee. "So, how's Dad?"

"He's worried about you."

"I'm worried about him."

She smiles. "I'm taking good care of him, but that's not to say this hasn't hurt him a lot. Both the thing with Chet, knowing how he hurt you and the kids, and, of course, the information Sandra doled out. Have you given any thought to how you're going to handle that?"

I set my elbows on the table and rest my head in my hands. Then I look back up at Cretia. "I have no idea. I've been so overwhelmed."

"I know. Well, either way, you have some work to do—with both Chet and your mother."

"What do you mean?"

"You have two significant people who've messed with your life in big ways. How you'll deal with that is a choice you need to make."

"You mean forgiving them?"

"That's one option."

"That's what you're suggesting though—that I forgive them?" I pick up my napkin and begin folding it into small sections.

"Honey, I'm not suggesting anything. But I will say this, remember that forgiveness isn't a feeling, it's a choice. And it's the one choice that may free you from bitterness."

"It's just…hard."

"Yes, it is. But here's the other thing to consider. Forgiveness and reconciliation are two different things. Forgiving someone doesn't always mean you restore the relationship. In some cases, restoration or reconciliation just isn't a wise choice, but you can still choose to forgive the person." She raises one eyebrow. "Or *people*, as the case may be."

I nod and then we sit in silence for a few minutes, both of us sipping our coffee.

"Honey, there's one more decision you'll have to make."

I know what she's going to say.

"You need to decide whether or not you want a paternity test. But don't think about it too long, okay? Your dad wants to give you time, but you can imagine, I'm sure, how hard this is on him."

I don't have to imagine, I *know* how hard it is on both of us.

Will the result of a paternity test make it any easier?

I will follow my instincts, be myself for good or ill, and see what will be the upshot.
John Muir

CHAPTER FORTY

Ted

THEY SAY, WHOEVER *they* are, that when it comes to women, men have a type. For example, once a leg man, always a leg man. That may be true for some men, but it's a broad generalization and one that doesn't apply to me. Sandra was a long-legged, dark-haired, dark-eyed woman with the broad cheekbones and features of her Native American heritage. She was a looker, no doubt about it. Cretia, on the other hand, is petite, with short, light-brown hair, and blue eyes. Also beautiful, and nothing like Sandra physically or in personality.

Sandra's looks lured me and her betrayal matured me.

When I met Cretia, although I was attracted to her physically, I looked beyond the exterior. I looked at her heart. Something I'd failed to notice in Sandra until it was too late.

Maybe when one type hurts you, you steer clear the next time around. I can't say for sure. One thing I can say is that Johnny married a woman who looked very much like Sandra.

Maybe that was just coincidence.

Or maybe not.

I pick up the cup of coffee the waitress just refilled for the third time. I got here thirty minutes early. I stare at the murky liquid and try to figure out if I'm doing the right thing.

Right or wrong, I'm doing the necessary thing. At least, that's what I tell myself. It's time to face reality. I may be four decades late, but it's time to deal with what I chose to deny the night Jessie was born.

Regardless of what Cretia thinks. And believe me, she's made no bones about what she thinks.

I shift my weight in the booth, trying to get comfortable. But this isn't a comfortable situation.

"Hello, my friend." Johnny comes up behind me, gives me a friendly slap on the back, then slides into the booth across from me. "It is, as always, good to see you."

I nod, then clear the gravel from my throat. I'm grateful when the waitress, who knows us, walks up to the table, flips Johnny's coffee cup over on its saucer, then fills it. "You two having pie this afternoon?"

I hold up one hand. "None for me."

Johnny pats his tummy. "I need to resist."

When she leaves, I shift in the booth again.

"So, Ted, you said there was something you needed to discuss with me when you called. From your expression, I see it's serious. What is it? Are you ill?"

"As fit as ever. It's nothing like that."

"Good to hear."

"How long've we been friends, Johnny?"

He laughs. "Too many years to count, old man."

I nod but don't smile with him. "I heard from Sandra a few weeks ago."

Johnny leans back in the booth and stares at me a moment. "Well…" His gaze never leaves mine. "It is about time. What did she have to say?"

I study Johnny's face, but his dark eyes reveal nothing.

"It's what she didn't say. That's what I want to talk to you about." I pick up my coffee cup, slurp a sip, then set it back down.

"Johnny's a straight shooter—a man of his word. You've always said that about him, Ted." Cretia's words nag at me.

"Speak your mind, Ted."

"Since Sandra left, trust hasn't come easily to you, honey. Be careful not to impose your issue on Johnny."

I pick up a packet of sugar and fidget with it. "She wrote me a letter. Said she needed to…clear her conscience."

Johnny waits.

"Well, I guess I'll start there—with what she did say, or the rest won't…"

"Honey, Johnny's your friend—he's always been your friend."

I sigh, set the sugar packet on the edge of the saucer, and pick up my cup again. Cretia's right, Johnny's a true friend, and not just to me but also to Jessie. For the first time since receiving Sandra's letter, I consider Johnny's friendship with Jessie. Why has he always taken such an interest in her? Is his friendship with her an extension of our friendship? Or is it something more? "It won't make sense unless I tell you all of it."

"I see this is hard for you, Ted. I am sorry."

I shake my head. "She told me there's a good chance that Jessie isn't mine. I may not be her biological father."

Johnny's mouth opens and his features go slack. He stares at me a moment, and it's evident he's shocked and trying to absorb the information.

I know how he feels.

He leans forward, puts his elbows on the table, and then bows his head in his hands. He sits that way for just a moment, then he straightens and squares his shoulders. "You are Jessica's father in every way that matters. Whether your DNA resides within her is of little concern. I don't mean to make light of the pain this news surely caused you, but in the end the only thing that matters is your relationship with your daughter."

I blink back tears and nod. "I know that, but…that girl has a right to know where she…comes from. You know her, Johnny—how important her heritage is to her. Not knowing her mother has driven her to lengths I don't fully understand. She's almost obsessed with creating and preserving a legacy for her own nuclear family—a legacy that, whether it makes sense to me or not, means something to her. And her entire career is built around preserving the cultural resources of her heritage—that link through her mother's lineage to the native people. I don't need to tell you all this, you know her." I shake my head again.

"Is Sandra telling the truth?"

"I don't know. I don't think truth was ever a priority for her. So why now? It's a question I've asked myself a hundred times over the last few weeks. It does seem just like her to make a selfish move like this—to want to clear her conscience for her own sake without regard for the pain it would cause others."

Johnny nods. "I assume from what you've said that Sandra didn't reveal the identity of the other man. Do you have any sense of who Sandra may have been involved with?"

The night of Jessie's birth replays as I look at Johnny across the table. Sandra's screams, the name she called out— the man she wanted by her side. I search my friend's face. Can I trust him or is he acting? I know what Cretia thinks. Do I accuse him?

Enough. Just say it!

I lean forward, elbows on the table. "Sandra called out another man's name the night she gave birth to Jessie, but I chose to ignore it. Chose to believe she was delirious from the pain of labor. I'm just an old fool, Johnny."

"No, my friend, you're just a man—human—and one who believes the best about those he loves. Whose name did she call?"

I lean back in the booth, stare at him a moment, then make my decision. "It doesn't matter now. It was no one I knew."

Long after Cretia's gone to bed, I sit at my desk and stare at a darkened computer screen, replaying not only my afternoon conversation with Johnny, but also the many years of our friendship. I chide myself for ever doubting him, yet this is what Sandra's actions did to me.

Or maybe it's what I let them do. Her actions planted doubt within me. But I am the one who allowed it to grow and harvested it, season after season. I can only hope Jessie doesn't allow Chet's actions to do the same to her. I hope, if nothing else, I can pass on the wisdom I've gained through my own mistakes.

I reach into the drawer, pull out the copy I made of the letter Sandra sent before I gave it to Jessie. I unfold the sheet of paper and read through it again, this time lingering on her closing paragraph—Sandra's explanation for the way in which she left us.

> The accusations of the evil spirits tormented me. And I knew they would soon punish me. Each time I held the sapling, her limbs reaching for me, I feared she too would suffer the inevitable punishment they would inflict. I could not risk her suffering for my actions, or hurting you further by endangering her.
>
> In the circular way of things, I imposed my own punishment, yet the evil ones have sneered and taunted me these many years anyway. May this truth I inflict finally silence them, as it silenced me.

Is it possible she still clung to the belief of her people—that evil spirits existed as a punishing force? Could she really have believed she was protecting Jessie? And me? Yet, in her attempt to protect, she caused the very suffering she claims she wanted to prevent.

Making sense of it is impossible. But maybe Jessie will find some comfort in knowing her mother tried, in her own way, to right the wrong she'd done.

I put the letter back into the drawer and turn off the lamp on my desk. It's time to put this to rest—to let the past go.

I just hope Jessie can do the same.

It would be far more pleasant to camp out...than to travel by
rule and make forced marches
to fixed points of...common confusion.
John Muir

CHAPTER FORTY-ONE

Haley

"HALEY, TIME TO get up." My mom opens the blinds in the den. "How's the sofa sleeper? Comfortable?"

I bury my head under my pillow. "I'm not going."

She lifts the pillow off my head. "You're going."

"But why? It's Friday. What difference does one more day make? I'll go back on Monday."

"Haley, we talked about this last night. You can't miss any more school. If you go today, you can get the assignments you need to make up and then you can work on them over the weekend." She stands next to the sofa sleeper and looks down at me. "I don't understand why you don't want to go. You've always loved school. Are you depressed? I know things are hard right—"

I fight a groan. "No. I'm not depressed." I put my arm over my eyes. It's too hard to explain it to her.

269

"Come on, get up then."

I move my arm and look at her. "If I said I was depressed, would you let me stay home?"

She smiles. "No. Then I'd *really* push you to get out of bed. And probably make an appointment for you with a counselor. Which, actually, if you'd like someone to talk to about—"

"No. Stop. I'm getting up."

"Haley, I'm serious."

"No. I don't need to talk to anybody. I talk to you. And...Chloe."

"Chloe? Is she helpful?"

I laugh. "No. Anyway, I didn't talk to her about...this."

"What about Zach? I know you told him. I thought he might come by this week."

I sit up and reach for my crutches. "He's got a lot going on." I don't look at her. Instead, I get up and head for the bathroom. But I can feel her staring at me as I go. When I reach the bathroom, I go in, close the door, then lean on the counter and stare at myself in the mirror, but not for long. I'm not beautiful, like Chloe, but I'm pretty okay with the way I look. I pull my brush out of the drawer. But sometimes, I don't know, I think Chloe might have an advantage.

Like Heather?

Where did that come from? I look back into the mirror. Zach's words about Heather come back to me now: *"She's hot... All the guys were trying to get her attention."*

All the guys?

That's not the kind of advantage I need.

I run the brush through my hair, then I open the drawer I moved all my makeup into when my mom helped me move my stuff downstairs. I look at the eye shadows, mascara, and lip glosses. I close the drawer and reach for my toothbrush.

The makeup's not worth the trouble today.

My mom pulls up to the stop sign, the one just before the school parking lot. Then she looks over at me. "Are you all right?"

"Why?" I didn't mean to snap.

She holds up one hand. "Sorry. I was just checking. You seem pretty subdued. And you didn't do much... I mean, it doesn't matter, you're beautiful, but usually you wear..."

"What?" I dare her to say whatever it was she was going to say. Not that I don't already know. She doesn't really wear much makeup, I mean, not on a daily basis, but I wear at least a little. Usually.

"Never mind. I'm just making sure you're okay."

"I told you I didn't want to go today."

She sighs. "Haley..."

I turn and stare out the window, but guilt gnaws on my conscience. I turn back. "I'm sorry. Okay? I'm just..." I exhale. "I don't know."

"You don't have to know. It is okay. Really, it is."

I nod, afraid to say anything else. Because the last thing I need is to get all emotional. "What are you doing today?"

"Well, I'm going into the office. I'm going to ask for a leave of absence."

"Um, it's fire season."

She turns into the parking lot. "I know."

"So, can you do that?"

She glances at me. "It's not great timing. At all. But I am doing it."

"What if they say no?"

"I'm doing it. I have to. I need to take some time..." She pulls up to the curb in front of the school, puts the truck in Park, and faces me. "I love my job, or...I think I do, but I need to make some changes and I need to take some time to decide what those changes will look like. I don't want to be irresponsible or leave them in a lurch, but I also won't do my job well until...I figure some things out."

"Okay. I hope it works out." I open the door.

"Hey, have a good day. It can't be that bad, right?"

I shrug. "Actually, yeah, it can. But I'll survive."

"Do you need help with your backpack?"

"No, I've got it." I get out of the car, grab my backpack off the floorboard, slip it over my shoulders, then lean in and grab my crutches from behind the seat. "See ya." I close the door and turn to go. I make my way up the curb and head toward the quad. But then I stop and my heart does some kind of acrobatic leap into my throat.

Chloe, who's wearing her short shorts and a top she'll probably get sent home for, is on tiptoe, whispering something into Zach's ear. He throws his head back and laughs and she shoves him, in some sort of, like, playful, hot-girl move.

A move, by the way, that he seems totally into.

He looks up and sees me. His expression blank at first, then he smiles and waves like nothing's wrong and starts walking toward me.

"Haley!" Chloe squeals. "You're here!"

This is exactly what I knew would happen today. What I know has been going on all week.

"Hey, I've missed you." Zach leans in to give me a hug, but my crutches get in the way, sort of. Or maybe I make sure they get in the way.

"I'm so glad you're back! School is sooo boring without you." Chloe reaches over and tugs on the sleeve of my shirt. "Cute top, by the way."

I look down at the *Go Climb a Mountain* T-shirt I threw on this morning. "It's a T-shirt, Chloe."

"It's a cute color."

"Here, let me take your backpack." Zach reaches for it.

"It's fine. I've got it."

"Okay. How's the leg?" He gestures to my cast.

"Fine. I need to go. I have a doctor's excuse I have to take to the office."

"I'll go with—"

"I can handle it, okay?" My tone is, like, so mean, and I see Chloe's expression register that things are not okay between us.

Between Chloe and me.

And Zach and me.

Well, they can just deal with it. I turn and head for the office. When I turn the corner at the hallway, I glance back. Chloe's off talking to someone else, but Zach is just watching me, standing alone, looking...sad. I go past the office and into the girls' restroom, where I lock myself in a stall. I pull toilet paper out of the dispenser and wipe my eyes and nose.

I swear, all I do anymore is cry.

I'm pathetic.

"What's up with you? Are you mad at me? And at Zach? You were so weird this morning." Chloe's whisper is a mixture of concern and frustration.

We have English together during third period and we sit next to each other. I can't avoid her.

"What'd we do?"

I don't look at her. "I'm sure you can figure it out, Chloe."

"So, are you, like, mad that I was talking to Zach?"

"Haley? Chloe? Do you ladies need to take that conversation outside?" Mrs. Chalmers gives us "the look" from the front of the classroom.

I slouch down in my seat and shake my head. Chloe does the same but then looks over at me and raises her eyebrows, like she's still expecting an answer to her question.

After class she follows me into the hallway. "Haley, you didn't answer me. Are you mad because I was talking to Zach?"

"You can talk to whoever you want to."

"Fine."

"Fine." But it's not fine and we both know it. "Where's Grant?"

"Grant?"

"Yeah, *your* boyfriend, remember?"

She rolls her eyes. "I don't know. Probably playing a video game somewhere." Then her tone softens. "We're not really together anymore."

Great. "Since when?"

She looks at me, then looks down at the ground. "Since last night."

When she looks at me again, there's something in her expression I can't read. But whatever it is worries me, and the anger that's followed me around all morning just sort of ditches me. "What happened?"

She shrugs. "Just, you know, stuff."

"You should have called me."

"Yeah, it was late, so…"

"Did you break up with him?"

There are tears in her big blue eyes, and she shakes her head.

"Oh… Sorry. But you weren't sure about him anyway, right?"

She looks down at the ground.

"Chloe? What happened?" Balancing my crutch under my arm, I reach out and put my hand on her shoulder. "Are you okay?"

She still doesn't look at me but mumbles, "I just need you to not be mad at me, okay?" She glances up at me.

"Okay." I mean, I'm not really mad at her, it's just…everything.

"I mean, if you don't want me to talk to Zach, I won't. I get it. But it doesn't mean anything. We're just friends, you know? He's so totally into you. I mean, he wouldn't ever even think about me like that. Really. Anyway, I would never do that to you, Haley. You're my best friend."

How could I have forgotten that? "I'm sorry I didn't…trust you. I'm just kind of messed up right now."

She sniffs and then reaches over and gives me a hug.

"But, are you okay?" I ask when she pulls away.

"I guess. I just thought…" She looks away again but doesn't say anything more.

I have to ask. "Did you sleep with him?"

She doesn't answer.

"Chloe?"

When she looks at me again the tears are gone. "No. I remembered what you said, you know, about respecting myself. But I thought maybe he'd just, you know, like me for me. But when I told him I wasn't going to…he broke up with me."

"That makes me so mad! Chloe, you deserve better than that. He isn't worth your tears or your time. What's with guys anyway?"

"But…not all guys are like that."

I shake my head. If only I could be sure about that.

I avoid Zach until I get a text from him asking if I want to get lunch with him. I don't know if he means go off campus and get lunch or just get lunch here. So I text back and tell him I can't leave without a note from my parents. I hope that will take care of it. But he texts back and says we can eat here. So I'm stuck.

When I go to meet him by the snack bar, he's standing with a group of his friends. I stay back until he notices me, which gives me a couple of minutes to try and get my mind straight, but it's not long enough.

As soon as he sees me he comes and joins me. "Hey. How are you?"

He seems kind of guarded or something, but I don't blame him after the way I acted this morning. And really, I've been pretty standoffish all week. "I'm fine."

"Good."

Okay. Now what? "How are you?"

He smiles. "Me? I'm good. But, you know, I've missed you. So things were a little crazy at home this week?"

I shrug. "A little."

"How's that whole thing with your parents going?"

I can tell by his expression that he really cares and wants to know, but… "Um, could we maybe talk about something else?"

He hesitates. "Yeah, sure." He looks around, then back at me. "What do you want for lunch?"

"I have a sandwich in my backpack."

His tone is deflated. "Oh."

"So maybe I'll go sit while you get something. It's kind of hard to just stand here."

"Definitely. Want to grab that table under the tree?" He points.

"Sure."

"Can I bring you a drink or a cookie or something?"

"No, I'm good."

The whole conversation is awkward, and I know it's my fault. When I get to the table, I lean my crutches against the bench and set my backpack down. My ankle hurts and my arms are tired from using the crutches to get around all morning. I sit on the bench and then fold my arms on the table and rest my head on my arms. I'm so tired. Tired of the noise. Tired of all the talking. I want to go someplace quiet. I close my eyes, but that's like turning up the volume and the talking turns to yelling. And I can't get away from it, because it's all inside my head.

"She's hot."

"I'm writing to apologize for my involvement with your husband."

"All the guys were trying to get her attention."

"When you discovered the affair…"

"Not all guys are like that, Haley."

I never thought my dad was. I trusted him. I mean, I never even thought about needing to trust him, I just did. And if he would do what he did, then any guy could do it.

"Haley?"

I open my eyes and jerk my head up.

"Sorry, were you asleep?" Zach sets his food down on the table.

I shake my head. "Um, no."

"Are you okay?"

I shake my head again and Zach becomes a blur through my tears. "I can't...I can't do this."

"Do what?" He reaches over to touch my arm, but I pull it away. "Haley?"

"This! I can't do this whole...relationship thing. I...I have to go." I get up from the table, or try to, but lifting my cast over the bench doesn't make for an easy getaway.

Zach jumps up and comes around to my side of the table. He stands there as I try to get my leg over the bench and then get to my feet. He talks the whole time.

"Wait, don't go. Please. Haley, whatever's going on, we can figure it out. I mean, I don't want to pressure you, but—"

"No!" I scramble to get my backpack on and then grab my crutches. "Just...just leave me alone!"

"Where"—I try to catch my breath—"are you?"

"Haley? You're crying? What's wrong?"

"Mom, can you....come get...me?" I sob. "Now?"

"Are you sick?"

"No, but can you just...come?"

"I just pulled into our driveway, but I'll turn around. I'll be there in ten or fifteen minutes, okay? Can you hang on?"

"Yeah. Can...you call"—I hiccup—"the school office?"

"Yes, I will. I'll tell them you're not feeling well, which sounds like it's true. I love you. I'll be there as soon as I can."

I stay on the bench in front of the school where I came after talking to Zach. I wish I had sunglasses in my backpack that I could hide behind. I wipe my face again and then sniff. *Stop crying. Just stop.*

I take a deep breath, and that helps for a second—but then the tears gush again.

*Nature is doing what she can...patiently trying
to heal every raw scar.*
John Muir

CHAPTER FORTY-TWO

Jessie

SINCE HALEY TURNED six, I've only seen her cry a handful of times, and usually because she was frustrated or angry. This week, she's shed more tears than not. And to hear her sobbing just now, oh…

I put my hand over my heart, then I put a little more pressure on the accelerator.

I can handle her attitude. And her anger. But her tears slay me.

A stream of grief and a rivulet of anger flow through me, as they have all week. Does Chet have any idea what he's done? The upheaval he's caused? My grip on the steering wheel tightens.

When I pull into the school parking lot, Haley is sitting on a bench out front. Her petite frame appears smaller than usual. Her shoulders are hunched forward and her head is down. Her long, dark hair hangs forward—a curtain veiling her face. Her casted leg is kicked out in front of her, and her crutches lean against the bench next to her. Oh, how I wish I could protect her—keep her from the pain of this reality.

She looks up when she hears the truck. Even from here I can see her complexion is mottled from crying. Her nose is red and her eyes swollen. I park, hop out, and go around to help her. I don't say anything, I just pick up her backpack, hand her the crutches, then put my hand on her back as she makes her way to the truck.

When I get into the truck, Haley is bent forward, hands covering her face, and her shoulders shake. Again, I reach over and put my hand on her shoulder and my own eyes well. I swallow the emotion lodged in my throat. "Haley? Honey?"

She doesn't respond, so I put the truck into gear and pull away from the curb. When she's ready to talk, there are better places for a conversation than sitting in front of her school. By the time I pull out of the parking lot, she's lifted her head and taken her hands away from her face.

She turns to me. "Tissue?"

"Oh, sorry. There may be some in the console."

She opens the console between us and holds up a couple of crumpled napkins. She raises her eyebrows.

"I guess that's all I have."

"Whatever," she mumbles.

This is new terrain for me with Haley, and I'm not sure which direction to go, but the direct route seems wise. "What happened?"

She blows her nose, then leans back against the seat of the truck. "Chloe…" She stares at the ceiling of the truck. "She told Grant, her boyfriend, that she wouldn't"—she glances over at me—"you know, like, sleep with him."

She seems to wait for a response from me, so I nod. I'm not shocked. "Okay."

"So he broke up with her."

"Oh, I'm sorry. But, obviously, he isn't good for her if that's all he wants." This seems like the appropriate response, but how does this connect to Haley's tears?

"So, anyway, at lunch…" She turns and stares out the window for a second, then turns back and looks straight ahead. "I broke up with Zach. I mean, I guess that's what…happened."

I glance her way and see her chin tremble.

"Were you having the same issue with Zach?" I can't imagine they've had enough time alone for him to be pressuring her about sex, but…

"Mom, no."

"Okay, so explain your decision to me."

"It wasn't a decision. It just sort of happened. But"— anger punctuates her tone—"that's all guys care about! You should totally get that after what dad did. I don't need that, you know? Zach will be the same way. I mean…how am I supposed to trust him? I can't even trust my own dad." She covers her face again.

The highway wavers as tears blur my vision. I pull off the road onto a wide shoulder, then drive a few more feet into a small rest area. I put the truck into Park, roll down the windows, and turn the ignition off. I use those few seconds to breathe, to think, to gather my own emotions. I have no idea what to say, but I trust as I open my mouth that something halfway intelligent will come out.

"Oh, Haley"—I take a deep breath—"it isn't all men. There are good, strong men. Look at your grandpa. Is he perfect? No. But he is a man of integrity. A man of his word. A man you can trust."

Haley sniffs and stares straight ahead. She's listening, so I keep talking. "And think about it. For every man who has an affair, there's a woman involved too."

She looks at me, her expression telling me she hadn't considered that.

"We're all susceptible to making really bad choices. Choices that hurt those we love."

"Yeah, but…it just seems like guys are more that way."

I'm just beginning to see, I know, the extent of the wounding Chet's actions caused.

In the same way my mother's actions wounded me? Oh...

"Haley, I understand what you're feeling. Not exactly, but I think I have a good idea."

My own fears, the burdens I've carried for over four decades, much like the tears in the basket of my dreams, weigh on my shoulders now. Yet in a brief moment of enlightenment, I'm also oddly grateful for the story I'm about to share with my daughter. It lets me understand a bit of her heartache. "Remember earlier in the week when I told you Grandpa told me something and I'd tell you about it later?"

She nods.

I take a deep breath and shift in my seat, "A few weeks ago, he received a letter from my—" The word feels foreign in my mouth. "Mother."

Her eyes widen.

I have wondered all week about the timing of the letter. Why now? But, in this moment, it all seems to make sense. "Sometime before I was born, around the time I would have been conceived, my mother had an affair."

"That's why she left?"

"Yes—so we both have parents who've made that choice, one male, one female. But there's more to it than that." I move one hand to the base of my neck and rub the knot of tension I find there. "Because of the timing of the affair, when she discovered she was pregnant, she wasn't sure..." Though I've considered the implications of my mother's actions this week, I haven't let myself fully delve into what they mean for me. Or for my dad.

"Oh no." Haley's horrified whisper splits the silence.

So I don't have to explain it to her, but I need to say it out loud anyway. I need to hear the truth—spoken in my own voice—to accept the truth delivered to me whether I want to or not.

I drop my hand back to my lap and stare straight ahead. My tone is flat, but I speak the words. "She wasn't sure who fathered me. If it was the man she had the affair with, or if it was"—I glance at Haley—"your grandpa. But it seems she thinks there's a good chance it was the other man."

"Who was the other man?"

"I don't know. She didn't say."

"But she stayed with Grandpa until after you were born, right?"

"Yes."

"But…did she go with the other man, or what? Why did she leave?"

"I've never known. Not until the letter." I look at Haley. This part of the story speaks of Chet as much as it does of my mother. "She was so burdened. So ashamed of her actions, that she couldn't stand staying. Native Americans believe that evil spirits punish them, and their families, for their wrong acts. So she feared my dad and I would also suffer whatever punishment she received. So she left." I lift my hands, palms up. "I don't know. I guess in some way she felt she was protecting us—me."

"But really, she punished herself, right? I mean, she didn't get to be your mom."

Haley speaks aloud what I've only begun to consider, and the reality of her words stabs me anew. "That's what she said." I sigh. "She suffered too. And, Haley, your dad will also suffer. His actions, whether he knows it now or not, will wound him as much as they've wounded you, and Tyler, and me."

"Yeah, but—"

"I'm not saying he isn't responsible for his actions. He is. He made a choice. But he will also suffer consequences. It isn't our place to judge him, but it's simple truth that consequences are part of the natural order of life." I shrug. "Maybe understanding that makes it easier to forgive because we aren't worrying about"—I turn from Haley and look out the front window of the truck—"making him pay for what he's done." I know I'm speaking to myself as much, or maybe more so, than I am to Haley.

We both stare out the windshield for a few minutes, until Haley breaks the silence. "Mom, are you going to do a test to find out if Grandpa is your real dad—your biological father?"

It's the same question Cretia asked me to consider—and not to linger too long in answering.

"Oh, Haley..." I lean my head back against the seat. "I don't know. Grandpa offered. Told me he was willing to do a paternity test if I want, but I don't know. I've had too much on my mind to really think it through."

She shrugs. "Maybe it doesn't matter."

I look over at her. "Maybe not."

Then she shrugs again. "Or, maybe it does."

I sigh again. "Exactly."

When we get home, I help Haley crawl into the bed we made up in the den. I think she's asleep before I finish propping her leg on a pillow. The storm of emotions she experienced today took their toll. Maybe I sent her back to school too soon, but then the conversation we had in the truck was so needed.

Things worked out as they should.

Wandering through conversation with my daughter isn't something I've had many opportunities to do. Which leads me back to the decision I made and executed this morning—to take a leave of absence.

Haley is right, fire season isn't good timing. But if I had any doubts about that choice, the call from her this afternoon affirmed it. Her life, and my own, are unpredictable right now. I want to be the steady force—the constant she can count on as we navigate the unknown.

As we drove home today, I made another decision. I pull my phone out of my back pocket and call Cretia.

"Hi, honey, what's up?"

I smile—her voice, her availability is such a comfort. "Hi, I want to ask you for a referral."

"What kind of referral?"

"A counselor. Someone who will help me through…everything. But also someone Haley can talk to. Do you think that could be the same person?"

"Sure it can. And honey, that's a good move. For both of you. I still have some contacts—I'll e-mail you a couple of names and numbers."

"Thanks."

After chatting with Cretia a few more minutes, I hang up, go to the refrigerator, pour myself a glass of iced tea, and then take it out to the patio where I land. I'm putting a permanent indent in one of the chair cushions this week. I put my feet up on the ottoman and stare out at the forest, the trees unmoving in the heat of afternoon.

If Chet and I divorce, how will I afford to live? Our income has been pretty equal in recent years, but we're dependent on both incomes to maintain the house. Oh, the thought of selling the house, finding another place to live…

I rub my shoulder.

I'd need a place for Haley and a room for Tyler when he's home on breaks from school. How would I afford a home like what we'd need on my own? I consider the equity we have in the house, an amount we'd split. It would help, but…

One step at a time.

This is becoming my mantra. If I look ahead, even a day, the enormity of it all crashes in on me.

I breathe deep and then lay my head back on the seat cushion. Instead of looking ahead to what *might* happen, I spend the next hour considering what, if I could rebuild our marriage, it might look like. I compile a mental list of changes both Chet and I need to make. I define a few of those boundaries that Cretia suggested I set. I even let myself dream about what could be…

When the doorbell rings, I hear it through an open window in the kitchen. I get up, annoyed. Who can that be? I go back inside and make my way through the house to the front door. When I open it, a large bouquet of sunflowers is thrust in my face.

"Delivery for"—the young delivery man looks down at a clipboard—"Haley Weaver."

"I'll take them."

I sign for the flowers and then take them into the kitchen and set the vase on the island. As I do, I hear the thud of Haley's crutches on the floor in the hallway. When she joins me in the kitchen, her eyes are still blurred with sleep.

"Sorry, did the doorbell wake you?"

She nods. "Who sent you those?"

"They're not mine. They're for you. There's a card attached." I point at the arrangement. "Zach, maybe?"

She reaches for the card, opens the small envelope, and then reads the message. She shakes her head, sets the card on the island, and then turns and goes back the way she came.

I pick up the card and read it.

Chipmunk,

You know I love you. Call me.

Dad

I take the card and go down the hall to the den, where Haley's back on the bed. "Want to talk about it?"

"No."

"Okay." If only I could help her in some way. "If you change your mind, I'm here." Then I turn to go.

"I don't want to talk about Dad. But…"

I turn back.

She sits up. "What do you think I should do about Zach?"

I sit on the end of the bed. "Well, what do you want your relationship with him to look like?"

She lifts one shoulder. "I don't know. I…I liked the way it was going. But…"

"You're afraid?"

She looks at me, her eyes wide. "Yeah."

"You know I wasn't thrilled with the idea of you having a boyfriend, but Zach seems like a nice guy. He certainly took good care of you out on the trail. I'm glad I got to meet him at the clinic and thank him."

"Yeah, he wasn't too happy when he found out I lied about getting permission to go on the hike. He was worried that you and Dad might think he'd encouraged me to go without asking for permission. Stuff like that is important to him."

"Well, that says a lot about his character, don't you think?"

"Maybe."

I look at my daughter, who's so much more mature than I was at her age. She's always had wisdom beyond her years while somehow still being a typical kid. I'm not sure how to advise her, but then something occurs to me and I smile.

I lean forward and put my hand on Haley's knee. "What's your heart telling you about Zach?"

"My heart?"

"Yeah, your heart. That's what your grandma Cretia always asks me. You can't always rely on your emotions, but it's good to pay attention to your instinct, or your heart, and factor it in when you're making a decision."

"Um, I'll think about it."

I pat her leg. "Okay."

As I leave Haley to her thoughts and wander back outside, it occurs to me that while I would never wish the pain of these circumstances on my daughter—*no* one should have to deal with betrayal—today I've witnessed something good sprouting from the soil of destruction. There is a new depth, maybe a new level of trust, in Haley's relationship with me.

If nothing else, the pain we're experiencing is drawing us together.

*No portion of the world is so barren as not to yield a rich and
precious harvest of divine truth.*
John Muir

CHAPTER FORTY-THREE

Haley

"I'M SICK OF this thing." I lift my leg off the bed,
the cast making the movement awkward.

"When do you get it off?" Chloe reaches for the remote
on my mom's nightstand.

"Like, five more weeks, at the earliest."

"Bummer." She flips on the TV. Then looks over at me.
"Wait, how many weeks until Winter Formal?"

I shrug. "It's not until December. Anyway, it doesn't
matter."

"Um, yeah it matters. You want that thing on under a
dress? You couldn't wear cute shoes."

"Chloe, December? Anyway, I'm not going."

"But you said Zach already asked you."

"Here, give me the remote."

Chloe sticks the remote behind her back. "Tell me why you're not going to Winter Formal, and then I'll give it to you."

"Chloe"—I roll my eyes—"I'm not going because I'm not with Zach anymore. I...sort of broke up with him during lunch yesterday."

"What? Is that why you left early? Oh, now I get it. That's why he was such a zombie yesterday afternoon. But he's so great. And he likes you sooo much. I don't get it. I totally don't get it. What happened?"

I put out my hand. "The remote?"

She pulls it out from behind her and starts to hand it to me. "What happened?"

"I don't know. I really don't. Can we just watch TV?"

She drops the remote on the bed between us. "Hey, at least we're both single now."

"Yeah." I pick up the remote. "So, he was a zombie?"

"Totally. I waved to him in the hall after last period. He looked at me and then walked right past me without saying anything. He was out of it."

"Do you think...?"

"What?"

"Do you think I hurt him?"

Chloe rolls her eyes. "Duh."

After Chloe leaves I go out to the kitchen where the vase of sunflowers is still sitting on the island. My mom put the card back in the little envelope and it's sitting next to the vase. I lean on my crutches and stare at the flowers for a long time. I finally reach for the card, open it, and read it again. For the first time since reading that stupid e-mail from Heather, I sort of miss my dad.

Or maybe I miss who I thought he was. I'm not sure. I toss the card back onto the counter.

"What are you going to do?"

I turn around. My mom is standing behind me—I didn't hear her come into the kitchen.

I shrug. "I don't know."

She comes around and stands next to me and looks at the flowers. Then she turns to me. "You know, your relationship with your dad is separate from my relationship with your dad."

"What do you mean?"

"You have your own relationship with him, and however you choose to handle that relationship is okay with me. In other words, if you want to call him, Haley, that's okay."

"What if I don't want to?"

"That's okay too. Cretia said something to me yesterday that made sense. She explained that forgiveness and reconciliation aren't the same thing. You can forgive someone without continuing the same relationship you've had with them."

Mom pulls out one of the bar stools for me and I sit down.

"I don't know what's going to happen between your dad and me, Haley, but even if our relationship can't be restored, that doesn't mean your relationship with him can't be."

I lean my elbows on the counter. "So, like, you could forgive Dad and still get a divorce, but you could forgive your mother and have a relationship with her?"

She stares at me for a few seconds, then pulls out the other bar stool and sits down before she says anything. "Theoretically. The difference is that I've never had a relationship with my mother, but you've had a relationship with your dad. A pretty close relationship."

"Yeah, but... Was it even real? I mean, the dad I thought I knew would never do what he did. I don't know what's true."

She sighs. "I know. I'm struggling with the same feeling. Remember when I asked you yesterday if you were depressed and I mentioned a counselor?"

"Yeah."

"Well, I'm thinking it might be a good idea for each of us to talk to someone. You know, someone objective who can help us deal with all of this. You could even talk about Zach, or anything else this…" She hesitates, like she can't think of the word she wants to use, but then comes up with it. "This upheaval has impacted in your life. Would you be willing to talk to someone?"

Would I? "I don't know. Maybe."

"Think about it, okay? Grandma Cretia sent me a couple of names of counselors and I'm going to make an appointment for myself. I'll make one for you too if you'll go. I think it could be helpful."

"I'll think about it."

"Okay." She gets up. "What do you want me to do with the flowers?"

Part of me wants to tell her to put them in the garbage, but sunflowers are my favorite. "Put them in the den, I guess."

"Okay." She does as I ask.

I pull my phone out of the pocket of my shorts and set it on the counter. I spin it around a few times, then pick it up. I should text Zach, but I don't know what to say. I type and delete, type and delete. Then I set the phone back down and rest my head on my arms on the counter.

I guess I should just tell him the truth.

I just wish I knew what it was.

Remember your penitential promises.
John Muir

CHAPTER FORTY-FOUR

Ted

I PULL THE piece of smooth pine off my lathe and then sand the edges. "That'll do." I sweep up the sawdust and leave the pieces of the project, one of Cretia's many *ideas*, on the workbench. I want to wait until she's here so I can test the stain color on a scrap of wood and get her approval. I'm not taking any chances and wasting an entire Saturday just because I picked the wrong color.

I shut off the garage light and head into the house, where my cell phone is vibrating on the kitchen counter. Guess I forgot to turn the volume back on after we got up this morning. I pick up the phone and see Chet's name on the screen. What in the world? Wish I'd turned the phone off altogether.

But I pick up the call. "Hello."

"Hi, Ted, thanks for answering."

"Curiosity got the best of me. Can't imagine what you'd have to say to me."

"I just want to set the record straight on something."

"You can try." My tone is gruff, I know, but as far as I'm concerned, Chet should be thankful I'm even giving him the time of day.

"Jess seems to have gotten a wrong idea, and I want to clear it up since it seems she's telling everyone the same story—my daughter included."

His daughter? I'm tempted to hang up on him right now, but again, I'm curious. "What story is that?"

"She seems to think the, uh, relationship I was involved in was more…intimate than it was. I told her it was an emotional thing."

"I see. So you told her it was an emotional thing or you told her it was *just* an emotional thing?"

He hesitates. "Listen, Ted, I was drawn to that woman—but it's not like I wanted to leave Jess. It was just a stupid mistake. I got in over my head. Actually, I was hoping maybe you'd talk to her—"

"Chet, if you expect me to listen to you, then you've got one option: honesty. And if you want your marriage to work, you've got the same option with Jessie. Anything less than total honesty is a waste of my time and hers."

"Of course, no question."

"All right then, was it also a physical relationship? Did you have relations with this woman? And what about the other women in question?"

"That depends on how you define relations."

"I'll tell you what, Chet. I know exactly how I define relations and I think you're smart enough to figure it out too. We're men. We know what we're talking about. And since we're discussing definitions, I suggest you go find yourself a dictionary and look up the word *honest*. And when you've figured out what that means, you call me back. Until then, don't bother. I'm hanging up now."

"Wait, Ted—"

Cretia comes in the back door with a bag of groceries.

I press the End button on my phone. I wasn't born yesterday. I know an evasive response when I hear one. *"That depends on how you define relations."*

My foot.

"From the look on your face, I'm almost afraid to ask who you were talking to." She sets the bag on the kitchen counter.

"That would be the idiot my daughter married."

"Oh, dear. Why did he call?"

"To manipulate me."

She raises her eyebrows and shakes her head. "Oh honey, don't be like that. What did he say?"

"Gave me some malarkey about an emotional affair with that woman. Said that's all it was."

"Yes, Jessie told me about that when I had coffee with her."

I just barely halt the growl that crawls up my throat. "And you didn't tell me?"

"Honey, you know me better than that. That was for her to share with you, not me. After talking to Chet, I take it you don't believe him?"

"Not as far as I could throw him, which at my age, isn't very far. I think he's more concerned with image management than he is with the truth. Or with saving his marriage, for that matter. I told him when he's ready to be honest, I'll consider listening to him."

"Good for you. Would you like a cup of coffee?"

I lean down and give Cretia a kiss. "Depends. Do we have anything sweet to go with the coffee?"

"I can probably find something."

"Great." I pat my tummy. "I deserve something good after that call. Are there more groceries in the car?"

"No, honey. You sit down. I just picked up a few things."

I take a seat at the kitchen table while Cretia makes a pot of decaf. I fiddle with my phone a minute, then make a decision. "It's time I call Jessie. Not about that mess with her mother, but to see how she's doing with the other mess in her life. And how Haley's doing."

Cretia's warm smile eases some of the tension in my gut. "I think that's a fine idea, Ted. She needs you."

When I called, Jessie told me to come on over. I pull my sedan into the driveway, get out, then follow the decomposed granite walkway I helped Chet put in to the front door. I lumber up the two stone steps to the porch and rap my knuckles on the craftsman-style front door Jessie stained herself when they built the place.

So much work went into this home and for what? I can't pretend to guess what Chet was thinking. Or wasn't thinking. I shake my head. Does the man ever think? Sure he does, but only about himse—

"Hi, Grandpa." Haley stands at the open door.

"Well, look at you. You must have the hang of those things by now"—I point at her crutches—"if your mom has you on door duty." I walk in and give her a kiss on one cheek.

"I told her I'd let you in, but yeah, I've gotten the hang of them."

"How's the ankle feeling?"

"It's okay, I guess."

"And how's that nice young man, Zachary?"

Haley rolls her eyes. "Don't ask."

"Uh-oh."

"Exactly."

"Well, honey, take it from someone with a lot of years of experience—these things tend to work out for the best."

"Maybe." She closes the front door. "Mom's outside—on the back porch. She has a glass of iced tea out there for you."

"Sounds good. The afternoon's heating up." I head for the back porch, then stop. "You're coming too, aren't you?"

Haley leans on her crutches in the entry hall. "Maybe later. I'm kind of in the middle of something."

"Okay, but don't wait too long. I want time with both my girls."

She smiles at me, but the usual light in her eyes has dimmed.

I so want to hunt Chet down and hurt him.

"Dad?" Jessie leans in the back door.

"I'm coming." I make my way through the living room and kitchen to join Jessie on the back porch, where, sure enough, two glasses of tea sit sweating on the table between the outdoor chairs. "This looks inviting."

"I've spent a lot of time out here this week."

"You heading back to work on Monday?" I take one of the chairs and pick up a glass.

Jessie sits down and then stares out at the trees behind the patch of lawn. "I took a leave of absence." She looks over at me.

I frown. "Surprised they let you."

"Me too, actually. But I was prepared to quit if they didn't, though I didn't threaten that, of course." She smiles, but like Haley, her gaze is vacant. "I'm all talk though. How could I quit when I may need that income more than ever now?"

"I suppose that might be true." I take a sip of the iced tea, then set the glass back on the table and shift toward Jessie so I can see her. "How're you holding up? And don't tell me fine. I want the real answer."

This time, there's no smile on her face. She knits her brow and then lifts her hands. "I don't know. That's the honest answer. I have moments of clarity, but they're matched by moments of confusion. And today…I'm just tired."

"Well, I guess that's to be expected. Give yourself time."

"I am."

"How's our girl?" I tilt my head, gesturing toward the house.

She sighs. "She's struggling. And Chet has no idea. He has no concept of the pain he's caused. Haley broke up with Zach this week because she doesn't know if she can trust him. She said if she can't trust her own dad, how can she trust Zach?" She rolls her shoulders back.

I can almost see the tension her body holds. I put my hands, palms down, on the arms of the chair and my jaw clenches. "Chet called me this morning."

Jessie's astonishment is clear on her features. "What? Why?"

"Wanted to set *me* straight. Well, not me personally, I guess. Wanted to set the record straight. As if that's possible. Gave me some baloney about an emotional affair with that woman."

"You don't believe him?"

"Do you?"

Her shoulders droop. "No. Anyway, it doesn't matter. I've decided I don't need details. If I'd trusted Chet in the first place, I wouldn't doubt him now. But when I look back, he's never given me reason to trust him. Instead, he just figured I'd comply with whatever he was doing. And, stupidly, I did. I didn't ask questions or challenge him." She waves her hand. "That's not new information to you. It's just new to me, and I'm still processing it."

She leans toward me. "Dad, what would you have done if you'd discovered my mother's affair? Would you have tried to make it work?"

I take my baseball cap off and set it in my lap. "Boy, that's not an easy question. Especially knowing what I do…" Well, no need to spell it out. It seems for today, we have a silent agreement not to talk about what we both know now. "I loved your mother, Jessie. And you were just a tiny thing. I think I'd have tried. I'd have set some ground rules, that's for sure, but if there'd been a chance to make things work…" I shrug. "It's hard to say all these years later."

Jessie's quiet for a few minutes, staring out at those trees again, then she looks back at me. "What kind of ground rules?"

"We talking about me now or you?"

"I'm...not sure."

I detect fear in her tone and my fists clench. *Chet!* I take a deep breath and then exhale between my teeth. That man doesn't deserve another chance, but that's not my decision to make. "Well, Cretia calls them *boundaries*, and if I were you, I'd set a boatload of 'em. But I can't tell you what they should be.

She sinks back in her chair and the slight shake of her head is almost imperceptible. "I can't begin to imagine Chet letting me set any type of boundary—"

"Letting you?" I growl. "This isn't about him *letting* you do anything. This is about him offering you what you need. This is about him taking responsibility for his actions. Letting you?" I grip the arm of the chair, wishing it were Chet's neck. That he's done this to my daughter...

Unbelievable.

"No, Jessie, you've got to get it into your head that you're only telling him what you need. And deserve."

Tears fill her eyes. "I don't know." She wipes a stray tear from her cheek. "You're right, but..."

As much as I love her, this isn't a time for tears. I straighten in the chair. "Jessie, where's that resolve I saw on Sunday? You told me you'd need accountability. So I'm holding you accountable. It isn't time for fear or to act like a pansy, you got that? You're a strong woman. Now is the time to be a strong wife. For your sake and Chet's. Cretia would no more let me treat her the way Chet treats you than she'd let a rattlesnake slither into her bed. You got that? I've kept quiet too long, Jessica, but no more. It is time for you to take a stand. A firm stand."

She sits a little taller in the chair, her shoulders no longer drooping, and the spark has returned to her eyes.

Anger, I'm guessing. Good. It's just what she needs. And I'll fan that spark until it blazes.

I lean back in my chair. "So what's it going to be, Jessie? What are *your* ground rules?"

*There are no unwritten pages in Nature, but
everywhere line upon line. In like manner every human heart
and mind is written upon as created.*
John Muir

CHAPTER FORTY-FIVE

Haley

I CRUTCH MY way out of the den, down the hall, and into the kitchen, where I pour myself a glass of milk. I stand in front of the refrigerator to drink it because it's impossible to carry anything and go anywhere at the same time. My mom and my grandpa's voices drift through the open window and more than once, I hear my dad's name.

Whatever. I'm sick of the drama.

I leave the glass on the counter and gimp my way back to the den, but when I get there, I just stand in the doorway. The flowers from my dad are on his desk, and my stuff is scattered across the room. Clothes hang over his desk chair. Books, magazines, and my laptop are piled on the floor next to the bed.

My stuff might be in here, but it's not my room.

And it doesn't feel like my room.

It doesn't feel—I think about it a minute—normal.

Normal? I swallow the lump in my throat. Nothing is normal anymore. And I want normal.

I, like, *need* normal.

I go into the den, make my way to the sofa-sleeper bed, pick up the pillow I've been using, and pull the pillowcase off. I lean my crutches against the wall, and then turn around and sit on the edge of the bed so I can bend to reach the pile on the floor. I pick up two books and drop them into the pillowcase, then I toss a couple of magazines, a tube of lip balm, and my comb in too. The last thing I put inside the pillowcase is my laptop. I set the full pillowcase on the bed, stand up, and make sure my phone is in my pocket. Then I reach for my crutches. With them held under my arms, I grab the pillowcase and wrap the top of it around my hand and then grab the handles of the crutches. The pillowcase dangles alongside one crutch.

I take a few steps toward the door of the den, the pillowcase swinging at my side, the laptop inside banging against the crutch. It's awkward, but it'll work.

I make my way out of the den and down the hall. It's slow, but I make it to the bottom of the stairs, where I stand for several seconds staring at the bottom step. This is stupid. I climb mountains—what's a few stairs? I put my crutches on the bottom stair, then my good foot, and I heave myself and my heavy bag of cargo up onto the step.

One stair at a time, I get myself up all fourteen steps. When I finally reach the landing, I'm just a few feet from my own bedroom door—a few feet from getting back to at least one normal thing.

"Haley? Where's my girl?"

I yell from my room. "I'm up here."

My grandpa's steps sound on the stairs. I close the lid of my laptop and reach over and set it on my desk.

"How'd you get up all those stairs, young lady?"

I smile. "Frustration."

He laughs. "It served you well. I'll bet it was coupled with a dose of determination too. Mind if I have a seat?" He points to the side of my bed.

I scoot over. "Go ahead."

"You know when you say, 'Don't ask' to your ol' grandpa, I'm going to ask. Your friend Zach seemed nice enough. What happened?"

"Things just got...hard, you know?"

"I'd guess most of life is pretty hard right now. How're you doing?"

"I just want things the way they were, but there's not much I can do about it."

"You're right, there's not. So do what you can, and let go of what you can't." He smiles. "Or something like that. In other words, if you can't do anything about it, try to move on. If you can change it, tackle it. Like you tackled those stairs."

I nod. "I guess so."

"I know so."

"Okay." I grab one of the throw pillows on my bed and hug it to my chest.

"Anytime you need a listening ear, I'll turn up my hearing aid for you."

I smile. "Thanks. So, not to change the subject or anything, but...Mom told me about what you found out. You know, about her mother."

The smile sort of fades from his eyes and he looks down at the floor, then back at me. "She told you that, did she?"

"Yeah, and I was thinking about it and I wanted to tell you something."

"What's that?"

"It's just that"—I shrug—"I mean, it doesn't make any difference to me, you know? Whatever happens, you'll always be my grandpa."

He stares at me for a minute and he looks like he might cry, but then he clears his throat. "They say blood is thicker than water."

"*They* aren't always right."

He chuckles, then reaches over and pats my knee. "You'll always be my girl."

"Good."

And it is good, because besides my mom, I'm not sure I'm anyone else's girl anymore.

After my grandpa leaves, I roll over on my side and reach out and trace the chevron pattern my mom and I painted on my wall. *"If you can change it, tackle it."*

I sit up and try to wedge my fingers between my cast and my leg. My leg itches so bad, but as usual, I can't reach the spot that itches. I slap the cast in frustration. What *can* I change?

I can't fix my broken ankle, except by waiting.

I can't undo what my dad did.

I can't guarantee Zach will never… I shake my head.

What can I change?

Nothing.

I lie back down and soon tears are sliding down my cheeks and puddling in my ears. But as I lie there, it occurs to me, there is something I can change. I can change me.

I mean, not that I don't like myself, but I can change what I do—how I handle things. I sit up. Like, just because I'm scared, doesn't mean I have to *act* scared.

I reach for some tissue. I wipe my eyes and nose, and then I grab my phone off my desk where I left it before I lay down. I look at the phone for a couple seconds, then I decide to do something I thought about earlier, but wasn't sure I was ready to do.

I open my messages and key in a text.

Hey, I was wondering if we could hang out. Maybe talk? If you picked me up, we could go to Brew's Up.

I reread the text a couple of times before I push Send. Then I lie back down, my stomach tying itself in knots.

He helps me into the truck and then closes the passenger-side door. I'd waited for him out by the driveway. When I saw him coming down the drive, I waved. He pulled in, parked, and then hopped out to help me get in. Neither of us said anything and the silence was—is—so awkward.

He comes around to the driver's side of the truck, climbs in, and glances over at me before putting the truck into gear and backing out. As we head down the long drive toward the highway, I stare out the window and my stomach growls. By the time he texted me back, it was almost dinnertime. So we decided to get dinner instead of coffee, but I don't know if I'll be able to eat. Now that I'm with him, I'm so—

"How's the leg, Chipmunk?"

I whip around and look at him. "Do *not* call me that. *Ever!*"

"You know, Haley, you were the one who asked to see me. So don't go off on me."

I don't yell again, but I can't keep the anger out of my tone. "And *you're* the one who blew it. You ruined everything! Why don't you get that?" My throat is thick with emotion, but I won't cry—I will not let him see me cry. I didn't plan on yelling, but I did plan on telling him how I feel. That's something I can do something about. I can be real, even if he isn't.

His words come out cold. "This isn't about you. This is between your mother and me." He pulls onto the highway.

I stare at him. *Really? Does he really think this isn't about me?* "Like, you're joking, right, Dad? Because this is *totally* about me and about Tyler. This is about our *family*. How can you not get that?"

"I get it. What I mean is that it's for your mother and me to work out. Okay?"

There's still sarcasm or something in his tone that makes me feel like he's just saying that so I'll shut up. So no, it's not okay.

"I screwed up. I blew it. That's obvious, so I shouldn't need to say it. But if that's what you need to hear, there it is."

He is unbelievable. "How about an apology? Like, a real one? Because you know what? You *hurt* me."

"I'm sorry." He stares straight ahead, his eyes on the road.

"Yeah, but here's the problem, I don't trust you anymore, so I don't even know if I can trust that what you say is real or not."

He doesn't look at me, and neither of us says anything else until he pulls into the parking lot of the South Gate Brewing Company—my favorite place—which, of course, he knows. My stomach growls again when I think about their beer-battered fish tacos.

He turns and looks at me. "This okay?"

I refuse to look at him. "Whatever."

After we've ordered and the waitress has taken our menus away, my dad reaches across the table like he's reaching for my hand, but then changes his mind. "Haley, I never…" He sighs. "I didn't mean to hurt you. *Really*." His expression is serious.

"Did you mean to hurt Mom?"

He leans back in the booth.

"*Did* you?"

"Haley, you're fifteen. You can't possibly understand."

"I know how old I am and I'm sick of you reminding me. I understand more than you think."

He stares at me.

I stare back. "Did you mean to hurt Mom?"

"I don't know."

It's the first thing he's said that I believe. "So here's the deal. I can't change what happened. You did what you did and that's your…issue. But I can decide how I want to handle the way it hurt me."

He raises his eyebrows.

I take a deep breath and keep my tone firm, but respectful. "I'm just going to be real about all of it. I'm going to tell you how I feel and I'm going to keep telling you how I feel. And then"—I shrug—"we'll see how things go. And right now, I feel really mad, and like I can't trust anyone. And I especially can't trust you."

He picks up his glass and takes a sip of water, then sets it back down. He looks across the table at me. "Anything else?"

"Yeah"—I swallow—"I...miss you."

After the waitress brings our meals, I eat both of my tacos and everything else on my plate. And then I'm ready to get back home so I can tackle something else I can change.

Or at least try to change.

*Down through the middle of the Valley flows the crystal
Merced, River of Mercy, peacefully quiet, reflecting lilies and
trees and the onlooking rocks; things frail and fleeting and
types of endurance meeting here and blending
in countless forms.*
John Muir

CHAPTER FORTY-SIX

Jessica

I DIG FOR the letter and find it wedged under my
phone charger, some loose change, and a tube of hand lotion
in my nightstand drawer. I tucked it in the drawer the night
my dad gave it to me and haven't looked at it since. But this
evening, with some time alone, I'm drawn to it again.

I pull the pages from the envelope. The edges of the
letter are dog-eared and the paper's soft to the touch, worn
smooth. How many times did my dad read this before giving
it to me? My vision blurs as I take in the slant of her words
on the page. How many tears did he shed after learning this
news—the possibility that I am not his flesh and blood?

I run my fingers over the blue ink on the page.

The first time I read the letter, I couldn't take in her words—couldn't comprehend most of what she'd written. It was only the confession, the possibility of what she wrote that, like a tick, burrowed into my brain.

I settle in one of the two leather chairs in our bedroom, switch on the lamp between the chairs, and begin reading. Beyond the obvious connection in subject matter— infidelity—I'm not sure what the letter has to do with my situation. But my sense is that there's something here that will inform my situation with Chet.

Some of the words are familiar; others it seems I'm reading for the first time. And much of the letter reads like a journal entry. Her reflections are a purging, it seems.

As I read the final paragraphs, my heart rate quickens. I'd stopped reading after learning of her doubts about the identity of my father, so this part of the letter is new to me.

I shift in the chair and read the paragraphs again:

> The stories of my people are passed from generation to generation—the legends, our legacies. But when I gave up the seed borne of my womb, I gave up my right to tell the stories, to pass them on to the next generation. Isn't that what punishment is? A loss of rights? If so, I sentenced myself.

> It is only now, when there is little to do but ponder the past, that I see the truth of my actions. I took the coward's path.

> May the River of Mercy cleanse us all from my transgressions.

The third time I read it, I realize my mother's given me a gift long overdue. The letter is her story. She's passed her legacy to me, her daughter, whether she realized she was doing so or not.

Will I live her legacy? Will I take the coward's path? Or will I create my own legacy? Will I pass weakness or strength to my children? I have a choice to make.

Like my mother, I sentenced myself. But instead of sentencing myself by fleeing from marriage—I sentenced myself *to* marriage. I married Chet because I was pregnant. I thought I had to do that to right my own wrong. Now, a generation later, I may not have considered pregnancy a reason to marry, but then…

Oh, I loved Chet. Or I thought I did. But really, I didn't know him well enough to commit to spending a lifetime with him.

And I didn't know myself at all.

I set the letter in my lap, lean my head back, and stare at the ceiling. Now, faced with the choice of doing it again, of returning to my marriage—or not—will I make a different choice? A choice that allows for the cleansing of mercy my mother speaks of?

The latch on the front door clicks. Haley, back from having dinner with her dad. As her crutches sound on the floor in the entry hall, the answer to my question settles in my soul.

Yes.

I will choose differently. Because one day, I will pass the legacy I create now to my children. And while I finally understand that I can't completely control the legacy, I can choose how I'd like to shape it.

🌲

Haley sits at the island eating a bowl of ice cream and reading something on her phone. We both slept in this morning and are taking this Sunday afternoon slow.

She sets her spoon in the bowl. "Grandpa says there's a fire in Oakhurst."

"Where in Oakhurst?"

"I don't know—it's not near them. But he said they're evacuating a whole neighborhood."

"Are you still planning on spending the night at their house?"

"Yeah. Are you taking me?"

"Sure." I wipe my hands on a dishtowel. "Did you tell them what time you'd be there?"

"No—just whenever—but before dinner." She looks at her phone again and smiles. "Hey, Zach said his mom heard they might close the schools tomorrow because of the fire."

"Zach?"

She glances at me and then looks back at her phone. "I texted him and told him I was sorry."

"So—"

"I don't know yet." She looks up at me.

Whatever took place between Chet and Haley last night seems to have lightened her spirits. Or maybe it has more to do with something between Zach and her. I trust she'll tell me in time. I smile. A few weeks ago, I wouldn't have felt that assurance. "I'm going to shower and get dressed, then we'll go."

"Okay."

My training and work as a firefighter lends credibility with those who fight the fires now. They know I understand and take into account the hardship that cutting a fire line around an owl's nest or a grinding stone may pose. That same credibility has landed me on a fire line a few times, working alongside the firefighters rather than issuing directives from an ICP.

But today, I'm only an observer.

After dropping Haley off at my dad's and Cretia's, I drove across town, parked, grabbed some gear I'd brought with me, and then flashed my ID at those keeping onlookers from invading the Bass Lake Heights neighborhood in Oakhurst. One call and I was in.

On foot, I thread my way through barricades, responder vehicles, and over hoses until I reach a spot where I can see a home engulfed in flames.

Where wild land and civilization meet, fire becomes a ravenous demon.

I stand a good distance from the house, but the heat from the fire still reaches out and caresses my cheeks. I take several steps back but can still see the flames dancing a frenzied recital—their hissing and popping almost rhythmic.

Within minutes, the flames have claimed their victim, and the roof of the house crashes inward. I consider the family who won't have a home to return to—the devastation they'll experience. They've lost everything. *No, not everything.* There's one important exception…

They still have each other.

"Chet may have started this fire, but you control it, Jessie."

I couldn't accept my dad's wisdom when he first spoke it while we drove to find Haley—she was my only focus then. But now, I understand. As I watch the destruction before me, I know my family faces a similar threat. But I can choose…

I can let the fire that's invaded our lives burn away the dross of our marriage and hope there's something to return to in the end.

Or I can let it run rampant destroying everything—and everyone—in its path.

My face flushes with the heat from the flames, my eyes never leaving the mesmerizing dance.

Which will it be?

There is really only one choice.

The final outcome is not mine alone to control, but I can certainly do my part to affect a desired outcome. No…not I can…

I must.

I toss my protective gear into the back seat of the SUV and then reach for my cell phone. Standing outside the open driver's door, smoke swirling as homes fall to the flames, I press Chet's number into my phone.

Just over a year ago I was dispatched to the ICP for the Rim Fire—a fire that spread so rapidly both on the ground and through the tree crowns that it consumed four hundred square miles of the Sierra Nevada forest and cost over one hundred million dollars to fight. Even now, so many months later, crews are still assessing the ultimate damage.

During the course of that fire there was a time where my primary focus was on two groves of trees within Yosemite National Park's boundaries—The Merced Grove and the Tuolumne Grove of giant sequoias. Trees that have stood since the beginning of time, or so it seems. Fire lines were cut and sprinklers were placed. Though the giant sequoias need fire to survive, the Rim Fire was too hot and too fast and would surely destroy what nature had produced. In the end...

The sequoias stood their ground.

My call goes to voice mail and I leave a message for Chet. "Hey, it's me. I'd like to talk. Can you meet me tomorrow at the Mariposa Grove?" I hesitate. "It's an odd request, I know, but I want to show you something. Let me know what time works for you, and I'll see you there." I end the call.

The Mariposa Grove is located at the southern end of the park, closer to home, and the walk in to see what I want to show Chet is less than a mile. But will he honor my request? He's not used to letting me call the shots.

I get into the SUV and take the drive home, slow, letting my mind consider the possibilities and weigh them against the probabilities.

As I do, hope and dread battle within.

No true invitation is ever declined.
John Muir

CHAPTER FORTY-SEVEN

Haley

"NO SCHOOL TODAY!" I look from my phone to my grandpa across their kitchen table and my excitement dies. Fast. "That must mean the fire is really bad."

He nods as he sips his coffee, then he sets his cup down. "A lot of homes lost and it's still burning, though it sounds like they're getting a handle on it."

"Bummer." How hard would that be?

My grandma's standing at the sink, cleaning up the breakfast dishes. "Honey, if there's no school, what are you going to do with yourself all day?"

"I don't know. I mean, I sort of know, but..."

"But what?" Grandpa looks at me over the newspaper he's just unfolded.

I shrug. "Um, Zach asked me if I'd want to go for a drive—maybe to Glacier Point. I mean, I can't do much with this stupid cast, but he thought a drive and a picnic, you know, if we didn't have school. He said we could at least look at the top of Half Dome together, since we didn't get to…well, you know."

"Sounds like a fine idea. Also sounds like you two are talking again?" He winks at me.

"Just as"—I look down and mumble—"friends."

"Nothing wrong with that." He sets the newspaper back on the table.

"I guess."

"What's the trouble, Haley?" Grandma walks over to the table, wiping her hands on a towel.

I sigh. "It's just that my mom and I made a pact that neither of us would run away from things anymore and instead we'd face them head-on."

She sits down at the table. "And…?"

"And Grandpa told me to change what I can and let go of everything else."

He looks at Grandma. "Wise words, don't you think?"

"I do." She smiles at him, then looks back to me. "So?"

"So I realized I was running away from Zach because I was scared. So after I had dinner with my dad last night, I called Zach and told him I was sorry." I look at Grandpa. "I figured I could at least change the way I was acting and, you know, apologize to Zach. Plus, I had to keep that pact with my mom."

"Good girl." He rests his elbows on the table.

Grandma leans over and gives one of his elbows a flick with her fingers, and he puts his arms back in his lap. Then she looks at me. "So honey, I'm still not sure what your hesitation is about today."

"I told Zach I just wanted to be friends, but maybe…" I crumple the napkin still in my lap and put it on the table. "I might want to be more than friends. And what if, I mean, after the way I treated him, he…doesn't want that?"

Grandma leans over and pats my shoulder. "Honey, you'll never know until you talk to him."

"But before you go off for a picnic with him"—Grandpa raises his eyebrows—"call your mom and get permission. For real, this time."

"I will. For real." I smile.

"My mom made us lunch, so you're missing out on another one of my great PB & Js." Zach smiles at me as he spreads a beach towel on a section of rock wall at Glacier Point.

"You make a pretty decent PB & J."

"One of my many talents." He laughs.

Before we sit down, we stand and look out at Half Dome and the cloud of smoke still hanging in the distance.

"My mom said the fire is 80 percent contained now."

Zach stares at the view. "It's hard to believe we were there. It's sort of surreal, you know? And I didn't really get how big the fire was until I made it to the top—from there"—he shakes his head—"man, it looked like a nuclear bomb had gone off. Then to see it all on the news. It was crazy."

"I know. It *was* crazy. But now, it seems like so long ago—so much has happened this week. Plus, I feel like I've had this cast forever." I lean my crutches against the low rock wall and then sit on the beach towel. "Hey, I never really thanked you, you know, for all you did that day. For the way you helped me."

Zach sits down but keeps a big space between us. "No problem. I was the one who talked you into going."

"Yeah, but if I hadn't been so tired and so freaked out about my parents, I probably wouldn't have fallen. Anyway, I hope we can do it again sometime."

"Really?" He looks like maybe he doesn't believe me.

"Of course. It's going to be a while"—I point to my cast—"but I definitely want to do it again."

"Cool."

Zach angles his body so he can look out at the view and still see me, but he doesn't say anything else. And even as much as I've rehearsed what I want to say today, my mind is blank and my tongue feels like it's sticking to the roof of my mouth. "Did you bring anything to drink?"

"Oh, yeah." Zach bends and opens the small ice chest at his feet. "Water or Gatorade?"

"Water's good."

He hands me a cold water bottle.

"Thanks for taking care of lunch and everything."

"Sure."

I take a swallow of water. It was so much easier to just text each other over the weekend. And the drive here wasn't bad because I spent most of it looking at pictures on Zach's phone—pictures of me being hoisted from the trail, of the fire from the top of Half Dome, of the helicopter that landed on the top of the dome, and even a group shot of everyone up on top waiting to be rescued.

But now, it's just so awkward. And what if I say what I've planned to say and he, like, doesn't want to…?

I sigh. How awkward will *that* be? Then what? Maybe I shouldn't say anything until we're on our way home.

"Are you okay?"

"Oh, yeah." I smile, but I know it's a lame attempt. "Totally." I turn and look back at Half Dome. "I mean, you know, I'm…sort of okay." I look back at him and the butterflies in my tummy—or my gut, as my grandpa calls it—flutter, like, full force.

"Sort of okay?" His forehead creases like he's concerned.

I wipe my palms on my shorts. "Okay, so I…" I stop, then reach for my water bottle and take another sip.

"Haley?"

"What?"

Zach raises his eyebrows.

"Oh, right. Um, so I wanted you to know that I'm really sorry. You know, for this past week and how I…treated you."

"Thanks. But you've already told me that. I mean, I appreciate it, but you don't have to apologize again. I know you've had a lot to deal with. And"—he shrugs—"stuff happens."

Stuff happens? I try to read his expression. Is he hurt or disappointed or…something? Does he care that we're just friends now? Was Chloe right when she said I'd hurt Zach, or is he maybe relieved?

"So are you thinking you might"—I take a deep breath—"ask someone else to Winter Formal now that we're just…" I look down at the water bottle I'm holding, then look back at Zach.

"*Just* friends?" Zach's smile has faded. "Does that mean you don't want to go as friends?"

I set my water bottle down. "No, I don't want to go as just friends."

Zach nods but doesn't look at me. "Oh, okay." He turns back and stares at the view again, his shoulders sort of drooping.

"Zach?"

"What?"

"Um, can you look at me?"

He waits a second or two, then turns and looks at me.

I take a deep breath. "I want to go, I mean…I was wondering if…could we still go as…more than friends?"

He frowns. "What do you mean? I thought—"

"I know, but—" I scoot closer to him, my heart ready to pound out of my chest. "It's been a hard week and I wasn't really myself and I wish I hadn't told you I couldn't do…the whole relationship thing." The final words come out in a whisper, like on the tail end of my courage. I look down, afraid to see Zach's expression.

When he doesn't say anything, I wish I could climb under a rock. I shouldn't have—

"But…what about now? Before Winter Formal?"

I look back up at him. "Oh, now?" I nod. "Now too."

His eyes crinkle at the corners as his lips curve into a smile. Then he leans toward me and rests his forehead on mine. "Really?"

"Really."

"Like right now?"

At his whisper, I lean back, just barely, and look at him and nod. Then I scoot even closer and put my hands on his shoulders and…my lips on his.

As we kiss, I'm glad, like *really* glad, I decided to change what I could.

Or at least try to.

Few are altogether deaf to the preaching of pine trees.
John Muir

CHAPTER FORTY-EIGHT

Jessica

I PULL INTO the Mariposa Grove parking area a few minutes before two o'clock—the time Chet told me worked for him. I park the SUV, then I run a comb through my hair, and dab a bit of gloss on my lips. I take a glance in the mirror. Satisfied, I get out of the SUV to wait for him. I lean against the passenger door trying to ignore my rattled nerves. I stand facing the entrance to the parking area and within a few minutes, I see Chet's truck come into the lot. He parks beside me, gets out, and points at the mirror on the SUV. "You got it fixed."

"I did. It looks good, right?"

"Yeah, considering the damage you did to it."

I nod, not sure how to take his comment. But rather than worry about it, I remind myself to stay focused, and I walk over and join him by his truck. "Thanks for coming."

"Sure." He puts his keys in his pocket, "So, what? You want to show me a tree?" The corners of his lips turn upward and there's a glint of humor, or is it sarcasm, in his eyes. Whatever it is, for just a moment, I see the man who kissed me the night we met—the man who made me feel like a woman for the first time. The memory stabs, and I remind myself, again, to focus.

"Yes, I want to show you a tree." I work to keep my tone neutral.

We take off toward the grove in silence. When we've gone no more than two hundred yards, Chet stops. "Jess, I'm ready to come home and put all this behind us."

I stop and look at him. "It isn't that easy."

"And seeing a tree is going to make it easier? You know, if you'd been around more, worked less—if you'd really loved me—none of this would have happened." He seems to plead with me. My soul sinks, but before I have a chance to respond, he holds up one hand. "Sorry. Forget it. Let's see what you want to show me."

We continue our walk, my stride just enough shorter than Chet's that I have to hustle to keep up with him.

He glances over at me. "I had dinner with Haley."

I nod. "How was it?"

"Fine. Sounds like her ankle is healing."

He gives nothing away and diverts the conversation from himself, or at least that's how I interpret his comment. I don't say anything more until the tree I want to show him comes into view. I slow my pace. "There." I point.

"Grizzly Giant?"

I nod and then stop well ahead of the tree. I want to see as much of it as possible.

"It's not like we've never seen this tree, Jess."

"I know." I catch my breath and try to push his earlier blame aside. "But I want to explain something. See the fire scar?" I point to the long, cone-shaped scar that runs up from the base of the sequoia. We both tilt our heads up, following the blackened scar with our eyes.

"Yeah, so?"

I look over at him. "The Courtney Fire in Oakhurst?"

"Yeah."

"By this afternoon, they're reporting thirty homes lost. I was over there yesterday. It's"—I shake my head—"sobering. But fire doesn't always destroy. Sometimes it causes an environment to thrive."

"Your point?"

Anger ripples through me at the impatience in his tone. "I think you can take the time to hear me out." He doesn't say anything, so I continue. "Chet, a fire has ripped through our marriage and now, I want to assess the damage and see if, maybe, we can save what's left. And maybe, in time, we'll realize it was exactly what was needed to create new life. Like the sequoias. Remember how their seeds are fire dependent? Without the heat of fire, the cones don't open and spill the seeds. Without fire, the overstory trees become overgrown and the seedlings don't receive the necessary light for growth." I look at him and though I want to say more, I know anything else I say will go unheard.

"Okay, so…" He turns toward me. "What's the damage? What's it going to take to *thrive*, as you put it?"

I stare at him. My husband. The father of my children. And…I take a step back from him. *The damage?* My tone is tight, guarded. "It will take a long time to assess the damage. It isn't something we can figure out right this moment."

A vein throbs in Chet's neck and his jaw tightens. "Okay. So what do you want from me, Jess?"

I step forward again. "It isn't what I want from you. It's what I want *for us*."

He nods, and his expression relaxes a bit. "And what's that?"

I hesitate. Why do this? Why expose myself and lay my soul bare? Because, I know I'll regret it if I don't. "I want…to be real. Both of us. I want us to enjoy the freedom, within our relationship, to just be…*ourselves*."

He sighs. "Sounds like the speech I got from Haley last night. Okay, go on."

Haley? I tuck that comment away for later. "I haven't been real, Chet. I haven't even gotten to know who I am. I've been so focused on the marriage, the family, the legacy—" I lift my shoulders. "I want more. I want to grow together and see what happens. I've lived under the overstory growth too long. I want to clear the forest and"—I raise my arms and turn slowly, taking in the grandeur surrounding us—"let the sun shine."

"C'mon, Jess. Enough of the metaphors, okay? Let's go home." He turns and begins walking toward the parking lot.

I drop my arms at my sides. "Wait…"

He turns around and looks down at the ground, then back at me, "What's this about? Really? Do I have to apologize again? Do you need to know I love you? What?"

My heart thrums, its beat steady as I inhale the dry, organic scent of the grove. My lungs expand as they fill. I exhale. And inhale again. The ease of breathing isn't lost on me. And as I breathe, a new realization, like the dawning of the morning sun, sheds light on something I felt yesterday— the battle between hope and dread.

I'd assumed I dreaded the probability that Chet wouldn't take responsibility for his actions, wouldn't show remorse for the pain he's caused me. That he's caused his children.

And I assumed I hoped for the possibility that we could work toward growth—a slow, steady growth of a new marriage for us, for our family.

I stand there, looking at Chet, and for the first time, I *see.* His impatience, his anger, throbs in his neck, and I recall all the times I've bowed to his impatience, cowered before his anger. How many times have I squelched my own feelings out of fear? I feared the repercussion of speaking up. Standing up. Fighting for what I believed.

Now, I see his dismissal of what I feel or need or want. I see his dismissal of me. But I also see my own culpability. I followed Chet's lead and dismissed myself. I allowed him to believe he could treat me with disrespect.

The weight of my responsibility in the demise of our relationship almost breaks me. I bend, hands on my knees, and swallow the feeling of nausea threatening me. I take a deep breath. Then another. When I rise back up, my eyes meeting Chet's, what I see—or rather, what I don't see— clarifies my struggle between dread and hope.

I don't see remorse.

I don't see him taking any responsibility for his actions.

And relief, like a cool spring rain, washes over me.

I take another step toward him. "This…is about something different than I thought." I point to Grizzly Giant. "I thought it was about burning the dross—the impurities—of our marriage and then, together, seeing what was left, determining what we could grow from the ashes. But…"

I shake my head and stare at the tree in wonder.

"But?"

I look at him. "I was wrong." The scarred sequoia towers over us, reaching heavenward. "Chet, what we have…what we've had?" I can say this now. It's the truth, and I can speak it. "There is no marriage. There's nothing left."

His eyes narrow.

I swallow the ache in my throat for what could have been. "The fire is fatal. The marriage won't survive."

But—hope spreads its wings—*I will.* And more than that…

I will thrive.

As I make the drive home, grief is my passenger. Sitting not in the seat next to me, but on top of me. Crushing me. There are no tears—the well is dry—there's just the weight, the burden of letting go of something I believed would last forever. And in the same way I understood Chet and I couldn't assess, in one afternoon, the damage his choices caused, I know grief will linger.

For days.

For weeks.

For as long as it takes.

The hours I spent pondering, considering what our marriage might look like after all this…how it might grow anew, the outcome was dependent on one thing: Chet's remorse. His own grief at hurting those he loved.

Something Cretia said comes back to me as I navigate what seems a new road ahead: *"Without remorse, without Chet owning his actions, healing in your marriage can't, won't, take place."*

It's what I desired, what I hoped for, and what I knew, deep within, I'd likely never witness.

I pull up in front of the house. Home. But not the home where I live. I turn off the ignition and sit, the reflection of the late-afternoon sun dancing on the windshield. The last time I parked here, the SUV had sustained almost irreparable damage. As had I. But this afternoon, fewer than ten days later, I cling to the assurance, an inexplicable knowing, that I too will survive.

I look up at the house, the lights inside beacons of love, warmth, and support. I don't navigate the unknown alone.

I get out of the SUV, walk up the path, and tap on the front door before opening the door myself and walking in. "Hello?"

"In here," Cretia calls.

I follow her voice into the kitchen, where Haley sits at the table, her casted leg propped on a chair, my dad across from her and Cretia at one end of the table. My dad and Cretia have mugs in front of them.

"Honey, sit." Cretia gets up. "I'll pour you a cup. We're having a little afternoon coffee klatch."

I head toward the empty seat at the table, but Cretia catches me before I reach the chair. She looks me in the eyes, then reaches up and puts her hands on my shoulders. "You look drained. Are you okay?"

"I'm beyond drained, but yes, I'm okay."

She squeezes my shoulders, then in a tone my dad and Haley can hear says, "Regular or decaf?"

"Decaf. I plan on sleeping tonight." I sit down and smile at my dad and Haley. Then I focus on Haley. "How was your picnic?"

"Good." Her smile tells me more than her words.

"Great. I look forward to hearing about it."

"And how was your…meeting?" My dad studies my face.

Haley looks at me, her expression inquisitive. "You saw Dad, right?"

I nod. "Right."

Cretia comes and sets a steaming mug of coffee in front of me and, though it isn't cold in the house, I wrap my hands around the mug, warming myself from its heat.

"Haley, want to watch some TV?" My dad points in the direction of the family room.

"No, Dad, it's okay." I look at Haley. "I'd like her to stay. She needs to hear this too."

Cretia sits down and picks up her mug. And the three of them watch me, waiting.

I lean forward and rest my arms on the table. I direct my attention to Haley. "Things with your dad…didn't go well."

Her eyes widen and her expression grows serious.

"It's not"—my eyes well with tears—"going to work." Though I had no tears left for myself, they flow now for my children.

"I know." Her tone is small, childlike.

"I'm…sorry."

"It's not your fault." She rests her head on her arms on the table and closes her eyes.

I turn and look at my dad and then at Cretia. I pick up the paper napkin she handed me with my mug of coffee and wipe my eyes.

Then Haley raises her head and looks at me again. "It's so weird. Zach and I got back together today, while you and Dad…broke up?"

I nod, afraid to speak for fear my tears will turn to sobs.

Haley looks across at my dad. "Change what you can and let go of what you can't."

My dad, his eyes misty, nods at Haley.

"I'm sure there will be lots to still work out."

I nod at Cretia's words. Then I lift the mug to my lips, hoping to still my tears. I take a sip, then find my voice again. "There will be lots to work through and"—I look at Haley—"lots for us to talk about along the way. Okay?"

She nods.

"But right now, I have something else to say." I gaze over at my dad, then reach for his hand. I give it a squeeze, then let go. "I made a decision this afternoon. Another decision."

"What's that?" His tone is gruff—filled with emotion.

"Well, as I was driving back from Mariposa Grove, I realized something." I lean forward. "My circumstances aren't my legacy."

"You've got that right, honey." Cretia smiles at me.

I look at Haley again. "Whether I'm married or not, employed or not, a mother or not, what matters most is love." I turn to my dad. "And Dad"—I take a deep breath—"it's love that binds us, not genetics."

He nods, tears pooling in his eyes.

"And that's all I need. And all I want."

He clears his throat. "What are you saying, Jessie?"

"I'm saying I don't need a paternity test. I know who my father is."

His tears fall as he nods again. He reaches over and grabs my hand, and this time he doesn't let go. When we both look at Cretia, she's wiping her eyes with her napkin.

"That's basically what I told Grandpa too."

I look over at Haley. "You did?"

She and Dad nod in unison and, as before, I bookmark the moment to consider later. "It seems you lead the way once again."

She shrugs. "Whatever."

"Honey, what about your mother? Are you going to contact her?" Cretia's gaze is so full of care for me.

I lean my head back and stretch my neck from one side to the other, then I lift my shoulders. "I don't know. Not now. But later…maybe." I squeeze Dad's hand again. "It isn't my priority right now. I have"—I look at Haley—"other things to take care of."

We're all silent for a moment, then my dad lets go of my hand and turns toward Cretia. "We need cookies."

She laughs, gets up, and then kisses him on the cheek before heading to the kitchen, where she takes home-baked cookies from a sealed container and puts them on a plate.

Cookies won't solve everything, I know.

But they're not a bad beginning.

Reading these grand mountain manuscripts displayed through every vicissitude of heat and cold, calm and storm, upheaving volcanoes and down-grinding glaciers, we see that everything in Nature called destruction must be creation—a change from beauty to beauty.
John Muir

CHAPTER FORTY-NINE

Jessica

I ZIP THE fleece jacket I put on at home before daylight this morning and then adjust the pack on my back before setting out from where I parked the SUV along the side of the road. The only way to reach the site of the fire is to make the trek on foot. The sun crests the eastern mountain range and splashes the gray sky with vibrant hues of pink, as though it performs for an audience of one. I breathe deep, my lungs filling with the chill of fall and my body filling with the energy of a new day—a new season. As I begin hiking, the muscles in my legs revolt, tight from lack of exercise since my leave of absence from work. I slow my pace until my muscles warm and stretch.

As I walk toward the site, straw-colored grass waves alongside the trail and dry leaves skitter around my feet. When the ache in my legs subsides, I push myself on the trail, enjoying the exertion as I gain altitude. Before long the grass and leaves give way to blackened, scorched earth, and the acrid scent of burnt foliage hangs in the air.

My desire—or is it need?—to see some of the area burnt by the Meadow Fire has baffled me for days. Maybe it's borne of habit, of years spent working fire sites, assessing the damage to natural and cultural resources. Or maybe it is something more. When I woke this morning, I decided to let desire lead the way. Now, attentive, I follow along not wanting to miss whatever the site may hold for me.

As I make my way deeper into the burn area, clouds drift overhead and the blush of morning turns gray and threatening. I stop on the trail and lift my face to the sky. Rain clouds. Oh, how we need the rain. Yet another year of drought is predicted.

Warmed by my exertion, I let the backpack drop from my shoulders, set it on the trail. I unzip and remove my jacket and tie it around my waist. Then I pick up the pack and slip it back on. I breathe deep again, inhaling the scent of burnt wood and ash, finding comfort, contentment even, in its familiarity.

I continue my hike into what was forested land. Tree trunks surround me. Some, felled by the fire, lie on the ground helter-skelter, like a child's pile of Lincoln Logs. Others, seemingly more stubborn, stand straight, their limbless, scorched trunks still pointing skyward. I stop on the trail again and make a slow turn. Nothing around me moves, despite an early morning breeze. And silence blankets the earth—all of life stilled by the fire.

What survived ran to safety. What didn't survive returned to the earth.

Not even a bird soars overhead.

I shudder. My aloneness stirs like a sharp, cold wind. I take a few more steps, but the energy I felt just moments ago lags. I stop, my breathing more shallow now. The blackened forest and foreboding clouds overhead press close.

"I'm surrounded by…death." I whisper it out loud, my breath catching as my focus turns inward.

In a few months, the finalization of our divorce will toll the death of our marriage. Our family. The fire that ripped through our lives left nothing standing. Nothing living.

I wrap my arms around myself as the pall of death knocks—a thief come to abscond with my peace.

But…

No.

I shake my head.

"No!" I shout into the void surrounding me. I stand silent waiting for the granite carved mountains to return my denial to me. *"No… No… No…"*

I've fought this intruder for months. Stood against its attacks. I won't succumb now.

The day I made the drive to the valley with my dad, I told him this journey would be like making my way through a foreign land without knowledge of the language spoken there. But I've learned the language now and it proved easier than I anticipated. Just one word is necessary. I speak it again.

"No."

I tighten the jacket around my waist and forge ahead, my stride swift and my steps sure. I navigate my way through the gray-scale landscape until I reach a vantage point. The rounded back of Half Dome stands to one side of me, its silvery granite surface barely highlighted against the charcoal sky.

Every inch of the surrounding palette is one shade or another of gray.

I view the panorama, not as an archeologist searching for resources, but as a woman searching for…

What did I think I'd find here? I'm not sure. I wait, hoping for some sign. Something that will point the way—direct my future.

But all is dull, still.

There's nothing for me here.

I smile and shake my head. A good hike is never wasted—at least I got some exercise. Whatever I hoped to find wasn't necessary, it seems. I turn back, intent on keeping a brisk pace on my way back to the SUV. "Endorphins," I say between breaths as I push myself forward. "That's what I came for."

As I make my way back down the trail and round a bend, something catches my attention. A dot of color spots the bleak terrain, then seems to disappear. I slow my pace as I search for it.

There…

I veer off the trail, leaving imprints in the ash, until I reach the bit of color I'd seen. I slow, almost reverent in my approach, then I stop.

And stare.

Poking out of the burnt crust of earth is a vibrant, living, green stem. Its delicate leaves bounce in the breeze. I have no idea what kind of plant it is, only that it's alive— living and thriving amidst destruction.

Regeneration.

I bend and run a finger over one of the soft leaves. As I do, a drop of water lands on my hand. Then another. And another.

I stand straight, step away from the seedling so as not to crush it, lift my face heavenward, and stretch out my arms.

Rain!

I smile as the sprinkling falls on my face, shoulders, and the thirsty earth, watering, cleansing, and offering…

Life.

Anew.

I pull into the parking spot, turn off the ignition, then reach and open the glove box. I pull out a comb, remove the band from my damp ponytail, and run the comb through my hair. I pull my hair back and secure it into a ponytail again.

Once I'd gotten back to the SUV, I'd put on a dry shirt, so while my pants are still damp, I'm mostly dry but still chilled.

I grab my purse and get out of the SUV, then I walk into the same café where I had coffee with Cretia the week after learning of Chet's affairs. It's become my new haunt—a place I've claimed as my own. I approach the counter and order my coffee. I pay for the drink and then slip my wallet back into my purse.

"Excuse me…"

I turn around. A tall, blonde woman, close to my own age, stands behind me. "Are you…" She hesitates, then smiles. "I'm sorry. I noticed you and thought you looked familiar—then I realized you look so much like someone I know—a friend of my son's. Are you Haley's mother?"

I'm drawn to the warmth of her smile. "Yes, I am."

"I'm Zach's mom."

"Oh, I'm so happy to meet you." I hold out my hand. "I'm sorry, I don't remember your name."

She clasps my hand in both of hers. "I wouldn't expect you to remember it. I'm Beth. And you're?"

"I'm…" I falter, unsure of how to introduce myself, which is ridiculous. But for the first time I wonder: am I Jess, or Jessie, or…? "I'm sorry. I'm Jessica."

"I'm so happy to run into you. I've wanted to meet you. I even got your phone number from Zach after their Half Dome disaster, but…" She shrugs. "I haven't called."

"Life gets busy, I know. And I've had your number too, but—"

"Life gets busy?" She laughs.

"Right."

As she places her order, I run my hand over my damp hair and then notice a leaf stuck in the lace of my right boot. But neither my hair nor the leaf bothers me. I am, it seems, comfortable.

After she's ordered her drink, she reaches for my elbow and guides me out of the way of other patrons waiting to place their orders. "Actually, Jessica, I really was planning on calling you this week. Zach just told me that you're…" She seems to weigh her words. "He told me you and your husband are separated. Divorcing."

I look from her face to the floor.

"It's just that I wanted you to know I understand. I mean, I don't know the particulars of your situation, but…"

I look back up and see what seems like compassion in her eyes. Along with the understanding she mentioned.

She shrugs. "I've been there."

"It still feels so…new. Foreign." I shake my head.

"I remember how challenging it was, and how helpful it was to talk with friends who'd gone through it. I don't want to intrude—"

"No." I reach out and place my hand on her arm. "It's not an intrusion. Really. I could use…a friend."

Beth glances at her watch as we move toward the coffee bar, where the barista has set our orders. "Are you in a hurry? Any chance you'd have time to sit down?" She gestures to a vacant table in a corner of the café. "We could get to know each other. If nothing else, we have Haley and Zach to talk about." She winks at me. "I'm sure they'll love hearing we discussed them over coffee."

I laugh. Then I pull my phone out of my pocket and check the time, though, really, what difference does it make? I have nowhere to go and no one waiting on me. I'm free.

Free.

I look back at Beth. "Yes, I can stay. I'd like that."

"Great."

We each reach for our drinks, then I follow her to the table. As I do, a photo on the wall catches my attention—a print of Ansel Adam's *Moon and Half Dome*—Tis-sa-ack's tears so evident, etched on her face until the end of time. I stop and gaze at the photo for a moment. Then I recall the vow I made: Tis-sa-ack's fate—her eternal tears—would not be mine.

I choose…

I take my seat across from Beth at the small table and take a sip of my steaming latte, letting it warm me from the inside out.

"So, Jessica, tell me about yourself. Who are you?"

I set my cup on the table, lean back in my chair, and consider my answer. Not long ago, if asked who I was, titles would have jumped to my lips: wife, mother, fire archeologist. Today, a new description pushes through the charred crust of my soul. I am…a seedling. Growing. Thriving.

I am a woman of strength.

Commitment.

And love.

Though I'm learning love doesn't always look the way others expect it to. Chet wouldn't likely describe my refusal to stay in our marriage as an act of love.

Yet, isn't that exactly what it was?

Loving Chet well means no longer accepting or enabling his disregard of others.

Loving my children well means exemplifying the truth that each person is deserving of respect.

Loving myself well means standing up for myself as a being of value.

These truths are taking root, flourishing within me.

"Jessica?"

I return my focus to Beth and smile. "Who am I?" Then I laugh. "How much time do you have?"

For the first time in my life, I know who I am.

I am a woman who preserves legacies. Most important of all…

The legacy of love.

ACKNOWLEDGEMENTS

I WROTE *FLAMES*—beginning to end—twice. The second version resembled the first only in title, setting, and theme. But the story, the second time around, differed dramatically, as did the characters. After writing the first version, I realized I didn't like my protagonist—and if I didn't like her, readers wouldn't like her. Frustrated, I set the manuscript aside, wrote it off to a learning experience, and moved on. Or…I tried to move on.

But the story nagged.

A year or so after scrapping the first manuscript, on a whim one morning I did an online search for fire archeologists. I was still intrigued by their work and though I'd searched for an archeologist who would help me with research as I wrote the first manuscript, I'd come up empty. But that morning, I discovered a Fire Archeology Facebook page and posted a request there. Within an hour or so, I had a response from an archeologist who told me I needed to connect with Yosemite National Park's Fire Archeologist, Jun Kinoshita. I laughed. Yeah, right. He was my dream interview. But I responded, and within minutes I received his contact information. By that afternoon, I had a phone appointment set with Jun Kinoshita.

Jun's experience as an archeologist, wildland firefighter, and training as one of the elite group of smoke jumpers made him an invaluable resource. But in addition to his experience, his enthusiasm for his job with the National Park Service and his willingness to share his knowledge with me were a gift. He was generous with both his time and information during our phone conversation and through many follow-up e-mails.

Working with Jun strengthened this story immeasurably, and I am so grateful for his contribution and for the work he does.

I also exchanged several e-mails with Lisa Hendy, Emergency Services Program Manager for Yosemite

National Park. Lisa also provided invaluable information regarding the Meadow Fire and the rescue process Haley would have experienced the day of that fire.

I've interacted with other National Park Service employees as well and found each to be welcoming and willing to share information. If you're not familiar with our National Park Service, please consider familiarizing yourself with the wonderful work they do to maintain and preserve the treasures that are our national parks. You may visit www.nps.gov to learn more.

Thank you to Andrea Berry who advised me as I developed Haley's character and read my first chapter from Haley's point of view to make sure I'd captured the voice and experiences of a fifteen-year-old girl. Andrea also accepted my friend requests on Facebook and Pinterest, which gave me further access to the life of a teenaged girl. As the mother of two adult sons, I was desperate for a young female's input, and Andrea was gracious and encouraging.

I am so thankful for my wonderful editors on this project, Karen Ball and Julee Schwarzburg, who challenged me, taught me, and encouraged me through the editing process. This story is stronger because of their experience and hard work. Both Karen and Julee also flexed their schedules for me multiple times as I dealt with family issues that prevented me from getting the manuscript to them as originally scheduled. I am without words when I consider the grace both Karen and Julee offered to me.

My dear friend Laurie Breining listens as I process each story I write and brainstorms with me when I'm stuck. As always, I value Laurie's consistent patience and her creative input.

My two wonderful sons, Justin and Jared, also endure chatter about the stories I'm working on and often offer important insight and encouragement as I'm writing.

I am also thankful for the men and women who've dared to share their own stories of betrayal with me. As I've spoken across the United States over the last five years, I've heard a variation of one story over and over: marriages destroyed by adultery. What surprised me most as I listened was that I rarely heard bitterness in the tones of those who shared with me. Instead, I heard strength. Yes, each story shared a foundation of heartbreak and dismay, but so many of those I spoke with had allowed brokenness to work its regenerating process. Many of the people I've met have grown paradoxically softer and stronger for the experience of suffering. May that be true of each of us when we endure suffering.

I offer special thanks to my own dear Ted and Cretia who allowed me to fictionalize their lives and use their names. The Ted and Cretia in this story are so close to who Ted and Cretia are as people: real, wise, loving, and gracious. But more than offering themselves as characters in this novel, they offer themselves as dear friends each and every day. They have supported me emotionally and unconditionally as a friend, and as a novelist. They also supported the publication of this book financially. I am so grateful for the gift of both of them.

I offer my deepest gratitude for the many family members, friends, and readers who donated to the crowdfunding campaign for the publication of this book. Simply put, this novel wouldn't exist without your belief in this project and your belief in me. This one is for you...

In the midst of this project, just as I was finalizing the manuscript for editing, my precious grandmother, at ninety-six years of age, suffered a major stroke. I set this manuscript aside, again, and during the next six months, I tended to my grandmother's needs. This wasn't a selfless act. Instead, I was simply emulating what I'd watched her do my entire life. She took care of her family. She took care of me. So it was time to offer what she had so freely given. I don't regret a moment of the time I spent with her before her death in July 2015. I learned what unconditional love looks like in practice from both my grandparents, and I learned what it means to set our own lives and goals aside for others when necessary. I fully recognize that the timing of this novel was always in the hands of Providence rather than my own hands.

Finally, I offer myself and my gratitude to the Creator who I see most clearly through the vast natural beauty of the earth in all its tangled wonder.

ABOUT THE AUTHOR

GINNY L. YTTRUP is the award-winning author of three inspirational novels with B&H Publishing group: Her debut novel, *Words*, won the Christy Award for Best First Novel, as well as being named *Foreword Reviews'* Inspirational Novel of the Year. *Publishers Weekly* called her second novel, *Lost and Found*, "as inspiring as it was entertaining." Her third novel, *Invisible*, was named *RT Reviews'* Inspirational Novel of the Year.

Ginny lives in northern California, which provides the rugged beauty for the settings of her novels. She enjoys gardening, cooking, dining with friends, and spending time with her two adult sons. She also adores her entitled Pomeranian, Bear.

Learn more about Ginny at www.ginnyyttrup.com.